FRANZ KAFKA

Metamorphosis

and

The Trial

Translated by David Wyllie

BORDERS.
CLASSICS

Please direct sales or editorial inquiries to:
BordersTradeBookInventoryQuestions@bordersgroupinc.com

This edition is published by
Borders Classics, an imprint of Borders Group, Inc.,
by special arrangement with
Ann Arbor Media Group, LLC
2500 South State Street, Ann Arbor, MI 48104

Printed and bound in the United States of America
by Edwards Brothers, Inc.

Quality Paperback ISBN 13: 978-1-58726-483-2
ISBN 10: 1-58726-483-8

11   10   09   08   07   10 9 8 7 6 5 4 3 2 1

CONTENTS

METAMORPHOSIS ◆ 1

THE TRIAL ◆ 51

METAMORPHOSIS

1

One morning, when Gregor Samsa woke from troubled dreams, he found himself transformed in his bed into a horrible vermin. He lay on his armour-like back, and if he lifted his head a little he could see his brown belly, slightly domed and divided by arches into stiff sections. The bedding was hardly able to cover it and seemed ready to slide off any moment. His many legs, pitifully thin compared to the size of the rest of him, waved about helplessly as he looked.

"What's happened to me?" he thought. It wasn't a dream. His room, a proper human room although a little too small, lay peacefully between its four familiar walls. A collection of textile samples lay spread out on the table—Samsa was a travelling salesman—and above it there hung a picture that he had recently cut out of an illustrated magazine and housed in a nice, gilded frame. It showed a lady fitted out with a fur hat and fur boa who sat upright, raising a heavy fur muff that covered the whole of her lower arm towards the viewer.

Gregor then turned to look out the window at the dull weather. Drops of rain could be heard hitting the pane, which made him feel quite sad. "How about if I sleep a little bit longer and forget all this nonsense," he thought, but that was something he was unable to do because he was used to sleeping on his right, and in his present state couldn't get into that position. However hard he threw himself onto his right, he always rolled back to where he was. He must have tried it a hundred times, shut his eyes so that he wouldn't have to look at the floundering legs, and only stopped when he began to feel a mild, dull pain there that he had never felt before.

"Oh, God," he thought, "what a strenuous career it is that I've chosen! Travelling day in and day out. Doing business like this takes much more effort than doing your own business at home, and on top of that there's the curse of travelling, worries about making train connections, bad and irregular food, contact with different people all the time so that you can never get to know anyone or become friendly with them. It can all go to Hell!" He felt a slight itch up on his belly; pushed himself slowly up on his back towards the headboard so that he could lift his head better; found where the itch was, and saw that it was covered with lots of little white spots which he didn't know what to make of; and when he tried to feel the place with one of his legs he drew it quickly back because as soon as he touched it he was overcome by a cold shudder.

He slid back into his former position. "Getting up early all the time," he thought, "it makes you stupid. You've got to get enough sleep. Other travelling salesmen live a life of luxury. For instance, whenever I go back to the guest house during the morning to copy out the contract, these gentlemen are always still sitting there eating their breakfasts. I ought to just try that with my boss; I'd get kicked out on the spot. But who knows, maybe that would be the best thing for me. If I didn't have my parents to think about I'd have given in my notice a long time ago, I'd have gone up to the boss and told him just what I think, tell him everything I would, let him know just what I feel. He'd fall right off his desk! And it's a funny sort of business to be sitting up there at your desk, talking down at your subordinates from up there, especially when you have to go right up close because the boss is hard of hearing. Well, there's still some hope; once I've got the money together to pay off my parents' debt to him—another five or six years I suppose—that's definitely what I'll do. That's when I'll make the big change. First of all though, I've got to get up, my train leaves at five."

And he looked over at the alarm clock, ticking on the chest of drawers. "God in Heaven!" he thought. It was half past six and the hands were quietly moving forwards, it was even later than half past, more like quarter to seven. Had the alarm clock not rung? He could see from the bed that it had been set for four o'clock as it should have been; it certainly must have rung. Yes, but was it possible to quietly sleep through that furniture-rattling noise? True, he had not slept peacefully, but probably all the more deeply because of that. What should he do now? The next train went at seven; if he were to catch that he would have to rush like mad and the collection of samples was still not packed, and he did not at all feel particularly fresh and lively. And even if he did catch the train he would not avoid his boss's anger as the office assistant would have been there to see the five o'clock train go, he would have put in his report about Gregor's not being there a long time ago. The office assistant was the boss's man, spineless, and with no understanding. What about if he reported sick? But that would be extremely strained and suspicious as in fifteen years of chaos. He told himself once more that it was not possible for him to stay in bed and that the most sensible thing to do would be to get free of it in whatever way he could at whatever sacrifice. At the same time, though, he did not forget to remind himself that calm consideration was much better than rushing to desperate conclusions. At times like this he would direct his eyes to the window and look out as clearly as he could, but unfortunately, even the other side of the narrow street was enveloped in morning fog and the view had little confidence or cheer to offer him. "Seven o'clock already," he said to himself when the clock struck again, "seven o'clock, and there's still a fog like this." And he lay there quietly a while longer, breathing lightly as if he perhaps expected the total stillness to bring things back to their real and natural state.

But then he said to himself: "Before it strikes quarter past seven I'll definitely have to have got properly out of bed. And by then somebody will have come round from work to ask what's happened to me as well, as they open up at work before seven o'clock." And so he set himself to the task of swinging the entire length of his body out of the bed all at the same time. If he succeeded in falling out of bed in this way and kept his head raised as he did so he could probably avoid injuring it. His back seemed to be quite hard, and probably nothing would happen to it falling onto the carpet. His main concern was for the loud noise he was bound to make, and which even through all the doors would probably raise concern if not alarm. But it was something that had to be risked.

When Gregor was already sticking halfway out of the bed—the new method was more of a game than an effort, all he had to do was rock back and forth—it occurred to him how simple everything would be if somebody came to help him. Two strong people—he had his father and the maid in mind—would have been more than enough; they would only have to push their arms under the dome of his back, peel him away from the bed, bend down with the load and then be patient and careful as he swang over onto the floor, where, hopefully, the little legs would find a use. Should he really call for help though, even apart from the fact that all the doors were locked? Despite all the difficulty he was in, he could not suppress a smile at this thought.

After a while he had already moved so far across that it would have been hard for him to keep his balance if he rocked too hard. The time was now ten past seven and he would have to make a final decision very soon. Then there was a ring at the door of the flat. "That'll be someone from work," he said to himself, and froze very still, although his little legs only became all the more lively as they danced around. For a moment everything remained quiet. "They're not opening the door," Gregor said to himself, caught in some nonsensical hope. But then of course, the maid's firm steps went to the door as ever and opened it. Gregor only needed to hear the visitor's first words of greeting and he knew who it was—the chief clerk himself. Why did Gregor have to be the only one condemned to work for a company where they immediately became highly suspicious at the slightest shortcoming? Were all employees, every one of them, louts, was there not one of them who was faithful and devoted who would go so mad with pangs of conscience that he couldn't get out of bed if he didn't spend at least a couple of hours in the morning on company business? Was it really not enough to let one of the trainees make enquiries—assuming enquiries were even necessary—did the chief clerk have to come himself, and did they have to show the whole, innocent family that this was so suspicious that only the chief clerk could be trusted to have the wisdom to investigate it? And more because these thoughts had made him upset than through any proper decision, he swang himself with all his force out of the bed. There was a loud thump, but it wasn't really a loud noise. His fall was softened a little by the carpet, and Gregor's back was also more elastic than he had thought, which made the sound muffled and not too noticeable. He had not held his head carefully enough, though, and hit it as he fell; annoyed and in pain, he turned it and rubbed it against the carpet.

"Something's fallen down in there," said the chief clerk in the room on the left. Gregor tried to imagine whether something of the sort that had happened to him today could ever happen to the chief clerk too; you had to concede that it was possible. But as if in gruff reply to this question, the chief clerk's firm footsteps in his highly polished boots could now be heard in the adjoining room. From the room on his right, Gregor's sister whispered to him to let him know: "Gregor, the chief clerk is here." "Yes, I know," said Gregor to himself; but without daring to raise his voice loud enough for his sister to hear him.

"Gregor," said his father now from the room to his left, "the chief clerk has come round and wants to know why you didn't leave on the early train. We don't know what to say to him. And anyway, he wants to speak to you personally. So please open up this door. I'm sure he'll be good enough to forgive the untidiness of your room." Then the chief clerk called "Good morning, Mr. Samsa." "He isn't well," said his mother to the chief clerk, while his father continued to speak through the door. "He isn't well, please believe me. Why else would Gregor have missed a train! The lad only ever thinks about the business. It nearly makes me cross the way he never goes out in the evenings; he's been in town for a week now but stayed home every evening. He sits with us in the kitchen and just reads the paper or studies train time-tables. His idea of relaxation is working with his fretsaw. He's made a little frame, for instance, it only took him two or three evenings, you'll be amazed how nice it is; it's hanging up in his room; you'll see it as soon as Gregor opens the door. Anyway, I'm glad you're here; we wouldn't have been able to get Gregor to open the door by ourselves; he's so stubborn; and I'm sure he isn't well, he said this morning that he is, but he isn't." "I'll be there in a moment," said Gregor slowly and thoughtfully, but without moving so that he would not miss any word of the conversation. "Well I can't think of any other way of explain-ing it, Mrs. Samsa," said the chief clerk, "I hope it's nothing serious. But on the other hand, I must say that if we people in commerce ever become slightly unwell then, fortunately or unfortunately as you like, we simply have to overcome it because of business considerations." "Can the chief clerk come in to see you now then?" asked his father impatiently, knocking at the door again. "No," said Gregor. In the room on his right there followed a painful silence; in the room on his left his sister began to cry.

So why did his sister not go and join the others? She had probably only just got up and had not even begun to get dressed. And why was she crying? Was it because he had not got up, and had not let the chief clerk in, because he was in danger of losing his job and if that happened his boss would once more pursue their parents with the same demands as before? There was no need to worry about things like that yet. Gregor was still there and had not the slightest intention of abandoning his family. For the time being he just lay there on the carpet, and no one who knew the condition he was in would seri-ously have expected him to let the chief clerk in. It was only a minor discourtesy, and a suitable excuse could easily be found for it later on, it was not something for which Gregor could be sacked on the spot. And it seemed to Gregor much more sensible to leave him now in peace instead of disturbing him with talking at him and crying. But the others didn't know what was happening, they were worried, that would excuse their behaviour.

The chief clerk now raised his voice, "Mr. Samsa," he called to him, "what is wrong? You barricade yourself in your room, give us no more than yes or no for an answer, you are causing serious and unnecessary concern to your parents and you fail—and I mention this just by the way—you fail to carry out your business duties in a way that is quite unheard of. I'm speaking here on behalf of your parents and of your employer, and really must request a clear and immediate explanation. I am astonished, quite astonished. I thought I knew you as a calm and sensible person, and now you suddenly seem to be showing off with peculiar whims. This morning, your employer did suggest a possible reason for your failure to appear, it's true—it had to do with the money that was recently entrusted to you—but I came near to giving him my word of honour that that could not be the right explanation. But now that I see your incomprehensible stubbornness I no longer feel any wish whatsoever to intercede on your behalf. And nor is your position all that secure. I had originally intended to say all this to you in private, but since you cause me to waste my time here for no good reason I don't see why your parents should not also learn of it. Your turnover has been very unsatisfactory of late; I grant you that it's not the time of year to do especially good business, we recognise that; but there simply is no time of year to do no business at all, Mr. Samsa, we cannot allow there to be."

"But Sir," called Gregor, beside himself and forgetting all else in the excitement, "I'll open up immediately, just a moment. I'm slightly unwell, an attack of dizziness, I haven't been able to get up. I'm still in bed now. I'm quite fresh again now, though. I'm just getting out of bed. Just a moment. Be patient! It's not quite as easy as I'd thought. I'm quite all right now, though. It's shocking, what can suddenly happen to a person! I was quite all right last night, my parents know about it, perhaps better than me, I had a small symptom of it last night already. They must have noticed it. I don't know why I didn't let you know at work! But you always think you can get over an illness without staying at home. Please, don't make my parents suffer! There's no basis for any of the accusations you're making; nobody's ever said a word to me about any of these things. Maybe you haven't read the latest contracts I sent in. I'll set off with the eight o'clock train, as well, these few hours of rest have given me strength. You don't need to wait, sir; I'll be in the office soon after you, and please be so good as to tell that to the boss and recommend me to him!"

And while Gregor gushed out these words, hardly knowing what he was saying, he made his way over to the chest of drawers—this was easily done, probably because of the practise he had already had in bed—where he now tried to get himself upright. He really did want to open the door, really did want to let them see him and to speak with the chief clerk; the others were being so insistent, and he was curious to learn what they would say when they caught sight of him. If they were shocked then it would no longer be Gregor's responsibility and he could rest. If, however, they took everything calmly he would still have no reason to be upset, and if he hurried he really could be at the station for eight o'clock. The first few times he tried to climb up on the smooth chest of drawers he just slid down again, but he finally gave himself one last swing and stood there upright; the lower part of his body was in serious pain but he no longer gave any attention to it. Now he let himself fall against the back of a nearby chair and held tightly to the edges of it with his little legs. By now he had also calmed down, and kept quiet so that he could listen to what the chief clerk was saying.

"Did you understand a word of all that?" the chief clerk asked his parents, "surely he's not trying to make fools of us." "Oh, God!" called his mother, who was already in tears, "he could be seriously ill and we're making him suffer. Grete! Grete!" she then cried. "Mother?" his sister called from the other side. They communicated across Gregor's room. "You'll have to go for the doctor straight away. Gregor is ill. Quick, get the doctor. Did you hear the way Gregor spoke just now?" "That was the voice of an animal," said the chief clerk, with a calmness that was in contrast with his mother's screams. "Anna! Anna!" his father called into the kitchen through the entrance hall, clapping his hands, "get a locksmith here, now!" And the two girls, their skirts swishing, immediately ran out through the hall, wrenching open the front door of the flat as they went. How had his sister managed to get dressed so quickly? There was no sound of the door banging shut again; they must have left it open; people often do in homes where something awful has happened.

Gregor, in contrast, had become much calmer. So they couldn't understand his words any more, although they seemed clear enough to him, clearer than before—perhaps his ears had become used to the sound. They had realised, though, that there was something wrong with him, and were ready to help. The first response to his situation had been confident and wise, and that made him feel better. He felt that he had been drawn back in among people, and from the doctor and the locksmith he expected great and surprising achievements—although he did not really distinguish one from the other. Whatever was said next would be crucial, so, in order to make his voice as clear as possible, he coughed a little, but taking care to do this not too loudly as even this might well sound different from the way that a human coughs and he was no longer sure he could judge this for himself. Meanwhile, it had become very quiet in the next room. Perhaps his parents were sat at the table whispering with the chief clerk, or perhaps they were all pressed against the door and listening.

Gregor slowly pushed his way over to the door with the chair. Once there he let go of it and threw himself onto the door, holding himself upright against it using the adhesive on the tips of his legs. He rested there a little while to recover from the effort involved and then set himself to the task of turning the key in the lock with his mouth. He seemed, unfortunately, to have no proper teeth—how was he, then, to grasp the key?—but the lack of teeth was, of course, made up for with a very strong jaw; using the jaw, he really was able to start the key turning, ignoring the fact that he must have been causing some kind of damage as a brown fluid came from his mouth, flowed over the key and dripped onto the floor. "Listen," said the chief clerk in the next room, "he's turning the key." Gregor was greatly encouraged by this; but they all should have been calling to him, his father and his mother too: "Well done, Gregor," they should have cried, "keep at it, keep hold of the lock!" And with the idea that they were all excitedly following his efforts, he bit on the key with all his strength, paying no attention to the pain he was causing himself. As the key turned round he turned around the lock with it, only holding himself upright with his mouth, and hung onto the key or pushed it down again with the whole weight of his body as needed. The clear sound of the lock as it snapped back was Gregor's sign that he could break his concentration, and as he regained his breath he said to himself: "So, I didn't need the locksmith after all." Then he lay his head on the handle of the door to open it completely.

Because he had to open the door in this way, it was already wide open before he could be seen. He had first to slowly turn himself around one of the double doors, and he had to do it very carefully if he did not want to fall flat on his back before entering the room. He was still occupied with this difficult movement, unable to pay attention to anything else, when he heard the chief clerk exclaim a loud "Oh!" which sounded like the soughing of the wind. Now he also saw him—he was the nearest to the door—his hand pressed against his open mouth and slowly retreating as if driven by a steady and invisible force. Gregor's mother, her hair still dishevelled from bed despite the chief clerk's being there, looked at his father. Then she unfolded her arms, took two steps forward towards Gregor and sank down onto the floor into her skirts that spread themselves out around her as her head disappeared down onto her breast. His father looked hostile, and clenched his fists as if wanting to knock Gregor back into his room. Then he looked uncertainly round the living room, covered his eyes with his hands and wept so that his powerful chest shook.

So Gregor did not go into the room, but leant against the inside of the other door which was still held bolted in place. In this way only half of his body could be seen, along with his head above it which he leant over to one side as he peered out at the others. Meanwhile the day had become much lighter; part of the endless, grey-black building on the other side of the street—which was a hospital—could be seen quite clearly with the austere and regular line of windows piercing its facade; the rain was still falling, now throwing down large, individual droplets which hit the ground one at a time. The washing up from breakfast lay on the table; there was so much of it because, for Gregor's father, breakfast was the most important meal of the day and he would stretch it out for several hours as he sat reading a number of different newspapers. On the wall exactly opposite there was photograph of Gregor when he was a lieutenant in the army, his sword in his hand and a carefree smile on his face as he called forth respect for his uniform and bearing. The door to the entrance hall was open and as the front door of the flat was also open he could see onto the landing and the stairs where they began their way down below.

"Now, then," said Gregor, well aware that he was the only one to have kept calm, "I'll get dressed straight away now, pack up my samples and set off. Will you please just let me leave? You can see," he said to the chief clerk, "that I'm not stubborn and I like to do my job; being a commercial traveller is arduous but without travelling I couldn't earn my living. So where are you going, in to the office? Yes? Will you report everything accurately, then? It's quite possible for someone to be temporarily unable to work, but that's just the right time to remember what's been achieved in the past and consider that later on, once the difficulty has been removed, he will certainly work with all the more diligence and concentration. You're well aware that I'm seriously in debt to our employer as well as having to look after my parents and my sister, so that I'm trapped in a difficult situation, but I will work my way out of it again. Please don't make things any harder for me than they are already, and don't take sides against me at the office. I know that nobody likes the travellers. They think we earn an enormous wage as well as having a soft time of it. That's just prejudice but they have no particular reason to think better it. But you, sir, you have a better overview than the rest of the staff, in fact, if I can say this in confidence, a better overview than the boss himself—it's very easy for a businessman like him to make mistakes about his employees and judge them more harshly than he should. And you're also well aware that we travellers spend almost the whole year away from the office, so that we can very easily fall victim to gossip and chance and groundless complaints, and it's almost impossible to defend yourself from that sort of thing, we don't usually even hear about them, or if at all it's when we arrive back home exhausted from a trip, and that's when we feel the harmful effects of what's been going on without even knowing what caused them. Please, don't go away, at least first say something to show that you grant that I'm at least partly right!"

But the chief clerk had turned away as soon as Gregor had started to speak, and, with protruding lips, only stared back at him over his trembling shoulders as he left. He did not keep still for a moment while Gregor was speaking, but moved steadily towards the door without taking his eyes off him. He moved very gradually, as if there had been some secret prohibition on leaving the room. It was only when he had reached the entrance hall that he made a sudden movement, drew his foot from the living room, and rushed forward in a panic. In the hall, he stretched his right hand far out towards the stairway as if out there, there were some supernatural force waiting to save him.

Gregor realised that it was out of the question to let the chief clerk go away in this mood if his position in the firm was not to be put into extreme danger. That was something his parents did not understand very well; over the years, they had become convinced that this job would provide for Gregor for his entire life, and besides, they had so much to worry about at present that they had lost sight of any thought for the future. Gregor, though, did think about the future. The chief clerk had to be held back, calmed down, convinced and finally won over; the future of Gregor and his family depended on it! If only his sister were here! She was clever; she was already in tears while Gregor was still lying peacefully on his back. And the chief clerk was a lover of women, surely she could persuade him; she would close the front door in the entrance hall and talk him out of his shocked state. But his sister was not there, Gregor would have to do the job himself. And without considering that he still was not familiar with how well he could move about in his present state, or that his speech still might not—or probably would not—be understood, he let go of the door; pushed himself through the opening; tried to reach the chief clerk on the landing who, ridiculously, was holding on to the banister with both hands; but Gregor fell immediately over and, with a little scream as he sought something to hold onto, landed on his numerous little legs. Hardly had that happened than, for the first time that day, he began to feel all right with his body; the little legs had the solid ground under them; to his pleasure, they did exactly as he told them; they were even making the effort to carry him where he wanted to go; and he was soon believing that all his sorrows would soon be finally at an end. He held back the urge to move but swayed from side to side as he crouched there on the floor. His mother was not far away in front of him and seemed, at first, quite engrossed in herself, but then she suddenly jumped up with her arms outstretched and her fingers spread shouting: "Help, for pity's sake, help!" The way she held her head suggested she wanted to see Gregor better, but the unthinking way she was hurrying backwards showed that she did not; she had forgotten that the table was behind her with all the breakfast things on it; when she reached the table she sat quickly down on it without knowing what she was doing; without even seeming to notice that the coffee pot had been knocked over and a gush of coffee was pouring down onto the carpet.

"Mother, mother," said Gregor gently, looking up at her. He had completely forgotten the chief clerk for the moment, but could not help himself snapping in the air with his jaws at the sight of the flow of coffee. That set his mother screaming anew, she fled from the table and into the arms of his father as he rushed towards her. Gregor, though, had no time to spare for his parents now; the chief clerk had already reached the stairs; with his chin on the banister, he looked back for the last time. Gregor made a run for him; he wanted to be sure of reaching him; the chief clerk must have expected something, as he leapt down several steps at once and disappeared; his shouts resounding all around the staircase. The flight of the chief clerk seemed, unfortunately, to put Gregor's father into a panic as well. Until then he had been relatively self controlled, but now, instead of running after the chief clerk himself, or at least not impeding Gregor as he ran after him, Gregor's father seized the chief clerk's stick in his right hand (the chief clerk had left it behind on a chair, along with his hat and overcoat), picked up a large newspaper from the table with his left, and used them to drive Gregor back into his room, stamping his foot at him as he went. Gregor's appeals to his father were of no help, his appeals were simply not understood, however much he humbly turned his head his father merely stamped his foot all the harder. Across the room, despite the chilly weather, Gregor's mother had pulled open a window, leant far out of it and pressed her hands to her face. A strong draught of air flew in from the street towards the stairway, the curtains flew up, the newspapers on the table fluttered and some of them were blown onto the floor. Nothing would stop Gregor's father as he drove him back, making hissing noises at him like a wild man. Gregor had never had any practice in moving backwards and was only able to go very slowly. If Gregor had only been allowed to turn round he would have been back in his room straight away, but he was afraid that if he took the time to do that his father would become impatient, and there was the threat of a lethal blow to his back or head from the stick in his father's hand any moment. Eventually, though, Gregor realised that he had no choice as he saw, to his disgust, that he was quite incapable of going backwards in a straight line; so he began, as quickly as possible and with frequent anxious glances at his father, to turn himself round. It went very slowly, but perhaps his father was able to see his good intentions as he did nothing to hinder him, in fact now and then he used the tip of his stick to give directions from a distance as to which way to turn. If only his father would stop that unbearable hissing! It was making Gregor quite confused. When he had nearly finished turning round, still listening to that hissing, he made a mistake and turned himself back a little the way he had just come. He was pleased when he finally had his head in front of the doorway, but then saw that it was too narrow, and his body was too broad to get through it without further difficulty. In his present mood, it obviously did not occur to his father to open the other of the double doors so that Gregor would have enough space to get through. He was merely fixed on the idea that Gregor should be got back into his room as quickly as possible. Nor would he ever have allowed Gregor the time to get himself upright as preparation for getting through the doorway. What he did, making more noise than ever, was to drive Gregor forwards all the harder as if there had been nothing in the way; it sounded to Gregor as if there was now more than one father behind him; it was not a pleasant experience, and Gregor pushed himself into the doorway without regard for what might happen. One side of his body lifted itself, he lay at an angle in the doorway, one flank scraped on the white door and was painfully injured, leaving vile brown flecks on it, soon he was stuck fast and would not have been able to move at all by himself, the little legs along one side hung quivering in the air while those on the other side were pressed painfully against the ground. Then his father gave him a hefty shove from behind which released him from where he was held and sent him flying, and heavily bleeding, deep into his room. The door was slammed shut with the stick, then, finally, all was quiet.

2

It was not until it was getting dark that evening that Gregor awoke from his deep and coma-like sleep. He would have woken soon afterwards anyway even if he hadn't been disturbed, as he had had enough sleep and felt fully rested. But he had the impression that some hurried steps and the sound of the door leading into the front room being carefully shut had woken him. The light from the electric street lamps shone palely here and there onto the ceiling and tops of the furniture, but down below, where Gregor was, it was dark. He pushed himself over to the door, feeling his way clumsily with his antennae—of which he was now beginning to learn the value—in order to see what had been happening there. The whole of his left side seemed like one, painfully stretched scar, and he limped badly on his two rows of legs. One of the legs had been badly injured in the events of that morning—it was nearly a miracle that only one of them had been—and dragged along lifelessly.

It was only when he had reached the door that he realised what it actually was that had drawn him over to it; it was the smell of something to eat. By the door there was a dish filled with sweetened milk with little pieces of white bread floating in it. He was so pleased he almost laughed, as he was even hungrier than he had been that morning, and immediately dipped his head into the milk, nearly covering his eyes with it. But he soon drew his head back again in disappointment; not only did the pain in his tender left side make it difficult to eat the food—he was only able to eat if his whole body worked together as a snuffling whole—but the milk did not taste at all nice. Milk like this was normally his favourite drink, and his sister had certainly left it there for him because of that, but he turned, almost against his own will, away from the dish and crawled back into the centre of the room.

Through the crack in the door, Gregor could see that the gas had been lit in the living room. His father at this time would normally be sat with his evening paper, reading it out in a loud voice to Gregor's mother, and sometimes to his sister, but there was now not a sound to be heard. Gregor's sister would often write and tell him about this reading, but maybe his father had lost the habit in recent times. It was so quiet all around too, even though there must have been somebody in the flat. "What a quiet life it is the family lead," said Gregor to himself, and, gazing into the darkness, felt a great pride that he was able to provide a life like that in such a nice home for his sister and parents. But what now, if all this peace and wealth and comfort should come to a horrible and frightening end? That was something that Gregor did not want to think about too much, so he started to move about, crawling up and down the room.

Once during that long evening, the door on one side of the room was opened very slightly and hurriedly closed again; later on the door on the other side did the same; it seemed that someone needed to enter the room but thought better of it. Gregor went and waited immediately by the door, resolved either to bring the timorous visitor into the room in some way or at least to find out who it was; but the door was opened no more that night and Gregor waited in vain. The previous morning while the doors were locked everyone had wanted to get in there to him, but now, now that he had opened up one of the doors and the other had clearly been unlocked some time during the day, no one came, and the keys were in the other sides.

It was not until late at night that the gaslight in the living room was put out, and now it was easy to see that parents and sister had stayed awake all that time, as they all could be distinctly heard as they went away together on tiptoe. It was clear that no one would come into Gregor's room any more until morning; that gave him plenty of time to think undisturbed about how he would have to re-arrange his life. For some reason, the tall, empty room where he was forced to remain made him feel uneasy as he lay there flat on the floor, even though he had been living in it for five years. Hardly aware of what he was doing other than a slight feeling of shame, he hurried under the couch. It pressed down on his back a little, and he was no longer able to lift his head, but he nonetheless felt immediately at ease and his only regret was that his body was too broad to get it all underneath.

He spent the whole night there. Some of the time he passed in a light sleep, although he frequently woke from it in alarm because of his hunger, and some of the time was spent in worries and vague hopes which, however, always led to the same conclusion: for the time being he must remain calm, he must show patience and the greatest

consideration so that his family could bear the unpleasantness that
he, in his present condition, was forced to impose on them.

Gregor soon had the opportunity to test the strength of his decisions, as early the next morning, almost before the night had ended,
his sister, nearly fully dressed, opened the door from the front room
and looked anxiously in. She did not see him straight away, but when
she did notice him under the couch—he had to be somewhere, for
God's sake, he couldn't have flown away—she was so shocked that she
lost control of herself and slammed the door shut again from outside.
But she seemed to regret her behaviour, as she opened the door again
straight away and came in on tiptoe as if entering the room of someone seriously ill or even of a stranger. Gregor had pushed his head
forward, right to the edge of the couch, and watched her. Would she
notice that he had left the milk as it was, realise that it was not from
any lack of hunger and bring him in some other food that was more
suitable? If she didn't do it herself he would rather go hungry than
draw her attention to it, although he did feel a terrible urge to rush
forward from under the couch, throw himself at his sister's feet and
beg her for something good to eat. However, his sister noticed the full
dish immediately and looked at it and the few drops of milk splashed
around it with some surprise. She immediately picked it up—using
a rag, not her bare hands—and carried it out. Gregor was extremely
curious as to what she would bring in its place, imagining the wildest
possibilities, but he never could have guessed what his sister, in her
goodness, actually did bring. In order to test his taste, she brought
him a whole selection of things, all spread out on an old newspaper.
There were old, half-rotten vegetables; bones from the evening meal,
covered in white sauce that had gone hard; a few raisins and almonds;
some cheese that Gregor had declared inedible two days before; a dry
roll and some bread spread with butter and salt. As well as all that she
had poured some water into the dish, which had probably been permanently set aside for Gregor's use, and placed it beside them. Then,
out of consideration for Gregor's feelings, as she knew that he would
not eat in front of her, she hurried out again and even turned the
key in the lock so that Gregor would know he could make things as
comfortable for himself as he liked. Gregor's little legs whirred, at last
he could eat. What's more, his injuries must already have completely
healed as he found no difficulty in moving. This amazed him, as
more than a month earlier he had cut his finger slightly with a knife,
he thought of how his finger had still hurt the day before yesterday.

"Am I less sensitive than I used to be, then?" he thought, and was already sucking greedily at the cheese which had immediately, almost compellingly, attracted him much more than the other foods on the newspaper. Quickly one after another, his eyes watering with pleasure, he consumed the cheese, the vegetables and the sauce; the fresh foods, on the other hand, he didn't like at all, and even dragged the things he did want to eat a little way away from them because he couldn't stand the smell. Long after he had finished eating and lay lethargic in the same place, his sister slowly turned the key in the lock as a sign to him that he should withdraw. He was immediately startled, although he had been half asleep, and he hurried back under the couch. But he needed great self-control to stay there even for the short time that his sister was in the room, as eating so much food had rounded out his body a little and he could hardly breathe in that narrow space. Half suffocating, he watched with bulging eyes as his sister unself-consciously took a broom and swept up the left-overs, mixing them in with the food he had not even touched at all as if it could not be used any more. She quickly dropped it all into a bin, closed it with its wooden lid, and carried everything out. She had hardly turned her back before Gregor came out again from under the couch and stretched himself.

This was how Gregor received his food each day now, once in the morning while his parents and the maid were still asleep, and the second time after everyone had eaten their meal at midday as his parents would sleep for a little while then as well, and Gregor's sister would send the maid away on some errand. Gregor's father and mother certainly did not want him to starve either, but perhaps it would have been more than they could stand to have any more experience of his feeding than being told about it, and perhaps his sister wanted to spare them what distress she could as they were indeed suffering enough.

It was impossible for Gregor to find out what they had told the doctor and the locksmith that first morning to get them out of the flat. As nobody could understand him, nobody, not even his sister, thought that he could understand them, so he had to be content to hear his sister's sighs and appeals to the saints as she moved about his room. It was only later, when she had become a little more used to everything—there was, of course, no question of her ever becoming fully used to the situation—that Gregor would sometimes catch a friendly comment, or at least a comment that could be construed as friendly. "He's enjoyed his dinner today," she might say when he had diligently cleared away all the food left for him, or if he left most of it, which slowly became more and more frequent, she would often say, sadly, "now everything's just been left there again."

Although Gregor wasn't able to hear any news directly he did listen to much of what was said in the next rooms, and whenever he heard anyone speaking he would scurry straight to the appropriate door and press his whole body against it. There was seldom any conversation, especially at first, that was not about him in some way, even if only in secret. For two whole days, all the talk at every mealtime was about what they should do now; but even between meals they spoke about the same subject as there were always at least two members of the family at home—nobody wanted to be at home by themselves and it was out of the question to leave the flat entirely empty. And on the very first day the maid had fallen to her knees and begged Gregor's mother to let her go without delay. It was not very clear how much she knew of what had happened but she left within a quarter of an hour, tearfully thanking Gregor's mother for her dismissal as if she had done her an enormous service. She even swore emphatically not to tell anyone the slightest about what had happened, even though no one had asked that of her.

Now Gregor's sister also had to help his mother with the cooking; although that was not so much bother as no one ate very much. Gregor often heard how one of them would unsuccessfully urge another to eat, and receive no more answer than "no thanks, I've had enough" or something similar. No one drank very much either. His sister would sometimes ask his father whether he would like a beer, hoping for the chance to go and fetch it herself. When his father then said nothing she would add, so that he would not feel selfish, that she could send the housekeeper for it, but then his father would close the matter with a big, loud "No," and no more would be said.

Even before the first day had come to an end, his father had explained to Gregor's mother and sister what their finances and prospects were. Now and then he stood up from the table and took some receipt or document from the little cash box he had saved from his business when it had collapsed five years earlier. Gregor heard how he opened the complicated lock and then closed it again after he had taken the item he wanted. What he heard his father say was some of the first good news that Gregor heard since he had first been incarcerated in his room. He had thought that nothing at all remained from his father's business, at least he had never told him anything different, and Gregor had never asked him about it anyway. Their business misfortune had reduced the family to a state of total despair, and Gregor's only concern at that time had been to arrange things so that they could all forget about it as quickly as possible. So then he started working especially hard, with a fiery vigour that raised him from a junior salesman to a travelling representative almost overnight, bringing with it the chance to earn money in quite different ways. Gregor converted his success at work straight into cash that he could lay on the table at home for the benefit of his astonished and delighted family. They had been good times and they had never come again, at least not with the same splendour, even though Gregor had later earned so much that he was in a position to bear the costs of the whole family, and did bear them. They had even got used to it, both Gregor and the family, they took the money with gratitude and he was glad to provide it, although there was no longer much warm affection given in return. Gregor only remained close to his sister now. Unlike him, she was very fond of music and a gifted and expressive violinist, it was his secret plan to send her to the conservatory next year even though it would cause great expense that would have to be made up for in some other way. During Gregor's short periods in town, conversation with his sister would often turn to the conservatory but it was only ever mentioned as a lovely dream that could never be realised. Their parents did not like to hear this innocent talk, but Gregor thought about it quite hard and decided he would let them know what he planned with a grand announcement of it on Christmas day.

That was the sort of totally pointless thing that went through his mind in his present state, pressed upright against the door and listening. There were times when he simply became too tired to continue listening, when his head would fall wearily against the door and he would pull it up again with a start, as even the slightest noise he caused would be heard next door and they would all go silent. "What's that he's doing now," his father would say after a while, clearly having gone over to the door, and only then would the interrupted conversation slowly be taken up again.

When explaining things, his father repeated himself several times, partly because it was a long time since he had been occupied with these matters himself and partly because Gregor's mother did not understand everything first time. From these repeated explanations Gregor learned, to his pleasure, that despite all their misfortunes there was still some money available from the old days. It was not a lot, but it had not been touched in the meantime and some interest had accumulated. Besides that, they had not been using up all the money that Gregor had been bringing home every month, keeping only a little for himself, so that that, too, had been accumulating. Behind the door, Gregor nodded with enthusiasm in his pleasure at this unexpected thrift and caution. He could actually have used this surplus money to reduce his father's debt to his boss, and the day when he could have freed himself from that job would have come much closer, but now it was certainly better the way his father had done things.

This money, however, was certainly not enough to enable the family to live off the interest; it was enough to maintain them for, perhaps, one or two years, no more. That's to say, it was money that should not really be touched but set aside for emergencies; money to live on had to be earned. His father was healthy but old, and lacking in self confidence. During the five years that he had not been working—the first holiday in a life that had been full of strain and no success—he had put on a lot of weight and become very slow and clumsy. Would Gregor's elderly mother now have to go and earn money? She suffered from asthma and it was a strain for her just to move about the home, every other day would be spent struggling for breath on the sofa by the open window. Would his sister have to go and earn money? She was still a child of seventeen, her life up till then had been very enviable, consisting of wearing nice clothes, sleeping late, helping out in the business, joining in with a few modest pleasures and most of all playing the violin. Whenever they began to talk of the need to earn money, Gregor would always first let go of the door and then throw himself onto the cool, leather sofa next to it, as he became quite hot with shame and regret.

He would often lie there the whole night through, not sleeping a wink but scratching at the leather for hours on end. Or he might go to all the effort of pushing a chair to the window, climbing up onto the sill and, propped up in the chair, leaning on the window to stare out of it. He had used to feel a great sense of freedom from doing this, but doing it now was obviously something more remembered than experienced, as what he actually saw in this way was becoming less distinct every day, even things that were quite near; he had used to curse the ever-present view of the hospital across the street, but now he could not see it at all, and if he had not known that he lived in Charlottenstrasse, which was a quiet street despite being in the middle of the city, he could have thought that he was looking out the window at a barren waste where the grey sky and the grey earth mingled inseparably. His observant sister only needed to notice the chair twice before she would always push it back to its exact position by the window after she had tidied up the room, and even left the inner pane of the window open from then on.

If Gregor had only been able to speak to his sister and thank her for all that she had to do for him it would have been easier for him to bear it; but as it was it caused him pain. His sister, naturally, tried as far as possible to pretend there was nothing burdensome about it, and the longer it went on, of course, the better she was able to do so, but as time went by Gregor was also able to see through it all so much better. It had even become very unpleasant for him, now, whenever she entered the room. No sooner had she come in than she would quickly close the door as a precaution so that no one would have to suffer the view into Gregor's room, then she would go straight to the window and pull it hurriedly open almost as if she were suffocating. Even if it was cold, she would stay at the window breathing deeply for a little while. She would alarm Gregor twice a day with this running about and noise making; he would stay under the couch shivering the whole while, knowing full well that she would certainly have liked to spare him this ordeal, but it was impossible for her to be in the same room with him with the windows closed.

One day, about a month after Gregor's transformation when his sister no longer had any particular reason to be shocked at his appearance, she came into the room a little earlier than usual and found him still staring out the window, motionless, and just where he would be most horrible. In itself, his sister's not coming into the room would have been no surprise for Gregor as it would have been difficult for her to immediately open the window while he was still there, but not only did she not come in, she went straight back and closed the door behind her, a stranger would have thought he had threatened her and tried to bite her. Gregor went straight to hide himself under the couch, of course, but he had to wait until midday before his sister came back and she seemed much more uneasy than usual. It made him realise that she still found his appearance unbearable and would continue to do so, she probably even had to overcome the urge to flee when she saw the little bit of him that protruded from under the couch. One day, in order to spare her even this sight, he spent four hours carrying the bedsheet over to the couch on his back and arranged it so that he

was completely covered and his sister would not be able to see him
even if she bent down. If she did not think this sheet was necessary
then all she had to do was take it off again, as it was clear enough that
it was no pleasure for Gregor to cut himself off so completely. She left
the sheet where it was. Gregor even thought he glimpsed a look of
gratitude one time when he carefully looked out from under the sheet
to see how his sister liked the new arrangement.

For the first fourteen days, Gregor's parents could not bring themselves to come into the room to see him. He would often hear them
say how they appreciated all the new work his sister was doing even
though, before, they had seen her as a girl who was somewhat useless
and frequently been annoyed with her. But now the two of them,
father and mother, would often both wait outside the door of Gregor's
room while his sister tidied up in there, and as soon as she went out
again she would have to tell them exactly how everything looked, what
Gregor had eaten, how he had behaved this time and whether, perhaps, any slight improvement could be seen. His mother also wanted
to go in and visit Gregor relatively soon but his father and sister at first
persuaded her against it. Gregor listened very closely to all this, and
approved fully. Later, though, she had to be held back by force, which
made her call out: "Let me go and see Gregor, he is my unfortunate
son! Can't you understand I have to see him?" and Gregor would
think to himself that maybe it would be better if his mother came in,
not every day of course, but one day a week, perhaps; she could understand everything much better than his sister who, for all her courage,
was still just a child after all, and really might not have had an adult's
appreciation of the burdensome job she had taken on.

Gregor's wish to see his mother was soon realised. Out of consideration for his parents, Gregor wanted to avoid being seen at the
window during the day, the few square meters of the floor did not
give him much room to crawl about, it was hard to just lie quietly
through the night, his food soon stopped giving him any pleasure at
all, and so, to entertain himself, he got into the habit of crawling up
and down the walls and ceiling. He was especially fond of hanging
from the ceiling; it was quite different from lying on the floor; he
could breathe more freely; his body had a light swing to it; and up
there, relaxed and almost happy, it might happen that he would surprise even himself by letting go of the ceiling and landing on the floor
with a crash. But now, of course, he had far better control of his body
than before and, even with a fall as great as that, caused himself no

damage. Very soon his sister noticed Gregor's new way of entertaining himself—he had, after all, left traces of the adhesive from his feet as he crawled about—and got it into her head to make it as easy as possible for him by removing the furniture that got in his way, especially the chest of drawers and the desk. Now, this was not something that she would be able to do by herself; she did not dare to ask for help from her father; the sixteen-year-old maid had carried on bravely since the cook had left but she certainly would not have helped in this, she had even asked to be allowed to keep the kitchen locked at all times and never to have to open the door unless it was especially important; so his sister had no choice but to choose some time when Gregor's father was not there and fetch his mother to help her. As she approached the room, Gregor could hear his mother express her joy, but once at the door she went silent. First, of course, his sister came in and looked round to see that everything in the room was all right; and only then did she let her mother enter. Gregor had hurriedly pulled the sheet down lower over the couch and put more folds into it so that everything really looked as if it had just been thrown down by chance. Gregor also refrained, this time, from spying out from under the sheet; he gave up the chance to see his mother until later and was simply glad that she had come. "You can come in, he can't be seen," said his sister, obviously leading her in by the hand. The old chest of drawers was too heavy for a pair of feeble women to be heaving about, but Gregor listened as they pushed it from its place, his sister always taking on the heaviest part of the work for herself and ignoring her mother's warnings that she would strain herself. This lasted a very long time. After labouring at it for fifteen minutes or more his mother said it would be better to leave the chest where it was, for one thing it was too heavy for them to get the job finished before Gregor's father got home and leaving it in the middle of the room it would be in his way even more, and for another thing it wasn't even sure that taking the furniture away would really be any help to him. She thought just the opposite; the sight of the bare walls saddened her right to her heart; and why wouldn't Gregor feel the same way about it, he'd been used to this furniture in his room for a long time and it would make him feel abandoned to be in an empty room like that. Then, quietly, almost whispering as if wanting Gregor (whose whereabouts she did not know) to hear not even the tone of her voice, as she was convinced that he did not understand her words, she added "and by taking the furniture away, won't it seem like we're showing that we've given up all hope of improvement and we're abandoning him to cope for himself? I think it'd be best to leave the room exactly the way it was before so that when Gregor comes back to us again he'll find everything unchanged and he'll be able to forget the time in between all the easier."

Hearing these words from his mother made Gregor realise that the lack of any direct human communication, along with the monotonous life led by the family during these two months, must have made him confused—he could think of no other way of explaining to himself why he had seriously wanted his room emptied out. Had he really wanted to transform his room into a cave, a warm room fitted out with the nice furniture he had inherited? That would have let him crawl around unimpeded in any direction, but it would also have let him quickly forget his past when he had still been human. He had come very close to forgetting, and it had only been the voice of his mother, unheard for so long, that had shaken him out of it. Nothing should be removed; everything had to stay; he could not do without the good influence the furniture had on his condition; and if the furniture made it difficult for him to crawl about mindlessly that was not a loss but a great advantage.

His sister, unfortunately, did not agree; she had become used to the idea, not without reason, that she was Gregor's spokesman to his parents about the things that concerned him. This meant that his mother's advice now was sufficient reason for her to insist on removing not only the chest of drawers and the desk, as she had thought at first, but all the furniture apart from the all-important couch. It was more than childish perversity, of course, or the unexpected confidence she had recently acquired, that made her insist; she had indeed noticed that Gregor needed a lot of room to crawl about in, whereas the furniture, as far as anyone could see, was of no use to him at all. Girls of that age, though, do become enthusiastic about things and feel they must get their way whenever they can. Perhaps this was what tempted Grete to make Gregor's situation seem even more shocking than it was so that she could do even more for him. Grete would probably be the only one who would dare enter a room dominated by Gregor crawling about the bare walls by himself.

So she refused to let her mother dissuade her. Gregor's mother already looked uneasy in his room, she soon stopped speaking and helped Gregor's sister to get the chest of drawers out with what strength she had. The chest of drawers was something that Gregor could do without if he had to, but the writing desk had to stay. Hardly had the two women pushed the chest of drawers, groaning, out of the room than Gregor poked his head out from under the couch to see what he could do about it. He meant to be as careful and considerate as he could, but, unfortunately, it was his mother who came back first while Grete in the next room had her arms round the chest, pushing and pulling at it from side to side by herself without, of course, moving it an inch. His mother was not used to the sight of Gregor, he might have made her ill, so Gregor hurried backwards to the far end of the couch. In his startlement, though, he was not able to prevent the sheet at its front from moving a little. It was enough to attract his mother's attention. She stood very still, remained there a moment, and then went back out to Grete.

Gregor kept trying to assure himself that nothing unusual was happening, it was just a few pieces of furniture being moved after all, but he soon had to admit that the women going to and fro, their little calls to each other, the scraping of the furniture on the floor, all these things made him feel as if he were being assailed from all sides. With his head and legs pulled in against him and his body pressed to the floor, he was forced to admit to himself that he could not stand all of this much longer. They were emptying his room out; taking away everything that was dear to him; they had already taken out the chest containing his fretsaw and other tools; now they threatened to remove the writing desk with its place clearly worn into the floor, the desk where he had done his homework as a business trainee, at high school, even while he had been at infant school—he really could not wait any longer to see whether the two women's intentions were good. He had nearly forgotten they were there anyway, as they were now too tired to say anything while they worked and he could only hear their feet as they stepped heavily on the floor.

So, while the women were leant against the desk in the other room catching their breath, he sallied out, changed direction four times not knowing what he should save first before his attention was suddenly caught by the picture on the wall—which was already denuded of everything else that had been on it—of the lady dressed in copious fur. He hurried up onto the picture and pressed himself against its glass, it held him firmly and felt good on his hot belly. This picture at least, now totally covered by Gregor, would certainly be taken away by no one. He turned his head to face the door into the living room so that he could watch the women when they came back.

They had not allowed themselves a long rest and came back quite soon; Grete had put her arm around her mother and was nearly carrying her. "What shall we take now, then?" said Grete and looked around. Her eyes met those of Gregor on the wall. Perhaps only because her mother was there, she remained calm, bent her face to her so that she would not look round and said, albeit hurriedly and with a tremor in her voice: "Come on, let's go back in the living room for a while?" Gregor could see what Grete had in mind, she wanted to take her mother somewhere safe and then chase him down from the wall. Well, she could certainly try it! He sat unyielding on his picture. He would rather jump at Grete's face.

But Grete's words had made her mother quite worried, she stepped to one side, saw the enormous brown patch against the flowers of the wallpaper, and before she even realised it was Gregor that she saw screamed: "Oh God, oh God!" Arms outstretched, she fell onto the couch as if she had given up everything and stayed there immobile. "Gregor!" shouted his sister, glowering at him and shaking her fist. That was the first word she had spoken to him directly since his transformation. She ran into the other room to fetch some kind of smelling salts to bring her mother out of her faint; Gregor wanted to help too—he could save his picture later, although he stuck fast to the glass and had to pull himself off by force; then he, too, ran into the next room as if he could advise his sister like in the old days; but he had to just stand behind her doing nothing; she was looking into various bottles, he startled her when she turned round; a bottle fell to the ground and broke; a splinter cut Gregor's face, some kind of caustic medicine splashed all over him; now, without delaying any longer, Grete took hold of all the bottles she could and ran with them in to her mother; she slammed the door shut with her foot. So now Gregor was shut out from his mother, who, because of him, might be near to death; he could not open the door if he did not want to chase his sister away, and she had to stay with his mother; there was nothing for him to do but wait; and, oppressed with anxiety and self-reproach, he began to crawl about, he crawled over everything, walls, furniture, ceiling, and finally in his confusion as the whole room began to spin around him he fell down into the middle of the dinner table.

He lay there for a while, numb and immobile, all around him it was quiet, maybe that was a good sign. Then there was someone at the door. The maid, of course, had locked herself in her kitchen so that Grete would have to go and answer it. His father had arrived home.

"What's happened?" were his first words; Grete's appearance must have made everything clear to him. She answered him with subdued voice, and openly pressed her face into his chest: "Mother's fainted, but she's better now. Gregor got out." "Just as I expected," said his father, "just as I always said, but you women wouldn't listen, would you." It was clear to Gregor that Grete had not said enough and that his father took it to mean that something bad had happened, that he was responsible for some act of violence. That meant Gregor would now have to try to calm his father, as he did not have the time to explain things to him even if that had been possible. So he fled to the door of his room and pressed himself against it so that his father, when he came in from the hall, could see straight away that Gregor had the best intentions and would go back into his room without delay, that it would not be necessary to drive him back but that they had only to open the door and he would disappear.

His father, though, was not in the mood to notice subtleties like that; "Ah!" he shouted as he came in, sounding as if he were both angry and glad at the same time. Gregor drew his head back from the door and lifted it towards his father. He really had not imagined his father the way he stood there now; of late, with his new habit of crawling about, he had neglected to pay attention to what was going on the rest of the flat the way he had done before. He really ought to have expected things to have changed, but still, still, was that really his father? The same tired man as used to be laying there entombed in his bed when Gregor came back from his business trips, who would receive him sitting in the armchair in his nightgown when he came back in the evenings; who was hardly even able to stand up but, as a sign of his pleasure, would just raise his arms and who, on the couple of times a year when they went for a walk together on a Sunday or public holiday wrapped up tightly in his overcoat between Gregor and his mother, would always labour his way forward a little more slowly than them, who were already walking slowly for his sake; who would place his stick down carefully and, if he wanted to say something would invariably stop and gather his companions around him. He was standing up straight enough now; dressed in a smart blue uniform with gold buttons, the sort worn by the employees at the banking institute; above the high, stiff collar of the coat his strong double-chin emerged; under the bushy eyebrows, his piercing, dark eyes looked out fresh and alert; his normally unkempt white hair was combed down painfully close to his scalp. He took his cap, with its gold monogram from, probably, some bank, and threw it in an arc right across the room onto the sofa, put his hands in his trouser pockets, pushing back the bottom of his long uniform coat, and, with look of determination, walked towards Gregor. He probably did not even know himself what he had in mind, but nonetheless lifted his feet unusually high. Gregor was amazed at the enormous size of the soles of his boots, but wasted no time with that—he knew full well, right from the first day of his new life, that his father thought it necessary to always be extremely strict with him. And so he ran up to his father, stopped when his father stopped, scurried forwards again when he moved, even slightly. In this way they went round the room several times without anything decisive happening, without even giving the impression of a chase as everything went so slowly. Gregor remained all this time on the floor, largely because he feared his father might see it as especially provoking if he fled onto the wall or ceiling. Whatever he did, Gregor had to admit that he certainly would not be able to keep up this running about for long, as for each step his father took he had to carry out countless movements. He became noticeably short of breath, even in his earlier life his lungs had not been very reliable. Now, as he lurched about in his efforts to muster all the strength he could for running he could hardly keep his eyes open; his thoughts became too slow for him to think of any other way of saving himself than running; he almost forgot that the walls were there for him to use although, here, they were concealed behind carefully carved furniture full of notches and protrusions—then, right beside him, lightly tossed, something flew down and rolled in front of him. It was an apple; then another one immediately flew at him; Gregor froze in shock; there was no longer any point in running as his father had decided to bombard him. He had filled his pockets with fruit from the bowl on the sideboard and now, without even taking the time for careful aim, threw one apple after another. These little red apples rolled about on the floor, knocking into each other as if they had electric motors. An apple thrown without much force glanced against Gregor's back and slid off without doing any harm. Another one however, immediately following it, hit squarely and lodged in his back; Gregor wanted to drag himself away, as if he could remove the surprising, the incredible pain by changing his position; but he felt as if nailed to the spot and spread himself out, all his senses in confusion. The last thing he saw was the door of his room being pulled open, his sister was screaming, his mother ran out in front of her in her blouse (as his sister had taken off some of her clothes after she had fainted to make it easier for her to breathe), she ran to his father, her skirts unfastened and sliding one after another to the ground, stumbling over the skirts she pushed herself to his father, her arms around him, uniting herself with him totally—now Gregor lost his ability to see anything—her hands behind his father's head begging him to spare Gregor's life.

3

No one dared to remove the apple lodged in Gregor's skin, so it remained there as a visible reminder of his injury. He had suffered it there for more than a month, and his condition seemed serious enough to remind even his father that Gregor, despite his current sad and revolting form, was a family member who could not be treated as an enemy. On the contrary, as a family there was a duty to swallow any revulsion for him and to be patient, just to be patient.

Because of his injuries, Gregor had lost much of his mobility—probably permanently. He had been reduced to the condition of an ancient invalid and it took him long, long minutes to crawl across his room—crawling over the ceiling was out of the question—but this deterioration in his condition was fully (in his opinion) made up for by the door to the living room being left open every evening. He got into the habit of closely watching it for one or two hours before it was opened and then, lying in the darkness of his room where he could not be seen from the living room, he could watch the family in the light of the dinner table and listen to their conversation—with everyone's permission, in a way, and thus quite differently from before.

They no longer held the lively conversations of earlier times, of course, the ones that Gregor always thought about with longing when he was tired and getting into the damp bed in some small hotel room. All of them were usually very quiet nowadays. Soon after dinner, his father would go to sleep in his chair; his mother and sister would urge each other to be quiet; his mother, bent deeply under the lamp, would sew fancy underwear for a fashion shop; his sister, who had taken a sales job, learned shorthand and French in the evenings so that she might be able to get a better position later on. Sometimes his father would wake up and say to Gregor's mother "you're doing so much sewing again today!" as if he did not know that he had been dozing—and then he would go back to sleep again while mother and sister would exchange a tired grin.

With a kind of stubbornness, Gregor's father refused to take his uniform off even at home; while his nightgown hung unused on its peg Gregor's father would slumber where he was, fully dressed, as if always ready to serve and expecting to hear the voice of his superior even here. The uniform had not been new to start with, but as a result of this it slowly became even shabbier despite the efforts of Gregor's mother and sister to look after it. Gregor would often spend the whole evening looking at all the stains on this coat, with its gold buttons always kept polished and shiny, while the old man in it would sleep, highly uncomfortable but peaceful.

As soon as it struck ten, Gregor's mother would speak gently to his father to wake him and try to persuade him to go to bed, as he couldn't sleep properly where he was and he really had to get his sleep if he was to be up at six to get to work. But since he had been in work he had become more obstinate and would always insist on staying longer at the table, even though he regularly fell asleep and it was then harder than ever to persuade him to exchange the chair for his bed. Then, however much mother and sister would importune him with little reproaches and warnings he would keep slowly shaking his head for a quarter of an hour with his eyes closed and refusing to get up. Gregor's mother would tug at his sleeve, whisper endearments into his ear, Gregor's sister would leave her work to help her mother, but nothing would have any effect on him. He would just sink deeper into his chair. Only when the two women took him under the arms he would abruptly open his eyes, look at them one after the other and say: "What a life! This is what peace I get in my old age!" And supported by the two women he would lift himself up carefully as if he were carrying the greatest load himself, let the women take him to the door, send them off and carry on by himself while Gregor's mother would throw down her needle and his sister her pen so that they could run after his father and continue being of help to him.

Who, in this tired and overworked family, would have had time to give more attention to Gregor than was absolutely necessary? The household budget became even smaller; so now the maid was dismissed; an enormous, thick-boned charwoman with white hair that flapped around her head came every morning and evening to do the heaviest work; everything else was looked after by Gregor's mother on top of the large amount of sewing work she did. Gregor even learned, listening to the evening conversation about what price they had hoped for, that several items of jewellery belonging to the family had been sold, even though both mother and sister had been very fond of wearing them at functions and celebrations. But the loudest complaint

was that although the flat was much too big for their present circumstances, they could not move out of it, there was no imaginable way
of transferring Gregor to the new address. He could see quite well,
though, that there were more reasons than consideration for him that
made it difficult for them to move, it would have been quite easy
to transport him in any suitable crate with a few air holes in it; the
main thing holding the family back from their decision to move was
much more to do with their total despair, and the thought that they
had been struck with a misfortune unlike anything experienced by
anyone else they knew or were related to. They carried out absolutely
everything that the world expects from poor people, Gregor's father
brought bank employees their breakfast, his mother sacrificed herself
by washing clothes for strangers, his sister ran back and forth behind
her desk at the behest of the customers, but they just did not have the
strength to do any more. And the injury in Gregor's back began to
hurt as much as when it was new. After they had come back from taking his father to bed Gregor's mother and sister would now leave their
work where it was and sit close together, cheek to cheek; his mother
would point to Gregor's room and say "Close that door, Grete," and
then, when he was in the dark again, they would sit in the next room
and their tears would mingle, or they would simply sit there staring
dry-eyed at the table.

Gregor hardly slept at all, either night or day. Sometimes he would
think of taking over the family's affairs, just like before, the next time
the door was opened; he had long forgotten about his boss and the
chief clerk, but they would appear again in his thoughts, the salesmen
and the apprentices, that stupid teaboy, two or three friends from
other businesses, one of the chambermaids from a provincial hotel, a
tender memory that appeared and disappeared again, a cashier from
a hat shop for whom his attention had been serious but too slow—all
of them appeared to him, mixed together with strangers and others he had forgotten, but instead of helping him and his family they
were all of them inaccessible, and he was glad when they disappeared.
Other times he was not at all in the mood to look after his family, he
was filled with simple rage about the lack of attention he was shown,
and although he could think of nothing he would have wanted, he
made plans of how he could get into the pantry where he could take
all the things he was entitled to, even if he was not hungry. Gregor's
sister no longer thought about how she could please him but would
hurriedly push some food or other into his room with her foot before

she rushed out to work in the morning and at midday, and in the evening she would sweep it away again with the broom, indifferent as to whether it had been eaten or—more often than not—had been left totally untouched. She still cleared up the room in the evening, but now she could not have been any quicker about it. Smears of dirt were left on the walls, here and there were little balls of dust and filth. At first, Gregor went into one of the worst of these places when his sister arrived as a reproach to her, but he could have stayed there for weeks without his sister doing anything about it; she could see the dirt as well as he could but she had simply decided to leave him to it. At the same time she became touchy in a way that was quite new for her and which everyone in the family understood—cleaning up Gregor's room was for her and her alone. Gregor's mother did once thoroughly clean his room, and needed to use several bucketfuls of water to do it—although that much dampness also made Gregor ill and he lay flat on the couch, bitter and immobile. But his mother was to be punished still more for what she had done, as hardly had his sister arrived home in the evening than she noticed the change in Gregor's room and, highly aggrieved, ran back into the living room where, despite her mother's raised and imploring hands, she broke into convulsive tears. Her father, of course, was startled out of his chair and the two parents looked on astonished and helpless; then they, too, became agitated; Gregor's father, standing to the right of his mother, accused her of not leaving the cleaning of Gregor's room to his sister; from her left, Gregor's sister screamed at her that she was never to clean Gregor's room again; while his mother tried to draw his father, who was beside himself with anger, into the bedroom; his sister, quaking with tears, thumped on the table with her small fists; and Gregor hissed in anger that no one had even thought of closing the door to save him the sight of this and all its noise.

Gregor's sister was exhausted from going out to work, and looking after Gregor as she had done before was even more work for her, but even so his mother ought certainly not to have taken her place. Gregor, on the other hand, ought not to be neglected. Now, though, the charwoman was here. This elderly widow, with a robust bone structure that made her able to withstand the hardest of things in her long life, wasn't really repelled by Gregor. Just by chance one day, rather than any real curiosity, she opened the door to Gregor's room and found herself face to face with him. He was taken totally by surprise, no one was chasing him but he began to rush to and fro while she just stood there in amazement with her hands crossed in front of her. From then on she never failed to open the door slightly every evening and morning and look briefly in on him. At first she would call to him as she did so with words that she probably considered friendly, such as "Come on then, you old dung beetle!" or "Look at the old dung beetle there!" Gregor never responded to being spoken to in that way, but just remained where he was without moving as if the door had never even been opened. If only they had told this charwoman to clean up his room every day instead of letting her disturb him for no reason whenever she felt like it! One day, early in the morning while a heavy rain struck the windowpanes, perhaps indicating that spring was coming, she began to speak to him in that way once again. Gregor was so resentful of it that he started to move toward her, he was slow and infirm, but it was like a kind of attack. Instead of being afraid, the charwoman just lifted up one of the chairs from near the door and stood there with her mouth open, clearly intending not to close her mouth until the chair in her hand had been slammed down into Gregor's back. "Aren't you coming any closer, then?" she asked when Gregor turned round again, and she calmly put the chair back in the corner.

Gregor had almost entirely stopped eating. Only if he happened to find himself next to the food that had been prepared for him he might take some of it into his mouth to play with it, leave it there a few hours and then, more often than not, spit it out again. At first he thought it was distress at the state of his room that stopped him eating, but he had soon got used to the changes made there. They had got into the habit of putting things into this room that they had no room for anywhere else, and there were now many such things as one of the rooms in the flat had been rented out to three gentlemen. These earnest gentlemen—all three of them had full beards, as Gregor learned peering through the crack in the door one day—were painfully insistent on things being tidy. This meant not only in their own room but, since they had taken a room in this establishment, in the entire flat and especially in the kitchen. Unnecessary clutter was something they could not tolerate, especially if it was dirty. They had moreover brought most of their own furnishings and equipment with them. For this reason, many things had become superfluous which, although they could not be sold, the family did not wish to discard. All these things found their way into Gregor's room. The dustbins from the kitchen found their way in there too. The charwoman was always in a hurry, and anything she couldn't use for the time being she would just chuck in there. He, fortunately, would usually see no more than the object and the hand that held it. The woman most likely meant to fetch the things back out again when she had time and the opportunity, or to throw everything out in one go, but what actually happened was that they were left where they landed when they had first been thrown unless Gregor made his way through the junk and moved it somewhere else. At first he moved it because, with no other room free where he could crawl about, he was forced to, but later on he came to enjoy it although moving about in the way left him sad and tired to death and he would remain immobile for hours afterwards.

The gentlemen who rented the room would sometimes take their evening meal at home in the living room that was used by everyone, and so the door to this room was often kept closed in the evening. But Gregor found it easy to give up having the door open, he had, after all, often failed to make use of it when it was open and, without the family having noticed it, lain in his room in its darkest corner. One time, though, the charwoman left the door to the living room slightly open, and it remained open when the gentlemen who rented the room came in in the evening and the light was put on. They sat up at the table where, formerly, Gregor had taken his meals with his father and mother, they unfolded the serviettes and picked up their knives and forks. Gregor's mother immediately appeared in the doorway with a dish of meat and soon behind her came his sister with a dish piled high with potatoes. The food was steaming, and filled the room with its smell. The gentlemen bent over the dishes set in front of them as if they wanted to test the food before eating it, and the gentleman in the middle, who seemed to count as an authority for the other two, did indeed cut off a piece of meat while it was still in its dish, clearly wishing to establish whether it was sufficiently cooked or whether it should be sent back to the kitchen. It was to his satisfaction, and Gregor's mother and sister, who had been looking on anxiously, began to breathe again and smiled.

The family themselves ate in the kitchen. Nonetheless, Gregor's father came into the living room before he went into the kitchen, bowed once with his cap in his hand and did his round of the table. The gentlemen stood as one, and mumbled something into their beards. Then, once they were alone, they ate in near perfect silence. It seemed remarkable to Gregor that above all the various noises of eating their chewing teeth could still be heard, as if they had wanted to Show Gregor that you need teeth in order to eat and it was not possible to perform anything with jaws that are toothless however nice they might be. "I'd like to eat something," said Gregor anxiously, "but not anything like they're eating. They do feed themselves. And here I am, dying!"

Throughout all this time, Gregor could not remember having heard the violin being played, but this evening it began to be heard from the kitchen. The three gentlemen had already finished their meal, the one in the middle had produced a newspaper, given a page to each of the others, and now they leant back in their chairs reading them and smoking. When the violin began playing they became attentive, stood up and went on tiptoe over to the door of the hallway where they stood pressed against each other. Someone must have heard them in the kitchen, as Gregor's father called out: "Is the playing perhaps unpleasant for the gentlemen? We can stop it straight away." "On the contrary," said the middle gentleman, "would the young lady not like to come in and play for us here in the room, where it is, after all, much more cosy and comfortable?" "Oh yes, we'd love to," called back Gregor's father as if he had been the violin player himself. The gentlemen stepped back into the room and waited. Gregor's father soon appeared with the music stand, his mother with the music and his sister with the violin. She calmly prepared everything for her to begin playing; his parents, who had never rented a room out before and therefore showed an exaggerated courtesy towards the three gentlemen, did not even dare to sit on their own chairs; his father leant against the door with his right hand pushed in between two buttons on his uniform coat; his mother, though, was offered a seat by one of the gentlemen and sat—leaving the chair where the gentleman happened to have placed it—out of the way in a corner.

His sister began to play; father and mother paid close attention, one on each side, to the movements of her hands. Drawn in by the playing, Gregor had dared to come forward a little and already had his head in the living room. Before, he had taken great pride in how considerate he was but now it hardly occurred to him that he had become so thoughtless about the others. What's more, there was now all the more reason to keep himself hidden as he was covered in the dust that lay everywhere in his room and flew up at the slightest movement; he carried threads, hairs, and remains of food about on his back and sides; he was much too indifferent to everything now to lay on his back and wipe himself on the carpet like he had used to do several times a day. And despite this condition, he was not too shy to move forward a little onto the immaculate floor of the living room.

No one noticed him, though. The family was totally preoccupied with the violin playing; at first, the three gentlemen had put their hands in their pockets and come up far too close behind the music stand to look at all the notes being played, and they must have disturbed Gregor's sister, but soon, in contrast with the family, they withdrew back to the window with their heads sunk and talking to each other at half volume, and they stayed by the window while Gregor's father observed them anxiously. It really now seemed very obvious that they had expected to hear some beautiful or entertaining violin playing but had been disappointed, that they had had enough of the whole performance and it was only now out of politeness that they allowed their peace to be disturbed. It was especially unnerving, the way they all blew the smoke from their cigarettes upwards from their mouth and noses. Yet Gregor's sister was playing so beautifully. Her face was leant to one side, following the lines of music with a careful and melancholy expression. Gregor crawled a little further forward, keeping his head close to the ground so that he could meet her eyes if the chance came. Was he an animal if music could captivate him so? It seemed to him that he was being shown the way to the unknown nourishment he had been yearning for. He was determined to make his way forward to his sister and tug at her skirt to show her she might come into his room with her violin, as no one appreciated her playing here as much as he would. He never wanted to let her out of his room, not while he lived, anyway; his shocking appearance should, for once, be of some use to him; he wanted to be at every door of his room at once to hiss and spit at the attackers; his sister should not be forced to stay with him, though, but stay of her own free will; she would sit beside him on the couch with her ear bent down to him while he told her how he had always intended to send her to the conservatory, how he would have told everyone about it last Christmas—had Christmas really come and gone already?—if this misfortune hadn't got in the way, and refuse to let anyone dissuade him from it. On hearing all this, his sister would break out in tears of emotion, and Gregor would climb up to her shoulder and kiss her neck, which, since she had been going out to work, she had kept free without any necklace or collar.

"Mr. Samsa!" shouted the middle gentleman to Gregor's father, pointing, without wasting any more words, with his forefinger at Gregor as he slowly moved forward. The violin went silent, the middle of the three gentlemen first smiled at his two friends, shaking his head, and then looked back at Gregor. His father seemed to think it more important to calm the three gentlemen before driving Gregor out, even though they were not at all upset and seemed to think Gregor was more entertaining that the violin playing had been. He rushed up to them with his arms spread out and attempted to drive them back into their room at the same time as trying to block their view of Gregor with his body. Now they did become a little annoyed, and it was not clear whether it was his father's behaviour that annoyed them or the dawning realisation that they had had a neighbour like Gregor in the next room without knowing it. They asked Gregor's father for explanations, raised their arms like he had, tugged excitedly at their beards and moved back towards their room only very slowly. Meanwhile Gregor's sister had overcome the despair she had fallen into when her playing was suddenly interrupted. She had let her hands drop and let violin and bow hang limply for a while but continued to look at the music as if still playing, but then she suddenly pulled herself together, lay the instrument on her mother's lap who still sat laboriously struggling for breath where she was, and ran into the next room which, under pressure from her father, the three gentlemen were more quickly moving toward. Under his sister's experienced hand, the pillows and covers on the beds flew up and were put into order and she had already finished making the beds and slipped out again before the three gentlemen had reached the room. Gregor's father seemed so obsessed with what he was doing that he forgot all the respect he owed to his tenants. He urged them and pressed them until, when he was already at the door of the room, the middle of the three gentlemen shouted like thunder and stamped his foot and thereby brought Gregor's father to a halt. "I declare here and now," he said, raising his hand and glancing at Gregor's mother and sister to gain their attention too, "that with regard to the repugnant conditions that prevail in this flat and with this family"—here he looked briefly but decisively at the floor—"I give immediate notice on my room. For the days that I have been living here I will, of course, pay nothing at all, on the contrary I will consider whether to proceed with some kind of action for damages from you, and believe me it would be very easy to set out the grounds for such an action." He was silent and looked straight ahead as if waiting for something. And indeed, his two friends joined in with the words: "And we also give immediate notice." With that, he took hold of the door handle and slammed the door.

Gregor's father staggered back to his seat, feeling his way with his hands, and fell into it; it looked as if he was stretching himself out for his usual evening nap but from the uncontrolled way his head kept nodding it could be seen that he was not sleeping at all. Throughout all this, Gregor had lain still where the three gentlemen had first seen him. His disappointment at the failure of his plan, and perhaps also because he was weak from hunger, made it impossible for him to move. He was sure that everyone would turn on him any moment, and he waited. He was not even startled out of this state when the violin on his mother's lap fell from her trembling fingers and landed loudly on the floor.

"Father, Mother," said his sister, hitting the table with her hand as introduction, "we can't carry on like this. Maybe you can't see it, but I can. I don't want to call this monster my brother, all I can say is: we have to try and get rid of it. We've done all that's humanly possible to look after it and be patient, I don't think anyone could accuse us of doing anything wrong."

"She's absolutely right," said Gregor's father to himself. His mother, who still had not had time to catch her breath, began to cough dully, her hand held out in front of her and a deranged expression in her eyes.

Gregor's sister rushed to his mother and put her hand on her forehead. Her words seemed to give Gregor's father some more definite ideas. He sat upright, played with his uniform cap between the plates left by the three gentlemen after their meal, and occasionally looked down at Gregor as he lay there immobile.

"We have to try and get rid of it," said Gregor's sister, now speaking only to her father, as her mother was too occupied with coughing to listen, "it'll be the death of both of you, I can see it coming. We can't all work as hard as we have to and then come home to be tortured like this, we can't endure it. I can't endure it any more." And she broke out so heavily in tears that they flowed down the face of her mother, and she wiped them away with mechanical hand movements.

"My child," said her father with sympathy and obvious understanding, "what are we to do?"

His sister just shrugged her shoulders as a sign of the helplessness and tears that had taken hold of her, displacing her earlier certainty.

"If he could just understand us," said his father almost as a question; his sister shook her hand vigorously through her tears as a sign that of that there was no question.

"If he could just understand us," repeated Gregor's father, closing his eyes in acceptance of his sister's certainty that that was quite impossible, "then perhaps we could come to some kind of arrangement with him. But as it is ..."

"It's got to go," shouted his sister, "that's the only way, Father. You've got to get rid of the idea that that's Gregor. We've only harmed ourselves by believing it for so long. How can that be Gregor? If it were Gregor he would have seen long ago that it's not possible for human beings to live with an animal like that and he would have gone of his own free will. We wouldn't have a brother any more, then, but we could carry on with our lives and remember him with respect. As it is this animal is persecuting us, it's driven out our tenants, it obviously wants to take over the whole flat and force us to sleep on the streets. Father, look, just look," she suddenly screamed, "he's starting again!" In her alarm, which was totally beyond Gregor's comprehension, his sister even abandoned his mother as she pushed herself vigorously out of her chair as if more willing to sacrifice her own mother than stay anywhere near Gregor. She rushed over to behind her father, who had become excited merely because she was and stood up half raising his hands in front of Gregor's sister as if to protect her.

But Gregor had had no intention of frightening anyone, least of all his sister. All he had done was begin to turn round so that he could go back into his room, although that was in itself quite startling as his pain-wracked condition meant that turning round required a great deal of effort and he was using his head to help himself do it, repeatedly raising it and striking it against the floor. He stopped and looked round. They seemed to have realised his good intention and had only been alarmed briefly. Now they all looked at him in unhappy silence. His mother lay in her chair with her legs stretched out and pressed against each other, her eyes nearly closed with exhaustion; his sister sat next to his father with her arms around his neck.

"Maybe now they'll let me turn round," thought Gregor and went back to work. He could not help panting loudly with the effort and had sometimes to stop and take a rest. No one was making him rush any more, everything was left up to him. As soon as he had finally finished turning round he began to move straight ahead. He was amazed at the great distance that separated him from his room, and could not understand how he had covered that distance in his weak state a little while before and almost without noticing it. He concentrated on crawling as fast as he could and hardly noticed that there was not a word, not any cry, from his family to distract him. He did not turn his head until he had reached the doorway. He did not turn it all the way round as he felt his neck becoming stiff, but it was nonetheless enough to see that nothing behind him had changed, only his sister had stood up. With his last glance he saw that his mother had now fallen completely asleep.

He was hardly inside his room before the door was hurriedly shut, bolted and locked. The sudden noise behind Gregor so startled him that his little legs collapsed under him. It was his sister who had been in so much of a rush. She had been standing there waiting and sprung forward lightly, Gregor had not heard her coming at all, and as she turned the key in the lock she said loudly to her parents "At last!"

"What now, then?" Gregor asked himself as he looked round in the darkness. He soon made the discovery that he could no longer move at all. This was no surprise to him, it seemed rather that being able to actually move around on those spindly little legs until then was unnatural. He also felt relatively comfortable. It is true that his entire body was aching, but the pain seemed to be slowly getting weaker and weaker and would finally disappear altogether. He could already hardly feel the decayed apple in his back or the inflamed area around it, which was entirely covered in white dust. He thought back of his family with emotion and love. If it was possible, he felt that he must go away even more strongly than his sister. He remained in this state of empty and peaceful rumination until he heard the clock tower strike three in the morning. He watched as it slowly began to get light everywhere outside the window too. Then, without his willing it, his head sank down completely, and his last breath flowed weakly from his nostrils.

When the cleaner came in early in the morning—they'd often asked her not to keep slamming the doors but with her strength and in her hurry she still did, so that everyone in the flat knew when she'd arrived and from then on it was impossible to sleep in peace—she made her usual brief look in on Gregor and at first found nothing special. She thought he was laying there so still on purpose, playing the martyr; she attributed all possible understanding to him. She happened to be holding the long broom in her hand, so she tried to tickle Gregor with it from the doorway. When she had no success with that she tried to make a nuisance of herself and poked at him a little, and only when she found she could shove him across the floor with no resistance at all did she start to pay attention. She soon realised what had really happened, opened her eyes wide, whistled to herself, but did not waste time to yank open the bedroom doors and shout loudly into the darkness of the bedrooms: "Come and 'ave a look at this, it's dead, just lying there, stone dead!"

Mr. and Mrs. Samsa sat upright there in their marriage bed and had to make an effort to get over the shock caused by the cleaner before they could grasp what she was saying. But then, each from his own side, they hurried out of bed. Mr. Samsa threw the blanket over his shoulders, Mrs. Samsa just came out in her nightdress; and that is how they went into Gregor's room. On the way they opened the door to the living room where Grete had been sleeping since the three gentlemen had moved in; she was fully dressed as if she had never been asleep, and the paleness of her face seemed to confirm this. "Dead?" asked Mrs. Samsa, looking at the charwoman enquiringly, even though she could have checked for herself and could have known it even without checking. "That's what I said," replied the cleaner, and to prove it she gave Gregor's body another shove with the broom, sending it sideways across the floor. Mrs. Samsa made a movement as if she wanted to hold back the broom, but did not complete it. "Now then," said Mr. Samsa, "let's give thanks to God for that." He crossed himself, and the three women followed his example. Grete, who had not taken her eyes from the corpse, said: "Just look how thin he was. He didn't eat anything for so long. The food came out again just the same as when it went in." Gregor's body was indeed completely dried up and flat, they had not seen it until then, but now he was not lifted up on his little legs, nor did he do anything to make them look away.

"Grete, come with us in here for a little while," said Mrs. Samsa with a pained smile, and Grete followed her parents into the bedroom but not without looking back at the body. The cleaner shut the door and opened the window wide. Although it was still early in the morning the fresh air had something of warmth mixed in with it. It was already the end of March, after all.

The three gentlemen stepped out of their room and looked round in amazement for their breakfasts; they had been forgotten about. "Where is our breakfast?" the middle gentleman asked the cleaner irritably. She just put her finger on her lips and made a quick and silent sign to the men that they might like to come into Gregor's room. They did so, and stood around Gregor's corpse with their hands in the pockets of their well-worn coats. It was now quite light in the room.

Then the door of the bedroom opened and Mr. Samsa appeared in his uniform with his wife on one arm and his daughter on the other. All of them had been crying a little; Grete now and then pressed her face against her father's arm.

"Leave my home. Now!" said Mr. Samsa, indicating the door and without letting the women from him. "What do you mean?" asked the middle of the three gentlemen somewhat disconcerted, and he smiled sweetly. The other two held their hands behind their backs and continually rubbed them together in gleeful anticipation of a loud quarrel which could only end in their favour. "I mean just what I said," answered Mr. Samsa, and, with his two companions, went in a straight line towards the man. At first, he stood there still, looking at the ground as if the contents of his head were rearranging themselves into new positions. "All right, we'll go then," he said, and looked up at Mr. Samsa as if he had been suddenly overcome with humility and wanted permission again from Mr. Samsa for his decision. Mr. Samsa merely opened his eyes wide and briefly nodded to him several times. At that, and without delay, the man actually did take long strides into the front hallway; his two friends had stopped rubbing their hands some time before and had been listening to what was being said. Now they jumped off after their friend as if taken with a sudden fear that Mr. Samsa might go into the hallway in front of them and break the connection with their leader. Once there, all three took their hats from the stand, took their sticks from the holder, bowed without a word and left the premises. Mr. Samsa and the two women followed them out onto the landing; but they had had no reason to mistrust the men's intentions and as they leaned over the landing they saw how the three gentlemen made slow but steady progress down the many steps. As they turned the corner on each floor they disappeared and would reappear a few moments later; the further down they went, the more that the Samsa family lost interest in them; when a butcher's boy, proud of posture with his tray on his head, passed them on his way up and came nearer than they were, Mr. Samsa and the women came away from the landing and went, as if relieved, back into the flat.

They decided the best way to make use of that day was for relaxation and to go for a walk; not only had they earned a break from work but they were in serious need of it. So they sat at the table and wrote three letters of excusal, Mr. Samsa to his employers, Mrs. Samsa to her contractor and Grete to her principal. The cleaner came in while they

were writing to tell them she was going, she'd finished her work for
that morning. The three of them at first just nodded without looking
up from what they were writing, and it was only when the cleaner still
did not seem to want to leave that they looked up in irritation. "Well?"
asked Mr. Samsa. The charwoman stood in the doorway with a smile
on her face as if she had some tremendous good news to report, but
would only do it if she was clearly asked to. The almost vertical little
ostrich feather on her hat, which had been source of irritation to Mr.
Samsa all the time she had been working for them, swayed gently in all
directions. "What is it you want then?" asked Mrs. Samsa, whom the
cleaner had the most respect for. "Yes," she answered, and broke into
a friendly laugh that made her unable to speak straight away, "well
then, that thing in there, you needn't worry about how you're going
to get rid of it. That's all been sorted out." Mrs. Samsa and Grete bent
down over their letters as if intent on continuing with what they were
writing; Mr. Samsa saw that the cleaner wanted to start describing
everything in detail but, with outstretched hand, he made it quite
clear that she was not to. So, as she was prevented from telling them
all about it, she suddenly remembered what a hurry she was in and,
clearly peeved, called out "Cheerio then, everyone," turned round
sharply and left, slamming the door terribly as she went.

"Tonight she gets sacked," said Mr. Samsa, but he received no reply
from either his wife or his daughter as the charwoman seemed to have
destroyed the peace they had only just gained. They got up and went
over to the window where they remained with their arms around each
other. Mr. Samsa twisted round in his chair to look at them and sat
there watching for a while. Then he called out: "Come here, then.
Let's forget about all that old stuff, shall we. Come and give me a bit
of attention." The two women immediately did as he said, hurrying
over to him where they kissed him and hugged him and then they
quickly finished their letters.

After that, the three of them left the flat together, which was something they had not done for months, and took the tram out to the
open country outside the town. They had the tram, filled with warm
sunshine, all to themselves. Leant back comfortably on their seats,
they discussed their prospects and found that on closer examination
they were not at all bad—until then they had never asked each other
about their work but all three had jobs which were very good and held
particularly good promise for the future. The greatest improvement
for the time being, of course, would be achieved quite easily by moving

house; what they needed now was a flat that was smaller and cheaper than the current one that had been chosen by Gregor, one that was in a better location and, most of all, more practical. All the time, Grete was becoming livelier. With all the worry they had been having of late her cheeks had become pale, but, while they were talking, Mr. and Mrs. Samsa were struck, almost simultaneously, with the thought of how their daughter was blossoming into a well built and beautiful young lady. They became quieter. Just from each other's glance and almost without knowing it they agreed that it would soon be time to find a good man for her. And, as if in confirmation of their new dreams and good intentions, as soon as they reached their destination Grete was the first to get up and stretch out her young body.

THE TRIAL

1

Arrest–
Conversation with Mrs. Grubach–
Then Miss Bürstner

Someone must have been telling lies about Josef K., he knew he had done nothing wrong, but one morning he was arrested. Every day at eight in the morning he was brought his breakfast by Mrs. Grubach's cook–Mrs. Grubach was his landlady–but today she didn't come. That had never happened before. K. waited a little while, looked from his pillow at the old woman who lived opposite and who was watching him with an inquisitiveness quite unusual for her, and finally, both hungry and disconcerted, rang the bell. There was immediately a knock at the door and a man entered. He had never seen the man in this house before. He was slim but firmly built, his clothes were black and close-fitting, with many folds and pockets, buckles and buttons and a belt, all of which gave the impression of being very practical but without making it very clear what they were actually for. "Who are you?" asked K., sitting half upright in his bed. The man, however, ignored the question as if his arrival simply had to be accepted, and merely replied, "You rang?" "Anna should have brought me my breakfast," said K. He tried to work out who the man actually was, first in silence, just through observation and by thinking about it, but the man didn't stay still long enough to be looked at. Instead he went over to the door, opened it slightly, and said to someone who was clearly standing immediately behind it, "He wants Anna to bring him his breakfast." There was a little laughter in the neighbouring room, it was not clear from the sound of it whether there were several people laughing. The strange man could not have learned anything from it that he hadn't known already, but now he said to K., as if making his report, "It is not possible." "It would be the first time that's happened," said K., as he jumped out of bed and quickly pulled on his trousers. "I want to see who that is in the next room, and why it is that Mrs. Grubach has let me be disturbed in this way." It immediately occurred to him that he needn't have said this out loud, and that he must to some extent have acknowledged their authority by doing so, but that didn't seem important to him at the time. That, at least, is how the stranger took it, as he said, "Don't you think you'd better stay where you are?" "I want neither to stay here nor to be spoken to by you until you've introduced yourself." "I meant it for your own good," said the stranger and opened the door, this time without being asked. The next room, which K. entered more slowly than he had intended, looked at first glance exactly the same as it had the previous evening. It was Mrs. Grubach's living room, overfilled with furniture, tablecloths, porcelain and photographs. Perhaps there was a little more space in there than usual today, but if so it was not immediately obvious, especially as the main difference was the presence of a man sitting by the open window with a book from which he now looked up. "You should have stayed in your room! Didn't Franz tell you?" "And what is it you want, then?" said K., looking back and forth between this new acquaintance and the one named Franz, who had remained in the doorway. Through the open window he noticed the old woman again, who had come close to the window opposite so that she could continue to see everything. She was showing an inquisitiveness that really made it seem like she was going senile. "I want to see Mrs. Grubach ..." said K., making a movement as if tearing himself away from the two men—even though they were standing well away from him—and wanted to go. "No," said the man at the window, who threw his book down on a coffee table and stood up. "You can't go away when you're under arrest." "That's how it seems," said K. "And why am I under arrest?" he then asked. "That's something we're not allowed to tell you. Go into your room and wait there. Proceedings are underway and you'll learn about everything all in good time. It's not really part of my job to be friendly towards you like this, but I hope no one, apart from Franz, will hear about it, and he's been more friendly towards you than he should have been, under the rules, himself. If you carry on having as much good luck as you have been with your arresting officers then you can reckon on things going well with you." K. wanted to sit down, but then he saw that, apart from the chair by the window, there was nowhere anywhere in the room where he could sit. "You'll get the chance to see for yourself how true all this is," said Franz and both men then walked up to K. They were significantly bigger than him, especially the second man, who frequently slapped him on the shoulder. The two of them felt K.'s nightshirt, and said he would now have to wear one that was of much lower quality, but that they would keep the nightshirt along with his other underclothes and return them to him if his case turned out well. "It's better for you if you give us the things than if you leave them in the storeroom," they said. "Things have a tendency to go missing in the storeroom, and after a certain amount of time they sell things off, whether the case involved has come to an end or not. And cases like this can last a long time, especially the ones that have been coming up lately. They'd give you the money they got for them, but it wouldn't be very much as it's not what they're offered for them when they sell them that counts, it's how much they get slipped on the side, and things like that lose their value anyway when they get passed on from hand to hand, year after year." K. paid hardly any attention to what they were saying, he did not place much value on what he may have still possessed or on who decided what happened to them. It was much more important to him to get a clear understanding of his position, but he could not think clearly while these people were here, the second policeman's belly—and they could only be policemen—looked friendly enough, sticking out towards him, but when K. looked up and saw his dry, boney face it did not seem to fit with the body. His strong nose twisted to one side as if ignoring K. and sharing an understanding with the other policeman. What sort of people were these? What were they talking about? What office did they belong to? K. was living in a free country, after all, everywhere was at peace, all laws were decent and were upheld, who was it who dared accost him in his own home? He was always inclined to take life as lightly as he could, to cross bridges when he came to them, pay no heed for the future, even when everything seemed under threat. But here that did not seem the right thing to do. He could have taken it all as a joke, a big joke set up by his colleagues at the bank for some unknown reason, or also perhaps because today was his thirtieth birthday, it was all possible of course, maybe all he had to do was laugh in the policemen's face in some way and they would laugh with him, maybe they were tradesmen from the corner of the street, they looked like they might be—but he was nonetheless determined, ever since he first caught sight of the one called Franz, not to lose any slight advantage he might have had over these people. There was a very slight risk that people would later say he couldn't understand a joke, but—although he wasn't normally in the habit of learning from experience—he might also have had a few unimportant occasions in mind when, unlike his more cautious friends, he had acted with no thought at all for what might follow and had been made to suffer for it. He didn't want that to happen again, not this time at least; if they were play-acting he would act along with them.

He still had time. "Allow me," he said, and hurried between the two policemen through into his room. "He seems sensible enough," he heard them say behind him. Once in his room, he quickly pulled open the drawer of his writing desk, everything in it was very tidy but in his agitation he was unable to find the identification documents he was looking for straight away. He finally found his bicycle permit and was about to go back to the policemen with it when it seemed to him too petty, so he carried on searching until he found his birth certificate. Just as he got back in the adjoining room the door on the other side opened and Mrs. Grubach was about to enter. He only saw her for an instant, for as soon as she recognised K. she was clearly embarrassed, asked for forgiveness and disappeared, closing the door behind her very carefully. "Do come in," K. could have said just then. But now he stood in the middle of the room with his papers in his hand and still looking at the door which did not open again. He stayed like that until he was startled out of it by the shout of the policeman who sat at the little table at the open window and, as K. now saw, was eating his breakfast. "Why didn't she come in?" he asked. "She's not allowed to," said the big policeman. "You're under arrest, aren't you." "But how can I be under arrest? And how come it's like this?" "Now you're starting again," said the policeman, dipping a piece of buttered bread in the honeypot. "We don't answer questions like that." "You will have to answer them," said K. "Here are my identification papers, now show me yours and I certainly want to see the arrest warrant." "Oh, my God!" said the policeman. "In a position like yours, and you think you can start giving orders, do you? It won't do you any good to get us on the wrong side, even if you think it will—we're probably more on your side than anyone else you know!" "That's true, you know, you'd better believe it," said Franz, holding a cup of coffee in his hand which he did not lift to his mouth but looked at K. in a way that was probably meant to be full of meaning but could not actually be understood. K. found himself, without intending it, in a mute dialogue with Franz, but then slapped his hand down on his papers and said, "Here are my identity documents." "And what do you want us to do about it?" replied the big policeman, loudly. "The way you're carrying on, it's worse than a child. What is it you want? Do you want to get this great, bloody trial of yours over with quickly by talking about ID and arrest warrants with us? We're just coppers, that's all we are. Junior officers like us hardly know one end of an ID card from another, all we've got to do with you is keep an eye on you for ten hours a day and get paid for it. That's all we are. Mind you, what we can do is make sure that the high officials we work for find out just what sort of person it is they're going to arrest, and why he should be arrested, before they issue the warrant. There's no mistake there. Our authorities as far as I know, and I only know the lowest grades, don't go out looking for guilt among the public; it's the guilt that draws them out, like it says in the law, and they have to send us police officers out. That's the law. Where d'you think there'd be any mistake there?" "I don't know this law," said K. "So much the worse for you, then," said the police-man. "It's probably exists only in your heads," said K., he wanted, in some way, to insinuate his way into the thoughts of the policemen, to re-shape those thoughts to his benefit or to make himself at home there. But the policeman just said dismissively, "You'll find out when it affects you." Franz joined in, and said, "Look at this, Willem, he admits he doesn't know the law and at the same time insists he's inno-cent." "You're quite right, but we can't get him to understand a thing," said the other. K. stopped talking with them; do I, he thought to himself, do I really have to carry on getting tangled up with the chat-tering of base functionaries like this?—and they admit themselves that they are of the lowest position. They're talking about things of which they don't have the slightest understanding, anyway. It's only because of their stupidity that they're able to be so sure of themselves. I just need few words with someone of the same social standing as myself and everything will be incomparably clearer, much clearer than a long conversation with these two can make it. He walked up and down the free space in the room a couple of times, across the street he could see the old woman who, now, had pulled an old man, much older than herself, up to the window and had her arms around him. K. had to put an end to this display, "Take me to your superior," he said. "As soon as he wants to see you. Not before," said the policeman, the one called Willem. "And now my advice to you," he added, "is to go into your room, stay calm, and wait and see what's to be done with you. If you take our advice, you won't tire yourself out thinking about things to no purpose, you need to pull yourself together as there's a lot that's going to be required of you. You've not behaved towards us the way we deserve after being so good to you, you forget that we, whatever we are, we're still free men and you're not, and that's quite an advantage. But in spite of all that we're still willing, if you've got the money, to go and get you some breakfast from the café over the road."

Without giving any answer to this offer, K. stood still for some time. Perhaps, if he opened the door of the next room or even the front door, the two of them would not dare to stand in his way, perhaps that would be the simplest way to settle the whole thing, by bringing it to a head. But maybe they would grab him, and if he were thrown down on the ground he would lose all the advantage he, in a certain respect, had over them. So he decided on the more certain solution, the way things would go in the natural course of events, and went back in his room without another word either from him or from the policemen.

He threw himself down on his bed, and from the dressing table he took the nice apple that he had put there the previous evening for his breakfast. Now it was all the breakfast he had and anyway, as he confirmed as soon as he took his first, big bite of it, it was far better than a breakfast he could have had through the good will of the policemen from the dirty café. He felt well and confident, he had failed to go into work at the bank this morning but that could easily be excused because of the relatively high position he held there. Should he really send in his explanation? He wondered about it. If nobody believed him, and in this case that would be understandable, he could bring Mrs. Grubach in as a witness, or even the old pair from across the street, who probably even now were on their way over to the window opposite. It puzzled K., at least it puzzled him looking at it from the policemen's point of view, that they had made him go into the room and left him alone there, where he had ten different ways of killing himself. At the same time, though, he asked himself, this time looking at it from his own point of view, what reason he could have to do so. Because those two were sitting there in the next room and had taken his breakfast, perhaps? It would have been so pointless to kill himself that, even if he had wanted to, the pointlessness would have made him unable. Maybe, if the policemen had not been so obviously limited in their mental abilities, it could have been supposed that they had come to the same conclusion and saw no danger in leaving him alone because of it. They could watch now, if they wanted, and see how he went over to the cupboard in the wall where he kept a bottle of good schnapps, how he first emptied a glass of it in place of his breakfast and how he then took a second glassful in order to give himself courage, the last one just as a precaution for the unlikely chance it would be needed.

Then he was so startled by a shout to him from the other room that he struck his teeth against the glass. "The supervisor wants to see you!" a voice said. It was only the shout that startled him, this curt, abrupt, military shout, that he would not have expected from the policeman called Franz. In itself, he found the order very welcome. "At last!" he called back, locked the cupboard and, without delay, hurried into the next room. The two policemen were standing there and chased him back into his bedroom as if that were a matter of course. "What d'you think you're doing?" they cried. "Think you're going to see the supervisor dressed in just your shirt, do you? He'd see to it you got a right thumping, and us and all!" "Let go of me for God's sake!" called K., who had already been pushed back as far as his wardrobe, "if you accost me when I'm still in bed you can't expect to find me in my evening dress." "That won't help you," said the policemen, who always became very quiet, almost sad, when K. began to shout, and in that way confused him or, to some extent, brought him to his senses. "Ridiculous formalities!" he grumbled, as he lifted his coat from the chair and kept it in both his hands for a little while, as if holding it out for the policemen's inspection. They shook their heads. "It's got to be a black coat," they said. At that, K. threw the coat to the floor and said—without knowing even himself what he meant by it—"Well it's not going to be the main trial, after all." The policemen laughed, but continued to insist, "It's got to be a black coat." "Well that's alright by me if it makes things go any faster," said K. He opened the wardrobe himself, spent a long time searching through all the clothes, and chose his best black suit which had a short jacket that had greatly surprised those who knew him, then he also pulled out a fresh shirt and began, carefully, to get dressed. He secretly told himself that he had succeeded in speeding things up by letting the policemen forget to make him have a bath. He watched them to see if they might remember after all, but of course it never occurred to them, although Willem did not forget to send Franz up to the supervisor with the message saying that K. was getting dressed.

Once he was properly dressed, K. had to pass by Willem as he went through the next room into the one beyond, the door of which was already wide open. K. knew very well that this room had recently been let to a typist named Miss Bürstner. She was in the habit of going out to work very early and coming back home very late, and K. had never exchanged more than a few words of greeting with her. Now, her bedside table had been pulled into the middle of the room to be used as a desk for these proceedings, and the supervisor sat behind it. He had his legs crossed, and had thrown one arm over the backrest of the chair.

In one corner of the room there were three young people looking at the photographs belonging to Miss Bürstner that had been put into a piece of fabric on the wall. Hung up on the handle of the open window was a white blouse. At the window across the street, there was the old pair again, although now their number had increased, as behind them, and far taller than they were, stood a man with an open shirt that showed his chest and a reddish goatee beard which he squeezed and twisted with his fingers. "Josef K.?" asked the supervisor, perhaps merely to attract K.'s attention as he looked round the room. K. nodded. "I daresay you were quite surprised by all that's been taking place this morning," said the supervisor as, with both hands, he pushed away the few items on the bedside table—the candle and box of matches, a book and a pin cushion which lay there as if they were things he would need for his own business. "Certainly," said K., and he began to feel relaxed now that, at last, he stood in front of someone with some sense, someone with whom he would be able to talk about his situation. "Certainly I'm surprised, but I'm not in any way very surprised." "You're not very surprised?" asked the supervisor, as he positioned the candle in the middle of the table and the other things in a group around it. "Perhaps you don't quite understand me," K. hurriedly pointed out. "What I mean is. . . ." here K. broke off and looked round for somewhere to sit. "I may sit down, mayn't I?" he asked. "That's not usual," the supervisor answered. "What I mean is . . ." said K. without delaying a second time, "that, yes, I am very surprised but when you've been in the world for thirty years already and had to make your own way through everything yourself, which has been my lot, then you become hardened to surprises and don't take them too hard. Especially not what's happened today." "Why especially not what's happened today?" "I wouldn't want to say that I see all of this as a joke, you seem to have gone to too much trouble making all these arrangements for that. Everyone in the house must be taking part in it as well as all of you, that would be going beyond what could be a joke. So I don't want to say that this is a joke." "Quite right," said the supervisor, looking to see how many matches were left in the box.

"But on the other hand," K. went on, looking round at everyone there and even wishing he could get the attention of the three who were looking at the photographs, "on the other hand this really can't be all that important. That follows from the fact that I've been indicted, but can't think of the slightest offence for which I could be indicted. But even that is all beside the point, the main question is: Who is issuing the indictment? What office is conducting this affair? Are you officials? None of you is wearing a uniform, unless what you are wearing"—here he turned towards Franz—"is meant to be a uniform, it's actually more of a travelling suit. I require a clear answer to all these questions, and I'm quite sure that once things have been made clear we can take our leave of each other on the best of terms." The supervisor slammed the box of matches down on the table. "You're making a big mistake," he said. "These gentlemen and I have got nothing to do with your business, in fact we know almost nothing about you. We could be wearing uniforms as proper and exact as you like and your situation wouldn't be any the worse for it. As to whether you're on a charge, I can't give you any sort of clear answer to that, I don't even know whether you are or not. You're under arrest, you're quite right about that, but I don't know any more than that. Maybe these officers have been chitchatting with you, well if they have that's all it is, chitchat. I can't give you an answer to your questions, but I can give you a bit of advice: You'd better think less about us and what's going to happen to you, and think a bit more about yourself. And stop making all this fuss about your sense of innocence; you don't make such a bad impression, but with all this fuss you're damaging it. And you ought to do a bit less talking, too. Almost everything you've said so far has been things we could have taken from your behaviour, even if you'd said no more than a few words. And what you have said has not exactly been in your favour."

K. stared at the supervisor. Was this man, probably younger than he was, lecturing him like a schoolmaster? Was he being punished for his honesty with a telling off? And was he to learn nothing about the reasons for his arrest or those who were arresting him? He became somewhat cross and began to walk up and down. No one stopped him doing this and he pushed his sleeves back, felt his chest, straightened his hair, went over to the three men, said, "It makes no sense," at which these three turned round to face him and came towards him with serious expressions. He finally came again to a halt in front of the supervisor's desk. "State Attorney Hasterer is a good friend of

mine," he said, "can I telephone him?" "Certainly," said the supervisor, "but I don't know what the point of that will be, I suppose you
must have some private matter you want to discuss with him." "What
the point is?" shouted K., more disconcerted that cross. "Who do you
think you are? You want to see some point in it while you're carrying
out something as pointless as it could be? It's enough to make you cry!
These gentlemen first accost me, and now they sit or stand about in
here and let me be hauled up in front of you. What point there would
be, in telephoning a state attorney when I'm ostensibly under arrest?
Very well, I won't make the telephone call." "You can call him if you
want to," said the supervisor, stretching his hand out towards the
outer room where the telephone was, "please, go on, do make your
phone call." "No, I don't want to any more," said K., and went over to
the window. Across the street, the people were still there at the window, and it was only now that K. had gone up to his window that they
seemed to become uneasy about quietly watching what was going on.
The old couple wanted to get up but the man behind them calmed
them down. "We've got some kind of audience over there," called K.
to the supervisor, quite loudly, as he pointed out with his forefinger.
"Go away," he then called across to them. And the three of them did
immediately retreat a few steps, the old pair even found themselves
behind the man who then concealed them with the breadth of his
body and seemed, going by the movements of his mouth, to be saying
something incomprehensible into the distance. They did not disappear entirely, though, but seemed to be waiting for the moment when
they could come back to the window without being noticed. "Intru-
sive, thoughtless people!" said K. as he turned back into the room.
The supervisor may have agreed with him, at least K. thought that was
what he saw from the corner of his eye. But it was just as possible that
he had not even been listening as he had his hand pressed firmly
down on the table and seemed to be comparing the length of his
fingers. The two policemen were sitting on a chest covered with a
coloured blanket, rubbing their knees. The three young people had
put their hands on their hips and were looking round aimlessly. Everything was still, like in some office that has been forgotten about.
"Now, gentlemen," called out K., and for a moment it seemed as if he
was carrying all of them on his shoulders, "it looks like your business
with me is over with. In my opinion, it's best now to stop wondering
about whether you're proceeding correctly or incorrectly, and to bring
the matter to a peaceful close with a mutual handshake. If you are of

the same opinion, then please …" and he walked up to the supervisor's desk and held out his hand to him. The supervisor raised his eyes, bit his lip and looked at K.'s outstretched hand; K. still believed the supervisor would do as he suggested. But instead, he stood up, picked up a hard round hat that was laying on Miss Bürstner's bed and put it carefully onto his head, using both hands as if trying on a new hat. "Everything seems so simple to you, doesn't it," he said to K. as he did so, "so you think we should bring the matter to a peaceful close, do you. No, no, that won't do. Mind you, on the other hand I certainly wouldn't want you to think there's no hope for you. No, why should you think that? You're simply under arrest, nothing more than that. That's what I had to tell you, that's what I've done and now I've seen how you've taken it. That's enough for one day and we can take our leave of each other, for the time being at least. I expect you'll want to go in to the bank now, won't you." "In to the bank?" asked K., "I thought I was under arrest." K. said this with a certain amount of defiance as, although his handshake had not been accepted, he was feeling more independent of all these people, especially since the supervisor had stood up. He was playing with them. If they left, he had decided he would run after them and offer to let them arrest him. That's why he even repeated, "How can I go in to the bank when I'm under arrest?" "I see you've misunderstood me," said the supervisor who was already at the door. "It's true that you're under arrest, but that shouldn't stop you from carrying out your job. And there shouldn't be anything to stop you carrying on with your usual life." "In that case it's not too bad, being under arrest," said K., and went up close to the supervisor. "I never meant it should be anything else," he replied. "It hardly seems to have been necessary to notify me of the arrest in that case," said K., and went even closer. The others had also come closer. All of them had gathered together into a narrow space by the door. "That was my duty," said the supervisor. "A silly duty," said K., unyielding. "Maybe so," replied the supervisor, "only don't let's waste our time talking on like this. I had assumed you'd be wanting to go to the bank. As you're paying close attention to every word I'll add this: I'm not forcing you to go to the bank, I'd just assumed you wanted to. And to make things easier for you, and to let you get to the bank with as little fuss as possible I've put these three gentlemen, colleagues of yours, at your disposal." "What's that?" exclaimed K., and looked at the three in astonishment. He could only remember seeing them in their group by the photographs, but these characterless, anae-

mic young people were indeed officials from his bank, not colleagues
of his, that was putting it too high and it showed a gap in the omnis-
cience of the supervisor, but they were nonetheless junior members of
staff at the bank. How could K. have failed to see that? How occupied
he must have been with the supervisor and the policemen not to have
recognised these three! Rabensteiner, with his stiff demeanour and
swinging hands, Kullich, with his blonde hair and deep-set eyes, and
Kaminer, with his involuntary grin caused by chronic muscle spasms.
"Good morning," said K. after a while, extending his hand to the
gentlemen as they bowed correctly to him. "I didn't recognise you at
all. So, we'll go into work now, shall we?" The gentlemen laughed and
nodded enthusiastically, as if that was what they had been waiting for
all the time, except that K. had left his hat in his room so they all
dashed, one after another, into the room to fetch it, which caused a
certain amount of embarrassment. K. stood where he was and watched
them through the open double doorway, the last to go, of course, was
the apathetic Rabensteiner who had broken into no more than an
elegant trot. Kaminer got to the hat and K., as he often had to do at
the bank, forcibly reminded himself that the grin was not deliberate,
that he in fact wasn't able to grin deliberately. At that moment Mrs.
Grubach opened the door from the hallway into the living room
where all the people were. She did not seem to feel guilty about anything at all, and K., as often before, looked down at the belt of her
apron which, for no reason, cut so deeply into her hefty body. Once
downstairs, K., with his watch in his hand, decided to take a taxi—he
had already been delayed by half an hour and there was no need to
make the delay any longer. Kaminer ran to the corner to summon it,
and the two others were making obvious efforts to keep K. diverted
when Kullich pointed to the doorway of the house on the other side
of the street where the large man with the blonde goatee beard
appeared and, a little embarrassed at first at letting himself be seen in
his full height, stepped back to the wall and leant against it. The old
couple were probably still on the stairs. K. was cross with Kullich for
pointing out this man whom he had already seen himself, in fact
whom he had been expecting. "Don't look at him!" he snapped, without noticing how odd it was to speak to free men in this way. But
there was no explanation needed anyway as just then the taxi arrived,
they sat inside and set off. Inside the taxi, K. remembered that he had
not noticed the supervisor and the policemen leaving—the supervisor
had stopped him noticing the three bank staff and now the three

bank staff had stopped him noticing the supervisor. This showed that K. was not very attentive, and he resolved to watch himself more carefully in this respect. Nonetheless, he gave it no thought as he twisted himself round and leant over onto the rear shelf of the car to catch sight of the supervisor and the policemen if he could. But he turned back round straight away and leant comfortably into the corner of the taxi without even having made the effort to see anyone. Although it did not seem like it, now was just the time when he needed some encouragement, but the gentlemen seemed tired just then, Rabensteiner looked out of the car to the right, Kullich to the left and only Kaminer was there with his grin at K.'s service. It would have been inhumane to make fun of that.

That spring, whenever possible, K. usually spent his evenings after work—he usually stayed in the office until nine o'clock—with a short walk, either by himself or in the company of some of the bank officials, and then he would go into a pub where he would sit at the regulars' table with mostly older men until eleven. There were, however, also exceptions to this habit, times, for instance, when K. was invited by the bank's manager (whom he greatly respected for his industry and trustworthiness) to go with him for a ride in his car or to eat dinner with him at his large house. K. would also go, once a week, to see a girl called Elsa who worked as a waitress in a wine bar through the night until late in the morning. During the daytime she only received visitors while still in bed.

That evening, though—the day had passed quickly with a lot of hard work and many respectful and friendly birthday greetings—K. wanted to go straight home. Each time he had any small break from the day's work he considered, without knowing exactly what he had in mind, that Mrs. Grubach's flat seemed to have been put into great disarray by the events of that morning, and that it was up to him to put it back into order. Once order had been restored, every trace of those events would have been erased and everything would take its previous course once more. In particular, there was nothing to fear from the three bank officials, they had immersed themselves back into their paperwork and there was no alteration to be seen in them. K. had called each of them, separately or all together, into his office that day for no other reason than to observe them; he was always satisfied and had always been able to let them go again.

At half past nine that evening, when he arrived back in front of the building where he lived, he met a young lad in the doorway who was standing there, his legs apart and smoking a pipe. "Who are you?" immediately asked K., bringing his face close to the lad's, as it was hard to see in the half light of the landing. "I'm the landlord's son, sir," answered the lad, taking the pipe from his mouth and stepping to one side. "The landlord's son?" asked K., and impatiently knocked on the ground with his stick. "Did you want anything, sir? Would you like me to fetch my father?" "No, no," said K., there was something forgiving in his voice, as if the boy had harmed him in some way and he was excusing him. "It's alright," he said then, and went on, but before going up the stairs he turned round once more.

He could have gone directly to his room, but as he wanted to speak with Mrs. Grubach he went straight to her door and knocked. She was sat at the table with a knitted stocking and a pile of old stockings in front of her. K. apologised, a little embarrassed at coming so late, but Mrs. Grubach was very friendly and did not want to hear any apology, she was always ready to speak to him, he knew very well that he was her best and her favourite tenant. K. looked round the room, it looked exactly as it usually did, the breakfast dishes, which had been on the table by the window that morning, had already been cleared away. "A woman's hands will do many things when no one's looking," he thought, he might himself have smashed all the dishes on the spot but certainly would not have been able to carry it all out. He looked at Mrs. Grubach with some gratitude. "Why are you working so late?" he asked. They were now both sitting at the table, and K. now and then sank his hands into the pile of stockings. "There's a lot of work to do," she said, "during the day I belong to the tenants; if I'm to sort out my own things there are only the evenings left to me." "I fear I may have caused you some exceptional work today." "How do you mean, Mr. K.?" she asked, becoming more interested and leaving her work in her lap. "I mean the men who were here this morning." "Oh, I see," she said, and went peacefully back to what she was doing, "that was no trouble, not especially." K. looked on in silence as she took up the knitted stocking once more. She seems surprised at my mentioning it, he thought, she seems to think it's improper for me to mention it. All the more important for me to do so. An old woman is the only person I can speak about it with. "But it must have caused some work for you," he said then, "but it won't happen again." "No, it can't happen again," she agreed, and smiled at K. in a way that was almost pained. "Do you mean that seriously?" asked K. "Yes," she said, more gently, "but the important thing is you mustn't take it too hard. There are so many awful things happening in the world! As you're being so honest with me, Mr. K., I can admit to you that I listened to a little of what was going on from behind the door, and that those two policemen told me one or two things as well. It's all to do with your happiness, and that's something that's quite close to my heart, perhaps more than it should be as I am, after all, only your landlady. Anyway, so I heard one or two things but I can't really say that it's about anything very serious. No. You have been arrested, but it's not in the same way as when they arrest a thief. If you're arrested in the same way as a thief, then it's bad, but an arrest like this.... It seems to me that it's something very complicated—forgive me if I'm saying something stupid—something very complicated that I don't understand, but something that you don't really need to understand anyway."

"There's nothing stupid about what you've said, Mrs. Grubach, or at least I partly agree with you, only, the way I judge the whole thing is harsher than yours, and think it's not only not something complicated but simply a fuss about nothing. I was just caught unawares, that's what happened. If I had got up as soon as I was awake without letting myself get confused because Anna wasn't there, if I'd got up and paid no regard to anyone who might have been in my way and come straight to you, if I'd done something like having my breakfast in the kitchen as an exception, asked you to bring my clothes from my room, in short, if I had behaved sensibly then nothing more would have happened, everything that was waiting to happen would have been stifled. People are so often unprepared. In the bank, for example, I am well prepared, nothing of this sort could possibly happen to me there, I have my own assistant there, there are telephones for internal and external calls in front of me on the desk, I continually receive visits from people, representatives, officials, but besides that, and most importantly, I'm always occupied with my work, that's to say I'm always alert, it would even be a pleasure for me to find myself faced with something of that sort. But now it's over with, and I didn't really even want to talk about it any more, only I wanted to hear what you, as a sensible woman, thought about it all, and I'm very glad to hear that we're in agreement. But now you must give me your hand, an agreement of this sort needs to be confirmed with a handshake. "

Will she shake hands with me? The supervisor didn't shake hands, he thought, and looked at the woman differently from before, examining her. She stood up, as he had also stood up, and was a little self-conscious, she hadn't been able to understand everything that K.

said. As a result of this self consciousness she said something that she
certainly did not intend and certainly was not appropriate. "Don't
take it so hard, Mr. K.," she said, with tears in her voice and also, of
course, forgetting the handshake. "I didn't know I was taking it hard,"
said K., feeling suddenly tired and seeing that if this woman did agree
with him it was of very little value.

Before going out the door he asked, "Is Miss Bürstner home?"
"No," said Mrs. Grubach, smiling as she gave this simple piece of
information, saying something sensible at last. "She's at the theatre.
Did you want to see her? Should I give her a message?" "I, er, I just
wanted to have a few words with her." "I'm afraid I don't know when
she's coming in; she usually gets back late when she's been to the
theatre." "It really doesn't matter," said K. his head hanging as he
turned to the door to leave, "I just wanted to give her my apology for
taking over her room today." "There's no need for that, Mr. K., you're
too conscientious, the young lady doesn't know anything about it,
she hasn't been home since early this morning and everything's been
tidied up again, you can see for yourself." And she opened the door
to Miss Bürstner's room. "Thank you, I'll take your word for it," said
K., but went nonetheless over to the open door. The moon shone
quietly into the unlit room. As far as could be seen, everything was
indeed in its place, not even the blouse was hanging on the window
handle. The pillows on the bed looked remarkably plump as they
lay half in the moonlight. "Miss Bürstner often comes home late,"
said K., looking at Mrs. Grubach as if that were her responsibility.
"That's how young people are!" said Mrs. Grubach to excuse herself.
"Of course, of course," said K., "but it can be taken too far." "Yes, it
can be," said Mrs. Grubach, "you're so right, Mr. K. Perhaps it is in
this case. I certainly wouldn't want to say anything nasty about Miss
Bürstner, she is a good, sweet girl, friendly, tidy, punctual, works hard,
I appreciate all that very much, but one thing is true, she ought to
have more pride, be a bit less forthcoming. Twice this month already,
in the street over the way, I've seen her with a different gentleman. I
really don't like saying this, you're the only one I've said this to, Mr.
K., I swear to God, but I'm going to have no choice but to have a few
words with Miss Bürstner about it myself. And it's not the only thing
about her that I'm worried about." "Mrs. Grubach, you are on quite
the wrong track," said K., so angry that he was hardly able to hide it,
"and you have moreover misunderstood what I was saying about Miss
Bürstner, that is not what I meant. In fact I warn you quite directly

not to say anything to her, you are quite mistaken, I know Miss Bürstner very well and there is no truth at all in what you say. And what's
more, perhaps I'm going too far, I don't want to get in your way, say to
her whatever you see fit. Good night." "Mr. K.," said Mrs. Grubach as
if asking him for something and hurrying to his door which he had
already opened, "I don't want to speak to Miss Bürstner at all, not
yet, of course I'll continue to keep an eye on her but you're the only
one I've told what I know. And it is, after all something that everyone
who lets rooms has to do if she's to keep the house decent, that's all
I'm trying to do." "Decent!" called out K. through the crack in the
door, "if you want to keep the house decent you'll first have to give me
notice." Then he slammed the door shut, there was a gentle knocking
to which he paid no more attention.

He did not feel at all like going to bed, so he decided to stay up,
and this would also give him the chance to find out when Miss Bürstner would arrive home. Perhaps it would also still be possible, even
if a little inappropriate, to have a few words with her. As he lay there
by the window, pressing his hands to his tired eyes, he even thought
for a moment that he might punish Mrs. Grubach by persuading Miss
Bürstner to give in her notice at the same time as he would. But
he immediately realised that that would be shockingly excessive, and
there would even be the suspicion that he was moving house because
of the incidents of that morning. Nothing would have been more
nonsensical and, above all, more pointless and contemptible.

When he had become tired of looking out onto the empty street
he slightly opened the door to the living room so that he could see
anyone who entered the flat from where he was and lay down on
the couch. He lay there, quietly smoking a cigar, until about eleven
o'clock. He wasn't able to hold out longer than that, and went a little
way into the hallway as if in that way he could make Miss Bürstner
arrive sooner. He had no particular desire for her, he could not even
remember what she looked like, but now he wanted to speak to her
and it irritated him that her late arrival home meant this day would
be full of unease and disorder right to its very end. It was also her
fault that he had not had any dinner that evening and that he had
been unable to visit Elsa as he had intended. He could still make up
for both of those things, though, if he went to the wine bar where
Elsa worked. He wanted to do so even later, after the discussion with
Miss Bürstner.

It was already gone half past eleven when someone could be heard in the stairway. K., who had been lost in his thoughts in the hallway, walking up and down loudly as if it were his own room, fled behind his door. Miss Bürstner had arrived. Shivering, she pulled a silk shawl over her slender shoulders as she locked the door. The next moment she would certainly go into her room, where K. ought not to intrude in the middle of the night; that meant he would have to speak to her now, but, unfortunately, he had not put the electric light on in his room so that when he stepped out of the dark it would give the impression of being an attack and would certainly, at the very least, have been quite alarming. There was no time to lose, and in his helplessness he whispered through the crack of the door, "Miss Bürstner." It sounded like he was pleading with her, not calling to her. "Is there someone there?" asked Miss Bürstner, looking round with her eyes wide open. "It's me," said K. and came out. "Oh, Mr. K.!" said Miss Bürstner with a smile. "Good evening," and offered him her hand. "I wanted to have a word with you, if you would allow me?" "Now?" asked Miss Bürstner, "does it have to be now? It is a little odd, isn't it?" "I've been waiting for you since nine o'clock." "Well, I was at the theatre, I didn't know anything about you waiting for me." "The reason I need to speak to you only came up today." "I see, well I don't see why not, I suppose, apart from being so tired I could drop. Come into my room for a few minutes then. We certainly can't talk out here, we'd wake everyone up and I think that would be more unpleasant for us than for them. Wait here till I've put the light on in my room, and then turn the light down out here." K. did as he was told, and then even waited until Miss Bürstner came out of her room and quietly invited him, once more, to come in. "Sit down," she said, indicating the ottoman, while she herself remained standing by the bedpost despite the tiredness she had spoken of; she did not even take off her hat, which was small but decorated with an abundance of flowers. "What is it you wanted, then? I'm really quite curious." She gently crossed her legs. "I expect you'll say," K. began, "that the matter really isn't all that urgent and we don't need to talk about it right now, but. ..." "I never listen to introductions," said Miss Bürstner. "That makes my job so much easier," said K. "This morning, to some extent through my fault, your room was made a little untidy, this happened because of people I did not know and against my will but, as I said, because of my fault; I wanted to apologise for it." "My room?" asked Miss Bürstner, and instead of looking round the room scrutinised K. "It is true," said K., and now, for the first time, they looked each other

in the eyes, "there's no point in saying exactly how this came about."
"But that's the interesting thing about it," said Miss Bürstner. "No,"
said K. "Well then," said Miss Bürstner, "I don't want to force my way
into any secrets, if you insist that it's of no interest I won't insist. I'm
quite happy to forgive you for it, as you ask, especially as I can't see
anything at all that's been left untidy." With her hand laid flat on her
lower hip, she made a tour around the room. At the mat where the
photographs were she stopped. "Look at this!" she cried. "My photographs really have been put in the wrong places. Oh, that's horrible.
Someone really has been in my room without permission." K. nodded,
and quietly cursed Kaminer who worked at his bank and who was
always active doing things that had neither use nor purpose. "It is
odd," said Miss Bürstner, "that I'm forced to forbid you to do something that you ought to have forbidden yourself to do, namely to come
into my room when I'm not here." "But I did explain to you," said K.,
and went over to join her by the photographs, "that it wasn't me who
interfered with your photographs; but as you don't believe me I'll have
to admit that the investigating committee brought along three bank
employees with them, one of them must have touched your photographs and as soon as I get the chance I'll ask to have him dismissed
from the bank. Yes, there was an investigating committee here," added
K., as the young lady was looking at him enquiringly. "Because of
you?" she asked. "Yes," answered K. "No!" the lady cried with a laugh.
"Yes, they were," said K., "you believe that I'm innocent then, do you?"
"Well now, innocent ..." said the lady, "I don't want to start making
any pronouncements that might have serious consequences, I don't
really know you after all, it means they're dealing with a serious criminal if they send an investigating committee straight out to get him.
But you're not in custody now—at least I take it you've not escaped
from prison considering that you seem quite calm—so you can't have
committed any crime of that sort." "Yes," said K., "but it might be that
the investigating committee could see that I'm innocent, or not so
guilty as had been supposed." "Yes, that's certainly a possibility," said
Miss Bürstner, who seemed very interested. "Listen," said K., "you
don't have much experience in legal matters." "No, that's true, I don't,"
said Miss Bürstner, "and I've often regretted it, as I'd like to know
everything and I'm very interested in legal matters. There's something
peculiarly attractive about the law, isn't there? But I'll certainly be
perfecting my knowledge in this area, as next month I start work in a
legal office." "That's very good," said K., "that means you'll be able to

give me some help with my trial." "That could well be," said Miss
Bürstner, "why not? I like to make use of what I know." "I mean it
quite seriously," said K., "or at least, half seriously, as you do. This
affair is too petty to call in a lawyer, but I could make good use of
someone who could give me advice." "Yes, but if I'm to give you advice
I'll have to know what it's all about," said Miss Bürstner. "That's
exactly the problem," said K., "I don't know that myself." "So you have
been making fun of me, then," said Miss Bürstner exceedingly disappointed, "you really ought not to try something like that on at this
time of night." And she stepped away from the photographs where
they had stood so long together. "Miss Bürstner, no," said K., "I'm not
making fun of you. Please believe me! I've already told you everything
I know. More than I know, in fact, as it actually wasn't even an investigating committee, that's just what I called them because I don't know
what else to call them. There was no cross questioning at all, I was
merely arrested, but by a committee." Miss Bürstner sat on the ottoman and laughed again. "What was it like then?" she asked. "It was
terrible" said K., although his mind was no longer on the subject, he
had become totally absorbed by Miss Bürstner's gaze who was supporting her chin on one hand—the elbow rested on the cushion of the
ottoman—and slowly stroking her hip with the other. "That's too
vague," said Miss Bürstner. "What's too vague?" asked K. Then he
remembered himself and asked, "Would you like me to show you what
it was like?" He wanted to move in some way but did not want to
leave. "I'm already tired," said Miss Bürstner. "You arrived back so
late," said K. "Now you've started telling me off. Well I suppose I
deserve it as I shouldn't have let you in here in the first place, and it
turns out there wasn't even any point." "Oh, there was a point, you'll
see now how important a point it was," said K. "May I move this table
away from your bedside and put it here?" "What do you think you're
doing?" said Miss Bürstner. "Of course you can't!" "In that case I can't
show you," said K., quite upset, as if Miss Bürstner had committed
some incomprehensible offence against him. "Alright then, if you
need it to show what you mean, just take the bedside table then," said
Miss Bürstner, and after a short pause added in a weak voice, "I'm so
tired I'm allowing more than I ought to." K. put the little table in the
middle of the room and sat down behind it. "You have to get a proper
idea of where the people were situated, it is very interesting. I'm the
supervisor, sitting over there on the chest are two policemen, standing
next to the photographs there are three young people. Hanging on the

handle of the window is a white blouse—I just mention that by the way. And now it begins. Ah yes, I'm forgetting myself, the most important person of all, so I'm standing here in front of the table. The supervisor is sitting extremely comfortably with his legs crossed and his arm hanging over the backrest here like some layabout. And now it really does begin. The supervisor calls out as if he had to wake me up, in fact he shouts at me, I'm afraid, if I'm to make it clear to you, I'll have to shout as well, and it's nothing more than my name that he shouts out." Miss Bürstner, laughing as she listened to him, laid her forefinger on her mouth so that K. would not shout, but it was too late. K. was too engrossed in his role and slowly called out, "Josef K.!" It was not as loud as he had threatened, but nonetheless, once he had suddenly called it out, the cry seemed gradually to spread itself all round the room.

There was a series of loud, curt and regular knocks at the door of the adjoining room. Miss Bürstner went pale and laid her hand on her heart. K. was especially startled, as for a moment he had been quite unable to think of anything other than the events of that morning and the girl for whom he was performing them. He had hardly pulled himself together when he jumped over to Miss Bürstner and took her hand. "Don't be afraid," he whispered, "I'll put everything right. But who can it be? It's only the living room next door, nobody sleeps in there." "Yes they do," whispered Miss Bürstner into K.'s ear, "a nephew of Mrs. Grubach's, a captain in the army, has been sleeping there since yesterday. There's no other room free. I'd forgotten about it too. Why did you have to shout like that? You've made me quite upset." "There is no reason for it," said K., and, now as she sank back onto the cushion, kissed her forehead. "Go away, go away," she said, hurriedly sitting back up, "get out of here, go, what is it you want, he's listening at the door he can hear everything. You're causing me so much trouble!" "I won't go," said K., "until you've calmed down a bit. Come over into the other corner of the room, he won't be able to hear us there." She let him lead her there. "Don't forget," he said, "although this might be unpleasant for you you're not in any real danger. You know how much esteem Mrs. Grubach has for me, she's the one who will make all the decisions in this, especially as the captain is her nephew, but she believes everything I say without question. What's more, she has borrowed a large sum of money from me and that makes her dependent on me. I will confirm whatever you say to explain our being here together, however inappropriate it might be, and I guarantee to make

sure that Mrs. Grubach will not only say she believes the explanation
in public but will believe it truly and sincerely. You will have no need
to consider me in any way. If you wish to let it be known that I have
attacked you then Mrs. Grubach will be informed of such and she
will believe it without even losing her trust in me, that's how much
respect she has for me." Miss Bürstner looked at the floor in front of
her, quiet and a little sunk in on herself. "Why would Mrs. Grubach
not believe that I've attacked you?" added K. He looked at her hair
in front of him, parted, bunched down, reddish and firmly held in
place. He thought she would look up at him, but without changing
her manner she said, "Forgive me, but it was the suddenness of the
knocking that startled me so much, not so much what the consequences of the captain being here might be. It was all so quiet after
you'd shouted, and then there was the knocking, that's was made me
so shocked, and I was sitting right by the door, the knocking was right
next to me. Thank you for your suggestions, but I won't accept them.
I can bear the responsibility for anything that happens in my room
myself, and I can do so with anyone. I'm surprised you don't realise
just how insulting your suggestions are and what they imply about
me, although I certainly acknowledge your good intentions. But now,
please go, leave me alone, I need you to go now even more than I did
earlier. The couple of minutes you asked for have grown into half an
hour, more than half an hour now." K. took hold of her hand, and
then of her wrist, "You're not cross with me, though?" he said. She
pulled her hand away and answered, "No, no, I'm never cross with
anyone." He grasped her wrist once more, she tolerated it now and,
in that way, lead him to the door. He had fully intended to leave. But
when he reached the door he came to a halt as if he hadn't expected
to find a door there, Miss Bürstner made use of that moment to get
herself free, open the door, slip out into the hallway and gently say
to K. from there, "Now, come along, please. Look," she pointed to
the captain's door, from under which there was a light shining, "he's
put a light on and he's laughing at us." "Alright, I'm coming," said K.,
moved forward, took hold of her, kissed her on the mouth and then
over her whole face like a thirsty animal lapping with its tongue when
it eventually finds water. He finally kissed her on her neck and her
throat and left his lips pressed there for a long time. He did not look
up until there was a noise from the captain's room. "I'll go now," he
said, he wanted to address Miss Bürstner by her Christian name, but
did not know it. She gave him a tired nod, offered him her hand to

kiss as she turned away as if she did not know what she was doing, and went back into her room with her head bowed. A short while later, K. was lying in his bed. He very soon went to sleep, but before he did he thought a little while about his behaviour, he was satisfied with it but felt some surprise that he was not more satisfied; he was seriously worried about Miss Bürstner because of the captain.

2

First Cross-Examination

K. was informed by telephone that there would be a small hearing concerning his case the following Sunday. He was made aware that these cross examinations would follow one another regularly, perhaps not every week but quite frequently. On the one hand it was in everyone's interest to bring proceedings quickly to their conclusion, but on the other hand every aspect of the examinations had to be carried out thoroughly without lasting too long because of the associated stress. For these reasons, it had been decided to hold a series of brief examinations following on one after another. Sunday had been chosen as the day for the hearings so that K. would not be disturbed in his professional work. It was assumed that he would be in agreement with this, but if he wished for another date then, as far as possible, he would be accommodated. Cross-examinations could even be held in the night, for instance, but K. would probably not be fresh enough at that time. Anyway, as long as K. made no objection, the hearing would be left on Sundays. It was a matter of course that he would have to appear without fail, there was probably no need to point this out to him. He would be given the number of the building where he was to present himself, which was in a street in a suburb well away from the city centre which K. had never been to before.

Once he had received this notice, K. hung up the receiver without giving an answer; he had decided immediately to go there that Sunday, it was certainly necessary, proceedings had begun and he had to face up to it, and this first examination would probably also be the last. He was still standing in thought by the telephone when he heard the voice of the deputy director behind him—he wanted to use the telephone but K. stood in his way. "Bad news?" asked the deputy director casually, not in order to find anything out but just to get K. away from the device. "No, no, " said K., he stepped to one side but did not go away entirely. The deputy director picked up the receiver and, as he waited for his connection, turned away from it and said to K., "One question, Mr. K.: Would you like to give me the pleasure of joining me on my sailing boat on Sunday morning? There's quite a few people coming, you're bound to know some of them. One of them is Hasterer, the state attorney. Would you like to come along? Do come along!" K. tried to pay attention to what the deputy director was saying. It was of no small importance for him, as this invitation from the deputy director, with whom he had never got on very well, meant that he was trying to improve his relations with him. It showed how important K. had become in the bank and how its second most important official seemed to value his friendship, or at least his impartiality. He was only speaking at the side of the telephone receiver while he waited for his connection, but in giving this invitation the deputy director was humbling himself. But K. would have to humiliate him a second time as a result, he said, "Thank you very much, but I'm afraid I will have no time on Sunday, I have a previous obligation." "Pity," said the deputy director, and turned to the telephone conversation that had just been connected. It was not a short conversation, but K., remained standing confused by the instrument all the time it was going on. It was only when the deputy director hung up that he was shocked into awareness and said, in order to partially excuse his standing there for no reason, "I've just received a telephone call, there's somewhere I need to go, but they forgot to tell me what time." "Ask them then," said the deputy director. "It's not that important," said K., although in that way his earlier excuse, already weak enough, was made even weaker. As he went, the deputy director continued to speak about other things. K. forced himself to answer, but his thoughts were mainly about that Sunday, how it would be best to get there for nine o'clock in the morning as that was the time that courts always start work on weekdays.

The weather was dull on Sunday. K. was very tired, as he had stayed out drinking until late in the night celebrating with some of the regulars, and he had almost overslept. He dressed hurriedly, without the time to think and assemble the various plans he had worked out during the week. With no breakfast, he rushed to the suburb he had been told about. Oddly enough, although he had little time to look around him, he came across the three bank officials involved in his case, Rabensteiner, Kullich and Kaminer. The first two were travelling in a tram that went across K.'s route, but Kaminer sat on the terrace of a café and leant curiously over the wall as K. came over. All of them seemed to be looking at him, surprised at seeing their superior running; it was a kind of pride that made K. want to go on foot, this was his affair and the idea of any help from strangers, however slight, was repulsive to him, he also wanted to avoid asking for anyone's help because that would initiate them into the affair even if only slightly. And after all, he had no wish at all to humiliate himself before the committee by being too punctual. Anyway, now he was running so that he would get there by nine o'clock if at all possible, even though he had no appointment for this time.

He had thought that he would recognise the building from a distance by some kind of sign, without knowing exactly what the sign would look like, or from some particular kind of activity outside the entrance. K. had been told that the building was in Juliusstrasse, but when he stood at the street's entrance it consisted on each side of almost nothing but monotonous, grey constructions, tall blocks of flats occupied by poor people. Now, on a Sunday morning, most of the windows were occupied, men in their shirtsleeves leant out smoking, or carefully and gently held small children on the sills. Other windows were piled up with bedding, above which the dishevelled head of a woman would briefly appear. People called out to each other across the street, one of the calls provoked a loud laugh about K. himself. It was a long street, and spaced evenly along it were small shops below street level, selling various kinds of foodstuffs, which you reached by going down a few steps. Women went in and out of them or stood chatting on the steps. A fruitmonger, taking his goods up to the windows, was just as inattentive as K. and nearly knocked him down with his cart. Just then, a gramophone, which in better parts of town would have been seen as worn out, began to play some murderous tune.

K. went further into the street, slowly, as if he had plenty of time now, or as if the examining magistrate were looking at him from one of the windows and therefore knew that K. had found his way there. It was shortly after nine. The building was quite far down the street, it covered so much area it was almost extraordinary, and the gateway in particular was tall and long. It was clearly intended for delivery wagons belonging to the various warehouses all round the yard which were now locked up and carried the names of companies some of which K. knew from his work at the bank. In contrast with his usual habits, he remained standing a while at the entrance to the yard taking in all these external details. Near him, there was a bare-footed man sitting on a crate and reading a newspaper. There were two lads swinging on a hand cart. In front of a pump stood a weak, young girl in a bedjacket who, as the water flowed into her can, looked at K. There was a piece of rope stretched between two windows in a corner of the yard, with some washing hanging on it to dry. A man stood below it calling out instructions to direct the work being done.

K. went over to the stairway to get to the room where the hearing was to take place, but then stood still again as besides these steps he could see three other stairway entrances, and there also seemed to be a small passageway at the end of the yard leading into a second yard. It irritated him that he had not been given more precise directions to the room, it meant they were either being especially neglectful with him or especially indifferent, and he decided to make that clear to them very loudly and very unambiguously. In the end he decided to climb up the stairs, his thoughts playing on something that he remembered the policeman, Willem, saying to him; that the court is attracted by the guilt, from which it followed that the courtroom must be on the stairway that K. selected by chance.

As he went up he disturbed a large group of children playing on the stairs who looked at him as he stepped through their rows. "Next time I come here," he said to himself, "I must either bring sweets with me to make them like me or a stick to hit them with." Just before he reached the first landing he even had to wait a little while until a ball had finished its movement, two small lads with sly faces like grown-up scoundrels held him by his trouser-legs until it had; if he were to shake them off he would have to hurt them, and he was afraid of what noise they would make by shouting.

On the first floor, his search began for real. He still felt unable to ask for the investigating committee, and so he invented a carpenter called Lanz—that name occurred to him because the captain, Mrs. Grubach's nephew, was called Lanz—so that he could ask at every flat whether Lanz the carpenter lived there and thus obtain a chance to look into the rooms. It turned out, though, that that was mostly possible without further ado, as almost all the doors were left open and the children ran in and out. Most of them were small, one-windowed rooms where they also did the cooking. Many women held babies in one arm and worked at the stove with the other. Half grown girls, who seemed to be dressed in just their pinafores worked hardest running to and fro. In every room, the beds were still in use by people who were ill, or still asleep, or people stretched out on them in their clothes. K. knocked at the flats where the doors were closed and asked whether

Lanz the carpenter lived there. It was usually a woman who opened the door, heard the enquiry and turned to somebody in the room who would raise himself from the bed. "The gentleman's asking if a carpenter called Lanz, lives here." "A carpenter, called Lanz?" he would ask from the bed." "That's right," K. would say, although it was clear that the investigating committee was not to be found there, and so his task was at an end. There were many who thought it must be very important for K. to find Lanz the carpenter and thought long about it, naming a carpenter who was not called Lanz or giving a name that had some vague similarity with Lanz, or they asked neighbours or accompanied K. to a door a long way away where they thought someone of that sort might live in the back part of the building or where someone would be who could advise K. better than they could themselves. K. eventually had to give up asking if he did not want to be led all round from floor to floor in this way. He regretted his initial plan, which had at first seemed so practical to him. As he reached the fifth floor, he decided to give up the search, took his leave of a friendly, young worker who wanted to lead him on still further and went down the stairs. But then the thought of how much time he was wasting made him cross, he went back again and knocked at the first door on the fifth floor. The first thing he saw in the small room was a large clock on the wall which already showed ten o'clock. "Is there a carpenter called Lanz who lives here?" he asked. "Pardon?" said a young woman with black, shining eyes who was, at that moment, washing children's underclothes in a bucket. She pointed her wet hand towards the open door of the adjoining room.

K. thought he had stepped into a meeting. A medium sized, two windowed room was filled with the most diverse crowd of people— nobody paid any attention to the person who had just entered. Close under its ceiling it was surrounded by a gallery which was also fully occupied and where the people could only stand bent down with their heads and their backs touching the ceiling. K., who found the air too stuffy, stepped out again and said to the young woman, who had probably misunderstood what he had said, "I asked for a carpenter, someone by the name of Lanz." "Yes," said the woman, "please go on in." K. would probably not have followed her if the woman had not gone up to him, taken hold of the door handle and said, "I'll have to close the door after you, no one else will be allowed in." "Very sensible," said K., "but it's too full already." But then he went back in anyway. He passed through between two men who were talking beside the door—one of them held both hands far out in front of himself making the movements of counting out money, the other looked him closely in the eyes—and someone took him by the hand. It was a small, red-faced youth. "Come in, come in," he said. K. let himself be led by him, and it turned out that there was—surprisingly in a densely packed crowd of people moving to and fro—a narrow passage which may have been the division between two factions; this idea was reinforced by the fact that in the first few rows to the left and the right of him there was hardly any face looking in his direction, he saw nothing but the backs of people directing their speech and their movements only towards members of their own side. Most of them were dressed in black, in old, long, formal frockcoats that hung down loosely around them. These clothes were the only thing that puzzled K., as he would otherwise have taken the whole assembly for a local political meeting.

At the other end of the hall where K. had been led there was a little table set at an angle on a very low podium which was as over-crowded as everywhere else, and behind the table, near the edge of the podium, sat a small, fat, wheezing man who was talking with someone behind him. This second man was standing with his legs crossed and his elbows on the backrest of the chair, provoking much laughter. From time to time he threw his arm in the air as if doing a caricature of someone. The youth who was leading K. had some dif-ficulty in reporting to the man. He had already tried twice to tell him something, standing on tiptoe, but without getting the man's atten-tion as he sat there above him. It was only when one of the people up on the podium drew his attention to the youth that the man turned to him and leant down to hear what it was he quietly said. Then he pulled out his watch and quickly looked over at K. "You should have been here one hour and five minutes ago," he said. K. was going to give him a reply but had no time to do so, as hardly had the man spoken than a general muttering arose all over the right hand side of the hall. "You should have been here one hour and five minutes ago," the man now repeated, raising his voice this time, and quickly looked round the hall beneath him. The muttering also became immediately louder and, as the man said nothing more, died away only gradually. Now the hall was much quieter than when K. had entered. Only the people up in the gallery had not stopped passing remarks. As far as could be distinguished, up in the half-darkness, dust and haze, they seemed to be less well dressed than those below. Many of them had brought pillows that they had put between their heads and the ceiling so that they would not hurt themselves pressed against it.

K. had decided he would do more watching than talking, so he did not defend himself for supposedly having come late, and simply said, "Well maybe I have arrived late, I'm here now." There followed loud applause, once more from the right hand side of the hall. Easy people to get on your side, thought K., and was bothered only by the quiet from the left hand side which was directly behind him and from which there was applause from only a few individuals. He wondered what he could say to get all of them to support him together or, if that were not possible, to at least get the support of the others for a while.

"Yes," said the man, "but I'm now no longer under any obligation to hear your case"—there was once more a muttering, but this time it was misleading as the man waved the people's objections aside with his hand and continued—"I will, however, as an exception, continue with it today. But you should never arrive late like this again. And now, step forward!" Someone jumped down from the podium so that there would be a place free for K., and K. stepped up onto it. He stood pressed closely against the table, the press of the crowd behind him was so great that he had to press back against it if he did not want to push the judge's desk down off the podium and perhaps the judge along with it.

The judge, however, paid no attention to that but sat very comfortably on his chair and, after saying a few words to close his discussion with the man behind him, reached for a little note book, the only item on his desk. It was like an old school exercise book and had become quite misshapen from much thumbing. "Now then," said the judge, thumbing through the book. He turned to K. with the tone of someone who knows his facts and said, "you are a house painter?" "No," said K., "I am the chief clerk in a large bank." This reply was followed by laughter among the right hand faction down in the hall, it was so hearty that K. couldn't stop himself joining in with it. The people supported themselves with their hands on their knees and shook as if suffering a serious attack of coughing. Even some of those in the gallery were laughing. The judge had become quite cross but seemed to have no power over those below him in the hall, he tried to reduce what harm had been done in the gallery and jumped up threatening them, his eyebrows, until then hardly remarkable, pushed themselves up and became big, black and bushy over his eyes.

The left hand side of the hall was still quiet, though, the people stood there in rows with their faces looking towards the podium listening to what was being said there, they observed the noise from the other side of the hall with the same quietness and even allowed some individuals from their own ranks, here and there, to go forward into the other faction. The people in the left faction were not only fewer in number than the right but probably were no more important than them, although their behaviour was calmer and that made it seem like they were. When K. now began to speak he was convinced he was doing it in the same way as them.

"Your question, My Lord, as to whether I am a house painter—in fact even more than that, you did not ask at all but merely imposed it on me—is symptomatic of the whole way these proceedings against me are being carried out. Perhaps you will object that there are no proceedings against me. You will be quite right, as there are proceedings only if I acknowledge that there are. But, for the moment, I do acknowledge it, out of pity for yourselves to a large extent. It's impossible not to observe all this business without feeling pity. I don't say things are being done without due care but I would like to make it clear that it is I who make the acknowledgement."

K. stopped speaking and looked down into the hall. He had spoken sharply, more sharply than he had intended, but he had been quite right. It should have been rewarded with some applause here and there but everything was quiet, they were all clearly waiting for what would follow, perhaps the quietness was laying the ground for an outbreak of activity that would bring this whole affair to an end. It was somewhat disturbing that just then the door at the end of the hall opened, the young washerwoman, who seemed to have finished her work, came in and, despite all her caution, attracted the attention of some of the people there. It was only the judge who gave K. any direct pleasure, as he seemed to have been immediately struck by K.'s words. Until then, he had listened to him standing, as K.'s speech had taken him by surprise while he was directing his attention to the gallery. Now, in the pause, he sat down very slowly, as if he did not want anyone to notice. He took out the notebook again, probably so that he could give the impression of being calmer.

"That won't help you, sir," continued K., "even your little book will only confirm what I say." K. was satisfied to hear nothing but his own quiet words in this room full of strangers, and he even dared casually to pick up the examining judge's notebook and, touching it only with the tips of his fingers as if it were something revolting, lifted it in the air, holding it just by one of the middle pages so that the others on each side of it, closely written, blotted and yellowing, flapped down. "Those are the official notes of the examining judge," he said, and let the notebook fall down onto the desk. "You can read in your book as much as you like, sir, I really don't have anything in this charge book to be afraid of, even though I don't have access to it as I wouldn't want it in my hand, I can only touch it with two fingers." The judge grabbed the notebook from where it had fallen on the desk—which could only have been a sign of his deep humiliation, or at least that is how it must have been perceived—tried to tidy it up a little, and held it once more in front of himself in order to read from it.

The people in the front row looked up at him, showing such tension on their faces that he looked back down at them for some time. Every one of them was an old man, some of them with white beards. Could they perhaps be the crucial group who could turn the whole assembly one way or the other? They had sunk into a state of motionlessness while K. gave his oration, and it had not been possible to raise them from this passivity even when the judge was being humiliated. "What has happened to me," continued K., with less of the vigour he had had earlier, he continually scanned the faces in the first row, and this gave his address a somewhat nervous and distracted character, "what has happened to me is not just an isolated case. If it were it would not be of much importance as it's not of much importance to me, but it is a symptom of proceedings which are carried out against many. It's on behalf of them that I stand here now, not for myself alone."

Without having intended it, he had raised his voice. Somewhere in the hall, someone raised his hands and applauded him shouting, "Bravo! Why not then? Bravo! Again I say, Bravo!" Some of the men in the first row groped around in their beards, none of them looked round to see who was shouting. Not even K. thought him of any importance but it did raise his spirits; he no longer thought it at all necessary that all of those in the hall should applaud him, it was enough if the majority of them began to think about the matter and if only one of them, now and then, was persuaded.

"I'm not trying to be a successful orator," said K. after this thought, "that's probably more than I'm capable of anyway. I'm sure the examining judge can speak far better than I can, it is part of his job after all. All that I want is a public discussion of a public wrong. Listen:

ten days ago I was placed under arrest, the arrest itself is something I laugh about but that's beside the point. They came for me in the morning when I was still in bed. Maybe the order had been given to arrest some house painter—that seems possible after what the judge has said—someone who is as innocent as I am, but it was me they chose. There were two police thugs occupying the next room. They could not have taken better precautions if I had been a dangerous robber. And these policemen were unprincipled riff-raff, they talked at me till I was sick of it, they wanted bribes, they wanted to trick me into giving them my clothes, they wanted money, supposedly so that they could bring me my breakfast after they had blatantly eaten my own breakfast in front of my eyes. And even that was not enough. I was led in front of the supervisor in another room. This was the room of a lady who I have a lot of respect for, and I was forced to look on while the supervisor and the policemen made quite a mess of this room because of me, although not through any fault of mine. It was not easy to stay calm, but I managed to do so and was completely calm when I asked the supervisor why it was that I was under arrest. If he were here he would have to confirm what I say. I can see him now, sitting on the chair belonging to that lady I mentioned—a picture of dull-witted arrogance. What do you think he answered? What he told me, gentlemen, was basically nothing at all; perhaps he really did know nothing, he had placed me under arrest and was satisfied. In fact he had done more than that and brought three junior employees from the bank where I work into the lady's room; they had made themselves busy interfering with some photographs that belonged to the lady and causing a mess. There was, of course, another reason for bringing these employees; they, just like my landlady and her maid, were expected to spread the news of my arrest and damage my public reputation and in particular to remove me from my position at the bank. Well they didn't succeed in any of that, not in the slightest, even my landlady, who is quite a simple person—and I will give you here her name in full respect, her name is Mrs. Grubach—even Mrs. Grubach was understanding enough to see that an arrest like this has no more significance than an attack carried out on the street by some youths who are not kept under proper control. I repeat, this whole affair has caused me nothing but unpleasantness and temporary irritation, but could it not also have had some far worse consequences?"

K. broke off here and looked at the judge, who said nothing. As he did so he thought he saw the judge use a movement of his eyes to

give a sign to someone in the crowd. K. smiled and said, "And now
the judge, right next to me, is giving a secret sign to someone among
you. There seems to be someone among you who is taking directions
from above. I don't know whether the sign is meant to produce boo-
ing or applause, but I'll resist trying to guess what its meaning is too
soon. It really doesn't matter to me, and I give his lordship the judge
my full and public permission to stop giving secret signs to his paid
subordinate down there and give his orders in words instead; let him
just say "Boo now!," and then the next time "Clap now!"

Whether it was embarrassment or impatience, the judge rocked
backwards and forwards on his seat. The man behind him, whom
he had been talking with earlier, leant forward again, either to give
him a few general words of encouragement or some specific piece of
advice. Below them in the hall the people talked to each other quietly
but animatedly. The two factions had earlier seemed to hold views
strongly opposed to each other but now they began to intermingle,
a few individuals pointed up at K., others pointed at the judge. The
air in the room was fuggy and extremely oppressive, those who were
standing furthest away could hardly even be seen through it. It must
have been especially troublesome for those visitors who were in the
gallery, as they were forced to quietly ask the participants in the assembly what exactly was happening, albeit with timid glances at the judge.
The replies they received were just as quiet, and given behind the
protection of a raised hand.

"I have nearly finished what I have to say," said K., and as there was
no bell available he struck the desk with his fist in a way that startled
the judge and his advisor and made them look up from each other.
"None of this concerns me, and I am therefore able to make a calm
assessment of it, and, assuming that this so-called court is of any real
importance, it will be very much to your advantage to listen to what
I have to say. If you want to discuss what I say, please don't bother to
write it down until later on, I don't have any time to waste and I'll
soon be leaving."

There was immediate silence, which showed how well K. was in
control of the crowd. There were no shouts among them as there had
been at the start, no one even applauded, but if they weren't already
persuaded they seemed very close to it.

K. was pleased at the tension among all the people there as they
listened to him, a rustling rose from the silence which was more invig-
orating than the most ecstatic applause could have been. "There is no

doubt," he said quietly, "that there is some enormous organisation determining what is said by this court. In my case this includes my arrest and the examination taking place here today, an organisation that employs policemen who can be bribed, oafish supervisors and judges of whom nothing better can be said than that they are not as arrogant as some others. This organisation even maintains a high-level judiciary along with its train of countless servants, scribes, policemen and all the other assistance that it needs, perhaps even executioners and torturers—I'm not afraid of using those words. And what, gentlemen, is the purpose of this enormous organisation? Its purpose is to arrest innocent people and wage pointless prosecutions against them which, as in my case, lead to no result. How are we to avoid those in office becoming deeply corrupt when everything is devoid of meaning? That is impossible, not even the highest judge would be able to achieve that for himself. That is why policemen try to steal the clothes off the back of those they arrest, that is why supervisors break into the homes of people they do not know, that is why innocent people are humiliated in front of crowds rather than being given a proper trial. The policemen only talked about the warehouses where they put the property of those they arrest, I would like to see these warehouses where the hard won possessions of people under arrest is left to decay, if, that is, it's not stolen by the thieving hands of the warehouse workers."

K. was interrupted by a screeching from the far end of the hall, he shaded his eyes to see that far, as the dull light of day made the smoke whitish and hard to see through. It was the washerwoman whom K. had recognised as a likely source of disturbance as soon as she had entered. It was hard to see now whether it was her fault or not. K. could only see that a man had pulled her into a corner by the door and was pressing himself against her. But it was not her who was screaming, but the man, he had opened his mouth wide and looked up at the ceiling. A small circle had formed around the two of them, the visitors near him in the gallery seemed delighted that the serious tone K. had introduced into the gathering had been disturbed in this way. K.'s first thought was to run over there, and he also thought that everyone would want to bring things back into order there or at least to make the pair leave the room, but the first row of people in front of him stayed were they were, no one moved and no one let K. through. On the contrary, they stood in his way, old men held out their arms in front of him and a hand from somewhere—he did not have the time to turn round—took hold of his collar. K., by this time, had forgotten about the pair, it seemed to him that his freedom was being limited as if his arrest was being taken seriously, and, without any thought for what he was doing, he jumped down from the podium. Now he stood face to face with the crowd. Had he judged the people properly? Had he put too much faith in the effect of his speech? Had they been putting up a pretence all the time he had been speaking, and now that he come to the end and to what must follow, were they tired of pretending? What faces they were, all around him! Dark, little eyes flickered here and there, cheeks drooped down like on drunken men, their long beards were thin and stiff, if they took hold of them it was more like they were making their hands into claws, not as if they were taking hold of their own beards. But underneath those beards—and this was the real discovery made by K.—there were badges of various sizes and colours shining on the collars of their coats. As far as he could see, every one of them was wearing one of these badges. All of them belonged to the same group, even though they seemed to be divided to the right and the left of him, and when he suddenly turned round he saw the same badge on the collar of the examining judge who calmly looked down at him with his hands in his lap. "So," called out K., throwing his arms in the air as if this sudden realisation needed more room, "all of you are working for this organisation, I see now that you are all the very bunch of cheats and liars I've just been speaking about, you've all pressed yourselves in here in order to listen in and snoop on me, you gave the impression of having formed into factions, one of you even applauded me to test me out, and you wanted to learn how to trap an innocent man! Well, I hope you haven't come here for nothing, I hope you've either had some fun from someone who expected you to defend his innocence or else—let go of me or I'll hit you," shouted K. to a quivery old man who had pressed himself especially close to him—"or else that you've actually learned something. And so I wish you good luck in your trade." He briskly took his hat from where it lay on the edge of the table and, surrounded by a silence caused perhaps by the completeness of their surprise, pushed his way to the exit. However, the examining judge seems to have moved even more quickly than K., as he was waiting for him at the doorway. "One moment," he said. K. stood where he was, but looked at the door with his hand already on its handle rather than at the judge. "I merely wanted to draw your attention," said the judge, "to something you seem not yet to be aware of: today, you have robbed yourself of the advantages that a hearing of this sort always gives to someone who is under arrest." K. laughed towards the door. "You bunch of louts," he called, "you can keep all your hearings as a present from me," then opened the door and hurried down the steps. Behind him, the noise of the assembly rose as it became lively once more and probably began to discuss these events as if making a scientific study of them.

3

In the Empty Courtroom— The Student–The Offices

Every day over the following week, K. expected another summons to arrive, he could not believe that his rejection of any more hearings had been taken literally, and when the expected summons really had not come by Saturday evening he took it to mean that he was expected, without being told, to appear at the same place at the same time. So on Sunday, he set out once more in the same direction, going without hesitation up the steps and through the corridors; some of the people remembered him and greeted him from their doorways, but he no longer needed to ask anyone the way and soon arrived at the right door. It was opened as soon as he knocked and, paying no attention to the woman he had seen last time who was standing at the doorway, he was about to go straight into the adjoining room when she said to him "There's no session today." "What do you mean; no session?" he asked, unable to believe it. But the woman persuaded him by opening the door to the next room. It was indeed empty, and looked even more dismal empty than it had the previous Sunday. On the podium stood the table exactly as it had been before with a few books laying on it. "Can I have a look at those books?" asked K., not because he was especially curious but so that he would not have come for nothing. "No," said the woman as she re-closed the door, "that's not allowed. Those books belong to the examining judge." "I see," said K., and nodded, "those books must be law books, and that's how this court does things, not only to try people who are innocent but even to try them without letting them know what's going on." "I expect you're right," said the woman, who had not understood exactly what he meant. "I'd better go away again, then," said K. "Should I give a message to the examining judge?" asked the woman. "Do you know him, then?" asked K. "Of course I know him," said the woman, "my husband is the court usher." It was only now that K. noticed that the room, which before had held nothing but a wash-tub, had been fitted out as a living room. The woman saw how surprised he was and said, "Yes, we're allowed to live here as we like, only we have to clear the room out when the court's in session. There's lots of disadvantages to my husband's job." "It's not so much the room that surprises me," said K., looking at her crossly, "it's your being married that shocks me." "Are you thinking about what happened last time the court was in session, when I disturbed what you were saying?" asked the woman. "Of course," said K., "it's in the past now and I've nearly forgotten about it, but at the time it made me furious. And now you tell me yourself that you are a married woman." "It wasn't any disadvantage for you to have your speech interrupted. The way they talked about you after you'd gone was really bad." "That could well be," said K., turning away, "but it does not excuse you." "There's no one I know who'd hold it against me," said the woman. "Him, who put his arms around me, he's been chasing after me for a long time. I might not be very attractive for most people, but I am for him. I've got no protection from him, even my husband has had to get used to it; if he wants to keep his job he's got to put up with it as that man's a student and he'll almost certainly be very powerful later on. He's always after me, he'd only just left when you arrived." "That fits in with everything else," said K., "I'm not surprised." "Do you want to make things a bit better here?" the woman asked slowly, watching him as if she were saying something that could be as dangerous for K. as for herself. "That's what I thought when I heard you speak, I really liked what you said. Mind you, I only heard part of it, I missed the beginning of it and at the end I was lying on the floor with the student—it's so horrible here," she said after a pause, and took hold of K.'s hand. "Do you believe you really will be able to make things better?" K. smiled and twisted his hand round a little in her soft hands. "It's really not my job to make things better here, as you put it," he said, "and if you said that to the examining judge he would laugh at you or punish you for it. I really would not have become involved in this matter if I could have helped it, and I would have lost no sleep worrying about how this court needs to be made better. But because I'm told that I have been arrested—and I am under arrest—it forces me to take some action, and to do so for my own sake. However, if I can be of some service to you in the process I will, of course, be glad to do so. And I will be glad to do so not only for the sake of charity but also because you can be of

some help to me." "How could I help you, then?" said the woman.
"You could, for example, show me the books on the table there." "Yes,
certainly," the woman cried, and pulled K. along behind her as she
rushed to them. The books were old and well worn, the cover of one
of them had nearly broken through in its middle, and it was held
together with a few threads. "Everything is so dirty here," said K.,
shaking his head, and before he could pick the books up the woman
wiped some of the dust off with her apron. K. took hold of the book
that lay on top and threw it open, an indecent picture appeared. A
man and a woman sat naked on a sofa, the base intent of whoever
drew it was easy to see but he had been so grossly lacking in skill that
all that anyone could really make out were the man and the woman
who dominated the picture with their bodies, sitting in overly upright
postures that created a false perspective and made it difficult for them
to approach each other. K. didn't thumb through that book any more,
but just threw open the next one at its title page, a novel entitled *What
Grete Suffered from Her Husband Hans*. "So this is the sort of law book
they study here," said K., "this is the sort of person sitting in judgement over me." "I can help you," said the woman, "would you like me
to?" "Could you really do that without placing yourself in danger? You
did say earlier on that your husband is wholly dependent on his superiors." "I still want to help you," said the woman, "come over here,
we've got to talk about it. Don't say any more about what danger I'm
in, I only fear danger where I want to fear it. Come over here." She
pointed to the podium and invited him to sit down on the step with
her. "You've got lovely dark eyes," she said after they had sat down,
looking up into K.'s face, "people say I've got nice eyes too, but yours
are much nicer. It was the first thing I noticed when you first came
here. That's even why I came in here, into the assembly room, afterwards, I'd never normally do that, I'm not really even allowed to." So
that's what all this is about, thought K., she's offering herself to me,
she's as degenerate as everything else around here, she's had enough
of the court officials, which is understandable I suppose, and so she
approaches any stranger and makes compliments about his eyes. With
that, K. stood up in silence as if he had spoken his thoughts out loud
and thus explained his action to the woman. "I don't think you can
be of any assistance to me," he said, "to be of any real assistance you
would need to be in contact with high officials. But I'm sure you only
know the lower employees, and there are crowds of them milling
about here. I'm sure you're very familiar with them and could achieve

a great deal through them, I've no doubt of that, but the most that could be done through them would have no bearing at all on the final outcome of the trial. You, on the other hand, would lose some of your friends as a result, and I have no wish of that. Carry on with these people in the same way as you have been, as it does seem to me to be something you cannot do without. I have no regrets in saying this as, in return for your compliment to me, I also find you rather attractive, especially when you look at me as sadly as you are now, although you really have no reason to do so. You belong to the people I have to combat, and you're very comfortable among them, you're even in love with the student, or if you don't love him you do at least prefer him to your husband. It's easy to see that from what you've been saying." "No!" she shouted, remained sitting where she was and grasped K.'s hand, which he failed to pull away fast enough. "You can't go away now, you can't go away when you've misjudged me like that! Are you really capable of going away now? Am I really so worthless that you won't even do me the favour of staying a little bit longer?" "You misunderstand me," said K., sitting back down, "if it's really important to you for me to stay here then I'll be glad to do so, I have plenty of time, I came here thinking there would be a trial taking place. All I meant with what I said just now was to ask you not to do anything on my behalf in the proceedings against me. But even that is nothing for you to worry about when you consider that there's nothing hanging on the outcome of this trial, and that, whatever the verdict, I will just laugh at it. And that's even presupposing it ever even reaches any conclusion, which I very much doubt. I think it's much more likely that the court officials will be too lazy, too forgetful, or even too fearful ever to continue with these proceedings and that they will soon be abandoned if they haven't been abandoned already. It's even possible that they will pretend to be carrying on with the trial in the hope of receiving a large bribe, although I can tell you now that that will be quite in vain as I pay bribes to no one. Perhaps one favour you could do me would be to tell the examining judge, or anyone else who likes to spread important news, that I will never be induced to pay any sort of bribe through any stratagem of theirs—and I'm sure they have many stratagems at their disposal. There is no prospect of that, you can tell them that quite openly. And what's more, I expect they have already noticed themselves, or even if they haven't, this affair is really not so important to me as they think. Those gentlemen would only save some work for themselves, or at least some unpleasantness for me, which, however, I am glad to endure if I know that each piece of unpleasantness for me is a blow against them. And I will make quite sure it is a blow against them. Do you actually know the judge?" "Course I do," said the woman, "he was the first one I thought of when I offered to help you. I didn't know he's only a minor official, but if you say so it must be true. Mind you, I still think the report he gives to his superiors must have some influence. And he writes so many reports. You say these officials are lazy, but they're certainly not all lazy, especially this examining judge, he writes ever such a lot. Last Sunday, for instance, that session went on till the evening. Everyone had gone, but the examining judge, he stayed in the hall, I had to bring him a lamp in, all I had was a little kitchen lamp but he was very satisfied with it and started to write straight away. Meantime my husband arrived, he always has the day off on Sundays, we got the furniture back in and got our room sorted out and then a few of the neighbours came, we sat and talked for a bit by a candle, in short, we forgot all about the examining judge and went to bed. All of a sudden in the night, it must have been quite late in the night, I wakes up, next to the bed, there's the examining judge shading the lamp with his hand so that there's no light from it falls on my husband, he didn't need to be as careful as that, the way my husband sleeps the light wouldn't have woken him up anyway. I was quite shocked and nearly screamed, but the judge was very friendly, warned me I should be careful, he whispered to me he's been writing all this time, and now he's brought me the lamp back, and he'll never forget how I looked when he found me there asleep. What I mean, with all this, I just wanted to tell you how the examining judge really does write lots of reports, especially about you as questioning you was definitely one of the main things on the agenda that Sunday. If he writes reports as long as that they must be of some importance. And besides all that, you can see from what happened that the examining judge is after me, and it's right now, when he's first begun to notice me, that I can have a lot of influence on him. And I've got other proof I mean a lot to him, too. Yesterday, he sent that student to me, the one he really trusts and who he works with, he sent him with a present for me, silk stockings. He said it was because I clear up in the courtroom but that's only a pretence, that job's no more than what I'm supposed to do, it's what my husband gets paid for. Nice stockings, they are, look"—she stretched out her leg, drew her skirt up to her knee and looked herself at the stocking—"they are nice stockings, but they're too good for me, really."

She suddenly interrupted herself and lay her hand on K.'s as if she wanted to calm him down, and whispered, "Be quiet, Berthold is watching us." K. slowly looked up. In the doorway to the courtroom stood a young man, he was short, his legs were not quite straight, and he continually moved his finger round in a short, thin, red beard with which he hoped to make himself look dignified. K. looked at him with some curiosity, he was the first student he had ever met of the unfamiliar discipline of jurisprudence, face to face at least, a man who would even most likely attain high office one day. The student, in contrast, seemed to take no notice of K. at all, he merely withdrew his finger from his beard long enough to beckon to the woman and went over to the window, the woman leant over to K. and whispered, "Don't be cross with me, please don't, and please don't think ill of me either, I've got to go to him now, to this horrible man, just look at his bent legs. But I'll come straight back and then I'll go with you if you'll take me, I'll go wherever you want, you can do whatever you like with me, I'll be happy if I can be away from here for as long as possible, it'd be best if I could get away from here for good." She stroked K.'s hand once more, jumped up and ran over to the window. Before he realised it, K. grasped for her hand but failed to catch it. He really was attracted to the woman, and even after thinking hard about it could find no good reason why he should not give in to her allure. It briefly crossed his mind that the woman meant to entrap him on behalf of the court, but that was an objection he had no difficulty in fending off. In what way could she entrap him? Was he not still free, so free that he could crush the entire court whenever he wanted, as least where it concerned him? Could he not have that much confidence in himself? And her offer of help sounded sincere, and maybe it wasn't quite worthless. And maybe there was no better revenge against the examining judge and his cronies than to take this woman from him and have her for himself. Maybe then, after much hard work writing dishonest reports about K., the judge would go to the woman's bed late one night and find it empty. And it would be empty because she belonged to K., because this woman at the window, this lush, supple, warm body in its sombre clothes of rough, heavy material belonged to him, totally to him and to him alone. Once he had settled his thoughts towards the woman in this way, he began to find the quiet

conversation at the window was taking too long, he rapped on the
podium with his knuckles, and then even with his fist. The student
briefly looked away from the woman to glance at K. over his shoulder
but did allow himself to be disturbed, in fact he even pressed himself
close to the woman and put his arms around her. She dropped her
head down low as if listening to him carefully, as she did so he kissed
her right on the neck, hardly even interrupting what he was saying.
K. saw this as confirmation of the tyranny the student held over the
woman and which she had already complained about, he stood up
and walked up and down the room. Glancing sideways at the student,
he wondered what would be the quickest possible way to get rid of
him, and so it was not unwelcome to him when the student, clearly
disturbed by K.'s to-ing and fro-ing which K. had now developed into
a stamping up and down, said to him, "You don't have to stay here,
you know, if you're getting impatient. You could have gone earlier, no
one would have missed you. In fact you should have gone, you should
have left as quickly as possible as soon as I got here." This comment
could have caused all possible rage to break out between them, but K.
also bore in mind that this was a prospective court official speaking to
a disfavoured defendant, and he might well have been taking pride in
speaking in this way. K. remained standing quite close to him and said
with a smile, "You're quite right, I am impatient, but the easiest way
to settle this impatience would be if you left us. On the other hand,
if you've come here to study—you are a student, I hear—I'll be quite
happy to leave the room to you and go away with the woman. I'm sure
you'll still have a lot of study to do before you're made into a judge.
It's true that I'm still not all that familiar with your branch of jurisprudence but I take it it involves a lot more than speaking roughly—and
I see you have no shame in doing that extremely well." "He shouldn't
have been allowed to move about so freely," said the student, as if he
wanted to give the woman an explanation for K.'s insults, "that was a
mistake. I've told the examining judge so. He should at least have been
detained in his room between hearings. Sometimes it's impossible to
understand what the judge thinks he's doing." "You're wasting your
breath," said K., then he reached his hand out towards the woman
and said, "come with me." "So that's it," said the student, "oh no,
you're not going to get her," and with a strength you would not have
expected from him, he glanced tenderly at her, lifted her up on one
arm and, his back bent under the weight, ran with her to the door.

In this way he showed, unmistakeably, that he was to some extent afraid of K., but he nonetheless dared to provoke him still further by stroking and squeezing the woman's arm with his free hand. K. ran the few steps up to him, but when he had reached him and was about to take hold of him and, if necessary, throttle him, the woman said, "It's no good, it's the examining judge who's sent for me, I daren't go with you, this little bastard ..." and here she ran her hand over the student's face, "this little bastard won't let me." "And you don't want to be set free!" shouted K., laying his hand on the student's shoulder, who then snapped at it with his teeth. "No!" shouted the woman, pushing K. away with both hands, "no, no don't do that, what d'you think you're doing!? That'd be the end of me. Let go of him, please just let go of him. He's only carrying out the judge's orders, he's carrying me to him." "Let him take you then, and I want to see nothing more of you," said K., enraged by his disappointment and giving the student a thump in the back so that he briefly stumbled and then, glad that he had not fallen, immediately jumped up all the higher with his burden. K. followed them slowly. He realised that this was the first unambiguous setback he had suffered from these people. It was of course nothing to worry about, he accepted the setback only because he was looking for a fight. If he stayed at home and carried on with his normal life he would be a thousand times superior to these people and could get any of them out of his way just with a kick. And he imagined the most laughable scene possible as an example of this, if this contemptible student, this inflated child, this knock-kneed redbeard, if he were kneeling at Elsa's bed wringing his hands and begging for forgiveness. K. so enjoyed imagining this scene that he decided to take the student along to Elsa with him if ever he should get the opportunity.

K. was curious to see where the woman would be taken and he hurried over to the door, the student was not likely to carry her through the streets on his arm. It turned out that the journey was far shorter. Directly opposite the flat there was a narrow flight of wooden steps which probably led up to the attic, they turned as they went so that it was not possible to see where they ended. The student carried the woman up these steps, and after the exertions of running with her he was soon groaning and moving very slowly. The woman waved down at K. and by raising and lowering her shoulders she tried to show that she was an innocent party in this abduction, although the gesture did not show a lot of regret. K. watched her without expression like a stranger, he wanted to show neither that he was disappointed nor that he would easily get over his disappointment.

The two of them had disappeared, but K. remained standing in the doorway. He had to accept that the woman had not only cheated him but that she had also lied to him when she said she was being taken to the examining judge. The examining judge certainly wouldn't be sitting and waiting in the attic. The wooden stairs would explain nothing to him however long he stared at them. Then K. noticed a small piece of paper next to them, went across to it and read, in a childish and unpractised hand, "Entrance to the Court Offices." Were the court offices here, in the attic of this tenement, then? If that was how they were accommodated it did not attract much respect, and it was some comfort for the accused to realise how little money this court had at its disposal if it had to locate its offices in a place where the tenants of the building, who were themselves among the poorest of people, would throw their unneeded junk. On the other hand, it was possible that the officials had enough money but that they squandered it on themselves rather than use it for the court's purposes. Going by K.'s experience of them so far, that even seemed probable, except that if the court were allowed to decay in that way it would not just humiliate the accused but also give him more encouragement than if the court were simply in a state of poverty. K. also now understood that the court was ashamed to summon those it accused to the attic of this building for the initial hearing, and why it preferred to impose upon them in their own homes. What a position it was that K. found himself in, compared with the judge sitting up in the attic! K., at the bank, had a big office with an anteroom, and had an enormous window through which he could look down at the activity in the square. It was true, though, that he had no secondary income from bribes and fraud, and he couldn't tell a servant to bring him a woman up to the office on his arm. K., however, was quite willing to do without such things, in this life at least. K. was still looking at the notice when a man came up the stairs, looked through the open door into the living room where it was also possible to see the courtroom, and finally asked K. whether he had just seen a woman there. "You're the court usher, aren't you?" asked K. "That's right," said the man, "oh, yes, you're defendant K., I recognise you now as well. Nice to see you here." And he offered K. his hand, which was far from what K. had expected. And when K. said nothing, he added, "There's no court session planned for today, though." "I know that," said K. as he looked at the usher's civilian coat which, beside its ordinary buttons, displayed two gilded ones as the only sign of his office and seemed to have been taken from an old army officer's coat. "I was speaking with your wife a little while ago. She is no longer here. The student has carried her off to the examining judge." "Listen to this," said the usher, "they're always carrying her away from me. It's Sunday today, and it's not part of my job to do any work today, but they send me off with some message which isn't even necessary just to get me away from here. What they do is they send me off not too far away so that I can still hope to get back on time if I really hurry. So off I go running as fast as I can, shout the message through the crack in the door of the office I've been sent to, so out of breath they'll hardly be able to under-stand it, run back here again, but the student's been even faster than I have—well he's got less far to go, he's only got to run down the steps. If I wasn't so dependent on them I'd have squashed the student against the wall here a long time ago. Right here, next to the sign. I'm always dreaming of doing that. Just here, just above the floor, that's where he's crushed onto the wall, his arms stretched out, his fingers spread apart, his crooked legs twisted round into a circle and blood squirted out all around him. It's only ever been a dream so far, though." "Is there nothing else you do?" asked K. with a smile. "Nothing that I know of," said the usher. "And it's going to get even worse now, up till now he's only been carrying her off for himself, now he's started car-rying her off for the judge and all, just like I'd always said he would." "Does your wife, then, not share some of the responsibility?" asked K. He had to force himself as he asked this question, as he, too, felt so jealous now. "Course she does," said the usher, "it's more her fault than theirs. It was her who attached herself to him. All he did, he just chases after any woman. There's five flats in this block alone where he's been thrown out after working his way in there. And my wife is the best looking woman in the whole building, but it's me who's not even allowed to defend himself." "If that's how things are, then there's nothing that can be done," said K. "Well why not?" asked the usher. "He's a coward that student, if he wants to lay a finger on my wife all you'd have to do is give him such a good hiding he'd never dare do it again. But I'm not allowed to do that, and nobody else is going to do me the favour as they're all afraid of his power. The only one who could do it is a man like you." "What, how could I do it?" asked K. in astonishment. "Well you're facing a charge, aren't you," said the usher.

"Yes, but that's all the more reason for me to be afraid. Even if he has no influence on the outcome of the trial he probably has some on the initial examination." "Yes, exactly," said the usher, as if K.'s view had been just as correct as his own. "Only we don't usually get any trials heard here with no hope at all." "I am not of the same opinion," said K., "although that ought not to prevent me from dealing with the student if the opportunity arises." "I would be very grateful to you," said the usher of the court, somewhat formally, not really seeming to believe that his highest wish could be fulfilled. "Perhaps," continued K., "perhaps there are some other officials of yours here, perhaps all of them, who would deserve the same." "Oh yes, yes," said the usher, as if this was a matter of course. Then he looked at K. trustingly which, despite all his friendliness, he had not done until then, and added, "they're always rebelling." But the conversation seemed to have become a little uncomfortable for him, as he broke it off by saying, "now I have to report to the office. Would you like to come with me?" "There's nothing for me to do there," said K. "You'd be able to have a look at it. No one will take any notice of you." "Is it worth seeing then?" asked K. hesitatingly, although he felt very keen to go with him. "Well," said the usher, "I thought you'd be interested in it." "Alright then," said K. finally, "I'll come with you." And, quicker than the usher himself, he ran up the steps.

At the entrance he nearly fell over, as behind the door there was another step. "They don't show much concern for the public," he said. "They don't show any concern at all," said the usher, "just look at the waiting room here." It consisted of a long corridor from which roughly made doors led out to the separate departments of the attic. There was no direct source of light but it was not entirely dark as many of the departments, instead of solid walls, had just wooden bars reaching up to the ceiling to separate them from the corridor. The light made its way in through them, and it was also possible to see individual officials through them as they sat writing at their desks or stood up at the wooden frameworks and watched the people on the corridor through the gaps. There were only a few people in the corridor, probably because it was Sunday. They were not very impressive. They sat, equally spaced, on two rows of long wooden benches which had been placed along both sides of the corridor. All of them were carelessly dressed although the expressions on their faces, their bearing, the style of their beards and many details which were hard to identify showed that they belonged to the upper classes. There were no coat hooks for them to use, and so they had placed their hats under the bench, each probably having followed the example of the others. When those who were sitting nearest the door saw K. and the usher of the court they stood up to greet them, and when the others saw that, they also thought they had to greet them, so that as the two of them went by all the people there stood up. None of them stood properly upright, their backs were bowed, their knees bent, they stood like beggars on the street. K. waited for the usher, who was following just behind him. "They must all be very dispirited," he said. "Yes," said the usher, "they are the accused, everyone you see here has been accused." "Really!" said K. "They're colleagues of mine then." And he turned to the nearest one, a tall, thin man with hair that was nearly grey. "What is it you are waiting for here?" asked K., politely, but the man was startled at being spoken to unexpectedly, which was all the more pitiful to see because the man clearly had some experience of the world and elsewhere would certainly have been able to show his superiority and would not have easily given up the advantage he had acquired. Here, though, he did not know what answer to give to such a simple question and looked round at the others as if they were under some obligation to help him, and as if no one could expect any answer from him without this help. Then the usher of the court stepped forward to him and, in order to calm him down and raise his spirits, said, "The gentleman here's only asking what it is you're waiting for. You can give him an answer." The voice of the usher was probably familiar to him, and had a better effect than K.'s. "I'm ... I'm waiting..." he began, and then came to a halt. He had clearly chosen this beginning so that he could give a precise answer to the question, but now he didn't know how to continue. Some of the others waiting had come closer and stood round the group, the usher of the court said to them, "Get out the way, keep the gangway free." They moved back slightly, but not as far as where they had been sitting before. In the meantime, the man whom K. had first approached had pulled himself together and even answered him with a smile. "A month ago I made some applications for evidence to be heard in my case, and I'm waiting for it to be settled." "You certainly seem to be going to a lot of effort," said K. "Yes," said the man, "it is my affair after all." "Not everyone thinks the same way as you do," said K. "I've been indicted as well but I swear on my soul that I've neither submitted evidence nor done anything else of the sort. Do you really think that's necessary?" "I don't really know, exactly," said the man, once more totally unsure of himself; he clearly thought K. was joking with him and therefore probably thought it best to repeat his earlier answer in order to avoid making any new mistakes. With K. looking at him impatiently, he just said, "as far as I'm concerned, I've applied to have this evidence heard." "Perhaps you don't believe I've been indicted?" asked K. "Oh, please, I certainly do," said the man, stepping slightly to one side, but there was more anxiety in his answer than belief. "You don't believe me then?" asked K., and took hold of his arm, unconsciously prompted by the man's humble demeanour, and as if he wanted to force him to believe him. But he did not want to hurt the man and had only taken hold of him very lightly. Nonetheless, the man cried out as if K. had grasped him not with two fingers but with red hot tongs. Shouting in this ridiculous way finally made K. tired of him, if he didn't believe he was indicted then so much the better; maybe he even thought K. was a judge. And before leaving, he held him a lot harder, shoved him back onto the bench and walked on. "These defendants are so sensitive, most of them," said the usher of the court. Almost all of those who had been waiting had now assembled around the man who, by now, had stopped shouting and they seemed to be asking him lots of precise questions about the incident. K. was approached by a security guard, identifiable mainly by his sword, of which the scabbard seemed to be made of aluminium. This greatly surprised K., and he reached out for it with his hand. The guard had come because of the shouting and asked what had been happening. The usher of the court said a few words to try and calm him down but the guard explained that he had to look into it himself, saluted, and hurried on, walking with very short steps, probably because of gout.

K. didn't concern himself long with the guard or these people, especially as he saw a turning off the corridor, about half way along it on the right hand side, where there was no door to stop him going that way. He asked the usher whether that was the right way to go, the usher nodded, and that is the way that K. went. The usher remained always one or two steps behind K., which he found irritating as in a place like this it could give the impression that he was being driven along by someone who had arrested him, so he frequently waited for the usher to catch up, but the usher always remained behind him. In order to put an end to his discomfort, K. finally said, "Now that I've seen what it looks like here, I'd like to go." "You haven't seen everything yet," said the usher ingenuously. "I don't want to see everything," said K., who was also feeling very tired, "I want to go, what is the way to the exit?" "You haven't got lost, have you?" asked the usher in amazement, "you go down this way to the corner, then right down the corridor straight ahead as far as the door." "Come with me," said K., "show me the way, I'll miss it, there are so many different ways here." "It's the only way there is," said the usher, who had now started to sound quite reproachful, "I can't go back with you again, I've got to hand in my report, and I've already lost a lot of time because of you as it is." "Come with me!" K. repeated, now somewhat sharper as if he had finally caught the usher out in a lie. "Don't shout like that," whispered the usher, "there's offices all round us here. If you don't want to go back by yourself come on a bit further with me or else wait here till I've sorted out my report, then I'll be glad to go back with you again." "No, no," said K., "I will not wait and you must come with me now." K. had still not looked round at anything at all in the room where he found himself, and it was only when one of the many wooden doors all around him opened that he noticed it. A young woman, probably summoned by the loudness of K.'s voice, entered and asked, "What is it the gentleman wants?" In the darkness behind her there was also a man approaching. K. looked at the usher. He had, after all, said that no one would take any notice of K., and now there were two people coming, it only needed a few and everyone in the office would become aware of him and asking for explanations as to why he was there. The only understandable and acceptable thing to say was that he was accused of something and wanted to know the date of his next hearing, but this was an explanation he did not want to give, especially as it was not true—he had only come out of curiosity. Or else, an explanation even less usable, he could say that he wanted to ascertain that the court was as revolting on the inside as it was on the outside. And it did seem that he had been quite right in this supposition, he had no wish to intrude any deeper, he was disturbed enough by what he had seen already, he was not in the right frame of mind just then to face a high official such as might appear from behind any door, and he wanted to go, either with the usher of the court or, if needs be, alone.

But he must have seemed very odd standing there in silence, and the young woman and the usher were indeed looking at him as if they thought he would go through some major metamorphosis any second which they didn't want to miss seeing. And in the doorway stood the man whom K. had noticed in the background earlier, he held firmly on to the beam above the low door swinging a little on the tips of his feet as if becoming impatient as he watched. But the young woman was the first to recognise that K.'s behaviour was caused by his feeling slightly unwell, she brought a chair and asked, "Would you not like to sit down?" K. sat down immediately and, in order to keep his place better, put his elbows on the armrests. "You're a little bit dizzy, aren't you?" she asked him. Her face was now close in front of him, it bore the severe expression that many young women have just when they're in the bloom of their youth. "It's nothing for you to worry about," she said, "that's nothing unusual here, almost everyone gets an attack like that the first time they come here. This is your first time is it? Yes, it's nothing unusual then. The sun burns down on the roof and the hot wood makes the air so thick and heavy. It makes this place rather unsuitable for offices, whatever other advantages it might offer. But the air is almost impossible to breathe on days when there's a lot of business, and that's almost every day. And when you think that there's a lot of washing put out to dry here as well—and we can't stop the tenants doing that—it's not surprising you started to feel unwell. But you get used to the air alright in the end. When you're here for the second or third time you'll hardly notice how oppressive the air is. Are you feeling any better now?" K. made no answer, he felt too embarrassed at being put at the mercy of these people by his sudden weakness, and learning the reason for feeling ill made him feel not better but a little worse. The girl noticed it straight away, and to make the air fresher for K., she took a window pole that was leaning against the wall and pushed open a small hatch directly above K.'s head that led to the outside. But so much soot fell in that the girl had to immediately close the hatch again and clean the soot off K.'s hands with her handkerchief, as K. was too tired to do that for himself. He would have liked just to sit quietly where he was until he had enough strength to leave, and the less fuss people made about him the sooner that would be. But then the girl said, "You can't stay here, we're in people's way here ..." K. looked at her as if to ask whose way they were impeding. "If you like, I can take you to the sick room," and turning to the man in the doorway said, "please help me." The man immediately came over to them, but K. did not want to go to the sick room, that was just what he wanted to avoid, being led further from place to place, the further he went the more difficult it must become. So he said, "I am able to walk now," and stood up, shaking after becoming used to sitting so comfortably. But then he was unable to stay upright. "I can't manage it," he said shaking his head, and sat down again with a sigh. He remembered the usher who, despite everything, would have been able to lead him out of there but who seemed to have gone long before. K. looked out between the man and the young woman who were standing in front of him but was unable to find the usher. "I think," said the man, who was elegantly dressed and whose appearance was made especially impressive with a grey waistcoat that had two long, sharply tailored points, "the gentleman is feeling unwell because of the atmosphere here, so the best thing, and what he would most prefer, would be not to take him to the sick room but get him out of the offices altogether." "That's right," exclaimed K., with such joy that he nearly interrupted what the man was saying, "I'm sure that'll make me feel better straight away, I'm really not that weak, all I need is a little support under my arms, I won't cause you much trouble, it's not such a long way anyway, lead me to the door and then I'll sit on the stairs for a while and soon recover, as I don't suffer from attacks like this at all, I'm surprised at it myself. I also work in an office and I'm quite used to office air, but here it seems to be too strong, you've said so yourselves. So please, be so kind as to help me on my way a little, I'm feeling dizzy, you see, and it'll make me ill if I stand up by myself." And with that he raised his shoulders to make it easier for the two of them to take him by the arms.

The man, however, didn't follow this suggestion but just stood there with his hands in his trouser pockets and laughed out loud. "There, you see," he said to the girl, "I was quite right. The gentleman is only unwell here, and not in general." The young woman smiled too, but lightly tapped the man's arm with the tips of her fingers as if he had allowed himself too much fun with K. "So what do you think, then?" said the man, still laughing, "I really do want to lead the gentleman out of here." "That's alright, then," said the girl, briefly inclining her charming head. "Don't worry too much about him laughing," said the girl to K., who had become unhappy once more and stared quietly in front of himself as if needing no further explanation. "This gentleman—may I introduce you?"—the man gave his permission with a wave of the hand—"so, this gentleman's job is to give out information. He gives all the information they need to people who are waiting, as our court and its offices are not very well known among the public he gets asked for quite a lot. He has an answer for every question, you can try him out if you feel like it. But that's not his only distinction, his other distinction is his elegance of dress. We, that's to say all of us who work in the offices here, we decided that the information-giver would have

to be elegantly dressed as he continually has to deal with the litigants
and he's the first one they meet, so he needs to give a dignified first
impression. The rest of us I'm afraid, as you can see just by looking at
me, dress very badly and old-fashioned; and there's not much point in
spending much on clothes anyway, as we hardly ever leave the offices,
we even sleep here. But, as I said, we decided that the information-
giver would have to have nice clothes. As the management here is
rather peculiar in this respect, and they would get them for us, we had
a collection—some of the litigants contributed too—and bought him
these lovely clothes and some others besides. So everything would be
ready for him to give a good impression, except that he spoils it again
by laughing and frightening people." "That's how it is," said the man,
mocking her, "but I don't understand why it is that you're explaining
all our intimate facts to the gentleman, or rather why it is that you're
pressing them on him, as I'm sure he's not all interested. Just look at
him sitting there, it's clear he's occupied with his own affairs." K. just
did not feel like contradicting him. The girl's intention may have been
good, perhaps she was under instructions to distract him or to give
him the chance to collect himself, but the attempt had not worked. "I
had to explain to him why you were laughing," said the girl. "I suppose
it was insulting." "I think he would forgive even worse insults if I
finally took him outside." K. said nothing, did not even look up, he
tolerated the two of them negotiating over him like an object, that was
even what suited him best. But suddenly he felt the information-giver's
hand on one arm and the young woman's hand on the other. "Up you
get then, weakling," said the information-giver. "Thank you both very
much," said K., pleasantly surprised, as he slowly rose and personally
guided these unfamiliar hands to the places where he most needed
support. As they approached the corridor, the girl said quietly into K.'s
ear, "I must seem to think it's very important to show the information-
giver in a good light, but you shouldn't doubt what I say, I just want
to say the truth. He isn't hard-hearted. It's not really his job to help
litigants outside if they're unwell but he's doing it anyway, as you can
see. I don't suppose any of us is hard-hearted, perhaps we'd all like to
be helpful, but working for the court offices it's easy for us to give the
impression we are hard-hearted and don't want to help anyone. It
makes me quite sad." "Would you not like to sit down here a while?"
asked the information-giver, they were already in the corridor and just
in front of the defendant whom K. had spoken to earlier. K. felt almost
ashamed to be seen by him, earlier he had stood so upright in front

of him and now he had to be supported by two others, his hat was held up by the information-giver balanced on outstretched fingers, his hair was dishevelled and hung down onto the sweat on his forehead. But the defendant seemed to notice nothing of what was going on and just stood there humbly, as if wanting to apologise to the information-giver for being there. The information-giver looked past him. "I know," he said, "that my case can't be settled today, not yet, but I've come in anyway, I thought, I thought I could wait here anyway, it's Sunday today, I've got plenty of time, and I'm not disturbing anyone here." "There's no need to be so apologetic," said the information-giver, "it's very commendable for you to be so attentive. You are taking up space here when you don't need to but as long as you don't get in my way I will do nothing to stop you following the progress of your case as closely as you like. When one has seen so many people who shamefully neglect their cases one learns to show patience with people like you. Do sit down." "He's very good with the litigants," whispered the girl. K. nodded, but started to move off again when the information-giver repeated, "Would you not like to sit down here a while?" "No, "said K., "I don't want to rest." He had said that as decisively as he could, but in fact it would have done him a lot of good to sit down. It was as if he were suffering sea-sickness. He felt as if he were on a ship in a rough sea, as if the water were hitting against the wooden walls, a thundering from the depths of the corridor as if the torrent were crashing over it, as if the corridor were swaying and the waiting litigants on each side of it rising and sinking. It made the calmness of the girl and the man leading him all the more incomprehensible. He was at their mercy, if they let go of him he would fall like a board. Their little eyes glanced here and there, K. could feel the evenness of their steps but could not do the same, as from step to step he was virtually being carried. He finally noticed they were speaking to him but he did not understand them, all he heard was a noise that filled all the space and through which there seemed to be an unchanging higher note sounding, like a siren. "Louder," he whispered with his head sunk low, ashamed at having to ask them to speak louder when he knew they had spoken loudly enough, even if it had been, for him, incomprehensible. At last, a draught of cool air blew in his face as if a gap had been torn out in the wall in front of him, and next to him he heard someone say, "First he says he wants to go, and then you can tell him a hundred times that this is the way out and he doesn't move." K. became aware that he was standing in front of the way out, and that the young woman had opened the door. It seemed to him that all his strength returned to him at once, and to get a foretaste of freedom he stepped straight on to one of the stairs and took his leave there of his companions, who bowed to him. "Thank you very much," he repeated, shook their hands once more and did not let go until he thought he saw that they found it hard to bear the comparatively fresh air from the stairway after being so long used to the air in the offices. They were hardly able to reply, and the young woman might even have fallen over if K. had not shut the door extremely fast. K. then stood still for a while, combed his hair with the help of a pocket mirror, picked up his hat from the next stair—the information-giver must have thrown it down there—and then he ran down the steps so fresh and in such long leaps that the contrast with his previous state nearly frightened him. His normally sturdy state of health had never prepared him for surprises such as this. Did his body want to revolt and cause him a new trial as he was bearing the old one with such little effort? He did not quite reject the idea that he should see a doctor the next time he had the chance, but whatever he did—and this was something on which he could advise himself—he wanted to spend all Sunday mornings in future better than he had spent this one.

4

Miss Bürstner's Friend

For some time after this, K. found it impossible to exchange even just a few words with Miss Bürstner. He tried to reach her in many and various ways but she always found a way to avoid it. He would come straight home from the office, remain in her room without the light on, and sit on the sofa with nothing more to distract him than keeping watch on the empty hallway. If the maid went by and closed the door of the apparently empty room he would get up after a while and open it again. He got up an hour earlier than usual in the morning so that he might perhaps find Miss Bürstner alone as she went to the office. But none of these efforts brought any success. Then he wrote her a letter, both to the office and the flat, attempting once more to justify his behaviour, offered to make whatever amends he could, promised never to cross whatever boundary she might set him and begged merely to have the chance to speak to her some time, especially as he was unable to do anything with Mrs. Grubach either until he had spoken with Miss Bürstner, he finally informed her that the following Sunday he would stay in his room all day waiting for a sign from her that there was some hope of his request being fulfilled, or at least that she would explain to him why she could not fulfil it even though he had promised to observe whatever stipulations she might make. The letters were not returned, but there was no answer either. However, on the following Sunday there was a sign that seemed clear enough. It was still early when K. noticed, through the keyhole, that there was an unusual level of activity in the hallway which soon abated. A French teacher, although she was German and called Montag, a pale and febrile girl with a slight limp who had previously occupied a room of her own, was moving into Miss Bürstner's room. She could be seen shuffling through the hallway for several hours, there was always another piece of clothing or a blanket or a book that she had forgotten and had to be fetched specially and brought into the new home.

When Mrs. Grubach brought K. his breakfast—ever since the time when she had made K. so cross she didn't trust the maid to do the slightest job—he had no choice but to speak to her, for the first time in five days. "Why is there so much noise in the hallway today?" he asked as she poured his coffee out, "Can't something be done about it? Does this clearing out have to be done on a Sunday?" K. did not look up at Mrs. Grubach, but he saw nonetheless that she seemed to feel some relief as she breathed in. Even sharp questions like this from Mr. K. she perceived as forgiveness, or as the beginning of forgiveness. "We're not clearing anything out, Mr. K.," she said, "it's just that Miss Montag is moving in with Miss Bürstner and is moving her things across." She said nothing more, but just waited to see how K. would take it and whether he would allow her to carry on speaking. But K. kept her in uncertainty, took the spoon and pensively stirred his coffee while he remained silent. Then he looked up at her and said, "What about the suspicions you had earlier about Miss Bürstner, have you given them up?" "Mr. K.," called Mrs. Grubach, who had been waiting for this very question, as she put her hands together and held them out towards him. "I just made a chance remark and you took it so badly. I didn't have the slightest intention of offending anyone, not you or anyone else. You've known me for long enough, Mr. K., I'm sure you're convinced of that. You don't know how I've been suffering for the past few days! That I should tell lies about my tenants! And you, Mr. K., you believed it! And said I should give you notice! Give you notice!" At this last outcry, Mrs. Grubach was already choking back her tears, she raised her apron to her face and blubbered out loud.

"Oh, don't cry Mrs. Grubach," said K., looking out the window, he was thinking only of Miss Bürstner and how she was accepting an unknown girl into her room. "Now don't cry," he said again as he turned his look back into the room where Mrs. Grubach was still crying. "I meant no harm either when I said that. It was simply a misunderstanding between us. That can happen even between old friends sometimes." Mrs. Grubach pulled her apron down to below her eyes to see whether K. really was attempting a reconciliation. "Well, yes, that's how it is," said K., and as Mrs. Grubach's behaviour indicated that the captain had said nothing he dared to add, "Do you really think, then, that I'd want to make an enemy of you for the sake of a girl we hardly know?" "Yes, you're quite right, Mr. K.," said Mrs. Grubach, and then, to her misfortune, as soon as she felt just a little freer to speak, she added something rather inept. "I kept asking myself why it was that Mr. K. took such an interest in Miss Bürstner. Why does he quarrel with me over her when he knows that any cross word from him and I can't sleep that night? And I didn't say anything about Miss Bürstner that I hadn't seen with my own eyes." K. said nothing in reply, he should have chased her from the room as soon as she had opened her mouth, and he didn't want to do that. He contented himself with merely drinking his coffee and letting Mrs. Grubach feel that she was superfluous. Outside, the dragging steps of Miss Montag could still be heard as she went from one side of the hallway to the other. "Do you hear that?" asked K. pointing his hand at the door. "Yes," said Mrs. Grubach with a sigh, "I wanted to give her some help and I wanted the maid to help her too but she's stubborn, she wants to move every-thing in herself. I wonder at Miss Bürstner. I often feel it's a burden for me to have Miss Montag as a tenant but Miss Bürstner accepts her into her room with herself." "There's nothing there for you to worry about" said K., crushing the remains of a sugar lump in his cup. "Does she cause you any trouble?" "No," said Mrs. Grubach, "in itself it's very good to have her there, it makes another room free for me and I can let my nephew, the captain, occupy it. I began to worry he might be disturbing you when I had to let him live in the living room next to you over the last few days. He's not very considerate." "What an idea!" said K. standing up, "there's no question of that. You seem to think that because I can't stand this to-ing and fro-ing of Miss Montag that I'm over-sensitive—and there she goes back again." Mrs. Grubach appeared quite powerless. "Should I tell her to leave moving the rest of her things over till later, then, Mr. K.? If that's what you want I'll do it immediately." "But she has to move in with Miss Bürstner!" said K. "Yes," said Mrs. Grubach, without quite understanding what K. meant. "So she has to take her things over there." Mrs. Grubach just nodded. K. was irritated all the more by this dumb helplessness which, seen from the outside, could have seemed like a kind of defi-ance on her part. He began to walk up and down the room between the window and the door, thus depriving Mrs. Grubach of the chance to leave, which she otherwise probably would have done.

Just as K. once more reached the door, someone knocked at it. It was the maid, to say that Miss Montag would like to have a few words with Mr. K., and therefore requested that he come to the dining room where she was waiting for him. K. heard the maid out thoughtfully,

and then looked back at the shocked Mrs. Grubach in a way that was
almost contemptuous. His look seemed to be saying that K. had been
expecting this invitation for Miss Montag for a long time, and that it
was confirmation of the suffering he had been made to endure that
Sunday morning from Mrs. Grubach's tenants. He sent the maid back
with the reply that he was on his way, then he went to the wardrobe
to change his coat, and in answer to Mrs. Grubach's gentle whining
about the nuisance Miss Montag was causing merely asked her to
clear away the breakfast things. "But you've hardly touched it," said
Mrs. Grubach. "Oh just take it away!" shouted K. It seemed to him
that Miss Montag was mixed up in everything and made it repulsive
to him.

As he went through the hallway he looked at the closed door of
Miss Bürstner's room. But it wasn't there that he was invited, but the
dining room, to which he yanked the door open without knocking.

The room was long but narrow with one window. There was only
enough space available to put two cupboards at an angle in the corner
by the door, and the rest of the room was entirely taken up with the
long dining table which started by the door and reached all the way to
the great window, which was thus made almost inaccessible. The table
was already laid for a large number of people, as on Sundays almost
all the tenants ate their dinner here at midday.

When K. entered, Miss Montag came towards him from the window along one side of the table. They greeted each other in silence.
Then Miss Montag, her head unusually erect as always, said, "I'm
not sure whether you know me." K. looked at her with a frown. "Of
course I do," he said, "you've been living here with Mrs. Grubach for
quite some time now." "But I get the impression you don't pay much
attention to what's going on in the lodging house," said Miss Montag.
"No," said K. "Would you not like to sit down?" said Miss Montag. In
silence, the two of them drew chairs out from the farthest end of the
table and sat down facing each other. But Miss Montag stood straight
up again as she had left her handbag on the window sill and went to
fetch it; she shuffled down the whole length of the room. When she
came back, the handbag lightly swinging, she said, "I'd like just to
have a few words with you on behalf of my friend. She would have
come herself, but she's feeling a little unwell today. Perhaps you'll be
kind enough to forgive her and listen to me instead. There's anyway
nothing that she could have said that I won't. On the contrary, in fact,
I think I can say even more than her because I'm relatively impartial.

Would you not agree?" "What is there to say, then?" answered K., who was tired of Miss Montag continuously watching his lips. In that way she took control of what he wanted to say before he said it. "Miss Bürstner clearly refuses to grant me the personal meeting that I asked her for." "That's how it is," said Miss Montag, "or rather, that's not at all how it is, the way you put it is remarkably severe. Generally speaking, meetings are neither granted nor the opposite. But it can be that meetings are considered unnecessary, and that's how it is here. Now, after your comment, I can speak openly. You asked my friend, verbally or in writing, for the chance to speak with her. Now my friend is aware of your reasons for asking for this meeting—or at least I suppose she is—and so, for reasons I know nothing about, she is quite sure that it would be of no benefit to anyone if this meeting actually took place. Moreover, it was only yesterday, and only very briefly, that she made it clear to me that such a meeting could be of no benefit for yourself either, she feels that it can only have been a matter of chance that such an idea came to you, and that even without any explanations from her, you will very soon come to realise yourself, if you have not done so already, the futility of your idea. My answer to that is that although it may be quite right, I consider it advantageous, if the matter is to be made perfectly clear, to give you an explicit answer. I offered my services in taking on the task, and after some hesitation my friend conceded. I hope, however, also to have acted in your interests, as even the slightest uncertainty in the least significant of matters will always remain a cause of suffering and if, as in this case, it can be removed without substantial effort, then it is better if that is done without delay." "I thank you," said K. as soon as Miss Montag had finished. He stood slowly up, looked at her, then across the table, then out the window—the house opposite stood there in the sun—and went to the door. Miss Montag followed him a few paces, as if she did not quite trust him. At the door, however, both of them had to step back as it opened and Captain Lanz entered. This was the first time that K. had seen him close up. He was a large man of about forty with a tanned, fleshy face. He bowed slightly, intending it also for K., and then went over to Miss Montag and deferentially kissed her hand. He was very elegant in the way he moved. The courtesy he showed towards Miss Montag made a striking contrast with the way she had been treated by K. Nonetheless, Miss Montag did not seem to be cross with K. as it even seemed to him that she wanted to introduce the captain. K. however, did not want to be introduced, he would not have been able to show any sort of friendliness either to Miss Montag or to the captain, the kiss on the hand had, for K., bound them into a group which would keep him at a distance from Miss Bürstner whilst at the same time seeming to be totally harmless and unselfish. K. thought, however, that he saw more than that, he thought he also saw that Miss Montag had chosen a means of doing it that was good, but two-edged. She exaggerated the importance of the relationship between K. and Miss Bürstner, and above all she exaggerated the importance of asking to speak with her and she tried at the same time to make out that K. was exaggerating everything. She would be disappointed, K. did not want to exaggerate anything, he was aware that Miss Bürstner was a little typist who would not offer him much resistance for long. In doing so he deliberately took no account of what Mrs. Grubach had told him about Miss Bürstner. All these things were going through his mind as he left the room with hardly a polite word. He wanted to go straight to his room, but a little laugh from Miss Montag that he heard from the dining room behind him brought him to the idea that he might prepare a surprise for the two of them, the captain and Miss Montag. He looked round and listened to find out if there might be any disturbance from any of the surrounding rooms, everywhere was quiet, the only thing to be heard was the conversation from the dining room and Mrs. Grubach's voice from the passage leading to the kitchen. This seemed an opportune time, K. went to Miss Bürstner's room and knocked gently. There was no sound so he knocked again but there was still no answer in reply. Was she asleep? Or was she really unwell? Or was she just pretending as she realised it could only be K. knocking so gently? K. assumed she was pretending and knocked harder, eventually, when the knocking brought no result, he carefully opened the door with the sense of doing something that was not only improper but also pointless. In the room there was no one. What's more, it looked hardly at all like the room K. had known before. Against the wall there were now two beds behind one another, there were clothes piled up on three chairs near the door, a wardrobe stood open. Miss Bürstner must have gone out while Miss Montag was speaking to him in the dining room. K. was not greatly bothered by this, he had hardly expected to be able to find Miss Bürstner so easily and had made this attempt for little more reason than to spite Miss Montag. But that made it all the more embarrassing for him when, as he was closing the door again, he saw Miss Montag and the captain talking in the open doorway of the dining room. They had probably been standing there ever since K. had opened the door, they avoided seeming to observe K. but chatted lightly and followed his movements with glances, the absent minded glances to the side such as you make during a conversation. But these glances were heavy for K., and he rushed alongside the wall back into his own room.

5

The Whip Man

One evening, a few days later, K. was walking along one of the corridors that separated his office from the main stairway—he was nearly the last one to leave for home that evening, there remained only a couple of workers in the light of a single bulb in the dispatch department—when he heard a sigh from behind a door that he had himself never opened but which he had always thought just led into a junk room. He stood in amazement and listened again to establish whether he might not be mistaken. For a while there was silence, but then came some more sighs. His first thought was to fetch one of the servitors, it might well have been worth having a witness present, but then he was taken by an uncontrollable curiosity that made him simply yank the door open. It was, as he had thought, a junk room. Old, unusable forms, empty stone ink bottles lay scattered behind the entrance. But in the cupboard-like room itself stood three men, crouching under the low ceiling. A candle fixed on a shelf gave them light. "What are you doing here?" asked K. quietly, but crossly and without thinking. One of the men was clearly in charge, and attracted attention by being dressed in a kind of dark leather costume which left his neck and chest and his arms exposed. He did not answer. But the other two called out, "Mr. K.! We're to be beaten because you made a complaint about us to the examining judge." And now, K. finally realised that it was actually the two policemen, Franz and Willem, and that the third man held a cane in his hand with which to beat them. "Well," said K., staring at them, "I didn't make any complaint, I only told what took place in my home. And your behaviour was not entirely unobjectionable, after all." "Mr. K.," said Willem, while Franz clearly tried to shelter behind him as protection from the third man, "if you knew how badly we get paid you wouldn't think so badly of us. I've got a family to feed, and Franz here wanted to get married, you just have to get more money where you can, you can't do it just by working hard, not however hard you try. I was sorely tempted by your fine clothes, policemen aren't allowed to do that sort of thing, course they aren't, and it wasn't right of us, but it's tradition that the clothes go to the officers, that's how it's always been, believe me; and it's understandable too, isn't it, what can things like that mean for anyone unlucky enough to be arrested? But if he starts talking about it openly then the punishment has to follow." "I didn't know about any of this that you've been telling me, and I made no sort of request that you be punished, I was simply acting on principle." "Franz," said Willem, turning to the other policeman, "didn't I tell you that the gentleman didn't say he wanted us to be punished? Now you can hear for yourself, he didn't even know we'd have to be punished." "Don't you let them persuade you, talking like that," said the third man to K., "this punishment is both just and unavoidable." "Don't listen to him," said Willem, interrupting himself only to quickly bring his hand to his mouth when it had received a stroke of the cane, "we're only being punished because you made a complaint against us. Nothing would have happened to us otherwise, not even if they'd found out what we'd done. Can you call that justice? Both of us, me especially, we'd proved our worth as good police officers over a long period—you've got to admit yourself that as far as official work was concerned we did the job well—things looked good for us, we had prospects, it's quite certain that we would've been made whip men too, like this one, only he had the luck not to have anyone make a complaint about him, as you really don't get many complaints like that. Only that's all finished now, Mr. K., our careers are at an end, we're going to have to do work now that's far inferior to police work and besides all this we're going to get this terrible, painful beating." "Can the cane really cause so much pain, then?" asked K., testing the cane that the whip man swang in front of him. "We're going to have to strip off totally naked," said Willem. "Oh, I see," said K., looking straight at the whip man, his skin was burned brown like a sailor's, and his face showed health and vigour. "Is there then no possibility of sparing these two their beating?" he asked him. "No," said the whip man, shaking his head with a laugh. "Get undressed!" he ordered the policemen. And to K. he said, "You shouldn't believe everything they tell you, it's the fear of being beaten, it's already made them a bit weak in the head. This one here, for instance," he pointed at Willem, "all that he told you about his career prospects, it's just

ridiculous. Look at him, look how fat he is—the first strokes of the
cane will just get lost in all that fat. Do you know what it is that's
made him so fat? He's in the habit of, everyone that gets arrested by
him, he eats their breakfast. Didn't he eat up your breakfast? Yeah, I
thought as much. But a man with a belly like that can't be made into
a whip man and never will be, that is quite out of the question."
"There are whip men like that," Willem insisted, who had just
released the belt of this trousers. "No," said the whip man, striking
him such a blow with the cane on his neck that it made him wince,
"you shouldn't be listening to this, just get undressed." "I would make
it well worth your while if you would let them go," said K., and without looking at the whip man again—as such matters are best carried
on with both pairs of eyes turned down—he pulled out his wallet.
"And then you'd try and put in a complaint against me, too," said the
whip man, "and get me flogged. No, no!" "Now, do be reasonable,"
said K., "if I had wanted to get these two punished I would not now
be trying to buy their freedom, would I. I could simply close the door
here behind me, go home and see or hear nothing more of it. But
that's not what I'm doing, it really is of much more importance to me
to let them go free; if I had realised they would be punished, or even
that they might be punished, I would never have named them in the
first place as they are not the ones I hold responsible. It's the organisation that's to blame, the high officials are the ones to blame."
"That's how it is!" shouted the policemen, who then immediately
received another blow on their backs, which were by now exposed.
"If you had a senior judge here beneath your stick," said K., pressing
down the cane as he spoke to stop it being raised once more, "I really
would do nothing to stop you, on the contrary, I would even pay you
money to give you all the more strength." "Yeah, that's all very plausi-
ble, what you're saying there," said the whip man, "only I'm not the
sort of person you can bribe. It's my job to flog people, so I flog
them." Franz, the policeman, had been fairly quiet so far, probably in
expectation of a good result from K.'s intervention, but now he
stepped forward to the door wearing just his trousers, kneeled down
hanging on to K.'s arm and whispered, "Even if you can't get mercy
shown for both of us, at least try and get me set free. Willem is older
than me, he's less sensitive than me in every way, he even got a light
beating a couple of years ago, but my record's still clean, I only did
things the way I did because Willem led me on to it, he's been my
teacher both for good and bad. Down in front of the bank my poor

bride is waiting for me at the entrance, I'm so ashamed of myself, it's pitiful." His face was flowing over with tears, and he wiped it dry on K.'s coat. "I'm not going to wait any longer," said the whip man, taking hold of the cane in both hands and laying in to Franz while Willem cowered back in a corner and looked on secretly, not even daring to turn his head. Then, the sudden scream that shot out from Franz was long and irrevocable, it seemed to come not from a human being but from an instrument that was being tortured, the whole corridor rang with it, it must have been heard by everyone in the building. "Don't shout like that!" called out K., unable to prevent himself, and, as he looked anxiously in the direction from which the servitor would come, he gave Franz a shove, not hard, but hard enough for him to fall down unconscious, clawing at the ground with his hands by reflex; he still did not avoid being hit; the rod still found him on the floor; the tip of the rod swang regularly up and down while he rolled to and fro under its blows. And now one of the servitors appeared in the distance, with another a few steps behind him. K. had quickly thrown the door shut, gone over to one of the windows overlooking the yard and opened it. The screams had completely stopped. So that the servitor wouldn't come in, he called out, "It's only me!" "Good evening, chief clerk," somebody called back. "Is there anything wrong?" "No, no," answered K., "it's only a dog yelping in the yard." There was no sound from the servitors so he added, "You can go back to what you were doing." He did not want to become involved with a conversation with them, and so he leant out of the window. A little while later, when he looked out in the corridor, they had already gone. Now, K. remained at the window, he did not dare go back into the junk room, and he did not want to go home either. The yard he looked down into was small and rectangular, all around it were offices, all the windows were now dark and only those at the very top caught a reflection of the moon. K. tried hard to see into the darkness of one corner of the yard, where a few handcarts had been left behind one another. He felt anguish at not having been able to prevent the flogging, but that was not his fault, if Franz had not screamed like that—clearly it must have caused a great deal of pain but it's important to maintain control of oneself at important moments—if Franz had not screamed then it was at least highly probable that K. would have been able to dissuade the whip man. If all the junior officers were contemptible why would the whip man, whose position was the most inhumane of all, be any exception, and K. had noticed very clearly how his eyes had lit up when he saw the banknotes, he had obviously only seemed serious about the flogging to raise the level of the bribe a little. And K. had not been ungenerous, he really had wanted to get the policemen freed; if he really had now begun to do something against the degeneracy of the court then it was a matter of course that he would have to do something here as well. But of course, it became impossible for him to do anything as soon as Franz started screaming. K. could not possibly have let the junior bank staff, and perhaps even all sorts of other people, come along and catch him by surprise as he haggled with those people in the junk room. Nobody could really expect that sort of sacrifice of him. If that had been his intention then it would almost have been easier, K. would have taken his own clothes off and offered himself to the whip man in the policemen's place. The whip man would certainly not have accepted this substitution anyway, as in that way he would have seriously violated his duty without gaining any benefit. He would most likely have violated his duty twice over, as court employees were probably under orders not to cause any harm to K. while he was facing charges, although there may have been special conditions in force here. However things stood, K. was able to do no more than throw the door shut, even though that would still do nothing to remove all the dangers he faced. It was regrettable that he had given Franz a shove, and it could only be excused by the heat of the moment.

In the distance, he heard the steps of the servitors; he did not want them to be too aware of his presence, so he closed the window and walked towards the main staircase. At the door of the junk room he stopped and listened for a little while. All was silent. The two policemen were entirely at the whip man's mercy; he could have beaten them to death. K. reached his hand out for the door handle but drew it suddenly back. He was no longer in any position to help anyone, and the servitors would soon be back; he did, though, promise himself that he would raise the matter again with somebody and see that, as far as it was in his power, those who really were guilty, the high officials whom nobody had so far dared point out to him, received their due punishment. As he went down the main stairway at the front of the bank, he looked carefully round at everyone who was passing, but there was no girl to be seen who might have been waiting for somebody, not even within some distance from the bank. Franz's claim that his bride was waiting for him was thus shown to be a lie, albeit one that was forgivable and intended only to elicit more sympathy.

The policemen were still on K.'s mind all through the following day; he was unable to concentrate on his work and had to stay in his office a little longer than the previous day so that he could finish it. On the way home, as he passed by the junk room again, he opened its door as if that had been his habit. Instead of the darkness he expected, he saw everything unchanged from the previous evening, and did not know how he should respond. Everything was exactly the same as he had seen it when he had opened the door the previous evening. The forms and bottles of ink just inside the doorway, the whip man with his cane, the two policemen, still undressed, the candle on the shelf, and the two policemen began to wail and call out "Mr. K.!" K. slammed the door immediately shut, and even thumped on it with his fists as if that would shut it all the firmer. Almost in tears, he ran to the servitors working quietly at the copying machine. "Go and get that junk room cleared out!" he shouted, and, in amazement, they stopped what they were doing. "It should have been done long ago, we're sinking in dirt!" They would be able to do the job the next day, K. nodded, it was too late in the evening to make them do it there and then as he had originally intended. He sat down briefly in order to keep them near him for a little longer, looked through a few of the copies to give the impression that he was checking them and then, as he saw that they would not dare to leave at the same time as himself, went home tired and with his mind numb.

6

K.'s Uncle—Leni

One afternoon—K. was very busy at the time, getting the mail ready—K.'s Uncle Karl, a small country landowner, came into the room, pushing his way between two of the staff who were bringing in some papers. K. had long expected his uncle to appear, but the sight of him now shocked K. far less than the prospect of it had done a long time before. His uncle was bound to come, K. had been sure of that for about a month. He already thought at the time he could see how his uncle would arrive, slightly bowed, his battered panama hat in his left hand, his right hand already stretched out over the desk long before he was close enough as he rushed carelessly towards K. knocking over everything that was in his way. K.'s uncle was always in a hurry, as he suffered from the unfortunate belief that he had a number things to do while he was in the big city and had to settle all of them in one day—his visits were only ever for one day—and at the same time thought he could not forgo any conversation or piece of business or pleasure that might arise by chance. Uncle Karl was K.'s former guardian, and so K. was dutybound to help him in all of this as well as to offer him a bed for the night. "I'm haunted by a ghost from the country,' he would say."

As soon as they had greeted each other—K. had invited him to sit in the armchair but Uncle Karl had no time for that—he said he wanted to speak briefly with K. in private. "It is necessary," he said with a tired gulp, "it is necessary for my peace of mind." K. immediately sent the junior staff from the room and told them to let no one in. "What's this that I've been hearing, Josef?" cried K.'s uncle when they were alone, as he sat on the table shoving various papers under himself without looking at them to make himself more comfortable. K. said nothing, he knew what was coming, but, suddenly relieved from the effort of the work he had been doing, he gave way to a pleasant lassitude and looked out the window at the other side of the street. From where he sat, he could see just a small, triangular section of it, part of the empty walls of houses between two shop windows. "You're staring out the window!" called out his uncle, raising his arms, "For God's sake, Josef, give me an answer! Is it true, can it really be true?" "Uncle Karl," said K., wrenching himself back from his daydreaming, "I really don't know what it is you want of me." "Josef," said his uncle in a warning tone, "as far as I know, you've always told the truth. Am I to take what you've just said as a bad sign?" "I think I know what it is you want," said K. obediently, "I expect you've heard about my trial." "That's right," answered his uncle with a slow nod, "I've heard about your trial." "Who did you hear it from, then?" asked K. "Erna wrote to me," said his uncle, "she doesn't have much contact with you, it's true, you don't pay very much attention to her, I'm afraid to say, but she learned about it nonetheless. I got her letter today and, of course, I came straight here. And for no other reason, but it seems to me that this is reason enough. I can read you out the part of the letter that concerns you." He drew the letter out from his wallet. "Here it is. She writes, 'I have not seen Josef for a long time, I was in the bank last week but Josef was so busy that they would not let me through; I waited there for nearly an hour but then I had to go home as I had my piano lesson. I would have liked to have spoken to him, maybe there will be a chance another time. He sent me a big box of chocolates for my name-day, that was very nice and attentive of him. I forgot to tell you about it when I wrote, and I only remember now that you ask me about it. Chocolate, as I am sure you are aware, disappears straight away in this lodging house, almost as soon as you know somebody has given you chocolate it is gone. But there is something else I wanted to tell you about Josef. Like I said, they would not let me through to see him at the bank because he was negotiating with some gentleman just then. After I had been waiting quietly for quite a long time I asked one of the staff whether his meeting would last much longer. He said it might well do, as it was probably about the legal proceedings, he said, that were being conducted against him. I asked what sort of legal proceedings it was that were being conducted against the chief clerk, and whether he was not making some mistake, but he said he was not making any mistake, there were legal proceedings underway and even that they were about something quite serious, but he did not know any more about it. He would have liked to have been of some help to the chief clerk himself, as the chief clerk was a gentleman, good and hon-

est, but he did not know what it was he could do and merely hoped
there would be some influential gentlemen who would take his side.
I'm sure that is what will happen and that everything will turn out for
the best in the end, but in the mean time things do not look at all
good, and you can see that from the mood of the chief clerk himself.
Of course, I did not place too much importance on this conversation,
and even did my best to put the bank clerk's mind at rest, he was quite
a simple man. I told him he was not to speak to anyone else about this,
and I think it is all just a rumour, but I still think it might be good if
you, Dear Father, if you looked into the matter the next time you visit.
It will be easy for you to find out more detail and, if it is really necessary, to do something about it through the great and influential people you know. But if it is not necessary, and that is what seems most
likely, then at least your daughter will soon have the chance to embrace
you and I look forward to it.' She's a good child," said K.'s uncle when
he had finished reading, and wiped a few tears from his eyes. K. nodded. With all the different disruptions he had had recently he had
completely forgotten about Erna, even her birthday, and the story of
the chocolates had clearly just been invented so that he wouldn't get
in trouble with his aunt and uncle. It was very touching, and even the
theatre tickets, which he would regularly send her from then on,
would not be enough to repay her, but he really did not feel, now, that
it was right for him to visit her in her lodgings and hold conversations
with a little, eighteen-year-old schoolgirl. "And what do you have to say
about that?" asked his uncle, who had forgotten all his rush and excitement as he read the letter, and seemed to be about to read it again.
"Yes, Uncle," said K., "it is true." "True!" called out his uncle. "What
is true? How can this be true? What sort of trial is it? Not a criminal
trial, I hope?" "It's a criminal trial," answered K. "And you sit quietly
here while you've got a criminal trial round your neck?" shouted his
uncle, getting ever louder. "The more calm I am, the better it will be
for the outcome," said K. in a tired voice, "don't worry." "How can I
help worrying?!" shouted his uncle, "Josef, my Dear Josef, think about
yourself, about your family, think about our good name! Up till now,
you've always been our pride, don't now become our disgrace. I don't
like the way you're behaving," he said, looking at K. with his head at
an angle, "that's not how an innocent man behaves when he's accused
of something, not if he's still got any strength in him. Just tell me what
it's all about so that I can help you. It's something to do with the bank,
I take it?" "No," said K. as he stood up, "and you're speaking too loud,

Uncle, I expect one of the staff is listening at the door and I find that rather unpleasant. It's best if we go somewhere else, then I can answer all your questions, as far as I can. And I know very well that I have to account to the family for what I do." "You certainly do!" his uncle shouted, "Quite right, you do. Now just get a move on, Josef, hurry up now!" "I still have a few documents I need to prepare," said K., and, using the intercom, he summoned his deputy who entered a few moments later. K.'s uncle, still angry and excited, gestured with his hand to show that K. had summoned him, even though there was no need whatever to do so. K. stood in front of the desk and explained to the young man, who listened calm and attentive, what would need to be done that day in his absence, speaking in a calm voice and making use of various documents. The presence of K.'s uncle while this was going on was quite disturbing; he did not listen to what was being said, but at first he stood there with eyes wide open and nervously biting his lips. Then he began to walk up and down the room, stopped now and then at the window, or stood in front of a picture always making various exclamations such as, "That is totally incomprehensible to me!" or "Now just tell me, what are you supposed to make of that?!" The young man pretended to notice nothing of this and listened to K.'s instructions through to the end, he made a few notes, bowed to both K. and his uncle and then left the room. K.'s uncle had turned his back to him and was looking out the window, bunching up the curtains with his outstretched hands. The door had hardly closed when he called out, "At last! Now that he's stopped jumping about we can go too!" Once they were in the front hall of the bank, where several members of staff were standing about and where, just then, the deputy director was walking across, there was unfortunately no way of stopping K.'s uncle from continually asking questions about the trial. "Now then, Josef," he began, lightly acknowledging the bows from those around them as they passed, "tell me everything about this trial; what sort of trial is it?" K. made a few comments which conveyed little information, even laughed a little, and it was only when they reached the front steps that he explained to his uncle that he had not wanted to talk openly in front of those people. "Quite right," said his uncle, "but now start talking." With his head to one side, and smoking his cigar in short, impatient draughts, he listened. "First of all, Uncle," said K., "it's not a trial like you'd have in a normal courtroom." "So much the worse," said his uncle. "How's that?" asked K., looking at him. "What I mean is, that's for the worse," he repeated. They were standing on the front steps of the bank; as the doorkeeper seemed to be listening to what they were saying K. drew his uncle down further, where they were absorbed into the bustle of the street. His uncle took K.'s arm and stopped asking questions with such urgency about the trial, they walked on for a while in silence. "But how did all this come about?" he eventually asked, stopping abruptly enough to startle the people walking behind, who had to avoid walking into him. "Things like this don't come all of a sudden, they start developing a long time beforehand, there must have been warning signs of it, why didn't you write to me? You know I'd do anything for you, to some extent I am still your guardian, and until today that's something I was proud of. I'll still help you, of course I will, only now, now that the trial is already underway, it makes it very difficult. But whatever; the best thing now is for you to take a short holiday staying with us in the country. You've lost weight, I can see that now. The country life will give you strength, that will be good, there's bound to be a lot of hard work ahead of you. But besides that it'll be a way of getting you away from the court, to some extent. Here they've got every means of show-ing the powers at their disposal and they're automatically bound to use them against you; in the country they'll either have to delegate authority to different bodies or just have to try and bother you by let-ter, telegram or telephone. And that's bound to weaken the effect, it won't release you from them but it'll give you room to breathe." "You could forbid me to leave," said K., who had been drawn slightly into his uncle's way of thinking by what he had been saying. "I didn't think you would do it," said his uncle thoughtfully, "you won't suffer too much loss of power by moving away." K. grasped his uncle under the arm to prevent him stopping still and said, "I thought you'd think all this is less important than I do, and now you're taking it so hard." "Josef," called his uncle trying to disentangle himself from him so that he could stop walking, but K. did not let go, "you've completely changed, you used to be so astute, are you losing it now? Do you want to lose the trial? Do you realise what that would mean? That would mean you would be simply destroyed. And that everyone you know would be pulled down with you or at the very least humiliated, dis-graced right down to the ground. Josef, pull yourself together. The way you're so indifferent about it, it's driving me mad. Looking at you I can almost believe that old saying: 'Having a trial like that means los-ing a trial like that.'" "My dear Uncle," said K., "it won't do any good to get excited, it's no good for you to do it and it'd be no good for me to do it. The case won't be won by getting excited, and please admit that my practical experience counts for something, just as I have always and still do respect your experience, even when it surprises me. You say that the family will also be affected by this trial; I really can't see how, but that's beside the point and I'm quite willing to follow your instructions in all of this. Only, I don't see any advantage in staying in the country, not even for you, as that would indicate flight and a sense of guilt. And besides, although I am more subject to persecution if I stay in the city I can also press the matter forward better here." "You're right," said his uncle in a tone that seemed to indicate they were finally coming closer to each other, "I just made the suggestion because, as I saw it, if you stay in the city the case will be put in danger by your indifference to it, and I thought it was better if I did the work for you. But will you push things forward yourself with all your strength, if so, that will naturally be far better." "We're agreed then," said K. "And do you have any suggestions for what I should do next?" "Well, naturally I'll have to think about it," said his uncle, "you must bear in mind that I've been living in the country for twenty years now, almost without a break, you lose your ability to deal with matters like this. But I do have some important connections with several people who, I expect, know their way around these things better than I do, and to contact them is a matter of course. Out there in the country I've been getting out of condition, I'm sure you're already aware of that. It's only at times like this that you notice it yourself. And this affair of yours came largely unexpected, although, oddly enough, I had expected something of the sort after I'd read Erna's letter, and today when I saw your face I knew it with almost total certainty. But all that is by the by, the important thing now is, we have no time to lose." Even while he was still speaking, K.'s uncle had stood on tiptoe to summon a taxi and now he pulled K. into the car behind himself as he called out an address to the driver. "We're going now to see Dr. Huld, the lawyer," he said, "we were at school together. I'm sure you know the name, don't you? No? Well that is odd. He's got a very good reputation as a defence barrister and for working with the poor. But I esteem him especially as someone you can trust." "It's alright with me, whatever you do," said K., although he was made uneasy by the rushed and urgent way his uncle was dealing with the matter. It was not very encouraging, as the accused, be to taken to a lawyer for poor people. "I didn't know," he said, "that you could take on a lawyer in matters like this." "Well of course you can," said his uncle, "that goes without saying. Why wouldn't you take on a lawyer? And now, so that I'm properly instructed in this matter, tell me what's been happening so far." K. instantly began telling his uncle about what had been happening, holding nothing back—being completely open with him was the only way that K. could protest at his uncle's belief that the trial was a great disgrace. He mentioned Miss Bürstner's name just once and in passing, but that did nothing to diminish his openness about the trial as Miss Bürstner had no connection with it. As he spoke, he looked out the window and saw how, just then, they were getting closer to the suburb where the court offices were. He drew this to his uncle's attention, but he did not find the coincidence especially remarkable. The taxi stopped in front of a dark building. K.'s uncle knocked at the very first door at ground level; while they waited he smiled, showing his big teeth, and whispered, "Eight o'clock; not the usual sort of time to be visiting a lawyer, but Huld won't mind it from me." Two large, black eyes appeared in the spy-hatch in the door, they stared at the two visitors for a while and then disappeared; the door, however, did not open. K. and his uncle confirmed to each other the fact that they had seen the two eyes. "A new maid, afraid of strangers," said K.'s uncle, and knocked again. The eyes appeared once more. This time they seemed almost sad, but the open gas flame that burned with a hiss close above their heads gave off little light and that may have merely created an illusion. "Open the door," called K.'s uncle, raising his fist against it, "we are friends of Dr. Huld, the lawyer!" "Dr. Huld is ill," whispered someone behind them. In a doorway at the far end of a narrow passage stood a man in his dressing gown, giving them this information in an extremely quiet voice. K.'s uncle, who had already been made very angry by the long wait, turned abruptly round and retorted, "Ill? You say he's ill?" and strode towards the gentleman in a way that seemed almost threatening, as if he were the illness himself. "They've opened the door for you, now," said the gentleman, pointing at the door of the lawyer. He pulled his dressing gown together and disappeared. The door had indeed been opened, a young girl—K. recognised the dark, slightly bulging eyes—stood in the hallway in a long white apron, holding a candle in her hand. "Next time, open up sooner!" said K.'s uncle instead of a greeting, while the girl made a slight curtsey. "Come along, Josef," he then said to K. who was slowly moving over towards the girl. "Dr. Huld is unwell," said the girl as K.'s uncle, without stopping, rushed towards one of the doors. K. continued to look at the girl in amazement as she turned round to block the way into the living room, she had a round face like a puppy's, not only the pale cheeks and the chin were round but the temples and the hairline were too. "Josef!" called his uncle once more, and he asked the girl, "It's trouble with his heart, is it?" "I think it is, sir," said the girl, who by now had found time to go ahead with the candle and open the door into the room. In one corner of the room, where the light of the candle did not reach, a face with a long beard looked up from the bed. "Leni, who's this coming in?" asked the lawyer, unable to recognise his guests because he was dazzled by the candle. "It's your old friend, Albert," said K.'s uncle. "Oh, Albert," said the lawyer, falling back onto his pillow as if this visit meant he would not need to keep up appearances. "Is it really as bad as that?" asked K.'s uncle, sitting on the edge of the bed. "I don't believe it is. It's a recurrence of your heart trouble and it'll pass over like the other times." "Maybe," said the lawyer quietly, "but it's just as much trouble as it's ever been. I can hardly breathe, I can't sleep at all and I'm getting weaker by the day." "I see," said K.'s uncle, pressing his panama hat firmly against his knee with his big hand. "That is bad news. But are you getting the right sort of care? And it's so depressing in here, it's so dark. It's a long time since I was last here, but it seemed to me friendlier then. Even your young lady here doesn't seem to have much life in her, unless she's just pretending." The maid was still standing by the door with the candle; as far as could be made out, she was watching K. more than she was watching his uncle even while the latter was still speaking about her. K. leant against a chair that he had pushed near to the girl. "When you're as ill as I am," said the lawyer, "you need to have peace. I don't find it depressing." After a short pause he added, "and Leni looks after me well, she's a good girl." But that was not enough to persuade K.'s uncle, he had visibly taken against his friend's carer and, even though he did not contradict the invalid, he persecuted her with his scowl as she went over to the bed, put the candle on the bedside table and, leaning over the bed, made a fuss of him by tidying the pillows. K.'s uncle nearly forgot the need to show any consideration for the man who lay ill in bed, he stood up, walked up and down behind the carer, and K. would not have been surprised if he had grabbed hold of her skirts behind her and dragged her away from the bed. K. himself looked on calmly, he was not even disappointed at finding the lawyer unwell, he had been able to do nothing to oppose the enthusiasm his uncle had developed for the matter, he was glad that this enthusiasm had now been distracted without his having to

do anything about it. His uncle, probably simply wishing to be offen-
sive to the lawyer's attendant, then said, "Young lady, now please leave
us alone for a while, I have some personal matters to discuss with my
friend." Dr. Huld's carer was still leant far over the invalid's bed and
smoothing out the cloth covering the wall next to it, she merely turned
her head and then, in striking contrast with the anger that first
stopped K.'s uncle from speaking and then let the words out in a gush,
she said very quietly, "You can see that Dr. Huld is so ill that he can't
discuss any matters at all." It was probably just for the sake of conven-
ience that she had repeated the words spoken by K.'s uncle, but an
onlooker might even have perceived it as mocking him and he, of
course, jumped up as if he had just been stabbed. "You damned . . ."
in the first gurglings of his excitement his words could hardly be
understood, K. was startled even though he had been expecting something of the sort and ran to his uncle with the intention, no doubt, of
closing his mouth with both his hands. Fortunately, though, behind
the girl, the invalid raised himself up, K.'s uncle made an ugly face as
if swallowing something disgusting and then, somewhat calmer, said,
"We have naturally not lost our senses, not yet; if what I am asking for
were not possible I would not be asking for it. Now please, go!" The
carer stood up straight by the bed directly facing K.'s uncle, K. thought
he noticed that with one hand she was stroking the lawyer's hand.
"You can say anything in front of Leni," said the invalid, in a tone that
was unmistakably imploring. "It's not my business," said K.'s uncle,
"and it's not my secrets." And he twisted himself round as if wanting
to go into no more negotiations but giving himself a little more time
to think. "Whose business is it then?" asked the lawyer in an exhausted
voice as he leant back again. "My nephew's," said K.'s uncle, "and I've
brought him along with me." And he introduced him, "Chief Clerk
Josef K." "Oh!" said the invalid, now with much more life in him, and
reached out his hand towards K. "Do forgive me, I didn't notice you
there at all." Then he then said to his carer, "Leni, go," stretching his
hand out to her as if this were a farewell that would have to last for a
long time. This time the girl offered no resistance. "So you," he finally
said to K.'s uncle, who had also calmed down and stepped closer, "you
haven't come to visit me because I'm ill but you've come on business."
The lawyer now looked so much stronger that it seemed the idea of
being visited because he was ill had somehow made him weak, he
remained supporting himself of one elbow, which must have been
rather tiring, and continually pulled at a lock of hair in the middle of

his beard. "You already look much better," said K.'s uncle, "now that that witch has gone outside." He interrupted himself, whispered, "I bet you she's listening!" and sprang over to the door. But behind the door there was no one, K.'s uncle came back not disappointed, as her not listening seemed to him worse than if she had been, but probably somewhat embittered. "You're mistaken about her," said the lawyer, but did nothing more to defend her; perhaps that was his way of indicating that she did not need defending. But in a tone that was much more committed he went on, "As far as your nephew's affairs are concerned, this will be an extremely difficult undertaking and I'd count myself lucky if my strength lasted out long enough for it; I'm greatly afraid it won't do, but anyway I don't want to leave anything untried; if I don't last out you can always get somebody else. To be honest, this matter interests me too much, and I can't bring myself to give up the chance of taking some part in it. If my heart does totally give out then at least it will have found a worthy affair to fail in." K. believed he understood not a word of this entire speech, he looked at his uncle for an explanation but his uncle sat on the bedside table with the candle in his hand, a medicine bottle had rolled off the table onto the floor, he nodded to everything the lawyer said, agreed to everything, and now and then looked at K. urging him to show the same compliance. Maybe K.'s uncle had already told the lawyer about the trial. But that was impossible, everything that had happened so far spoke against it. So he said, "I don't understand ..." "Well, maybe I've misunderstood what you've been saying," said the lawyer, just as astonished and embarrassed as K. "Perhaps I've been going too fast. What was it you wanted to speak to me about? I thought it was to do with your trial." "Of course it is," said K.'s uncle, who then asked K., "So what is it you want?" "Yes, but how is it that you know anything about me and my case?" asked K. "Oh, I see," said the lawyer with a smile. "I am a lawyer, I move in court circles, people talk about various different cases and the more interesting ones stay in your mind, especially when they concern the nephew of a friend. There's nothing very remarkable about that." "What is it you want, then?" asked K.'s uncle once more, "You seem so uneasy about it" "You move in this court's circles?" asked K. "Yes," said the lawyer. "You're asking questions like a child," said K.'s uncle. "What circles should I move in, then, if not with members of my own discipline?" the lawyer added. It sounded so indisputable that K. gave no answer at all. "But you work in the High Court, not that court in the attic," he had wanted to say but could not bring

himself to actually utter it. "You have to realise," the lawyer continued, in a tone as if he were explaining something obvious, unnecessary and incidental, "you have to realise that I also derive great
advantage for my clients from mixing with those people, and do so in
many different ways, it's not something you can keep talking about all
the time. I'm at a bit of a disadvantage now, of course, because of my
illness, but I still get visits from some good friends of mine at the court
and I learn one or two things. It might even be that I learn more than
many of those who are in the best of health and spend all day in court.
And I'm receiving a very welcome visit right now, for instance." And
he pointed into a dark corner of the room. "Where?" asked K., almost
uncouth in his surprise. He looked round uneasily; the little candle
gave off far too little light to reach as far as the wall opposite. And
then, something did indeed begin to move there in the corner. In the
light of the candle held up by K.'s uncle an elderly gentleman could be
seen sitting beside a small table. He had been sitting there for so long
without being noticed that he could hardly have been breathing. Now
he stood up with a great deal of fuss, clearly unhappy that attention
had been drawn to him. It was as if, by flapping his hands about like
short wings, he hoped to deflect any introductions and greetings, as
if he wanted on no account to disturb the others by his presence and
seemed to be exhorting them to leave him back in the dark and forget
about his being there. That, however, was something that could no
longer be granted him. "You took us by surprise, you see," said the
lawyer in explanation, cheerfully indicating to the gentleman that he
should come closer, which, slowly, hesitatingly, looking all around
him, but with a certain dignity, he did. "The office director—oh, yes,
forgive me, I haven't introduced you—this is my friend Albert K., this
is his nephew, the chief clerk Josef K., and this is the office director—so, the office director was kind enough to pay me a visit. It's only
possible to appreciate just how valuable a visit like this is if you've been
let into the secret of what a pile of work the office director has heaped
over him. Well, he came anyway, we were having a peaceful chat, as
far as I was able when I'm so weak, and although we hadn't told Leni
she mustn't let anyone in as we weren't expecting anyone, we still
would rather have remained alone, but then along came you, Albert,
thumping your fists on the door, the office director moved over into
the corner pulling his table and chair with him, but now it turns out
we might have, that is, if that's what you wish, we might have something to discuss with each other and it would be good if we can all

come back together again. Office director …" he said with his head
on one side, pointing with a humble smile to an armchair near the
bed. "I'm afraid I'll only be able to stay a few minutes more," smiled
the office director as he spread himself out in the armchair and looked
at the clock. "Business calls. But I wouldn't want to miss the chance
of meeting a friend of my friend." He inclined his head slightly toward
K.'s uncle, who seemed very happy with his new acquaintance, but he
was not the sort of person to express his feelings of deference and
responded to the office director's words with embarrassed, but loud,
laughter. A horrible sight! K. was able to quietly watch everything as
nobody paid any attention to him, the office director took over as
leader of the conversation as seemed to be his habit once he had been
called forward, the lawyer listened attentively with his hand to his ear,
his initial weakness having perhaps only had the function of driving
away his new visitors, K.'s uncle served as candle-bearer—balancing the
candle on his thigh while the office director frequently glanced nervously at it—and was soon free of his embarrassment and was quickly
enchanted not only by the office director's speaking manner but also
by the gentle, waving hand-movements with which he accompanied it.
K., leaning against the bedpost, was totally ignored by the office director, perhaps deliberately, and served the old man only as audience.
And besides, he had hardly any idea what the conversation was about
and his thoughts soon turned to the care assistant and the ill treat-
ment she had suffered from his uncle. Soon after, he began to wonder
whether he had not seen the office director somewhere before, perhaps among the people who were at his first hearing. He may have
been mistaken, but thought the office director might well have been
among the old gentlemen with the thin beards in the first row.

There was then a noise that everyone heard from the hallway as if
something of porcelain were being broken. "I'll go and see what's happened," said K., who slowly left the room as if giving the others the
chance to stop him. He had hardly stepped into the hallway, finding
his bearings in the darkness with his hand still firmly holding the
door, when another small hand, much smaller than K.'s own, placed
itself on his and gently shut the door. It was the carer who had been
waiting there. "Nothing has happened," she whispered to him, "I just
threw a plate against the wall to get you out of there." "I was thinking
about you, as well," replied K. uneasily. "So much the better," said the
carer. "Come with me." A few steps along, they came to a frosted glass
door which the carer opened for him. "Come in here," she said. It was

clearly the lawyer's office, fitted out with old, heavy furniture, as far
as could be seen in the moonlight which now illuminated just a small,
rectangular section of the floor by each of the three big windows.
"This way," said the carer, pointing to a dark trunk with a carved,
wooden backrest. When he had sat down, K. continued to look round
the room, it was a large room with a high ceiling, the clients of this
lawyer for the poor must have felt quite lost in it. K. thought he could
see the little steps with which visitors would approach the massive
desk. But then he forgot about all of this and had eyes only for the
carer who sat very close beside him, almost pressing him against the
armrest. "I did think," she said "you would come out here to me by
yourself without me having to call you first. It was odd. First you stare
at me as soon as you come in, and then you keep me waiting. And you
ought to call me Leni, too," she added quickly and suddenly, as if no
moment of this conversation should be lost. "Gladly," said K. "But as
for its being odd, Leni, that's easy to explain. Firstly, I had to listen to
what the old men were saying and couldn't leave without a good reason, but secondly I'm not a bold person, if anything I'm quite shy, and
you, Leni, you didn't really look like you could be won over in one
stroke, either." "That's not it," said Leni, laying one arm on the armrest and looking at K., "you didn't like me, and I don't suppose you
like me now, either." "Liking wouldn't be very much," said K., eva-
sively. "Oh!" she exclaimed with a smile, thus making use of K.'s comment to gain an advantage over him. So K. remained silent for a while.
By now, he had become used to the darkness in the room and was able
to make out various fixtures and fittings. He was especially impressed
by a large picture hanging to the right of the door, he leant forward in
order to see it better. It depicted a man wearing a judge's robes; he was
sitting on a lofty throne gilded in a way that shone forth from the
picture. The odd thing about the picture was that this judge was not
sitting there in dignified calm but had his left arm pressed against the
back and armrest, his right arm, however, was completely free and
only grasped the armrest with his hand, as if about to jump up any
moment in vigorous outrage and make some decisive comment or
even to pass sentence. The accused was probably meant to be imagined at the foot of the steps, the top one of which could be seen in the
picture, covered with a yellow carpet. "That might be my judge," said
K., pointing to the picture with one finger. "I know him," said Leni
looking up at the picture, "he comes here quite often. That picture is
from when he was young, but he can never have looked anything like

it, as he's tiny, minute almost. But despite that, he had himself made to look bigger in the picture as he's madly vain, just like everyone round here. But even I'm vain and that makes me very unhappy that you don't like me." K. replied to that last comment merely by embracing Leni and drawing her towards him, she lay her head quietly on his shoulder. To the rest of it, though, he said, "What rank is he?" "He's an examining judge," she said, taking hold of the hand with which K. held her and playing with his fingers. "Just an examining judge once again," said K. in disappointment, "the senior officials keep themselves hidden. But here he is sitting on a throne." "That's all just made up," said Leni with her face bent over K.'s hand, "really he's sitting on a kitchen chair with an old horse blanket folded over it. But do you have to be always thinking about your trial?" she added slowly. "No, not at all," said K., "I probably even think too little about it." "That's not the mistake you're making," said Leni, "you're too unyielding, that's what I've heard." "Who said that?" asked K., he felt her body against his chest and looked down on her rich, dark, tightly bound hair. "I'd be saying too much if I told you that," answered Leni. "Please don't ask for names, but do stop making these mistakes of yours, stop being so unyielding, there's nothing you can do to defend yourself from this court, you have to confess. So confess to them as soon as you get the chance. It's only then that they give you the chance to get away, not till then. Only, without help from outside even that's impossible, but you needn't worry about getting this help as I want to help you myself." "You understand a lot about this court and what sort of tricks are needed," said K. as he lifted her, since she was pressing in much too close to him, onto his lap. "That's alright, then," she said, and made herself comfortable on his lap by smoothing out her skirt and adjusting her blouse. Then she hung both her arms around his neck, leant back and took a long look at him. "And what if I don't confess, could you not help me then?" asked K. to test her out. I'm accumulating women to help me, he thought to himself almost in amazement, first Miss Bürstner, then the court usher's wife, and now this little care assistant who seems to have some incomprehensible need for me. The way she sits on my lap as if it were her proper place! "No," answered Leni, slowly shaking her head, "I couldn't help you then. But you don't want my help anyway, it means nothing to you, you're too stubborn and won't be persuaded." Then, after a while she asked, "Do you have a lover?" "No," said K. "Oh, you must have," she said. "Well, I have really," said K. "Just think, I've even betrayed her while I'm carrying her photograph with me." Leni insisted he show her a photograph of Elsa, and then, hunched on his lap, studied the picture closely. The photograph was not one that had been taken while Elsa was posing for it, it showed her just after she had been in a wild dance such as she liked to do in wine bars, her skirt was still flung out as she span round, she had placed her hands on her firm hips and, with her neck held taut, looked to one side with a laugh; you could not see from the picture whom her laugh was intended for. "She's very tightly laced," said Leni, pointing to the place where she thought this could be seen. "I don't like her, she's clumsy and crude. But maybe she's gentle and friendly towards you, that's the impression you get from the picture. Big, strong girls like that often don't know how to be anything but gentle and friendly. Would she be capable of sacrificing herself for you, though?" "No," said K., "she isn't gentle or friendly, and nor would she be capable of sacrificing herself for me. But I've never yet asked any of those things of her. I've never looked at this picture as closely as you." "You can't think much of her, then," said Leni. "She can't be your lover after all." "Yes she is," said K., "I'm not going to take my word back on that." "Well she might be your lover now, then," said Leni, "but you wouldn't miss her much if you lost her or if you exchanged her for somebody else, me for instance." "That is certainly conceivable," said K. with a smile, "but she does have one major advantage over you, she knows nothing about my trial, and even if she did she wouldn't think about it. She wouldn't try to persuade me to be less unyielding." "Well that's no advantage," said Leni. "If she's got no advantage other than that, I can keep on hoping. Has she got any bodily defects?" "'Bodily defects'?" asked K. "Yeah," said Leni, "as I do have a bodily defect, just a little one. Look." She spread the middle and ring fingers of her right hand apart from each other. Between those fingers the flap of skin connecting them reached up almost as far as the top joint of the little finger. In the darkness, K. did not see at first what it was she wanted to show him, so she led his hand to it so that he could feel. "What a freak of nature," said K., and when he had taken a look at the whole hand he added, "What a pretty claw!" Leni looked on with a kind of pride as K. repeatedly opened and closed her two fingers in amazement, until, finally, he briefly kissed them and let go. "Oh!" she immediately exclaimed, "you kissed me!" Hurriedly, and with her mouth open, she clambered up K.'s lap with her knees. He was almost aghast as he looked up at her, now that she was so close to him there was a bitter, irritating smell from her, like pepper, she grasped his head, leant out over him, and bit and kissed his neck, even biting into his hair. "I've taken her place!" she exclaimed from time to time. "Just look, now you've taken me instead of her!" Just then, her knee slipped out and, with a little cry, she nearly fell down onto the carpet, K. tried to hold her by putting his arms around her and was pulled down with her. "Now you're mine," she said. Her last words to him as he left were, "Here's the key to the door, come whenever you want," and she planted an undirected kiss on his back. When he stepped out the front door there was a light rain falling, he was about to go to the middle of the street to see if he could still glimpse Leni at the window when K.'s uncle leapt out of a car that K., thinking of other things, had not seen waiting outside the building. He took hold of K. by both arms and shoved him against the door as if he wanted to nail him to it. "Young man," he shouted, "how could you do a thing like that?! Things were going well with this business of yours, now you've caused it terrible damage. You slope off with some dirty, little thing who, moreover, is obviously the lawyer's beloved, and stay away for hours. You don't even try to find an excuse, don't try to hide anything, no, you're quite open about it, you run off with her and stay there. And meanwhile we're sitting there, your uncle who's going to such effort for you, the lawyer who needs to be won over to your side, and above all the office director, a very important gentleman who is in direct command of your affair in its present stage. We wanted to discuss how best to help you, I had to handle the lawyer very carefully, he had to handle the office director carefully, and you had most reason of all to at least give me some support. Instead of which you stay away. Eventually we couldn't keep up the pretence any longer, but these are polite and highly capable men, they didn't say anything about it so as to spare my feelings but in the end not even they could continue to force themselves and, as they couldn't speak about the matter in hand, they became silent. We sat there for several minutes, listening to see whether you wouldn't finally come back. All in vain. In the end the office director stood up, as he had stayed far longer than he had originally intended, made his farewell, looked at me in sympathy without being able to help, he waited at the door for a long time although it's more than I can understand why he was being so good, and then he went. I, of course, was glad he'd gone, I'd been holding my breath all this time. All this had even more affect on the lawyer lying there ill, when I took my leave of him, the good man, he was quite unable to speak. You have probably contributed to his total collapse and so brought the very man who you are dependent on closer to his death. And me, your own uncle, you leave me here in the rain—just feel this, I'm wet right through—waiting here for hours, sick with worry."

7

Lawyer—Manufacturer—Painter

One winter morning—snow was falling in the dull light outside—K. was sitting in his office, already extremely tired despite the early hour. He had told the servitor he was engaged in a major piece of work and none of the junior staff should be allowed in to see him, so he would not be disturbed by them at least. But instead of working he turned round in his chair, slowly moved various items around his desk, but then, without being aware of it, he lay his arm stretched out on the desk top and sat there immobile with his head sunk down on his chest.

He was no longer able to get the thought of the trial out of his head. He had often wondered whether it might not be a good idea to work out a written defence and hand it in to the court. It would contain a short description of his life and explain why he had acted the way he had at each event that was in any way important, whether he now considered he had acted well or ill, and his reasons for each. There was no doubt of the advantages a written defence of this sort would have over relying on the lawyer, who was anyway not without his shortcomings. K. had no idea what actions the lawyer was taking; it was certainly not a lot, it was more than a month since the lawyer had summoned him, and none of the previous discussions had given K. the impression that this man would be able to do much for him. Most importantly, he had asked him hardly any questions. And there were so many questions here to be asked. Asking questions were the most important thing. K. had the feeling that he would be able to ask all the questions needed here himself. The lawyer, in contrast, did not ask questions but did all the talking himself or sat silently facing him, leant forward slightly over the desk, probably because he was hard of hearing, pulled on a strand of hair in the middle of his beard and looked down at the carpet, perhaps at the very spot where K. had lain

with Leni. Now and then he would give K. some vague warning of the
sort you give to children. His speeches were as pointless as they were
boring, and K. decided that when the final bill came he would pay not
a penny for them. Once the lawyer thought he had humiliated K. sufficiently, he usually started something that would raise his spirits
again. He had already, he would then say, won many such cases, partly
or in whole, cases which may not really have been as difficult as this
one but which, on the face of it, had even less hope of success. He had
a list of these cases here in the drawer—here he would tap on one or
other of the drawers in his desk—but could, unfortunately, not show
them to K. as they dealt with official secrets. Nonetheless, the great
experience he had acquired through all these cases would, of course,
be of benefit to K. He had, of course, begun work straight away and
was nearly ready to submit the first documents. They would be very
important because the first impression made by the defence will often
determine the whole course of the proceedings. Unfortunately,
though, he would still have to make it clear to K. that the first documents submitted are sometimes not even read by the court. They simply put them with the other documents and point out that, for the
time being, questioning and observing the accused are much more
important than anything written. If the applicant becomes insistent,
then they add that before they come to any decision, as soon as all the
material has been brought together, with due regard, of course, to all
the documents, then these first documents to have been submitted
will also be checked over. But unfortunately, even this is not usually
true, the first documents submitted are usually mislaid or lost completely, and even if they do keep them right to the end they are hardly
read, although the lawyer only knew about this from rumour. This is
all very regrettable, but not entirely without its justifications. But K.
should not forget that the trial would not be public, if the court deems
it necessary it can be made public but there is no law that says it has
to be. As a result, the accused and his defence don't have access even
to the court records, and especially not to the indictment, and that
means we generally don't know—or at least not precisely—what the first
documents need to be about, which means that if they do contain
anything of relevance to the case it's only by a lucky coincidence. If
anything about the individual charges and the reasons for them comes
out clearly or can be guessed at while the accused is being questioned,
then it's possible to work out and submit documents that really direct
the issue and present proof, but not before. Conditions like this, of

course, place the defence in a very unfavourable and difficult position. But that is what they intend. In fact, defence is not really allowed under the law, it's only tolerated, and there is even some dispute about whether the relevant parts of the law imply even that. So strictly speaking, there is no such thing as a counsel acknowledged by the court, and anyone who comes before this court as counsel is basically no more than a barrack room lawyer. The effect of all this, of course, is to remove the dignity of the whole procedure, the next time K. is in the court offices he might like to have a look in at the lawyers' room, just so that he's seen it. He might well be quite shocked by the people he sees assembled there. The room they've been allocated, with its narrow space and low ceiling, will be enough to show what contempt the court has for these people. The only light in the room comes through a little window that is so high up that, if you want to look out of it, you first have to get one of your colleagues to support you on his back, and even then the smoke from the chimney just in front of it will go up your nose and make your face black. In the floor of this room—to give yet another example of the conditions there—there is a hole that's been there for more than a year, it's not so big that a man could fall through, but it is big enough for your foot to disappear through it. The lawyers' room is on the second floor of the attic; if your foot does go through it will hang down into the first floor of the attic underneath it, and right in the corridor where the litigants are waiting. It's no exaggeration when lawyers say that conditions like that are a disgrace. Complaints to the management don't have the slightest effect, but the lawyers are strictly forbidden to alter anything in the room at their own expense. But even treating the lawyers in this way has its reasons. They want, as far as possible, to prevent any kind of defence, everything should be made the responsibility of the accused. Not a bad point of view, basically, but nothing could be more mistaken than to think from that that lawyers are not necessary for the accused in this court. On the contrary, there is no court where they are less needed than here. This is because proceedings are generally kept secret not only from the public but also from the accused. Only as far as that is possible, of course, but it is possible to a very large extent. And the accused doesn't get to see the court records either, and it's very difficult to infer what's in the court records from what's been said during questioning based on them, especially for the accused who is in a difficult situation and is faced with every possible worry to distract him. This is when the defence begins. Counsel for the defence are not normally allowed to be present while the accused is being questioned, so afterwards, and if possible still at the door of the interview room, he has to learn what he can about it from him and extract whatever he can that might be of use, even though what the accused has to report is often very confused. But that is not the most important thing, as there's really not a lot that can be learned in this way, although in this, as with anything else, a competent man will learn more than another. Nonetheless, the most important thing is the lawyer's personal connections, that's where the real value of taking counsel lies. Now K. will most likely have already learned from his own experience that, among its very lowest orders, the court organisation does have its imperfections, the court is strictly closed to the public, but staff who forget their duty or who take bribes do, to some extent, show where the gaps are. This is where most lawyers will push their way in, this is where bribes are paid and information extracted, there have even, in earlier times at least, been incidents where documents have been stolen. There's no denying that some surprisingly favourable results have been attained for the accused in this way, for a limited time, and these petty advocates then strut to and fro on the basis of them and attract new clients, but for the further course of the proceedings it signifies either nothing or nothing good. The only things of real value are honest personal contacts, contacts with higher officials, albeit higher officials of the lower grades, you understand. That is the only way the progress of the trial can be influenced, hardly noticeable at first, it's true, but from then on it becomes more and more visible. There are, of course, not many lawyers who can do this, and K. has made a very good choice in this matter. There were probably no more than one or two who had as many contacts as Dr. Huld, but they don't bother with the company of the lawyers' room and have nothing to do with it. This means they have all the less contact with the court officials. It is not at all necessary for Dr. Huld to go to the court, wait in the anterooms for the examining judges to turn up, if they turn up, and try to achieve something which, according to the judges' mood is usually more apparent than real and most often not even that. No, K. has seen for himself that the court officials, including some who are quite high up, come forward without being asked, are glad to give information which is fully open or at least easy to understand, they discuss the next stages in the proceedings, in fact in some cases they can be won over and are quite willing to adopt the other person's point of view. However, when this happens, you should never trust them too far, as however firmly they may have declared this new point of view in favour of the defendant they might well go straight back to their offices and write a report for the court that says just the opposite, and might well be even harder on the defendant than the original view, the one they insist they've been fully dissuaded from. And, of course, there's no way of defending yourself from this, something said in private is indeed in private and cannot then be used in public, it's not something that makes it easy for the defence to keep those gentlemen's favour. On the other hand, it's also true that the gentlemen don't become involved with the defence—which will of course be done with great expertise—just for philanthropic reasons or in order to be friendly, in some respects it would be truer to say that they, too, have it allocated to them. This is where the disadvantages of a court structure that, right from the start, stipulates that all proceedings take place in private, come into force. In normal, mediocre trials its officials have contact with the public, and they're very well equipped for it, but here they don't; normal trials run their course all by themselves, almost, and just need a nudge here and there; but when they're faced with cases that are especially difficult they're as lost as they often are with ones that are very simple; they're forced to spend all their time, day and night, with their laws, and so they don't have the right feel for human relationships, and that's a serious shortcoming in cases like this. That's when they come for advice to the lawyer, with a servant behind them carrying the documents which normally are kept so secret. You could have seen many gentlemen at this window, gentlemen of whom you would least expect it, staring out this window in despair on the street below while the lawyer is at his desk studying the documents so that he can give them good advice. And at times like that it's also possible to see how exceptionally seriously these gentlemen take their professions and how they are thrown into great confusion by difficulties which it's just not in their natures to overcome. But they're not in an easy position, to regard their positions as easy would be to do them an injustice. The different ranks and hierarchies of the court are endless, and even someone who knows his way around them cannot always tell what's going to happen. But even for the junior officials, the proceedings in the courtrooms are usually kept secret, so they are hardly able to see how the cases they work with proceed, court affairs appear in their range of vision often without their knowing where they come from and they move on further without their learning where they go. So civil servants like this are not able to learn the things you can learn from studying the successive stages that individual trials go through, the final verdict or the reasons for it. They're only allowed to deal with that part of the trial which the law allocates them, and they usually know less about the results of their work after it's left them than the defence does, even though the defence will usually stay in contact with the accused until the trial is nearly at its end, so that the court officials can learn many useful things from the defence. Bearing all this in mind, does it still surprise K. that the officials are irritated and often express themselves about the litigants in unflattering ways—which is an experience shared by everyone. All the officials are irritated, even when they appear calm. This causes many difficulties for the junior advocates, of course. There is a story, for instance, that has very much the ring of truth about it. It goes like this: One of the older officials, a good and peaceful man, was dealing with a difficult matter for the court which had become very confused, especially thanks to the contributions from the lawyers. He had been studying it for a day and a night without a break—as these officials are indeed hard working, no one works as hard as they do. When it was nearly morning, and he had been working for twenty-four hours with probably very little result, he went to the front entrance, waited there in ambush, and every time a lawyer tried to enter the building he would throw him down the steps. The lawyers gathered together down in front of the steps and discussed with each other what they should do; on the one hand they had actually no right to be allowed into the building so that there was hardly anything that they could legally do to the official and, as I've already mentioned, they would have to be careful not to set all the officials against them. On the other hand, any day not spent in court is a day lost for them and it was a matter of some importance to force their way inside. In the end, they agreed that they would try to tire the old man out. One lawyer after another was sent out to run up the steps and let himself be thrown down again, offering what resistance he could as long as it was passive resistance, and his colleagues would catch him at the bottom of the steps. That went on for about an hour until the old gentleman, who was already exhausted from working all night, was very tired and went back to his office. Those who were at the bottom of the steps could not believe it at first, so they sent somebody out to go and look behind the door to see if there really was no one there, and only then did they all gather together and probably didn't even dare to complain, as it's far from being the lawyers' job to introduce any improvements in the court system, or even to want to. Even the most junior lawyer can understand the relationship there to some extent, but one significant point is that almost every defendant, even very simple people, begins to think of suggestions for improving the court as soon as his proceedings have begun, many of them often even spend time and energy on the matter that could be spent far better elsewhere. The only right thing to do is to learn how to deal with the situation as it is. Even if it were possible to improve any detail of it— which is anyway no more than superstitious nonsense—the best that they could achieve, although doing themselves incalculable harm in the process, is that they will have attracted the special attention of the officials for any case that comes up in the future, and the officials are always ready to seek revenge. Never attract attention to yourself! Stay calm, however much it goes against your character! Try to gain some insight into the size of the court organism and how, to some extent, it remains in a state of suspension, and that even if you alter something in one place you'll draw the ground out from under your feet and might fall, whereas if an enormous organism like the court is disrupted in any one place it finds it easy to provide a substitute for itself somewhere else. Everything is connected with everything else and will continue without any change or else, which is quite probable, even more closed, more attentive, more strict, more malevolent. So it's best to leave the work to the lawyers and not to keep disturbing them. It doesn't do much good to make accusations, especially if you can't make it clear what they're based on and their full significance, but it must be said that K. caused a great deal of harm to his own case by his behaviour towards the office director, he was a very influential man but now he might as well be struck off the list of those who might do anything for K. If the trial is mentioned, even just in passing, it's quite obvious that he's ignoring it. These officials are in many ways just like children. Often, something quite harmless—although K.'s behaviour could unfortunately not be called harmless—will leave them feeling so offended that they will even stop talking with good friends of theirs, they turn away when they see them and do everything they can to oppose them. But then, with no particular reason, surprisingly enough, some little joke that was only ever attempted because everything seemed so hopeless will make them laugh and they'll be reconciled. It's both difficult and hard at the same time to deal with them, and there's hardly any reason for it. It's sometimes quite astonishing that a single, average life is enough to encompass so much that it's at all possible ever to have any success in one's work here. On the other hand, there are also dark moments, such as everyone has, when you think you've achieved nothing at all, when it seems that the only trials to come to a good end are those that were determined to have a good end from the start and would do so without any help, while all the others are lost despite all the running to and fro, all the effort, all the little, apparent successes that gave such joy. Then you no longer feel very sure of anything and, if asked about a trial that was doing well by its own nature but which was turned for the worse because you assisted in it, would not even dare deny that. And even that is a kind of self-confidence, but then it's the only one that's left. Lawyers are especially vulnerable to fits of depression of that sort—and they are no more than fits of depression of course—when a case is suddenly taken out of their hands after they've been conducting it satisfactorily for some time. That's probably the worst that can happen to a lawyer. It's not that the accused takes the case away from him, that hardly ever happens, once a defendant has taken on a certain lawyer he has to stay with him whatever happens. How could he ever carry on by himself after he's taken on help from a lawyer? No, that just doesn't happen, but what does sometimes happen is that the trial takes on a course where the lawyer may not go along with it. Client and trial are both simply taken away from the lawyer; and then even contact with the court officials won't help, however good they are, as they don't know anything themselves. The trial will have entered a stage where no more help can be given, where it's being processed in courts to which no one has any access, where the defendant cannot even be contacted by his lawyer. You come home one day and find all the documents you've submitted, which you've worked hard to create and which you had the best hopes for, lying on the desk, they've been sent back as they can't be carried through to the next stage in the trial, they're just worthless scraps of paper. It doesn't mean that the case has been lost, not at all, or at least there is no decisive reason for supposing so, it's just that you don't know anything more about the case and won't be told anything of what's happening. Well, cases like that are the exceptions, I'm glad to say, and even if K.'s trial is one of them, it's still, for the time being, a long way off. But there was still plenty of opportunity for lawyers to get to work, and K. could be sure they would be made use of. As he had said, the time for submitting documents was still in the future and there was no rush to prepare them, it was much more important to start the initial discussions with the appropriate officials, and they had already taken place. With varying degrees of success, it must be said. It was much better not to give away any details before their time, as in that way K. could only be influenced unfavourably and his hopes might be raised or he might be made too anxious, better just to say that some individuals have spoken very favourably and shown themselves very willing to help, although others have spoken less favourably, but even they have not in any way refused to help. So all in all, the results are very encouraging, only you should certainly not draw any particular conclusions as all preliminary proceedings begin in the same way and it was only the way they developed further that would show what the value of these preliminary proceedings has been. Anyway, nothing has been lost yet, and if we can succeed in getting the office director, despite everything, on our side—and several actions have been undertaken to this end—then everything is a clean wound, as a surgeon would say, and we can wait for the results with some comfort.

When he started talking on in this way the lawyer was quite tireless. He went through it all again every time K. went to see him. There was always some progress, but he could never be told what sort of progress it was. The first set of documents to be submitted were being worked on but still not ready, which usually turned out to be a great advantage the next time K. went to see him as the earlier occasion would have been a very bad time to put them in, which they could not then have known. If K., stupefied from all this talking, ever pointed out that even considering all these difficulties progress was very slow, the lawyer would object that progress was not slow at all, but that they might have progressed far further if K. had come to him at the right time. But he had come to him late and that lateness would bring still further difficulties, and not only where time was concerned. The only welcome interruption during these visits was always when Leni contrived to bring the lawyer his tea while K. was there. Then she would stand behind K.—pretending to watch the lawyer as he bent greedily over his cup, poured the tea in and drank—and secretly let K. hold her hand. There was always complete silence. The lawyer drank. K. squeezed Leni's hand and Leni would sometimes dare to gently stroke K.'s hair. "Still here, are you?" the lawyer would ask when he was ready. "I wanted to take the dishes away," said Leni, they would give each other's hands a final squeeze, the lawyer would wipe his mouth and then start talking at K. again with renewed energy.

Was the lawyer trying to comfort K. or to confuse him? K. could

not tell, but it seemed clear to him that his defence was not in good
hands. Maybe everything the lawyer said was quite right, even though
he obviously wanted to make himself as conspicuous as possible and
probably had never even taken on a case as important as he said K.'s
was. But it was still suspicious how he continually mentioned his
personal contacts with the civil servants. Were they to be exploited
solely for K.'s benefit? The lawyer never forgot to mention that they
were dealing only with junior officials, which meant officials who
were dependent on others, and the direction taken in each trial could
be important for their own furtherment. Could it be that they were
making use of the lawyer to turn trials in a certain direction, which
would, of course, always be at the cost of the defendant? It certainly
did not mean that they would do that in every trial, that was not likely
at all, and there were probably also trials where they gave the lawyer
advantages and all the room he needed to turn it in the direction he
wanted, as it would also be to their advantage to keep his reputation
intact. If that really was their relationship, how would they direct K.'s
trial which, as the lawyer had explained, was especially difficult and
therefore important enough to attract great attention from the very
first time it came to court? There could not be much doubt about
what they would do. The first signs of it could already be seen in the
fact that the first documents still had not been submitted even though
the trial had already lasted several months, and that, according to the
lawyer, everything was still in its initial stages, which was very effec-
tive, of course, in making the defendant passive and keeping him
helpless. Then he could be suddenly surprised with the verdict, or at
least with a notification that the hearing had not decided in his favour
and the matter would be passed on to a higher office.

It was essential that K. take a hand in it himself. On winter's mornings such as this, when he was very tired and everything dragged itself
lethargically through his head, this belief of his seemed irrefutable. He
no longer felt the contempt for the trial that he had had earlier. If he
had been alone in the world it would have been easy for him to ignore
it, although it was also certain that, in that case, the trial would never
have arisen in the first place. But now, his uncle had already dragged
him to see the lawyer, he had to take account of his family; his job was
no longer totally separate from the progress of the trial, he himself
had carelessly—with a certain, inexplicable complacency—mentioned
it to acquaintances and others had learned about it in ways he did not
know, his relationship with Miss Bürstner seemed to be in trouble

because of it. In short, he no longer had any choice whether he would accept the trial or turn it down, he was in the middle of it and had to defend himself. If he was tired, then that was bad.

But there was no reason to worry too much before he needed to. He had been capable of working himself up to his high position in the bank in a relatively short time and to retain it with respect from everyone, now he simply had to apply some of the talents that had made that possible for him to the trial, and there was no doubt that it had to turn out well. The most important thing, if something was to be achieved, was to reject in advance any idea that he might be in any way guilty. There was no guilt. The trial was nothing but a big piece of business, just like he had already concluded to the benefit of the bank many times, a piece of business that concealed many lurking dangers waiting in ambush for him, as they usually did, and these dangers would need to be defended against. If that was to be achieved then he must not entertain any idea of guilt, whatever he did, he would need to look after his own interests as closely as he could. Seen in this way, there was no choice but to take his representation away from the lawyer very soon, at best that very evening. The lawyer had told him, as he talked to him, that that was something unheard of and would probably do him a great deal of harm, but K. could not tolerate any impediment to his efforts where his trial was concerned, and these impediments were probably caused by the lawyer himself. But once he had shaken off the lawyer the documents would need to be submitted straight away and, if possible, he would need to see to it that they were being dealt with every day. It would of course not be enough, if that was to be done, for K. to sit in the corridor with his hat under the bench like the others. Day after day, he himself, or one of the women or somebody else on his behalf, would have to run after the officials and force them to sit at their desks and study K.'s documents instead of looking out on the corridor through the grating. There could be no let-up in these efforts, everything would need to be organised and supervised, it was about time that the court came up against a defendant who knew how to defend and make use of his rights.

But when K. had the confidence to try and do all this the difficulty of composing the documents was too much for him. Earlier, just a week or so before, he could only have felt shame at the thought of being made to write out such documents himself; it had never entered his head that the task could also be difficult. He remembered one morning when, already piled up with work, he suddenly shoved

everything to one side and took a pad of paper on which he sketched
out some of his thoughts on how documents of this sort should proceed. Perhaps he would offer them to that slow-witted lawyer, but
just then the door of the manager's office opened and the deputy-
director entered the room with a loud laugh. K. was very embarrassed,
although the deputy-director, of course, was not laughing at K.'s documents, which he knew nothing about, but at a joke he had just heard
about the stock-exchange, a joke which needed an illustration if it was
to be understood, and now the deputy-director leant over K.'s desk,
took his pencil from his hand, and drew the illustration on the writing pad that K. had intended for his ideas about his case.

K. now had no more thoughts of shame, the documents had to be
prepared and submitted. If, as was very likely, he could find no time
to do it in the office he would have to do it at home at night. If the
nights weren't enough he would have to take a holiday. Above all, he
could not stop half way, that was nonsense not only in business but
always and everywhere. Needless to say, the documents would mean
an almost endless amount of work. It was easy to come to the belief,
not only for those of an anxious disposition, that it was impossible
ever to finish it. This was not because of laziness or deceit, which were
the only things that might have hindered the lawyer in preparing it,
but because he did not know what the charge was or even what consequences it might bring, so that he had to remember every tiny action
and event from the whole of his life, looking at them from all sides
and checking and reconsidering them. It was also a very disheartening
job. It would have been more suitable as a way of passing the long days
after he had retired and become senile. But now, just when K. needed
to apply all his thoughts to his work, when he was still rising and
already posed a threat to the deputy-director, when every hour passed
so quickly and he wanted to enjoy the brief evenings and nights as a
young man, this was the time he had to start working out these documents. Once more, he began to feel resentment. Almost involuntarily,
only to put an end to it, his finger felt for the button of the electric
bell in the anteroom. As he pressed it he glanced up to the clock. It
was eleven o'clock, two hours, he had spent a great deal of his costly
time just dreaming and his wits were, of course, even more dulled
than they had been before. But the time had, nonetheless, not been
wasted, he had come to some decisions that could be of value. As well
as various pieces of mail, the servitors brought two visiting cards from
gentlemen who had already been waiting for K. for some time. They

were actually very important clients of the bank who should not really have been kept waiting under any circumstances. Why had they come at such an awkward time, and why, the gentlemen on the other side of the closed door seemed to be asking, was the industrious K. using up the best business time for his private affairs? Tired from what had gone before, and tired in anticipation of what was to follow, K. stood up to receive the first of them.

He was a short, jolly man, a manufacturer who K. knew well. He apologised for disturbing K. at some important work, and K., for his part, apologised for having kept the manufacturer waiting for so long. But even this apology was spoken in such a mechanical way and with such false intonation that the manufacturer would certainly have noticed if he had not been fully preoccupied with his business affairs. Instead, he hurriedly pulled calculations and tables out from all his pockets, spread them out in front of K., explained several items, corrected a little mistake in the arithmetic that he noticed as he quickly glanced over it all, and reminded K. of a similar piece of business he'd concluded with him about a year before, mentioning in passing that this time there was another bank spending great effort to get his business, and finally stopped speaking in order to learn K.'s opinion on the matter. And K. had indeed, at first, been closely following what the manufacturer was saying, he too was aware of how important the deal was, but unfortunately it did not last, he soon stopped listening, nodded at each of the manufacturer's louder exclamations for a short while, but eventually he stopped doing even that and did no more than stare at the bald head bent over the papers, asking himself when the manufacturer would finally realise that everything he was saying was useless. When he did stop talking, K. really thought at first that this was so that he would have the chance to confess that he was incapable of listening. Instead, seeing the anticipation on the manufacturer's face, obviously ready to counter any objections made, he was sorry to realise that the business discussion had to be continued. So he bent his head as if he'd been given an order and began slowly to move his pencil over the papers, now and then he would stop and stare at one of the figures. The manufacturer thought there must be some objection, perhaps his figures weren't really sound, perhaps they weren't the decisive issue, whatever he thought, the manufacturer covered the papers with his hand and began once again, moving very close to K., to explain what the deal was all about. "It is difficult," said K., pursing his lips. The only thing that could offer him any guidance were the papers, and the manufacturer had covered them from his view, so he just sank back against the arm of the chair. Even when the door of the manager's office opened and revealed not very clearly, as if through a veil, the deputy director, he did no more than look up weakly. K. thought no more about the matter, he merely watched the immediate effect of the deputy director's appearance and, for him, the effect was very pleasing; the manufacturer immediately jumped up from his seat and hurried over to meet the deputy director, although K. would have liked to make him ten times livelier as he feared the deputy director might disappear again. He need not have worried, the two gentlemen met each other, shook each other's hand and went together over to K.'s desk. The manufacturer said he was sorry to find the chief clerk so little inclined to do business, pointing to K. who, under the view of the deputy director, had bent back down over the papers. As the two men leant over the desk and the manufacturer made some effort to gain and keep the deputy director's attention, K. felt as if they were much bigger than they really were and that their negotiations were about him. Carefully and slowly turning his eyes upwards, he tried to learn what was taking place above him, took one of the papers from his desk without looking to see what it was, lay it on the flat of his hand and raised it slowly up as he rose up to the level of the two men himself. He had no particular plan in mind as he did this, but merely felt this was how he would act if only he had finished preparing that great document that was to remove his burden entirely. The deputy director had been paying all his attention to the conversation and did no more than glance at the paper, he did not read what was written on it at all as what was important for the chief clerk was not important for him, he took it from K.'s hand saying, "Thank you, I'm already familiar with everything," and lay it calmly back on the desk. K. gave him a bitter, sideways look. But the deputy director did not notice this at all, or if he did notice it it only raised his spirits, he frequently laughed out loud, one time he clearly embarrassed the manufacturer when he raised an objection in a witty way but drew him immediately back out of his embarrassment by commenting adversely on himself, and finally invited him into his office where they could bring the matter to its conclusion. "It's a very important matter," said the manufacturer. "I understand that completely. And I'm sure the chief clerk . . ."—even as he said this he was actually speaking only to the manufacturer—"will be very glad to have us take it off his hands. This is something that needs calm consideration. But he seems to be overburdened today, there are even some people in the room outside who've been waiting there for hours for him." K. still had enough control of himself to turn away from the deputy director and direct his friendly, albeit stiff, smile only at the manufacturer, he made no other retaliation, bent down slightly and supported himself with both hands on his desk like a clerk, and watched as the two gentlemen, still talking, took the papers from his desk and disappeared into the manager's office. In the doorway, the manufacturer turned and said he wouldn't make his farewell with K. just yet, he would of course let the chief clerk know about the success of his discussions but he also had a little something to tell him about.

At last, K. was by himself. It did not enter his head to show anyone else into his office and only became vaguely aware of how nice it was that the people outside thought he was still negotiating with the manufacturer and, for this reason, he could not let anyone in to see him, not even the servitor. He went over to the window, sat down on the ledge beside it, held firmly on to the handle and looked down onto the square outside. The snow was still falling, the weather still had not brightened up at all.

He remained a long time sitting in this way, not knowing what it actually was that made him so anxious, only occasionally did he glance, slightly startled, over his shoulder at the door to the outer room where, mistakenly, he thought he'd heard some noise. No one came, and that made him feel calmer, he went over to the wash stand, rinsed his face with cold water and, his head somewhat clearer, went back to his place by the window. The decision to take his defence into his own hands now seemed more of a burden than he had originally assumed. All the while he had left his defence up to the lawyer his trial had had little basic affect on him, he had observed it from afar as something that was scarcely able to reach him directly, when it suited him he looked to see how things stood but he was also able to draw his head back again whenever he wanted. Now, in contrast, if he was to conduct his defence himself, he would have to devote himself entirely to the court—for the time being, at least—success would mean, later on, his complete and conclusive liberation, but if he was to achieve this he would have to place himself, to start with, in far greater danger than he had been in so far. If he ever felt tempted to doubt this, then his experience with the deputy director and the manufacturer that day would be quite enough to convince him of it. How could he have sat there totally convinced of the need to do his own defence? How would it be later? What would his life be like in the days ahead? Would he find the way through it all to a happy conclusion? Did a carefully worked out defence—and any other sort would have made no sense—did a carefully worked out defence not also mean he would need to shut himself off from everything else as much as he could? Would he survive that? And how was he to succeed in conducting all this at the bank? It involved much more than just submitting some documents that he could probably prepare in a few days' leave, although it would have been great temerity to ask for time off from the bank just at that time, it was a whole trial and there was no way of seeing how long it might last. This was an enormous difficulty that had suddenly been thrown into K.'s life!

And was he supposed to be doing the bank's work at a time like this? He looked down at his desk. Was he supposed to let people in to see him and go into negotiations with them at a time like this? While his trial trundled on, while the court officials upstairs in the attic room sat looking at the papers for this trial, should he be worrying about the business of the bank? Did this not seem like a kind of torture, acknowledged by the court, connected with the trial and which followed him around? And is it likely that anyone in the bank, when judging his work, would take any account of his peculiar situation? No one and never. There were those who knew about his trial, although it was not quite clear who knew about it or how much. But he hoped rumours had not reached as far as the deputy director, otherwise he would obviously soon find a way of making use of it to harm K., he would show neither comradeship nor humaneness. And what about the director? It was true that he was well disposed towards K., and as soon as he heard about the trial he would probably try to do everything he could to make it easier for him, but he would certainly not devote himself to it. K. at one time had provided the counter-balance to what the deputy director said but the director was now coming more and more under his influence, and the deputy director would also exploit the weakened condition of the director to strengthen his own power. So what could K. hope for? Maybe considerations of this sort weakened his power of resistance, but it was still necessary not to deceive oneself and to see everything as clearly as it could be seen at that moment.

For no particular reason, just to avoiding returning to his desk for a while, he opened the window. It was difficult to open and he had to turn the handle with both his hands. Then, through the whole height and breadth of the window, the mixture of fog and smoke was drawn into the room, filling it with a slight smell of burning. A few flakes of snow were blown in with it. "It's a horrible autumn," said the manufacturer, who had come into the room unnoticed after seeing the deputy director and now stood behind K. K. nodded and looked uneasily at the manufacturer's briefcase, from which he would now probably take the papers and inform K. of the result of his negotiations with the deputy director. However, the manufacturer saw where K. was looking, knocked on his briefcase and without opening it said, "You'll be wanting to hear how things turned out. I've already got the contract in my pocket, almost. He's a charming man, your deputy director—he's got his dangers, though." He laughed as he shook K.'s hand and wanted to make him laugh with him. But to K., it once more seemed suspicious that the manufacturer did not want to show him the papers and saw nothing about his comments to laugh at. "Chief clerk," said the manufacturer, "I expect the weather's been affecting your mood, has it? You're looking so worried today." "Yes," said K., raising his hand and holding the temple of his head, "headaches, worries in the family." "Quite right," said the manufacturer, who was always in a hurry and could never listen to anyone for very long, "everyone has his cross to bear." K. had unconsciously made a step towards the door as if wanting to show the manufacturer out, but the manufacturer said, "Chief clerk, there's something else I'd like to mention to you. I'm very sorry if it's something that'll be a burden to you today of all days but I've been to see you twice already, lately, and each time I forgot all about it. If I delay it any longer it might well lose its point altogether. That would be a pity, as I think what I've got to say does have some value." Before K. had had the time to answer, the manufacturer came up close to him, tapped his knuckle lightly on his chest and said quietly, "You've got a trial going on, haven't you?" K. stepped back and immediately exclaimed, "That's what the deputy director's been telling you!" "No, no," said the manufacturer, "how would the deputy director know about it?" "And what about you?" asked K., already more in control of himself. "I hear things about the court here and there," said the manufacturer, "and that even applies to what it is that I wanted to tell you about." "There are so many people who have connections with the court!" said K. with lowered head, and he led the manufacturer over to his desk. They sat down where they had been before, and the manufacturer said, "I'm afraid it's not very much that I've got to tell you about. Only, in matters like this, it's best not to overlook the tiniest details. Besides, I really want to help you in some way, however modest my help might be. We've been good business partners up till now, haven't we? Well then." K. wanted to apologise for his behaviour in the conversation earlier that day, but the manufacturer would tolerate no interruption, shoved his briefcase up high in his armpit to show that he was in a hurry, and carried on. "I know about your case through a certain Titorelli. He's a painter, Titorelli's just his artistic name, I don't even know what his real name is. He's been coming to me in my office for years from time to time, and brings little pictures with him which I buy more or less just for the sake of charity as he's hardly more than a beggar. And they're nice pictures, too, moorland landscapes and that sort of thing. We'd both got used to doing business in this way and it always went smoothly. Only, one time these visits became a bit too frequent, I began to tell him off for it, we started talking and I became interested how it was that he could earn a living just by painting, and then I learned to my amazement that his main source of income was painting portraits. 'I work for the court,' he said, 'what court?' said I. And that's when he told me about the court. I'm sure you can imagine how amazed I was at being told all this. Ever since then I learn something new about the court every time he comes to visit, and so little by little I get to under-stand something of how it works. Anyway, Titorelli talks a lot and I often have to push him away, not only because he's bound to be lying but also, most of all, because a businessman like me who's already close to breaking point under the weight of his own business worries can't pay too much attention to other people's. But all that's just by the by. Perhaps—this is what I've been thinking—perhaps Titorelli might be able to help you in some small way, he knows lots of judges and even if he can't have much influence himself he can give you some advice about how to get some influential people on your side. And even if this advice doesn't turn out to make all the difference I still think it'll be very important once you've got it. You're nearly a lawyer yourself. That's what I always say, Mr. K. the chief clerk is nearly a lawyer. Oh I'm sure this trial of yours will turn out all right. So do you want to go and see Titorelli, then? If I ask him to he'll certainly do everything he possibly can. I really do think you ought to go. It needn't be today, of course, just some time, when you get the chance. And anyway—I want to tell you this too—you don't actually have to go and see Titorelli, this advice from me doesn't place you under any obligation at all. No, if you think you can get by without Titorelli it'll certainly be better to leave him completely out of it. Maybe you've already got a clear idea of what you're doing and Titorelli could upset your plans. No, if that's the case then of course you shouldn't go there under any circumstances! And it certainly won't be easy to take advice from a lad like that. Still, it's up to you. Here's the letter of recommendation and here's the address."

Disappointed, K. took the letter and put it in his pocket. Even at best, the advantage he might derive from this recommendation was incomparably smaller than the damage that lay in the fact of the manufacturer knowing about his trial, and that the painter was spreading the news about. It was all he could mange to give the manufacturer, who was already on his way to the door, a few words of thanks. "I'll go there," he said as he took his leave of the manufacturer at the door, "or, as I'm very busy at present, I'll write to him, perhaps he would like to come to me in my office some time." "I was sure you'd find the best solution," said the manufacturer. "Although I had thought you'd prefer to avoid inviting people like this Titorelli to the bank and talking about the trial here. And it's not always a good idea to send letters to people like Titorelli, you don't know what might happen to them. But you're bound to have thought everything through and you know what you can and can't do." K. nodded and accompanied the manufacturer on through the anteroom. But despite seeming calm on the outside he was actually very shocked; he had told the manufacturer he would write to Titorelli only to show him in some way that he valued his recommendations and would consider the opportunity to speak with Titorelli without delay, but if he had thought Titorelli could offer any worthwhile assistance he would not have delayed. But it was only the manufacturer's comment that made K. realise what dangers that could lead to. Was he really able to rely on his own understanding so little? If it was possible that he might invite a questionable character into the bank with a clear letter, and ask advice from him about his trial, separated from the deputy director by no more than a door, was it not possible or even very likely that there were also other dangers he had failed to see or that he was even running towards? There was not always someone beside him to warn him. And just now, just when he would have to act with all the strength he could muster, now a number of doubts of a sort he had never before known had presented themselves and affected his own vigilance! The difficulties he had been feeling in carrying out his office work; were they now going to affect the trial too? Now, at least, he found himself quite unable to understand how he could have intended to write to Titorelli and invite him into the bank.

He shook his head at the thought of it once more as the servitor came up beside him and drew his attention to the three gentlemen who were waiting on a bench in the anteroom. They had already been waiting to see K. for a long time. Now that the servitor was speaking with K. they had stood up and each of them wanted to make use of the opportunity to see K. before the others. It had been negligent of the bank to let them waste their time here in the waiting room, but none of them wanted to draw attention to this. "Mr. K., ..." one of them was saying, but K. had told the servitor to fetch his winter coat and said to the three of them, as the servitor helped him to put it on, "Please forgive me, gentlemen, I'm afraid I have no time to see you at present. Please do forgive me but I have some urgent business to settle and have to leave straight away. You've already seen yourselves how long I've been delayed. Would you be so kind as to come back tomorrow or some time? Or perhaps we could settle your affairs by telephone? Or perhaps you would like to tell me now, briefly, what it's about and I can then give you a full answer in writing. Whatever, the best thing will be for you to come here again." The gentlemen now saw that their wait had been totally pointless, and these suggestions of K.'s left them so astounded that they looked at each other without a word. "That's agreed then, is it?" asked K., who had turned toward the servitor bringing him his hat. Through the open door of K.'s office they could see that the snowfall outside had become much heavier. So K. turned the collar of his coat up and buttoned it up high under his chin. Just then the deputy director came out of the adjoining room, smiled as he saw K. negotiating with the gentlemen in his winter coat, and asked, "Are you about to go out?" "Yes," said K., standing more upright, "I have to go out on some business." But the deputy director had already turned towards the gentlemen. "And what about these gentlemen?" he asked. "I think they've already been waiting quite a long time." "We've already come to an understanding," said K. But now the gentlemen could be held back no longer, they surrounded K. and explained that they would not have been waiting for hours if it had not been about something important that had to be discussed now, at length and in private. The deputy director listened to them for a short while, he also looked at K. as he held his hat in his hand cleaning the dust off it here and there, and then he said, "Gentlemen, there is a very simple way to solve this. If you would prefer it, I'll be very glad to take over these negotiations instead of the chief clerk. Your business does, of course, need to be discussed without delay. We are businessmen like yourselves and know the value of a businessman's time. Would you like to come this way?" And he opened the door leading to the anteroom of his own office.

The deputy director seemed very good at appropriating everything that K. was now forced to give up! But was K. not giving up more than he absolutely had to? By running off to some unknown painter, with, as he had to admit, very little hope of any vague benefit, his renown was suffering damage that could not be repaired. It would probably be much better to take off his winter coat again and, at the very least, try to win back the two gentlemen who were certainly still waiting in the next room. If K. had not then glimpsed the deputy director in his office, looking for something from his bookshelves as if they were his own, he would probably even have made the attempt. As K., somewhat agitated, approached the door the deputy director called out, "Oh, you've still not left!" He turned his face toward him—its many deep folds seemed to show strength rather than age—and immediately began once more to search. "I'm looking for a copy of a contract," he said, "which this gentleman insists you must have. Could you help me look for it, do you think?" K. made a step forward, but the deputy director said, "thank you, I've already found it," and with a big package of papers, which certainly must have included many more documents than just the copy of the contract, he turned and went back into his own office.

"I can't deal with him right now," K. said to himself, "but once my personal difficulties have been settled, then he'll certainly be the first to get the effect of it, and he certainly won't like it." Slightly calmed by these thoughts, K. gave the servitor, who had already long been holding the door to the corridor open for him, the task of telling the director, when he was able, that K. was going out of the bank on a business matter. As he left the bank he felt almost happy at the thought of being able to devote more of himself to his own business for a while.

He went straight to the painter, who lived in an outlying part of town which was very near to the court offices, although this area was even poorer, the houses were darker, the streets were full of dirt that slowly blew about over the half-melted snow. In the great gateway to the building where the painter lived only one of the two doors was open, a hole had been broken open in the wall by the other door, and as K. approached it a repulsive, yellow, steaming liquid shot out causing some rats to scurry away into the nearby canal. Down by the staircase there was a small child lying on its belly crying, but it could hardly be heard because of the noise from a metal-workshop on the other side of the entrance hall, drowning out any other sound. The door to the workshop was open, three workers stood in a circle around some piece of work that they were beating with hammers. A large tin plate hung on the wall, casting a pale light that pushed its way in between two of the workers, lighting up their faces and their work-aprons. K. did no more than glance at any of these things, he wanted to get things over with here as soon as possible, to exchange just a few words to find out how things stood with the painter and go straight back to the bank. Even if he had just some tiny success here it would still have a good effect on his work at the bank for that day. On the third floor he had to slow down his pace, he was quite out of breath—the steps, just like the height of each floor, were much higher than they needed to be and he'd been told that the painter lived right up in the attic. The air was also quite oppressive, there was no proper stairwell and the narrow steps were closed in by walls on both sides with no more than a small, high window here and there. Just as K. paused for a while some young girls ran out of one of the flats and rushed higher up the stairs, laughing. K. followed them slowly, caught up with one of the girls who had stumbled and been left behind by the others, and asked her as they went up side by side, "Is there a painter, Titorelli, who lives here?" The girl, hardly thirteen years old and somewhat hunchbacked, jabbed him with her elbow and looked at him sideways. Her youth and her bodily defects had done nothing to stop her being already quite depraved. She did not smile once, but looked at K. earnestly, with sharp, acquisitive eyes. K. pretended not to notice her behaviour and asked, "Do you know Titorelli, the painter?" She nodded and asked in reply, "What d'you want to see him for?" K. thought it would be to his advantage quickly to find out something more about Titorelli. "I want to have him paint my portrait," he said. "Paint your portrait?" she asked, opening her mouth too wide and lightly hitting K. with her hand as if he had said something extraordinarily surprising or clumsy, with both hands she lifted her skirt, which was already very short, and, as fast as she could, she ran off after the other girls whose indistinct shouts lost themselves in the heights. At the next turn of the stairs, however, K. encountered all the girls once more. The hunchbacked girl had clearly told them about K.'s intentions and they were waiting for him. They stood on both sides of the stairs, pressing themselves against the wall so that K. could get through between them, and smoothed their aprons down with their hands. All their faces, even in this guard of honour, showed a mixture of childishness and depravity. Up at the head of the line of girls, who now, laughing, began to close in around K., was the hunchback who had taken on the role of leader. It was thanks to her that K. found the right direction without delay—he would have continued up the stairs straight in front of him, but she showed him that to reach Titorelli he would need to turn off to one side. The steps that led up to the painter were especially narrow, very long without any turning, the whole length could be seen in one glance and, at the top, at Titorelli's closed door, it came to its end. This door was much better illuminated than the rest of the stairway by the light from a small skylight set obliquely above it, it had been put together from unpainted planks of wood and the name 'Titorelli' was painted on it in broad, red brushstrokes. K. was no more than half way up the steps, accompanied by his retinue of girls, when, clearly the result of the noise of all those footsteps, the door opened slightly and in the crack a man who seemed to be dressed in just his nightshirt appeared. "Oh!" he cried, when he saw the approaching crowd, and vanished. The hunchbacked girl clapped her hands in glee and the other girls crowded in behind K. to push him faster forward.

They still had not arrived at the top, however, when the painter up above them suddenly pulled the door wide open and, with a deep bow, invited K. to enter. The girls, on the other hand, he tried to keep away, he did not want to let any of them in however much they begged him and however much they tried to get in—if they could not get in with his permission they would try to force their way in against his will. The only one to succeed was the hunchback when she slipped through under his outstretched arm, but the painter chased after her, grabbed her by the skirt, span her once round and set her down again by the door with the other girls who, unlike the first, had not dared to cross the doorstep while the painter had left his post. K. did not know what he was to make of all this, as they all seemed to be having fun. One behind the other, the girls by the door stretched their necks up high and called out various words to the painter which were meant in jest but which K. did not understand, and even the painter laughed as the hunchback whirled round in his hand. Then he shut the door, bowed once more to K., offered him his hand and introduced him-

self, saying, "Titorelli, painter." K. pointed to the door, behind which
the girls were whispering, and said, "You seem to be very popular in
this building." "Ach, those brats!" said the painter, trying in vain to
fasten his nightshirt at the neck. He was also bare-footed and, apart
from that, was wearing nothing more than a loose pair of yellowish
linen trousers held up with a belt whose free end whipped to and fro.
"Those kids are a real burden for me," he continued. The top button
of his nightshirt came off and he gave up trying to fasten it, fetched
a chair for K. and made him sit down on it. "I painted one of them
once—she's not here today—and ever since then they've been following
me about. If I'm here they only come in when I allow it, but as soon
as I've gone out there's always at least one of them in here. They had
a key made to my door and lend it round to each other. It's hard to
imagine what a pain that is. Suppose I come back home with a lady
I'm going to paint, I open the door with my own key and find the
hunchback there or something, by the table painting her lips red with
my paintbrush, and meanwhile her little sisters will be keeping guard
for her, moving about and causing chaos in every corner of the room.
Or else, like happened yesterday, I might come back home late in the
evening—please forgive my appearance and the room being in a mess,
it is to do with them—so, I might come home late in the evening and
want to go to bed, then I feel something pinching my leg, look under
the bed and pull another of them out from under it. I don't know why
it is they bother me like this, I expect you've just seen that I do nothing to encourage them to come near me. And they make it hard for
me to do my work too, of course. If I didn't get this studio for nothing
I'd have moved out a long time ago." Just then, a little voice, tender
and anxious, called out from under the door, "Titorelli, can we come
in now?" "No," answered the painter. "Not even just me, by myself?"
the voice asked again. "Not even just you," said the painter, as he went
to the door and locked it.

Meanwhile, K. had been looking round the room, if it had not been
pointed out it would never have occurred to him that this wretched
little room could be called a studio. It was hardly long enough or
broad enough to make two steps. Everything, floor, walls and ceiling,
was made of wood, between the planks narrow gaps could be seen.
Across from where K. was, the bed stood against the wall under a
covering of many different colours. In the middle of the room a picture stood on an easel, covered over with a shirt whose arms dangled
down to the ground. Behind K. was the window through which the

fog made it impossible to see further than the snow covered roof of the neighbouring building.

The turning of the key in the lock reminded K. that he had not wanted to stay too long. So he drew the manufacturer's letter out from his pocket, held it out to the painter and said, "I learned about you from this gentleman, an acquaintance of yours, and it's on his advice that I've come here." The painter glanced through the letter and threw it down onto the bed. If the manufacturer had not said very clearly that Titorelli was an acquaintance of his, a poor man who was dependent on his charity, then it would really have been quite possible to believe that Titorelli did not know him or at least that he could not remember him. This impression was augmented by the painter's asking, "Were you wanting to buy some pictures or did you want to have yourself painted?" K. looked at the painter in astonishment. What did the letter actually say? K. had taken it as a matter of course that the manufacturer had explained to the painter in his letter that K. wanted nothing more with him than to find out more about his trial. He had been far too rash in coming here! But now he had to give the painter some sort of answer and, glancing at the easel, said, "Are you working on a picture currently?" "Yes," said the painter, and he took the shirt hanging over the easel and threw it onto the bed after the letter. "It's a portrait. Quite a good piece of work, although it's not quite finished yet." This was a convenient coincidence for K., it gave him a good opportunity to talk about the court as the picture showed, very clearly, a judge. What's more, it was remarkably similar to the picture in the lawyer's office, although this one showed a quite different judge, a heavy man with a full beard which was black and bushy and extended to the sides far up the man's cheeks. The lawyer's picture was also an oil painting, whereas this one had been made with pastel colours and was pale and unclear. But everything else about the picture was similar, as this judge, too, was holding tightly to the arm of his throne and seemed ominously about to rise from it. At first K. was about to say, "He certainly is a judge," but he held himself back for the time being and went closer to the picture as if he wanted to study it in detail. There was a large figure shown in middle of the throne's back rest which K. could not understand and asked the painter about it. That'll need some more work done on it, the painter told him, and taking a pastel crayon from a small table he added a few strokes to the edges of the figure but without making it any clearer as far as K. could make out. "That's the figure of justice," said the painter, finally. "Now I see," said K., "here's the blindfold and here are the scales. But aren't those wings on her heels, and isn't she moving?" "Yes," said the painter, "I had to paint it like that according to the contract. It's actually the figure of justice and the goddess of victory all in one." "That is not a good combination," said K. with a smile. "Justice needs to remain still, otherwise the scales will move about and it won't be possible to make a just verdict." "I'm just doing what the client wanted," said the painter. "Yes, certainly," said K., who had not meant to criticise anyone by that comment. "You've painted the figure as it actually appears on the throne." "No," said the painter, "I've never seen that figure or that throne, it's all just invention, but they told me what it was I had to paint." "How's that?" asked K. pretending not fully to understand what the painter said. "That is a judge sitting on the judge's chair, isn't it?" "Yes, " said the painter, "but that judge isn't very high up and he's never sat on any throne like that." "And he has himself painted in such a grand pose? He's sitting there just like the president of the court." "Yeah, gentlemen like this are very vain," said the painter. "But they have permission from higher up to get themselves painted like this. It's laid down quite strictly just what sort of portrait each of them can get for himself. Only it's a pity that you can't make out the details of his costume and pose in this picture, pastel colours aren't really suitable for showing people like this." "Yes," said K., "it does seem odd that it's in pastel colours." "That's what the judge wanted," said the painter, "it's meant to be for a woman." The sight of the picture seemed to make him feel like working, he rolled up his shirtsleeves, picked up a few of the crayons, and K. watched as a reddish shadow built up around the head of the judge under their quivering tips and radiated out the to edges of the picture. This shadow play slowly surrounded the head like a decoration or lofty distinction. But around the figure of Justice, apart from some coloration that was barely noticeable, it remained light, and in this brightness the figure seemed to shine forward so that it now looked like neither the God of Justice nor the God of Victory, it seemed now, rather, to be a perfect depiction of the God of the Hunt. K. found the painter's work more engrossing than he had wanted; but finally he reproached himself for staying so long without having done anything relevant to his own affair. "What's the name of this judge?" he asked suddenly. "I'm not allowed to tell you that," the painter answered. He was bent deeply over the picture and clearly neglecting his guest who, at first, he had received with such care. K. took this to be just a foible of the painter's, and it irritated him as it made him lose time. "I take it you must be a trustee of the court," he said. The painter immediately put his crayons down, stood upright, rubbed his hands together and looked at K. with a smile. "Always straight out with the truth," he said. "You want to learn something about the court, like it says in your letter of recommendation, but then you start talking about my pictures to get me on your side. Still, I won't hold it against you, you weren't to know that that was entirely the wrong thing to try with me. Oh, please!" he said sharply, repelling K.'s attempt to make some objection. He then continued, "And besides, you're quite right in your comment that I'm a trustee of the court." He made a pause, as if wanting to give K. the time to come to terms with this fact. The girls could once more be heard from behind the door. They were probably pressed around the keyhole, perhaps they could even see into the room through the gaps in the planks. K. forewent the opportunity to excuse himself in some way as he did not wish to distract the painter from what he was saying, or else perhaps he didn't want him to get too far above himself and in this way make himself to some extent unattainable, so he asked, "Is that a publicly acknowledged position?" "No," was the painter's curt reply, as if the question prevented him saying any more. But K. wanted him to continue speaking and said, "Well, positions like that, that aren't officially acknowledged, can often have more influence than those that are." "And that's how it is with me," said the painter, and nodded with a frown. "I was talking about your case with the manufacturer yesterday, and he asked me if I wouldn't like to help you, and I answered: 'He can come and see me if he likes,' and now I'm pleased to see you here so soon. This business seems to be quite important to you, and, of course, I'm not surprised at that. Would you not like to take your coat off now?" K. had intended to stay for only a very short time, but the painter's invitation was nonetheless very welcome. The air in the room had slowly become quite oppressive for him, he had several times looked in amazement at a small, iron stove in the corner that certainly could not have been lit, the heat of the room was inexplicable. As he took off his winter overcoat and also unbuttoned his frock-coat the painter said to him in apology, "I must have warmth. And it is very cosy here, isn't it. This room's very good in that respect." K. made no reply, but it was actually not the heat that made him uncomfortable but, much more, the stuffiness, the air that almost made it more difficult to breathe, the room had probably not been ventilated for a long time. The unpleasantness of this was made all the stronger for K. when the painter invited him to sit on the bed while he himself sat down on the only chair in the room in front of the easel. The painter even seemed to misunderstand why K. remained at the edge of the bed and urged K. to make himself comfortable, and as he hesitated he went over to the bed himself and pressed K. deep down into the bedclothes and pillows. Then he went back to his seat and at last he asked his first objective question, which made K. forget everything else. "You're innocent, are you?" he asked. "Yes," said K. He felt a simple joy at answering this question, especially as the answer was given to a private individual and therefore would have no consequences. Up till then no one had asked him this question so openly. To make the most of his pleasure he added, "I am totally innocent." "So," said the painter, and he lowered his head and seemed to be thinking. Suddenly he raised his head again and said, "Well if you're innocent it's all very simple." K. began to scowl, this supposed trustee of the court was talking like an ignorant child. "My being innocent does not make things simple," said K. Despite everything, he couldn't help smiling and slowly shook his head. "There are many fine details in which the court gets lost, but in the end it reaches into some place where originally there was nothing and pulls enormous guilt out of it." "Yeah, yeah, sure," said the painter, as if K. had been disturbing his train of thought for no reason. "But you are innocent, aren't you?" "Well of course I am," said K. "That's the main thing," said the painter. There was no counter-argument that could influence him, but although he had made up his mind it was not clear whether he was talking this way because of conviction or indifference. K., then, wanted to find out and said therefore, "I'm sure you're more familiar with the court than I am, I know hardly more about it than what I've heard, and that's been from many very different people. But they were all agreed on one thing, and that was that when ill thought-out accusations are made they are not ignored, and that once the court has made an accusation it is convinced of the guilt of the defendant and it's very hard to make it think otherwise." "Very hard?" the painter asked, throwing one hand up in the air. "It's impossible to make it think otherwise. If I painted all the judges next to each other here on canvas, and you were trying to defend yourself in front of it, you'd have more success with them than you'd ever have with the real court." "Yes," said K. to himself, forgetting that he had only gone there to investigate the painter.

One of the girls behind the door started up again, and asked,

"Titorelli, is he going to go soon?" "Quiet!" shouted the painter at the door, "Can't you see I'm talking with the gentleman?" But this was not enough to satisfy the girl and she asked, "You going to paint his picture?" And when the painter didn't answer she added, "Please don't paint him, he's an awful man." There followed an incomprehensible, interwoven babble of shouts and replies and calls of agreement. The painter leapt over to the door, opened it very slightly—the girls' clasped hands could be seen stretching through the crack as if they wanted something—and said, "If you're not quiet I'll throw you all down the stairs. Sit down here on the steps and be quiet." They probably did not obey him immediately, so that he had to command, "Down on the steps!" Only then it became quiet.

"I'm sorry about that," said the painter as he returned to K. K. had hardly turned towards the door, he had left it completely up to the painter whether and how he would place him under his protection if he wanted to. Even now, he made hardly any movement as the painter bent over him and, whispering into his ear in order not to be heard outside, said, "These girls belong to the court as well." "How's that?" asked K., as he leant his head to one side and looked at the painter. But the painter sat back down on his chair and, half in jest, half in explanation, "Well, everything belongs to the court." "That is something I had never noticed until now," said K. curtly, this general comment of the painter's made his comment about the girls far less disturbing. Nonetheless, K. looked for a while at the door, behind which the girls were now sitting quietly on the steps. Except, that one of them had pushed a drinking straw through a crack between the planks and was moving it slowly up and down. "You still don't seem to have much general idea of what the court's about," said the painter, who had stretched his legs wide apart and was tapping loudly on the floor with the tip of his foot. "But as you're innocent you won't need it anyway. I'll get you out of this by myself." "How do you intend to do that?" asked K. "You did say yourself not long ago that it's quite impossible to go to the court with reasons and proofs." "Only impossible for reasons and proofs you take to the court yourself" said the painter, raising his forefinger as if K. had failed to notice a fine distinction. "It goes differently if you try to do something behind the public court, that's to say in the consultation rooms, in the corridors or here, for instance, in my studio." K. now began to find it far easier to believe what the painter was saying, or rather it was largely in agreement with what he had also been told by others. In fact it was even quite promis-

ing. If it really was so easy to influence the judges through personal
contacts as the lawyer had said then the painter's contacts with these
vain judges was especially important, and at the very least should not
be undervalued. And the painter would fit in very well in the circle of
assistants that K. was slowly gathering around himself. He had been
noted at the bank for his talent in organising, here, where he was
placed entirely on his own resources, would be a good opportunity to
test that talent to its limits. The painter observed the effect his explanation had had on K. and then, with a certain unease, said, "Does
it not occur to you that the way I'm speaking is almost like a lawyer?
It's the incessant contact with the gentlemen of the court has that
influence on me. I gain a lot by it, of course, but I lose a lot, artistically speaking." "How did you first come into contact with the judges,
then?" asked K., he wanted first to gain the painter's trust before he
took him into his service. "That was very easy," said the painter, "I
inherited these contacts. My father was court painter before me. It's
a position that's always inherited. They can't use new people for it,
the rules governing how the various grades of officials are painted are
so many and varied, and, above all, so secret that no one outside of
certain families even knows them. In the drawer there, for instance,
I've got my father's notes, which I don't show to anyone. But you're
only able to paint judges if you know what they say. Although, even
if I lost them no one could ever dispute my position because of all
the rules I just carry round in my head. All the judges want to be
painted like the old, great judges were, and I'm the only one who
can do that." "You are to be envied," said K., thinking of his position
at the bank. "Your position is quite unassailable, then?" "Yes, quite
unassailable," said the painter, and he raised his shoulders in pride.
"That's how I can even afford to help some poor man facing trial now
and then." "And how do you do that?" asked K., as if the painter had
not just described him as a poor man. The painter did not let himself
be distracted, but said, "In your case, for instance, as you're totally
innocent, this is what I'll do." The repeated mention of K.'s innocence
was becoming irksome to him. It sometimes seemed to him as if the
painter was using these comments to make a favourable outcome to
the trial a precondition for his help, which of course would make the
help itself unnecessary. But despite these doubts K. forced himself not
to interrupt the painter. He did not want to do without the painter's
help, that was what he had decided, and this help did not seem in any
way less questionable than that of the lawyer. K. valued the painter's

help far more highly because it was offered in a way that was more harmless and open.

The painter had pulled his seat closer to the bed and continued in a subdued voice: "I forgot to ask you; what sort of acquittal is it you want? There are three possibilities: absolute acquittal, apparent acquittal and deferment. Absolute acquittal is the best, of course, only there's nothing I could do to get that sort of outcome. I don't think there's anyone at all who could do anything to get an absolute acquittal. Probably the only thing that could do that is if the accused is innocent. As you are innocent it could actually be possible and you could depend on your innocence alone. In that case you won't need me or any other kind of help."

At first, K. was astonished at this orderly explanation, but then, just as quietly as the painter, he said, "I think you're contradicting yourself." "How's that?" asked the painter patiently, leaning back with a smile. This smile made K. feel as if he were examining not the words of the painter but seeking out inconsistencies in the procedures of the court itself. Nonetheless, he continued unabashed and said, "You remarked earlier that the court cannot be approached with reasoned proofs, you later restricted this to the open court, and now you go so far as to say that an innocent man needs no assistance in court. That entails a contradiction. Moreover, you said earlier that the judges can be influenced personally but now you insist that an absolute acquittal, as you call it, can never be attained through personal influence. That entails a second contradiction." "It's quite easy to clear up these contradictions," said the painter. "We're talking about two different things here, there's what it says in the law and there's what I know from my own experience, you shouldn't get the two confused. I've never seen it in writing, but the law does, of course, say on the one hand that the innocent will be set free, but on the other hand it doesn't say that the judges can be influenced. But in my experience it's the other way round. I don't know of any absolute acquittals but I do know of many times when a judge has been influenced. It's possible, of course, that there was no innocence in any of the cases I know about. But is that likely? Not a single innocent defendant in so many cases? When I was a boy I used to listen closely to my father when he told us about court cases at home, and the judges that came to his studio talked about the court, in our circles nobody talks about anything else; I hardly ever got the chance to go to court myself but always made use of it when I could, I've listened to countless trials at important stages in their development, I've followed them closely as far as they could be followed, and I have to say that I've never seen a single acquittal." "So. Not a single acquittal," said K., as if talking to himself and his hopes. "That confirms the impression I already have of the court. So there's no point in it from this side either. They could replace the whole court with a single hangman." "You shouldn't generalise," said the painter, dissatisfied, "I've only been talking about my own experience." "Well that's enough," said K., "or have you heard of any acquittals that happened earlier?" "They say there have been some acquittals earlier," the painter answered, "but it's very hard to be sure about it. The courts don't make their final conclusions public, not even the judges are allowed to know about them, so that all we know about these earlier cases are just legends. But most of them did involve absolute acquittals, you can believe that, but they can't be proved. On the other hand, you shouldn't forget all about them either, I'm sure there is some truth to them, and they are very beautiful, I've painted a few pictures myself depicting these legends." "My assessment will not be altered by mere legends," said K. "I don't suppose it's possible to cite these legends in court, is it?" The painter laughed. "No, you can't cite them in court," he said. "Then there's no point in talking about them," said K., he wanted, for the time being, to accept anything the painter told him, even if he thought it unlikely or contradicted what he had been told by others. He did not now have the time to examine the truth of everything the painter said or even to disprove it, he would have achieved as much as he could if the painter would help him in any way even if his help would not be decisive. As a result, he said, "So let's pay no more attention to absolute acquittal, but you mentioned two other possibilities." "Apparent acquittal and deferment. They're the only possibilities," said the painter. "But before we talk about them, would you not like to take your coat off? You must be hot." "Yes," said K., who until then had paid attention to nothing but the painter's explanations, but now that he had had the heat pointed out to him his brow began to sweat heavily. "It's almost unbearable." The painter nodded as if he understood K.'s discomfort very well. "Could we not open the window?" asked K. "No," said the painter. "It's only a fixed pane of glass, it can't be opened." K. now realised that all this time he had been hoping the painter would suddenly go over to the window and pull it open. He had prepared himself even for the fog that he would breathe in through his open mouth. The thought that here he was entirely cut off from the air made him feel dizzy. He tapped lightly on the bedspread beside him and, with a weak voice, said, "That is very inconvenient and unhealthy." "Oh no," said the painter in defence of his window, "as it can't be opened this room retains the heat better than if the window were double glazed, even though it's only a single pane. There's not much need to air the room as there's so much ventilation through the gaps in the wood, but when I do want to I can open one of my doors, or even both of them." K. was slightly consoled by this explanation and looked around to see where the second door was. The painter saw him do so and said, "It's behind you, I had to hide it behind the bed." Only then was K. able to see the little door in the wall. "It's really much too small for a studio here," said the painter, as if he wanted to anticipate an objection K. would make. "I had to arrange things as well as I could. That's obviously a very bad place for the bed, in front of the door. For instance when the judge I'm painting at present comes he always comes through the door by the bed, and I've even given him a key to this door so that he can wait for me here in the studio when I'm not home. Although nowadays he usually comes early in the morning when I'm still asleep. And of course, it always wakes me up when I hear the door opened beside the bed, however fast asleep I am. If you could hear the way I curse him as he climbs over my bed in the morning you'd lose all respect for judges. I suppose I could take the key away from him but that'd only make things worse. It only takes a tiny effort to break any of the doors here off their hinges." All the time the painter was speaking, K. was considering whether he should take off his coat, but he finally realised that, if he didn't do so, he would be quite unable to stay here any longer, so he took off his frockcoat and lay it on his knee so that he could put it back on again as soon as the conversation was over. He had hardly done this when one of the girls called out, "Now he's taken his coat off!" and they could all be heard pressing around the gaps in the planks to see the spectacle for themselves. "The girls think I'm going to paint your portrait," said the painter, "and that's why you're taking your coat off." "I see," said K., only slightly amused by this, as he felt little better than he had before even though he now sat in his shirtsleeves. With some irritation he asked, "What did you say the two other possibilities were?" He had already forgotten the terms used. "Apparent acquittal and deferment," said the painter. "It's up to you which one you choose. You can get either of them if I help you, but it'll take some effort of course, the difference between them is that apparent acquittal needs concentrated effort for a while and that deferment takes much less effort but it has to be sustained. Now then, apparent acquittal. If that's what you want I'll write down an assertion of your innocence on a piece of paper. The text for an assertion of this sort was passed down to me from my father and it's quite unassailable. I take this assertion round to the judges I know. So I'll start off with the one I'm currently painting, and put the assertion to him when he comes for his sitting this evening. I'll lay the assertion in front of him, explain that you're innocent and give him my personal guarantee of it. And that's not just a superficial guarantee, it's a real one and it's binding." The painter's eyes seemed to show some reproach of K. for wanting to impose that sort of responsibility on him. "That would be very kind of you," said K. "And would the judge then believe you and nonetheless not pass an absolute acquittal?" "It's like I just said," answered the painter. "And anyway, it's not entirely sure that all the judges would believe me, many of them, for instance, might want me to bring you to see them personally. So then you'd have to come along too. But at least then, if that happens, the matter is half way won, especially as I'd teach you in advance exactly how you'd need to act with the judge concerned, of course. What also happens, though, is that there are some judges who'll turn me down in advance, and that's worse. I'll certainly make several attempts, but still, we'll have to forget about them, but at least we can afford to do that as no one judge can pass the decisive verdict. Then when I've got enough judges' signatures on this document I take it to the judge who's concerned with your case. I might even have his signature already, in which case things develop a bit quicker than they would do otherwise. But there aren't usually many hold ups from then on, and that's the time that the defendant can feel most confident. It's odd, but true, that people feel more confidence in this time than they do after they've been acquitted. There's no particular exertion needed now. When he has the document asserting the defendant's innocence, guaranteed by a number of other judges, the judge can acquit you without any worries, and although there are still several formalities to be gone through there's no doubt that that's what he'll do as a favour to me and several other acquaintances. You, however, walk out the court and you're free." "So, then I'll be free," said K., hesitantly. "That's right," said the painter, "but only apparently free or, to put it a better way, temporarily free, as the most junior judges, the ones I know, they don't have the right to give the final acquittal. Only the highest judge can do that, in the court that's quite out of reach for you, for me and for all of us. We don't know how things look there and, incidentally, we don't want to know. The right to acquit people is a major privilege and our judges don't have it, but they do have the right to free people from the indictment. That's to say, if they're freed in this way then for the time being the charge is withdrawn but it's still hanging over their heads and it only takes an order from higher up to bring it back into force. And as I'm in such good contact with the court I can also tell you how the difference between absolute and apparent acquittal is described, just in a superficial way, in the directives to the court offices. If there's an absolute acquittal all proceedings should stop, everything disappears from the process, not just the indictment but the trial and even the acquittal disappears, everything just disappears. With an apparent acquittal it's different. When that happens, nothing has changed except that the case for your innocence, for your acquittal and the grounds for the acquittal have been made stronger. Apart from that, proceedings go on as before, the court offices continue their business and the case gets passed to higher courts, gets passed back down to the lower courts and so on, backwards and forwards, sometimes faster, sometimes slower, to and fro. It's impossible to know exactly what's happening while this is going on. Seen from outside it can sometimes seem that everything has been long since forgotten, the documents have been lost and the acquittal is complete. No one familiar with the court would believe it. No documents ever get lost, the court forgets nothing. One day—no one expects it—some judge or other picks up the documents and looks more closely at them, he notices that this particular case is still active, and orders the defendant's immediate arrest. I've been talking here as if there's a long delay between apparent acquittal and re-arrest, that is quite possible and I do know of cases like that, but it's just as likely that the defendant goes home after he's been acquitted and finds somebody there waiting to re-arrest him. Then, of course, his life as a free man is at an end." "And does the trial start over again?" asked K., finding it hard to believe. "The trial will always start over again," said the painter, "but there is, once again as before, the possibility of getting an apparent acquittal. Once again, the accused has to muster all his strength and mustn't give up." The painter said that last phrase possibly as a result of the impression that K., whose shoulders had dropped somewhat, gave on him. "But to get a second acquittal," asked K., as if in anticipation of further revelations by the painter, "is that not harder to get than the first time?" "As far as that's concerned," answered the painter, "there's nothing you can say for certain. You mean, do you, that the second arrest would have an adverse influence on the judge and the verdict he passes on the defendant? That's not how it happens. When the acquittal is passed the judges are already aware that re-arrest is likely. So when it happens it has hardly any effect. But there are countless other reasons why the judges' mood and their legal acumen in the case can be altered, and efforts to obtain the second acquittal must therefore be suited to the new conditions, and generally just as vigorous as the first." "But this second acquittal will once again not be final," said K., shaking his head. "Of course not," said the painter, "the second acquittal is followed by the third arrest, the third acquittal by the fourth arrest and so on. That's what is meant by the term apparent acquittal." K. was silent. "You clearly don't think an apparent acquittal offers much advantage," said the painter, "perhaps deferment would suit you better. Would you like me to explain what deferment is about?" K. nodded. The painter had leant back and spread himself out in his chair, his nightshirt was wide open, he had pushed his hand inside and was stroking his breast and his sides. "Deferment," said the painter, looking vaguely in front of himself for a while as if trying to find a perfectly appropriate explanation, "deferment consists of keeping proceedings permanently in their earliest stages. To do that, the accused and those helping him need to keep in continuous personal contact with the court, especially those helping him. I repeat, this doesn't require so much effort as getting an apparent acquittal, but it probably requires a lot more attention. You must never let the trial out of your sight, you have to go and see the appropriate judge at regular intervals as well as when something in particular comes up and, whatever you do, you have to try and remain friendly with him; if you don't know the judge personally you have to influence him through the judges you do know, and you have to do it without giving up on the direct discussions. As long as you don't fail to do any of these things you can be reasonably sure the trial won't get past its first stages. The trial doesn't stop, but the defendant is almost as certain of avoiding conviction as if he'd been acquitted. Compared with an apparent acquittal, deferment has the advantage that the defendant's future is less uncertain, he's safe from the shock of being suddenly re-arrested and doesn't need to fear the exertions and stress involved in getting an apparent acquittal just when everything else in his life would make it most difficult. Deferment does have certain disadvantages of its own though, too, and they shouldn't be underestimated. I don't mean by this that the defendant is never free, he's never free in the proper sense of the word with an apparent acquittal either. There's another disadvantage. Proceedings can't be prevented from moving forward unless there are some at least ostensible reasons given. So something needs to seem to be happening when looked at from the outside. This means that from time to time various injunctions have to be obeyed, the accused has to be questioned, investigations have to take place and so on. The trial's been artificially constrained inside a tiny circle, and it has to be continuously spun round within it. And that, of course, brings with it certain unpleasantnesses for the accused, although you shouldn't imagine they're all that bad. All of this is just for show, the interrogations, for instance, they're only very short, if you ever don't have the time or don't feel like going to them you can offer an excuse, with some judges you can even arrange the injunctions together a long time in advance, in essence all it means is that, as the accused, you have to report to the judge from time to time." Even while the painter was speaking those last words K. had laid his coat over his arm and had stood up. Immediately, from outside the door, there was a cry of 'He's standing up now!' "Are you leaving already?" asked the painter, who had also stood up. "It must be the air that's driving you out. I'm very sorry about that. There's still a lot I need to tell you. I had to put everything very briefly but I hope at least it was all clear." "Oh yes," said K., whose head was aching from the effort of listening. Despite this affirmation the painter summed it all up once more, as if he wanted to give K. something to console him on his way home. "Both have in common that they prevent the defendant being convicted," he said. "But they also prevent his being properly acquitted," said K. quietly, as if ashamed to acknowledge it. "You've got it, in essence," said the painter quickly. K. placed his hand on his winter overcoat but could not bring himself to put it on. Most of all he would have liked to pack everything together and run out to the fresh air. Not even the girls could induce him to put his coat on, even though they were already loudly telling each other that he was doing so. The painter still had to interpret K.'s mood in some way, so he said, "I expect you've deliberately avoided deciding between my suggestions yet. That's good. I would even have advised against making a decision straight away. There's no more than a hair's breadth of difference between the advantages and disadvantages. Everything has to be carefully weighed up. But the most important thing is you shouldn't lose too much time." "I'll come back here again soon," said

K., who had suddenly decided to put his frockcoat on, threw his overcoat over his shoulder and hurried over to the door behind which the
girls now began to scream. K. thought he could even see the screaming girls through the door. "Well, you'll have to keep your word," said
the painter, who had not followed him, "otherwise I'll come to the
bank to ask about it myself." "Will you open this door for me," said K.
pulling at the handle which, as he noticed from the resistance, was
being held tightly by the girls on the other side. "Do you want to be
bothered by the girls?" asked the painter. "It's better if you use the
other way out," he said, pointing to the door behind the bed. K.
agreed to this and jumped back to the bed. But instead of opening
that door the painter crawled under the bed and from underneath it
asked K., "Just a moment more, would you not like to see a picture I
could sell to you?" K. did not want to be impolite, the painter really
had taken his side and promised to help him more in the future, and
because of K.'s forgetfulness there had been no mention of any pay-
ment for the painter's help, so K. could not turn him down now and
allowed him to show him the picture, even though he was quivering
with impatience to get out of the studio. From under the bed, the
painter withdrew a pile of unframed paintings. They were so covered
in dust that when the painter tried to blow it off the one on top the
dust swirled around in front of K.'s eyes, robbing him of breath for
some time. "Moorland landscape," said the painter passing the picture
to K. It showed two sickly trees, well separated from each other in
dark grass. In the background there was a multi-coloured sunset.
"That's nice," said K. "I'll buy it." K. expressed himself in this curt way
without any thought, so he was glad when the painter did not take
this amiss and picked up a second painting from the floor. "This is a
counterpart to the first picture," said the painter. Perhaps it had been
intended as a counterpart, but there was not the slightest difference
to be seen between it and the first picture, there were the trees, there
the grass and there the sunset. But this was of little importance to K.
"They are beautiful landscapes," he said, "I'll buy them both and hang
them in my office." "You seem to like this subject," said the painter,
picking up a third painting, "good job I've still got another, similar
picture here." The picture though, was not similar, rather it was exactly
the same moorland landscape. The painter was fully exploiting this
opportunity to sell off his old pictures. "I'll take this one too," said K.
"How much do the three paintings cost?" "We can talk about that
next time," said the painter. "You're in a hurry now, and we'll still be

in contact. And besides, I'm glad you like the paintings, I'll give you all the paintings I've got down here. They're all moorland landscapes, I've painted a lot of moorland landscapes. A lot of people don't like that sort of picture because they're too gloomy, but there are others, and you're one of them, who love gloomy themes." But K. was not in the mood to hear about the professional experiences of this painter cum beggar. "Wrap them all up!" he called out, interrupting the painter as he was speaking, "my servant will come to fetch them in the morning." "There's no need for that," said the painter. "I expect I can find a porter for you who can go with you now." And, at last, he leant over the bed and unlocked the door. "Just step on the bed, don't worry about that," said the painter, "that's what everyone does who comes in here." Even without this invitation, K. had shown no compunction in already placing his foot in the middle of the bed covers, then he looked out through the open door and drew his foot back again. "What is that?" he asked the painter. "What are you so surprised at?" he asked, surprised in his turn. "Those are court offices. Didn't you know there are court offices here? There are court offices in almost every attic, why should this building be any different? Even my studio is actually one of the court offices but the court put it at my disposal." It was not so much finding court offices even here that shocked K., he was mainly shocked at himself, at his own naïvety in court matters. It seemed to him that one of the most basic rules governing how a defendant should behave was always to be prepared, never allow surprises, never to look, unsuspecting, to the right when the judge stood beside him to his left—and this was the very basic rule that he was continually violating. A long corridor extended in from of him, air blew in from it which, compared with the air in the studio, was refreshing. There were benches set along each side of the corridor just as in the waiting area for the office he went to himself. There seemed to be precise rules governing how offices should be equipped. There did not seem to be many people visiting the offices that day. There was a man there, half sitting, half laying, his face was buried in his arm on the bench and he seemed to be sleeping; another man was standing in the half-dark at the end of the corridor. K. now climbed over the bed, the painter followed him with the pictures. They soon came across a servant of the court—K. was now able to recognise all the servants of the court from the gold buttons they wore on their civilian clothes below the normal buttons—and the painter instructed him to go with K. carrying the pictures. K. staggered more than he walked, his handkerchief pressed over his mouth. They had nearly reached the exit when the girls stormed in on them, so K. had not been able to avoid them. They had clearly seen that the second door of the studio had been opened and had gone around to impose themselves on him from this side. "I can't come with you any further!" called out the painter with a laugh as the girls pressed in. "Goodbye, and don't hesitate too long!" K. did not even look round at him. Once on the street he took the first cab he came across. He now had to get rid of the servant, whose gold button continually caught his eye even if it caught no one else's. As a servant, the servant of the court was going to sit on the coach-box. But K. chased him down from there. It was already well into the afternoon when K. arrived in front of the bank. He would have liked to leave the pictures in the cab but feared there might be some occasion when he would have to let the painter see he still had them. So he had the pictures taken to his office and locked them in the lowest drawer of his desk so that he could at least keep them safe from the deputy director's view for the next few days.

Block, the Businessman—
Dismissing the Lawyer

K. had at last made the decision to withdraw his defence from the
lawyer. It was impossible to remove his doubts as to whether this was
the right decision, but this was outweighed by his belief in its neces-
sity. This decision, on the day he intended to go to see the lawyer,
took a lot of the strength he needed for his work, he worked exceptionally slowly, he had to remain in his office a long time, and it was
already past ten o'clock when he finally stood in front of the lawyer's
front door. Even before he rang he considered whether it might not
be better to give the lawyer notice by letter or telephone, a personal
conversation would certainly be very difficult. Nonetheless, K. did not
actually want to do without it, if he gave notice by any other means
it would be received in silence or with a few formulated words, and
unless Leni could discover anything K. would never learn how the
lawyer had taken his dismissal and what its consequences might be,
in the lawyer's not unimportant opinion. But sitting in front of him
and taken by surprise by his dismissal, K. would be able easily to infer
everything he wanted from the lawyer's face and behaviour, even if
he could not be induced to say very much. It was not even out of the
question that K. might, after all, be persuaded that it would be best to
leave his defence to the lawyer and withdraw his dismissal.

As usual, there was at first no response to K.'s ring at the door.
"Leni could be a bit quicker," thought K. But he could at least be glad
there was nobody else interfering as usually happened, be it the man
in his nightshirt or anyone else who might bother him. As K. pressed
on the button for the second time he looked back at the other door,
but this time it, too, remained closed. At last, two eyes appeared at the
spy-hatch in the lawyer's door, although they weren't Leni's eyes.

Someone unlocked the door, but kept himself pressed against it as he called back inside, "It's him!" and only then did he open the door properly. K. pushed against the door, as behind him he could already hear the key being hurriedly turned in the lock of the door to the other flat. When the door in front of him finally opened, he stormed straight into the hallway. Through the corridor which led between the rooms he saw Leni, to whom the warning cry of the door opener had been directed, still running away in her nightshirt . He looked at her for a moment and then looked round at the person who had opened the door. It was a small, wizened man with a full beard, he held a candle in his hand. "Do you work here?" asked K. "No," answered the man, "I don't belong here at all, the lawyer is only representing me, I'm here on legal business." "Without your coat?" asked K., indicating the man's deficiency of dress with a gesture of his hand. "Oh, do for-give me!" said the man, and he looked at himself in the light of the candle he was holding as if he had not known about his appearance until then. "Is Leni your lover?" asked K. curtly. He had set his legs slightly apart, his hands, in which he held his hat, were behind his back. Merely by being in possession of a thick overcoat he felt his advantage over this thin little man. "Oh God," he said and, shocked, raised one hand in front of his face as if in defence, "no, no, what can you be thinking?" "You look honest enough," said K. with a smile, "but come along anyway." K. indicated with his hat which way the man was to go and let him go ahead of him. "What is your name then?" asked K. on the way. "Block. I'm a businessman," said the small man, twisting himself round as he thus introduced himself, although K. did not allow him to stop moving. "Is that your real name?" asked K. "Of course it is," was the man's reply, "why do you doubt it?" "I thought you might have some reason to keep your name secret," said K. He felt himself as much at liberty as is normally only felt in foreign parts when speaking with people of lower standing, keeping every-thing about himself to himself, speaking only casually about the inter-ests of the other, able to raise him to a level above one's own, but also able, at will, to let him drop again. K. stopped at the door of the law-yer's office, opened it and, to the businessman who had obediently gone ahead, called, "Not so fast! Bring some light here!" K. thought Leni might have hidden in here, he let the businessman search in every corner, but the room was empty. In front of the picture of the judge K. took hold of the businessman's braces to stop him moving on. "Do you know him?" he asked, pointing upwards with his finger.

The businessman lifted the candle, blinked as he looked up and said, "It's a judge." "An important judge?" asked K., and stood to the side and in front of the businessman so that he could observe what impression the picture had on him. The businessman was looking up in admiration. "He's an important judge." "You don't have much insight," said K. "He is the lowest of the lowest examining judges." "I remember now," said the businessman as he lowered the candle, "that's what I've already been told." "Well of course you have," called out K., "I'd forgotten about it, of course you would already have been told." "But why, why?" asked the businessman as he moved forwards towards the door, propelled by the hands of K. Outside in the corridor K. said, "You know where Leni's hidden, do you?" "Hidden?" said the businessman, "No, but she might be in the kitchen cooking soup for the lawyer." "Why didn't you say that immediately?" asked K. "I was going to take you there, but you called me back again," answered the businessman, as if confused by the contradictory commands. "You think you're very clever, don't you," said K., "now take me there!" K. had never been in the kitchen, it was surprisingly big and very well equipped. The stove alone was three times bigger than normal stoves, but it was not possible to see any detail beyond this as the kitchen was at the time illuminated by no more than a small lamp hanging by the entrance. At the stove stood Leni, in a white apron as always, breaking eggs into a pot standing on a spirit lamp. "Good evening, Josef," she said with a glance sideways. "Good evening," said K., pointing with one hand to a chair in a corner which the businessman was to sit on, and he did indeed sit down on it. K. however went very close behind Leni's back, leant over her shoulder and asked, "Who is this man?" Leni put one hand around K. as she stirred the soup with the other, she drew him forward toward herself and said, "He's a pitiful character, a poor businessman by the name of Block. Just look at him." The two of them looked back over their shoulders. The businessman was sitting on the chair that K. had directed him to, he had extinguished the candle whose light was no longer needed and pressed on the wick with his fingers to stop the smoke. "You were in your nightshirt," said K., putting his hand on her head and turning it back towards the stove. She was silent. "Is he your lover?" asked K. She was about to take hold of the pot of soup, but K. took both her hands and said, "Answer me!" She said, "Come into the office, I'll explain everything to you." "No," said K., "I want you to explain it here." She put her arms around him and wanted to kiss him. K., though, pushed her away and said, "I don't want you to kiss me now." "Josef," said Leni, looking at K. imploringly but frankly in the eyes, "you're not going to be jealous of Mr. Block now, are you? Rudi," she then said, turning to the businessman, "help me out will you, I'm being suspected of something, you can see that, leave the candle alone." It had looked as though Mr. Block had not been paying attention but he had been following closely. "I don't even know why you might be jealous," he said ingenuously. "Nor do I, actually," said K., looking at the businessman with a smile. Leni laughed out loud and while K. was not paying attention took the opportunity of embracing him and whispering, "Leave him alone, now, you can see what sort of person he is. I've been helping him a little bit because he's an important client of the lawyer's, and no other reason. And what about you? Do you want to speak to the lawyer at this time of day? He's very unwell today, but if you want I'll tell him you're here. But you can certainly spend the night with me. It's so long since you were last here, even the lawyer has been asking about you. Don't neglect your case! And I've got some things to tell you that I've learned about. But now, before anything else, take your coat off!" She helped him off with his coat, took the hat off his head, ran with the things into the hallway to hang them up, then she ran back and saw to the soup. "Do you want me to tell him you're here straight away or take him his soup first?" "Tell him I'm here first," said K. He was in a bad mood, he had originally intended a detailed discussion of his business with Leni, especially the question of his giving the lawyer notice, but now he no longer wanted to because of the presence of the businessman. Now he considered his affair too important to let this little businessman take part in it and perhaps change some of his decisions, and so he called Leni back even though she was already on her way to the lawyer. "Bring him his soup first," he said, "I want him to get his strength up for the discussion with me, he'll need it." "You're a client of the lawyer's too, aren't you," said the businessman quietly from his corner as if he were trying to find this out. It was not, however, taken well. "What business is that of yours?" said K., and Leni said, "Will you be quiet—I'll take him his soup first then, shall I?" And she poured the soup into a dish. "The only worry then is that he might go to sleep soon after he's eaten." "What I've got to say to him will keep him awake," said K., who still wanted to intimate that he intended some important negotiations with the lawyer, he wanted Leni to ask him what it was and only then to ask her advice. But instead, she just promptly carried out the order he had given her.

When she went over to him with the dish she deliberately brushed against him and whispered, "I'll tell him you're here as soon as he's eaten the soup so that I can get you back as soon as possible." "Just go," said K., "just go." "Be a bit more friendly," she said and, still holding the dish, turned completely round once more in the doorway.

K. watched her as she went; the decision had finally been made that the lawyer was to be dismissed, it was probably better that he had not been able to discuss the matter any more with Leni beforehand; she hardly understood the complexity of the matter, she would certainly have advised him against it and perhaps would even have prevented him from dismissing the lawyer this time, he would have remained in doubt and unease and eventually have carried out his decision after a while anyway as this decision was something he could not avoid. The sooner it was carried out the more harm would be avoided. And moreover, perhaps the businessman had something to say on the matter.

K. turned round, the businessman hardly noticed it as he was about to stand up. "Stay where you are," said K. and pulled up a chair beside him. "Have you been a client of the lawyer's for a long time?" asked K. "Yes," said the businessman, "a very long time." "How many years has he been representing you so far, then?" asked K. "I don't know how you mean," said the businessman, "he's been my business lawyer—I buy and sell cereals—he's been my business lawyer since I took the business over, and that's about twenty years now, but perhaps you mean my own trial and he's been representing me in that since it started, and that's been more than five years. Yes, well over five years," he then added, pulling out an old briefcase, "I've got everything written down; I can tell you the exact dates if you like. It's so hard to remember everything. Probably, my trial's been going on much longer than that, it started soon after the death of my wife, and that's been more than five and a half years now." K. moved in closer to him. "So the lawyer takes on ordinary legal business, does he?" he asked. This combination of criminal and commercial business seemed surprisingly reassuring for K. "Oh yes," said the businessman, and then he whispered, "They even say he's more efficient in jurisprudence than he is in other matters." But then he seemed to regret saying this, and he laid a hand on K.'s shoulder and said, "Please don't betray me to him, will you." K. patted his thigh to reassure him and said, "No, I don't betray people." "He can be so vindictive, you see," said the businessman. "I'm sure he won't do anything against such a faithful client

as you," said K. "Oh, he might do," said the businessman, "when he
gets cross it doesn't matter who it is, and anyway, I'm not really faithful to him." "How's that then?" asked K. "I'm not sure I should tell you
about it," said the businessman hesitantly. "I think it'll be alright,"
said K. "Well then," said the businessman, "I'll tell you about some of
it, but you'll have to tell me a secret too, then we can support each
other with the lawyer." "You are very careful," said K., "but I'll tell you
a secret that will set your mind completely at ease. Now tell me, in
what way have you been unfaithful to the lawyer?" "I've …" said the
businessman hesitantly, and in a tone as if he were confessing something dishonourable, "I've taken on other lawyers besides him."
"That's not so serious," said K., a little disappointed. "It is, here," said
the businessman, who had had some difficulty breathing since making his confession but who now, after hearing K.'s comment, began to
feel more trust for him. "That's not allowed. And it's allowed least of
all to take on petty lawyers when you've already got a proper one. And
that's just what I have done, besides him I've got five petty lawyers."
"Five!" exclaimed K., astonished at this number, "Five lawyers besides
this one?" The businessman nodded. "I'm even negotiating with a
sixth one." "But why do you need so many lawyers?" asked K. "I need
all of them," said the businessman. "Would you mind explaining that
to me?" asked K. "I'd be glad to," said the businessman. "Most of all,
I don't want to lose my case, well that's obvious. So that means I
mustn't neglect anything that might be of use to me; even if there's
very little hope of a particular thing being of any use I can't just throw
it away. So everything I have I've put to use in my case. I've taken all
the money out of my business, for example, the offices for my business
used to occupy nearly a whole floor, but now all I need is a little room
at the back where I work with one apprentice. It wasn't just using up
the money that caused the difficulty, of course, it was much more to
do with me not working at the business as much as I used to. If you
want to do something about your trial you don't have much time for
anything else." "So you're also working at the court yourself?" asked
K. "That's just what I want to learn more about." "I can't tell you very
much about that," said the businessman, "at first I tried to do that too
but I soon had to give it up again. It wears you out too much, and it's
really not much use. And it turned out to be quite impossible to work
there yourself and to negotiate, at least for me it was. It's a heavy strain
there just sitting and waiting. You know yourself what the air is like
in those offices." "How do you know I've been there, then?" asked K.

"I was in the waiting room myself when you went through." "What a coincidence that is!" exclaimed K., totally engrossed and forgetting how ridiculous the businessman had seemed to him earlier. "So you saw me! You were in the waiting room when I went through. Yes, I did go through it one time." "It isn't such a big coincidence," said the businessman, "I'm there nearly every day." "I expect I'll have to go there quite often myself now," said K., "although I can hardly expect to be shown the same respect as I was then. They all stood up for me. They must have thought I was a judge." "No," said the businessman, "we were greeting the servant of the court. We knew you were a defendant. That sort of news spreads very quickly." "So you already knew about that," said K., "the way I behaved must have seemed very arrogant to you. Did you criticise me for it afterwards?" "No," said the businessman, "quite the opposite. That was just stupidity." "What do you mean 'stupidity'?" asked K. "Why are you asking about it?" said the businessman in some irritation. "You still don't seem to know the people there and you might take it wrong. Don't forget in proceedings like this there are always lots of different things coming up to talk about, things that you just can't understand with reason alone, you just get too tired and distracted for most things and so, instead, people rely on superstition. I'm talking about the others, but I'm no better myself. One of these superstitions, for example, is that you can learn a lot about the outcome of a defendant's case by looking at his face, especially the shape of his lips. There are lots who believe that, and they said they could see from the shape of your lips that you'd definitely be found guilty very soon. I repeat that all this is just a ridiculous superstition, and in most cases it's completely disproved by the facts, but when you live in that society it's hard to hold yourself back from beliefs like that. Just think how much effect that superstition can have. You spoke to one of them there, didn't you? He was hardly able to give you an answer. There are lots of things there that can make you confused, of course, but one of them, for him, was the appearance of your lips. He told us all later he thought he could see something in your lips that meant he'd be convicted himself." "On my lips?" asked K., pulling out a pocket mirror and examining himself. "I can see nothing special about my lips. Can you?" "Nor can I," said the businessman, "nothing at all." "These people are so superstitious!" exclaimed K. "Isn't that what I just told you?" asked the businessman. "Do you then have that much contact with each other, exchanging each other's opinions?" said K. "I've kept myself completely apart so far." "They don't normally have much contact with each other," said the businessman, "that would be impossible, there are so many of them. And they don't have much in common either. If a group of them ever thinks they have found something in common it soon turns out they were mistaken. There's nothing you can do as a group where the court's concerned. Each case is examined separately, the court is very painstaking. So there's nothing to be achieved by forming into a group, only sometimes an individual will achieve something in secret; and it's only when that's been done the others learn about it; nobody knows how it was done. So there's no sense of togetherness, you meet people now and then in the waiting rooms, but we don't talk much there. The superstitious beliefs were established a long time ago and they spread all by themselves." "I saw those gentlemen in the waiting room," said K., "it seemed so pointless for them to be waiting in that way." "Waiting is not pointless," said the businessman, "it's only pointless if you try and interfere yourself. I told you just now I've got five lawyers besides this one. You might think—I thought it myself at first—you might think I could leave the whole thing entirely up to them now. That would be entirely wrong. I can leave it up to them less than when I had just the one. Maybe you don't understand that, do you?" "No," said K., and to slow the businessman down, who had been speaking too fast, he laid his hand on the businessman's to reassure him, "but I'd like just to ask you to speak a little more slowly, these are many very important things for me, and I can't follow exactly what you're saying." "You're quite right to remind me of that," said the businessman, "you're new to all this, a junior. Your trial is six months old, isn't it? Yes, I've heard about it. Such a new case! But I've already thought all these things through countless times, to me they're the most obvious things in the world." "You must be glad your trial has already progressed so far, are you?" asked K., he did not wish to ask directly how the businessman's affairs stood, but received no clear answer anyway. "Yes, I've been working at my trial for five years now," said the businessman as his head sank, "that's no small achievement." Then he was silent for a while. K. listened to hear whether Leni was on her way back. On the one hand he did not want her to come back too soon as he still had many questions to ask and did not want her to find him in this intimate discussion with the businessman, but on the other hand it irritated him that she stayed so long with the lawyer when K. was there, much longer than she needed to give him his soup. "I still remember it exactly," the businessman began again, and K.

immediately gave him his full attention, "when my case was as old as yours is now. I only had this one lawyer at that time but I wasn't very satisfied with him." Now I'll find out everything, thought K., nodding vigorously as if he could thereby encourage the businessman to say everything worth knowing. "My case," the businessman continued, "didn't move on at all, there were some hearings that took place and I went to every one of them, collected materials, handed all my business books to the court—which I later found was entirely unnecessary—I ran back and forth to the lawyer, and he submitted various documents to the court too. ...." "Various documents?" asked K. "Yes, that's right," said the businessman. "That's very important for me," said K., "in my case he's still working on the first set of documents. He still hasn't done anything. I see now that he's been neglecting me quite disgracefully." "There can be lots of good reasons why the first documents still aren't ready," said the businessman, "and anyway, it turned out later on that the ones he submitted for me were entirely worthless. I even read one of them myself, one of the officials at the court was very helpful. It was very learned, but it didn't actually say anything. Most of all, there was lots of Latin, which I can't understand, then pages and pages of general appeals to the court, then lots of flattery for particular officials, they weren't named, these officials, but anyone familiar with the court must have been able to guess who they were, then there was self-praise by the lawyer where he humiliated himself to the court in a way that was downright doglike, and then endless investigations of cases from the past which were supposed to be similar to mine. Although, as far as I was able to follow them, these investigations had been carried out very carefully. Now, I don't mean to criticise the lawyer's work with all of this, and the document I read was only one of many, but even so, and this is something I will say, at that time I couldn't see any progress in my trial at all." "And what sort of progress had you been hoping for?" asked K. "That's a very sensible question," said the businessman with a smile, "it's only very rare that you see any progress in these proceedings at all. But I didn't know that then. I'm a businessman, much more in those days than now, I wanted to see some tangible progress, it should have all been moving to some conclusion or at least should have been moving on in some way according to the rules. Instead of which there were just more hearings, and most of them went through the same things anyway; I had all the answers off pat like in a church service; there were messengers from the court coming to me at work several times a week, or they came to me at home or anywhere else they could find me; and that was very disturbing of course (but at least now things are better in that respect, it's much less disturbing when they contact you by telephone), and rumours about my trial even started to spread among some of the people I do business with, and especially my relations, so I was being made to suffer in many different ways but there was still not the slightest sign that even the first hearing would take place soon. So I went to the lawyer and complained about it. He explained it all to me at length, but refused to do anything I asked for, no one has any influence on the way the trial proceeds, he said, to try and insist on it in any of the documents submitted—like I was asking— was simply unheard of and would do harm to both him and me. I thought to myself: What this lawyer can't or won't do another lawyer will. So I looked round for other lawyers. And before you say anything: none of them asked for a definite date for the main trial and none of them got one, and anyway, apart from one exception which I'll talk about in a minute, it really is impossible, that's one thing this lawyer didn't mislead me about; but besides, I had no reason to regret turning to other lawyers. Perhaps you've already heard how Dr. Huld talks about the petty lawyers, he probably made them sound very contemptible to you, and he's right, they are contemptible. But when he talks about them and compares them with himself and his colleagues there's a small error running through what he says, and, just for your interest, I'll tell you about it. When he talks about the lawyers he mixes with he sets them apart by calling them the 'great lawyers.' That's wrong, anyone can call himself 'great' if he wants to, of course, but in this case only the usage of the court can make that distinction. You see, the court says that besides the petty lawyers there are also minor lawyers and great lawyers. This one and his colleagues are only minor lawyers, and the difference in rank between them and the great lawyers, who I've only ever heard about and never seen, is incomparably greater than between the minor lawyers and the despised petty lawyers." "The great lawyers?" asked K. "Who are they then? How do you contact them?" "You've never heard about them, then?" said the businessman. "There's hardly anyone who's been accused who doesn't spend a lot of time dreaming about the great lawyers once he's heard about them. It's best if you don't let yourself be misled in that way. I don't know who the great lawyers are, and there's probably no way of contacting them. I don't know of any case I can talk about with certainty where they've taken any part. They do defend a lot of people, but you can't get hold of them by your own efforts, they only defend those who they want to defend. And I don't suppose they ever take on cases that haven't already got past the lower courts. Anyway, it's best not to think about them, as if you do it makes the discussions with the other lawyers, all their advice and all that they do manage to achieve, seem so unpleasant and useless, I had that experience myself, just wanted to throw everything away and lay at home in bed and hear nothing more about it. But that, of course, would be the stupidest thing you could do, and you wouldn't be left in peace in bed for very long either." "So you weren't thinking about the great lawyers at that time?" asked K. "Not for very long," said the businessman, and smiled again, "you can't forget about them entirely, I'm afraid, especially in the night when these thoughts come so easily. But I wanted immediate results in those days, so I went to the petty lawyers."

"Well look at you two sat huddled together!" called Leni as she came back with the dish and stood in the doorway. They were indeed sat close together, if either of them turned his head even slightly it would have knocked against the other's, the businessman was not only very small but also sat hunched down, so that K. was also forced to bend down low if he wanted to hear everything. "Not quite yet!" called out K., to turn Leni away, his hand, still resting on the businessman's hand, twitching with impatience. "He wanted me to tell him about my trial," said the businessman to Leni. "Carry on, then, carry on," she said. She spoke to the businessman with affection but, at the same time, with condescension. K. did not like that, he had begun to learn that the man was of some value after all, he had experience at least, and he was willing to share it. Leni was probably wrong about him. He watched her in irritation as Leni now took the candle from the businessman's hand—which he had been holding on to all this time—wiped his hand with her apron and then knelt beside him to scratch off some wax that had dripped from the candle onto his trousers. "You were about to tell me about the petty lawyers," said K., shoving Leni's hand away with no further comment. "What's wrong with you today?" asked Leni, tapped him gently and carried on with what she had been doing. "Yes, the petty lawyers," said the businessman, putting his hand to his brow as if thinking hard. K. wanted to help him and said, "You wanted immediate results and so went to the petty lawyers." "Yes, that's right," said the businessman, but did not continue with what he'd been saying. "Maybe he doesn't want to speak about it in front of Leni," thought K., suppressing his impatience to hear the rest straight away, and stopped trying to press him.

"Have you told him I'm here?" he asked Leni. "Course I have," she said, "he's waiting for you. Leave Block alone now, you can talk to Block later, he'll still be here." K. still hesitated. "You'll still be here?" he asked the businessman, wanting to hear the answer from him and not wanting Leni to speak about the businessman as if he weren't there, he was full of secret resentment towards Leni today. And once more it was only Leni who answered. "He often sleeps here." "He sleeps here?" exclaimed K., he had thought the businessman would just wait there for him while he quickly settled his business with the lawyer, and then they would leave together to discuss everything thoroughly and undisturbed. "Yes," said Leni, "not everyone's like you, Josef, allowed to see the lawyer at any time you like. You don't even seem surprised that the lawyer, despite being ill, still receives you at eleven o'clock at night. You take it far too much for granted, what your friends do for you. Well, your friends, or at least I do, we like to do things for you. I don't want or need any more thanks than that you're fond of me." "Fond of you?" thought K. at first, and only then it occurred to him, "Well, yes, I am fond of her." Nonetheless, what he said, forgetting all the rest, was, "He receives me because I am his client. If I needed anyone else's help I'd have to beg and show gratitude whenever I do anything." "He's really nasty today, isn't he?" Leni asked the businessman. "Now it's me who's not here," thought K., and nearly lost his temper with the businessman when, with the same rudeness as Leni, he said, "The lawyer also has other reasons to receive him. His case is much more interesting than mine. And it's only in its early stages too, it probably hasn't progressed very far so the lawyer still likes to deal with him. That'll all change later on." "Yeah, yeah," said Leni, looking at the businessman and laughing. "He doesn't half talk!" she said, turning to face K. "You can't believe a word he says. He's as talkative as he is sweet. Maybe that's why the lawyer can't stand him. At least, he only sees him when he's in the right mood. I've already tried hard to change that but it's impossible. Just think, there are times when I tell him Block's here and he doesn't receive him until three days later. And if Block isn't on the spot when he's called then everything's lost and it all has to start all over again. That's why I let Block sleep here, it wouldn't be the first time Dr. Huld has wanted to see him in the night. So now Block is ready for that. Sometimes, when he knows Block is still here, he'll even change his mind about letting him in to see him." K. looked questioningly at the businessman. The latter nodded and, although he had spoken quite openly with K. earlier, seemed to be confused with shame as he said, "Yes, later on you become very dependent on your lawyer." "He's only pretending to mind," said Leni. "He likes to sleep here really, he's often said so." She went over to a little door and shoved it open. "Do you want to see his bedroom?" she asked. K. went over to the low, windowless room and looked in from the doorway. The room contained a narrow bed which filled it completely, so that to get into the bed you would need to climb over the bedpost. At the head of the bed there was a niche in the wall where, fastidiously tidy, stood a candle, a bottle of ink, and a pen with a bundle of papers which were probably to do with the trial. "You sleep in the maid's room?" asked K., as he went back to the businessman. "Leni's let me have it," answered the businessman, "it has many advantages." K. looked long at him; his first impression of the businessman had perhaps not been right; he had experience as his trial had already lasted a long time, but he had paid a heavy price for this experience. K. was suddenly unable to bear the sight of the businessman any longer. "Bring him to bed, then!" he called out to Leni, who seemed to understand him. For himself, he wanted to go to the lawyer and, by dismissing him, free himself from not only the lawyer but also from Leni and the businessman. But before he had reached the door the businessman spoke to him gently. "Excuse me, sir," he said, and K. looked round crossly. "You've forgotten your promise," said the businessman, stretching his hand out to K. imploringly from where he sat. "You were going to tell me a secret." "That is true," said K., as he glanced at Leni, who was watching him carefully, to check on her. "So listen; it's hardly a secret now anyway. I'm going to see the lawyer now to sack him." "He's sacking him!" yelled the businessman, and he jumped up from his chair and ran around the kitchen with his arms in the air. He kept on shouting, "He's sacking his lawyer!" Leni tried to rush at K. but the businessman got in her way so that she shoved him away with her fists. Then, still with her hands balled into fists, she ran after K. who, however, had been given a long start. He was already inside the lawyer's room by the time Leni caught up with him. He had almost closed the door behind himself, but Leni held the door open with her foot, grabbed his arm and tried to pull him back. But he put such pressure on her wrist that, with a sigh, she was forced to release him. She did not dare go into the room straight away, and K. locked the door with the key.

"I've been waiting for you a very long time," said the lawyer from his bed. He had been reading something by the light of a candle but now he laid it onto the bedside table and put his glasses on, looking at K. sharply through them. Instead of apologising K. said, "I'll be leaving again soon." As he had not apologised the lawyer ignored what K. said, and replied, "I won't let you in this late again next time." "I find that quite acceptable," said K. The lawyer looked at him quizzically. "Sit down," he said. "As you wish," said K., drawing a chair up to the bedside table and sitting down. "It seemed to me that you locked the door," said the lawyer. "Yes," said K., "it was because of Leni." He had no intention of letting anyone off lightly. But the lawyer asked him, "Was she being importunate again?" "Importunate?" asked K. "Yes," said the lawyer, laughing as he did so, had a fit of coughing and then, once it had passed, began to laugh again. "I'm sure you must have noticed how importunate she can be sometimes," he said, and patted K.'s hand which K. had rested on the bedside table and which he now snatched back. "You don't attach much importance to it, then," said the lawyer when K. was silent, "so much the better. Otherwise I might have needed to apologise to you. It is a peculiarity of Leni's. I've long since forgiven her for it, and I wouldn't be talking of it now, if you hadn't locked the door just now. Anyway, perhaps I should at least explain this peculiarity of hers to you, but you seem rather disturbed, the way you're looking at me, and so that's why I'll do it, this peculiarity of hers consists in this; Leni finds most of the accused attractive. She attaches herself to each of them, loves each of them, even seems to be loved by each of them; then she sometimes entertains me by telling me about them when I allow her to. I am not so astonished by all of this as you seem to be. If you look at them in the right way the accused really can be attractive, quite often. But that is a remarkable and to some extent scientific phenomenon. Being indicted does not cause any clear, precisely definable change in a person's appearance, of course. But it's not like with other legal matters, most of them remain in their usual way of life and, if they have a good lawyer looking after them, the trial doesn't get in their way. But there are nonetheless those who have experience in these matters who can look at a crowd, however big, and tell you which among them is facing a charge. How can they do that, you will ask.

My answer will not please you. It is simply that those who are facing a charge are the most attractive. It cannot be their guilt that makes them attractive as not all of them are guilty—at least that's what I, as a lawyer, have to say—and nor can it be the proper punishment that has made them attractive as not all of them are punished, so it can only be that the proceedings levelled against them take some kind of hold on them. Whatever the reason, some of these attractive people are indeed very attractive. But all of them are attractive, even Block, pitiful worm that he is." As the lawyer finished what he was saying, K. was fully in control of himself, he had even nodded conspicuously at his last few words in order to confirm to himself the view he had already formed; that the lawyer was trying to confuse him, as he always did, by making general and irrelevant observations, and thus distract him from the main question of what he was actually doing for K.'s trial. The lawyer must have noticed that K. was offering him more resistance than before, as he became silent, giving K. the chance to speak himself, and then, as K. also remained silent, he asked, "Did you have a particular reason for coming to see me today?" "Yes," said K., putting his hand up to slightly shade his eyes from the light of the candle so that he could see the lawyer better, "I wanted to tell you that I'm withdrawing my representation from you, with immediate effect." "Do I understand you rightly?" asked the lawyer as he half raised himself in his bed and supported himself with one hand on the pillow. "I think you do," said K., sitting stiffly upright as if waiting in ambush. "Well we can certainly discuss this plan of yours," said the lawyer after a pause. "It's not a plan any more," said K. "That may be," said the lawyer, "but we still mustn't rush anything." He used the word 'we,' as if he had no intention of letting K. go free, and as if, even if he could no longer represent him, he could still at least continue as his adviser. "Nothing is being rushed," said K., standing slowly up and going behind his chair, "everything has been well thought out and probably even for too long. The decision is final." "Then allow me to say a few words," said the lawyer, throwing the bed cover to one side and sitting on the edge of the bed. His naked, white-haired legs shivered in the cold. He asked K. to pass him a blanket from the couch. K. passed him the blanket and said, "You are running the risk of catching cold for no reason." "The circumstances are important enough," said the lawyer as he wrapped the bed cover around the top half of his body and then the blanket around his legs. "Your uncle is my friend and in the course of time

I've become fond of you as well. I admit that quite openly. There's nothing in that for me to be ashamed of." It was very unwelcome for K. to hear the old man speak in this touching way, as it forced him to explain himself more fully, which he would rather have avoided, and he was aware that it also confused him even though it could never make him reverse his decision. "Thank you for feeling so friendly toward me," he said, "and I also realise how deeply involved you've been in my case, as deeply as possible for yourself and to bring as much advantage as possible to me. Nonetheless, I have recently come to the conviction that it is not enough. I would naturally never attempt, considering that you are so much older and more experienced than I am, to convince you of my opinion; if I have ever unintentionally done so then I beg your forgiveness, but, as you have just said yourself, the circumstances are important enough and it is my belief that my trial needs to be approached with much more vigour than has so far been the case." "I see," said the lawyer, "you've become impatient." "I am not impatient," said K., with some irritation and he stopped paying so much attention to his choice of words. "When I first came here with my uncle you probably noticed I wasn't greatly concerned about my case, and if I wasn't reminded of it by force, as it were, I would forget about it completely. But my uncle insisted I should allow you to represent me and I did so as a favour to him. I could have expected the case to be less of a burden than it had been, as the point of taking on a lawyer is that he should take on some of its weight. But what actually happened was the opposite. Before, the trial was never such a worry for me as it has been since you've been representing me. When I was by myself I never did anything about my case, I was hardly aware of it, but then, once there was someone representing me, everything was set for something to happen, I was always, without cease, waiting for you to do something, getting more and more tense, but you did nothing. I did get some information about the court from you that I probably could not have got anywhere else, but that can't be enough when the trial, supposedly in secret, is getting closer and closer to me." K. had pushed the chair away and stood erect, his hands in the pockets of his frockcoat. "After a certain point in the proceedings," said the lawyer quietly and calmly, "nothing new of any importance ever happens. So many litigants, at the same stage in their trials, have stood before me just like you are now and spoken in the same way." "Then these other litigants," said K., "have all been right, just as I am. That does not show that I'm not." "I wasn't trying to show that you were mistaken," said the lawyer, "but I wanted to add that I expected better judgement from you than from the others, especially as I've given you more insight into the workings of the court and my own activities than I normally do. And now I'm forced to accept that, despite everything, you have too little trust in me. You don't make it easy for me." How the lawyer was humiliating himself to K.! He was showing no regard for the dignity of his position, which on this point, must have been at its most sensitive. And why did he do that? He did seem to be very busy as a lawyer as well a rich man, neither the loss of income nor the loss of a client could have been of much importance to him in themselves. He was moreover unwell and should have been thinking of passing work on to others. And despite all that he held on tightly to K. Why? Was it something personal for his uncle's sake, or did he really see K.'s case as one that was exceptional and hoped to be able to distinguish himself with it, either for K.'s sake or—and this possibility could never be excluded—for his friends at the court? It was not possible to learn anything by looking at him, even though K. was scrutinizing him quite brazenly. It could almost be supposed he was deliberately hiding his thoughts as he waited to see what effect his words would have. But he clearly deemed K.'s silence to be favourable for himself and he continued, "You will have noticed the size of my office, but that I don't employ any staff to help me. That used to be quite different, there was a time when several young lawyers were working for me but now I work alone. This is partly to do with changes in the way I do business, in that I concentrate nowadays more and more on matters such as your own case, and partly to do with the ever deeper understanding that I acquire from these legal matters. I found that I could never let anyone else deal with this sort of work unless I wanted to harm both the client and the job I had taken on. But the decision to do all the work myself had its obvious result: I was forced to turn almost everyone away who asked me to represent them and could only accept those I was especially interested in—well there are enough creatures who leap at every crumb I throw down, and they're not so very far away. Most importantly, I became ill from over-work. But despite that I don't regret my decision, quite possibly I should have turned more cases away than I did, but it did turn out to be entirely necessary for me to devote myself fully to the cases I did take on, and the successful results showed that it was worth it. I once read a description of the difference between representing someone in ordinary legal matters and in legal matters of this sort, and the writer expressed it very well. This is what he said: some lawyers lead their clients on a thread until judgement is passed, but there are others who immediately lift their clients onto their shoulders and carry them all the way to the judgement and beyond. That's just how it is. But it was quite true when I said I never regret all this work. But if, as in your case, they are so fully misunderstood, well, then I come very close to regretting it." All this talking did more to make K. impatient than to persuade him. From the way the lawyer was speaking, K. thought he could hear what he could expect if he gave in, the delays and excuses would begin again, reports of how the documents were progressing, how the mood of the court officials had improved, as well as all the enormous difficulties—in short all that he had heard so many times before would be brought out again even more fully, he would try to mislead K. with hopes that were never specified and to make him suffer with threats that were never clear. He had to put a stop to that, so he said, "What will you undertake on my behalf if you continue to represent me?" The lawyer quietly accepted even this insulting question, and answered, "I should continue with what I've already been doing for you." "That's just what I thought," said K., "and now you don't need to say another word." "I will make one more attempt," said the lawyer as if whatever had been making K. so annoyed was affecting him too. "You see, I have the impression that you have not only misjudged the legal assistance I have given you but also that that misjudgement has led you to behave in this way, you seem, although you are the accused, to have been treated too well or, to put it a better way, handled with neglect, with apparent neglect. Even that has its reason; it is often better to be in chains than to be free. But I would like to show you how other defendants are treated, perhaps you will succeed in learning something from it. What I will do is I will call Block in, unlock the door and sit down here beside the bedside table." "Be glad to," said K., and did as the lawyer suggested; he was always ready to learn something new. But to make sure of himself for any event he added, "but you do realise that you are no longer to be my lawyer, don't you?" "Yes," said the lawyer. "But you can still change your mind today if you want to." He lay back down in the bed, pulled the quilt up to his chin and turned to face the wall. Then he rang.

    Leni appeared almost the moment he had done so. She looked hurriedly at K. and the lawyer to try and learn what had happened;

she seemed to be reassured by the sight of K. sitting calmly at the lawyer's bed. She smiled and nodded to K., K. looked blankly back at her. "Fetch Block," said the lawyer. But instead of going to fetch him, Leni just went to the door and called out, "Block! To the lawyer!" Then, probably because the lawyer had turned his face to the wall and was paying no attention, she slipped in behind K.'s chair. From then on, she bothered him by leaning forward over the back of the chair or, albeit very tenderly and carefully, she would run her hands through his hair and over his cheeks. K. eventually tried to stop her by taking hold of one hand, and after some resistance Leni let him keep hold of it. Block came as soon as he was called, but he remained standing in the doorway and seemed to be wondering whether he should enter or not. He raised his eyebrows and lowered his head as if listening to find out whether the order to attend the lawyer would be repeated. K. could have encouraged to enter, but he had decided to make a final break not only with the lawyer but with everything in his home, so he kept himself motionless. Leni was also silent. Block noticed that at least no one was chasing him away, and, on tiptoe, he entered the room, his face was tense, his hands were clenched behind his back. He left the door open in case he needed to go back again. K. did not even glance at him, he looked instead only at the thick quilt under which the lawyer could not be seen as he had squeezed up very close to the wall. Then his voice was heard: "Block here?" he asked. Block had already crept some way into the room but this question seemed to give him first a shove in the breast and then another in the back, he seemed about to fall but remained standing, deeply bowed, and said, "At your service, sir." "What do you want?" asked the lawyer, "you've come at a bad time." "Wasn't I summoned?" asked Block, more to himself than the lawyer. He held his hands in front of himself as protection and would have been ready to run away any moment. "You were summoned," said the lawyer, "but you have still come at a bad time." Then, after a pause he added, "You always come at a bad time." When the lawyer started speaking Block had stopped looking at the bed but stared rather into one of the corners, just listening, as if the light from the speaker were brighter than Block could bear to look at. But it was also difficult for him to listen, as the lawyer was speaking into the wall and speaking quickly and quietly. "Would you like me to go away again, sir?" asked Block. "Well you're here now," said the lawyer. "Stay!" It was as if the lawyer had not done as Block had wanted but instead threatened him with a stick, as now Block really

began to shake. "I went to see," said the lawyer, "the third judge yesterday, a friend of mine, and slowly brought the conversation round
to the subject of you. Do you want to know what he said?" "Oh, yes
please," said Block. The lawyer did not answer immediately, so Block
repeated his request and lowered his head as if about to kneel down.
But then K. spoke to him: "What do you think you're doing?" he
shouted. Leni had wanted to stop him from calling out and so he took
hold of her other hand. It was not love that made him squeeze it and
hold on to it so tightly, she sighed frequently and tried to disengage
her hands from him. But Block was punished for K.'s outburst, as the
lawyer asked him, "Who is your lawyer?" "You are, sir," said Block.
"And who besides me?" the lawyer asked. "No one besides you, sir,"
said Block. "And let there be no one besides me," said the lawyer.
Block fully understood what that meant, he glowered at K., shaking
his head violently. If these actions had been translated into words they
would have been coarse insults. K. had been friendly and willing to
discuss his own case with someone like this! "I won't disturb you any
more," said K., leaning back in his chair. "You can kneel down or
creep on all fours, whatever you like. I won't bother with you any
more." But Block still had some sense of pride, at least where K. was
concerned, and he went towards him waving his fists, shouting as
loudly as he dared while the lawyer was there. "You shouldn't speak
to me like that, that's not allowed. Why are you insulting me? Especially here in front of the lawyer, where both of us, you and me, we're
only tolerated because of his charity. You're not a better person than
me, you've been accused of something too, you're facing a charge too.
If, in spite of that, you're still a gentleman then I'm just as much a
gentleman as you are, if not even more so. And I want to be spoken
to as a gentleman, especially by you. If you think being allowed to sit
there and quietly listen while I creep on all fours as you put it makes
you something better than me, then there's an old legal saying you
ought to bear in mind: If you're under suspicion it's better to be moving than still, as if you're still you can be in the pan of the scales
without knowing it and be weighed along with your sins." K. said
nothing. He merely looked in amazement at this distracted being, his
eyes completely still. He had gone through such changes in just the
last few hours! Was it the trial that was throwing him from side to side
in this way and stopped him knowing who was friend and who was
foe? Could he not see the lawyer was deliberately humiliating him and
had no other purpose today than to show off his power to K., and

perhaps even thereby subjugate K.? But if Block was incapable of seeing that, or if he so feared the lawyer that no such insight would even
be of any use to him, how was it that he was either so sly or so bold as
to lie to the lawyer and conceal from him the fact that he had other
lawyers working on his behalf? And how did he dare to attack K., who
could betray his secret any time he liked? But he dared even more
than this, he went to the lawyer's bed and began there to make complaints about K. "Dr. Huld, sir," he said, "did you hear the way this
man spoke to me? You can count the length of his trial in hours, and
he wants to tell me what to do when I've been involved in a legal case
for five years. He even insults me. He doesn't know anything, but he
insults me, when I, as far as my weak ability allows, when I've made a
close study of how to behave with the court, what we ought to do and
what the court practices are." "Don't let anyone bother you," said the
lawyer, "and do what seems to you to be right." "I will," said Block, as
if speaking to himself to give himself courage, and with a quick glance
to the side he kneeled down close beside the bed. "I'm kneeling now
Dr. Huld, sir," he said. But the lawyer remained silent. With one hand,
Block carefully stroked the bed cover. In the silence while he did so,
Leni, as she freed herself from K.'s hands, said, "You're hurting me.
Let go of me. I'm going over to Block." She went over to him and sat
on the edge of the bed. Block was very pleased at this and with lively,
but silent, gestures he immediately urged her to intercede for him with
the lawyer. It was clear that he desperately needed to be told something by the lawyer, although perhaps only so that he could make use
of the information with his other lawyers. Leni probably knew very
well how the lawyer could be brought round, pointed to his hand and
pursed her lips as if making a kiss. Block immediately performed the
hand-kiss and, at further urging from Leni, repeated it twice more.
But the lawyer continued to be silent. Then Leni leant over the lawyer,
as she stretched out, the attractive shape of her body could be seen,
and, bent over close to his face, she stroked his long white hair. That
now forced him to give an answer. "I'm rather wary of telling him,"
said the lawyer, and his head could be seen shaking slightly, perhaps
so that he would feel the pressure of Leni's hand better. Block listened
closely with his head lowered, as if by listening he were breaking an
order. "What makes you so wary about it?" asked Leni. K. had the
feeling he was listening to a contrived dialogue that had been repeated
many times, that would be repeated many times more, and that for
Block alone it would never lose its freshness. "What has his behaviour

been like today?" asked the lawyer instead of an answer. Before Leni
said anything she looked down at Block and watched him a short
while as he raised his hands towards her and rubbed them together
imploringly. Finally she gave a serious nod, turned back to the lawyer
and said, "He's been quiet and industrious." This was an elderly businessman, a man whose beard was long, and he was begging a young
girl to speak on his behalf. Even if there was some plan behind what
he did, there was nothing that could reinstate him in the eyes of his
fellow man. K. could not understand how the lawyer could have
thought this performance would win him over. Even if he had done
nothing earlier to make him want to leave then this scene would have
done so. It was almost humiliating even for the onlooker. So these
were the lawyer's methods, which K. fortunately had not been exposed
to for long, to let the client forget about the whole world and leave him
with nothing but the hope of reaching the end of his trial by this
deluded means. He was no longer a client, he was the lawyer's dog. If
the lawyer had ordered him to crawl under the bed as if it were a ken-
nel and to bark out from under it, then he would have done so with
enthusiasm. K. listened to all of this, testing it and thinking it over as
if he had been given the task of closely observing everything spoken
here, inform a higher office about it and write a report. "And what has
he been doing all day?" asked the lawyer. "I kept him locked in the
maid's room all day," said Leni, "so that he wouldn't stop me doing
my work. That's where he usually stays. From time to time I looked in
through the spyhole to see what he was doing, and each time he was
kneeling on the bed and reading the papers you gave him, propped
up on the window sill. That made a good impression on me; as the
window only opens onto an air shaft and gives hardly any light. It
showed how obedient he is that he was even reading in those conditions." "I'm pleased to hear it," said the lawyer. "But did he understand what he was reading?" While this conversation was going on,
Block continually moved his lips and was clearly formulating the
answers he hoped Leni would give. "Well I can't give you any certain
answer to that of course," said Leni, "but I could see that he was reading thoroughly. He spent all day reading the same page, running his
finger along the lines. Whenever I looked in on him he sighed as if
this reading was a lot of work for him. I expect the papers you gave
him were very hard to understand." "Yes," said the lawyer, "they certainly are that. And I really don't think he understood anything of
them. But they should at least give him some inkling of just how hard

a struggle it is and how much work it is for me to defend him. And who am I doing all this hard work for? I'm doing it—it's laughable even to say it—I'm doing it for Block. He ought to realise what that means, too. Did he study without a pause?" "Almost without a pause," answered Leni. "Just the once he asked me for a drink of water, so I gave him a glassful through the window. Then at eight o'clock I let him out and gave him something to eat." Block glanced sideways at K., as if he were being praised and had to impress K. as well. He now seemed more optimistic, he moved more freely and rocked back and forth on his knees. This made his astonishment all the more obvious when he heard the following words from the lawyer: "You speak well of him," said the lawyer, "but that's just what makes it difficult for me. You see, the judge did not speak well of him at all, neither about Block nor about his case." "Didn't speak well of him?" asked Leni. "How is that possible?" Block looked at her with such tension he seemed to think that although the judge's words had been spoken so long before she would be able to change them in his favour. "Not at all," said the lawyer. "In fact he became quite cross when I started to talk about Block to him. 'Don't talk to me about Block,' he said. 'He is my client,' said I. 'You're letting him abuse you,' he said. 'I don't think his case is lost yet,' said I. 'You're letting him abuse you,' he repeated. 'I don't think so,' said I. 'Block works hard in his case and always knows where it stands. He practically lives with me so that he always knows what's happening. You don't always find such enthusiasm as that. He's not very pleasant personally, I grant you, his manners are terrible and he's dirty, but as far as the trial's concerned he's quite immaculate.' I said immaculate, but I was deliberately exaggerating. Then he said, 'Block is sly, that's all. He's accumulated plenty of experience and knows how to delay proceedings. But there's more that he doesn't know than he does. What do you think he'd say if he learned his trial still hasn't begun, if you told him they haven't even rung the bell to announce the start of proceedings?' Alright Block, alright," said the lawyer, as at these words Block had begun to raise himself on his trembling knees and clearly wanted to plead for some explanation. It was the first time the lawyer had spoken any clear words directly to Block. He looked down with his tired eyes, half blankly and half at Block, who slowly sank back down on his knees under this gaze. "What the judge said has no meaning for you," said the lawyer. "You needn't be frightened at every word. If you do it again I won't tell you anything else at all. It's impossible to start a sentence without you looking at me as if you

were receiving your final judgement. You should be ashamed of yourself here in front of my client! And you're destroying the trust he has
for me. Just what is it you want? You're still alive, you're still under my
protection. There's no point in worrying! Somewhere you've read that
the final judgement can often come without warning, from anyone at
any time. And, in the right circumstances, that's basically true, but it's
also true that I dislike your anxiety and fear and see that you don't
have the trust in me you should have. Now what have I just said? I
repeated something said by one of the judges. You know that there are
so many various opinions about the procedure that they form into a
great big pile and nobody can make any sense of them. This judge, for
instance, sees proceedings as starting at a different point from where
I do. A difference of opinion, nothing more. At a certain stage in the
proceedings tradition has it that a sign is given by ringing a bell. This
judge sees that as the point at which proceedings begin. I can't set out
all the opinions opposed to that view here, and you wouldn't understand it anyway, suffice it to say that there are many reasons to disa-
gree with him." Embarrassed, Block ran his fingers through the pile
of the carpet, his anxiety about what the judge had said had let him
forget his inferior status towards the lawyer for a while, he thought
only about himself and turned the judges words round to examine
them from all sides. "Block," said Leni, as if reprimanding him, and,
taking hold of the collar of his coat, pulled him up slightly higher.
"Leave the carpet alone and listen to what the lawyer is saying."

[This chapter was left unfinished.]

In the Cathedral

A very important Italian business contact of the bank had come to visit the city for the first time and K. was given the task of showing him some of its cultural sights. At any other time he would have seen this job as an honour but now, when he was finding it hard even to maintain his current position in the bank, he accepted it only with reluctance. Every hour that he could not be in the office was a cause of concern for him, he was no longer able to make use of his time in the office anything like as well as he had previously, he spent many hours merely pretending to do important work, but that only increased his anxiety about not being in the office. Then he sometimes thought he saw the deputy director, who was always watching, come into K.'s office, sit at his desk, look through his papers, receive clients who had almost become old friends of K., and lure them away from him, perhaps he even discovered mistakes, mistakes that seemed to threaten K. from a thousand directions when he was at work now, and which he could no longer avoid. So now, if he was ever asked to leave the office on business or even needed to make a short business trip, however much an honour it seemed—and tasks of this sort happened to have increased substantially recently—there was always the suspicion that they wanted to get him out of his office for a while and check his work, or at least the idea that they thought he was dispensable. It would not have been difficult for him to turn down most of these jobs, but he did not dare to do so because, if his fears had the slightest foundation, turning the jobs down would have been an acknowledgement of them. For this reason, he never demurred from accepting them, and even when he was asked to go on a tiring business trip lasting two days he said nothing about having to go out in the rainy autumn weather when he had a severe chill, just in order to avoid the risk of not being asked to go. When, with a raging headache, he arrived back from this trip he learned that he had been chosen to accompany the Italian business contact the following day. The temptation for once to turn the job down was very great, especially as it had no direct connection with business, but there was no denying that social obligations towards this business contact were in themselves important enough, only not for K., who knew quite well that he needed some successes at work if he was to maintain his position there and that, if he failed in that, it would not help him even if this Italian somehow found him quite charming; he did not want to be removed from his workplace for even one day, as the fear of not being allowed back in was too great, he knew full well that the fear was exaggerated but it still made him anxious. However, in this case it was almost impossible to think of an acceptable excuse, his knowledge of Italian was not great but still good enough; the deciding factor was that K. had earlier known a little about art history and this had become widely known around the bank in extremely exaggerated form, and that K. had been a member of the Society for the Preservation of City Monuments, albeit only for business reasons. It was said that this Italian was an art lover, so the choice of K. to accompany him was a matter of course.

It was a very rainy and stormy morning when K., in a foul temper at the thought of the day ahead of him, arrived early at seven o'clock in the office so that he could at least do some work before his visitor would prevent him. He had spent half the night studying a book of Italian grammar so that he would be somewhat prepared and was very tired; his desk was less attractive to him than the window where he had spent far too much time sitting of late, but he resisted the temptation and sat down to his work. Unfortunately, just then the servitor came in and reported that the director had sent him to see whether the chief clerk was already in his office; if he was, then would he please be so kind as to come to his reception room as the gentleman from Italy was already there. "I'll come straight away," said K. He put a small dictionary in his pocket, took a guide to the city's tourist sites under his arm that he had compiled for strangers, and went through the deputy director's office into that of the director. He was glad he had come into the office so early and was able to be of service immediately, nobody could seriously have expected that of him. The deputy director's office was, of course, still as empty as the middle of the night, the servitor had probably been asked to summon him too but without success. As K. entered the reception room two men stood up from the deep armchairs where they had been sitting. The director gave him a friendly smile, he was clearly very glad that K. was there, he immediately introduced him to the Italian who shook K.'s hand vigorously and joked that somebody was an early riser. K. did not quite understand whom he had in mind, it was moreover an odd expression to use and it took K. a little while to guess its meaning. He replied with a few bland phrases which the Italian received once more with a laugh, passing his hand nervously and repeatedly over his blue-grey, bushy moustache. This moustache was obviously perfumed, it was almost tempting to come close to it and sniff. When they had all sat down and begun a light preliminary conversation, K. was disconcerted to notice that he understood no more than fragments of what the Italian said. When he spoke very calmly he understood almost everything, but that was very infrequent, mostly the words gushed from his mouth and he seemed to be enjoying himself so much his head shook. When he was talking in this way his speech was usually wrapped up in some kind of dialect which seemed to K. to have nothing to do with Italian but which the director not only understood but also spoke, although K. ought to have foreseen this as the Italian came from the south of his country where the director had also spent several years. Whatever the cause, K. realised that the possibility of communicating with the Italian had been largely taken from him, even his French was difficult to understand, and his moustache concealed the movements of his lips which might have offered some help in understanding what he said. K. began to anticipate many difficulties, he gave up trying to understand what the Italian said—with the director there, who could understand him so easily, it would have been pointless effort—and for the time being did no more than scowl at the Italian as he relaxed sitting deep but comfortable in the armchair, as he frequently pulled at his short, sharply tailored jacket and at one time lifted his arms in the air and moved his hands freely to try and depict something that K. could not grasp, even though he was leaning forward and did not let the hands out of his sight. K. had nothing to occupy himself but mechanically watch the exchange between the two men and his tiredness finally made itself felt, to his alarm, although fortunately in good time, he once caught himself nearly getting up, turning round and leaving. Eventually the Italian looked at the clock and jumped up. After taking his leave from the director he turned to K., pressing himself so close to him that K. had to push his chair back just so that he could move. The director had, no doubt, seen the anxiety in K.'s eyes as he tried to cope with this dialect of Italian, he joined in with this conversation in a way that was so adroit and unobtrusive that he seemed to be adding no more than minor comments, whereas in fact he was swiftly and patiently breaking into what the Italian said so that K. could understand. K. learned in this way that the Italian first had a few business matters to settle, that he unfortunately had only a little time at his disposal, that he certainly did not intend to rush round to see every monument in the city, that he would much rather—at least as long as K. would agree, it was entirely his decision—just see the cathedral and to do so thoroughly. He was extremely pleased to be accompanied by someone who was so learned and so pleasant—by this he meant K., who was occupied not with listening to the Italian but the director—and asked if he would be so kind, if the time was suitable, to meet him in the cathedral in two hours' time at about ten o'clock. He hoped he would certainly be able to be there at that time. K. made an appropriate reply, the Italian shook first the director's hand and then K.'s, then the director's again and went to the door, half turned to the two men who followed him and continuing to talk without a break. K. remained together with the director for a short while, although the director looked especially unhappy today. He thought he needed to apologise to K. for something and told him— they were standing intimately close together—he had thought at first he would accompany the Italian himself, but then—he gave no more precise reason than this—then he decided it would be better to send K. with him. He should not be surprised if he could not understand the Italian at first, he would be able to very soon, and even if he really could not understand very much he said it was not so bad, as it was really not so important for the Italian to be understood. And anyway, K.'s knowledge of Italian was surprisingly good, the director was sure he would get by very well. And with that, it was time for K. to go. He spent the time still remaining to him with a dictionary, copying out obscure words he would need to guide the Italian round the cathedral. It was an extremely irksome task, servitors brought him the mail, bank staff came with various queries and, when they saw that K. was busy, stood by the door and did not go away until he had listened to them, the deputy director did not miss the opportunity to disturb K. and came in frequently, took the dictionary from his hand and flicked through its pages, clearly for no purpose, when the door to the anteroom opened even clients would appear from the half darkness and bow timidly to him—they wanted to attract his attention but were not sure whether he had seen them—all this activity was circling around

K. with him at its centre while he compiled the list of words he would need, then looked them up in the dictionary, then wrote them out, then practised their pronunciation and finally tried to learn them by heart. The good intentions he had had earlier, though, seemed to have left him completely, it was the Italian who had caused him all this effort and sometimes he became so angry with him that he buried the dictionary under some papers firmly intending to do no more preparation, but then he realised he could not walk up and down in the cathedral with the Italian without saying a word, so, in an even greater rage, he pulled the dictionary back out again.

At exactly half past nine, just when he was about to leave, there was a telephone call for him, Leni wished him good morning and asked how he was, K. thanked her hurriedly and told her it was impossible for him to talk now as he had to go to the cathedral. "To the cathedral?" asked Leni. "Yes, to the cathedral." "What do you have to go to the cathedral for?" said Leni. K. tried to explain it to her briefly, but he had hardly begun when Leni suddenly said, "They're harassing you." One thing that K. could not bear was pity that he had not wanted or expected, he took his leave of her with two words, but as he put the receiver back in its place he said, half to himself and half to the girl on the other end of the line who could no longer hear him, "Yes, they're harassing me."

By now the time was late and there was almost a danger he would not be on time. He took a taxi to the cathedral, at the last moment he had remembered the album that he had had no opportunity to give to the Italian earlier and so took it with him now. He held it on his knees and drummed impatiently on it during the whole journey. The rain had eased off slightly but it was still damp chilly and dark, it would be difficult to see anything in the cathedral but standing about on cold flagstones might well make K.'s chill much worse. The square in front of the cathedral was quite empty, K. remembered how even as a small child he had noticed that nearly all the houses in this narrow square had the curtains at their windows closed most of the time, although today, with the weather like this, it was more understandable. The cathedral also seemed quite empty, of course no one would think of going there on a day like this. K. hurried along both the side naves but saw no one but an old woman who, wrapped up in a warm shawl, was kneeling at a picture of the Virgin Mary and staring up at it. Then, in the distance, he saw a church official who limped away through a doorway in the wall. K. had arrived on time, it had struck ten just as he was entering the building, but the Italian still was not there. K. went back to the main entrance, stood there indecisively for a while, and then walked round the cathedral in the rain in case the Italian was waiting at another entrance. He was nowhere to be found. Could the director have misunderstood what time they had agreed on? How could anyone understand someone like that properly anyway? Whatever had happened, K. would have to wait for him for at least half an hour. As he was tired he wanted to sit down, he went back inside the cathedral, he found something like a small carpet on one of the steps, he moved it with his foot to a nearby pew, wrapped himself up tighter in his coat, put the collar up and sat down. To pass the time he opened the album and flicked through the pages a little but soon had to give up as it became so dark that when he looked up he could hardly make out anything in the side nave next to him.

In the distance there was a large triangle of candles flickering on the main altar, K. was not certain whether he had seen them earlier. Perhaps they had only just been lit. Church staff creep silently as part of their job, you don't notice them. When K. happened to turn round he also saw a tall, stout candle attached to a column not far behind him. It was all very pretty, but totally inadequate to illuminate the pictures which were usually left in the darkness of the side altars, and seemed to make the darkness all the deeper. It was discourteous of the Italian not to come but it was also sensible of him, there would have been nothing to see, they would have had to content themselves with seeking out a few pictures with K.'s electric pocket torch and looking at them one small part at a time. K. went over to a nearby side chapel to see what they could have hoped for, he went up a few steps to a low marble railing and leant over it to look at the altar picture by the light of his torch. The eternal light hung disturbingly in front of it. The first thing that K. partly saw and partly guessed at was a large knight in armour who was shown at the far edge of the painting. He was leaning on his sword that he had stuck into the naked ground in front of him where only a few blades of grass grew here and there. He seemed to be paying close attention to something that was being played out in front of him. It was astonishing to see how he stood there without going any closer. Perhaps it was his job to stand guard. It was a long time since K. had looked at any pictures and he studied the knight for a long time even though he had continually to blink as he found it difficult to bear the green light of his torch. Then when he moved the light to the other parts of the picture he found an interment of Christ shown in the usual way, it was also a comparatively new painting. He put his torch away and went back to his place.

There seemed to be no point in waiting for the Italian any longer, but outside it was certainly raining heavily, and as it was not so cold in the cathedral as K. had expected he decided to stay there for the time being. Close by him was the great pulpit, there were two plain golden crosses attached to its little round roof which were lying almost flat and whose tips crossed over each other. The outside of the pulpit's balustrade was covered in green foliage which continued down to the column supporting it, little angels could be seen among the leaves, some of them lively and some of them still. K. walked up to the pulpit and examined it from all sides, its stonework had been sculpted with great care, it seemed as if the foliage had trapped a deep darkness between and behind its leaves and held it there prisoner, K. lay his hand in one of these gaps and cautiously felt the stone, until then he had been totally unaware of this pulpit's existence. Then K. happened to notice one of the church staff standing behind the next row of pews, he wore a loose, creased, black cassock, he held a snuff box in his left hand and he was watching K. Now what does he want? thought K. Do I seem suspicious to him? Does he want a tip? But when the man in the cassock saw that K. had noticed him he raised his right hand, a pinch of snuff still held between two fingers, and pointed in some vague direction. It was almost impossible to understand what this behaviour meant, K. waited a while longer but the man in the cassock did not stop gesturing with his hand and even augmented it by nodding his head. "Now what does he want?" asked K. quietly, he did not dare call out loud here; but then he drew out his purse and pushed his way through the nearest pews to reach the man. He, however, immediately gestured to turn down this offer, shrugged his shoulders and limped away. As a child K. had imitated riding on a horse with the same sort of movement as this limp. "This old man is like a child," thought K., "he doesn't have the sense for anything more than serving in a church. Look at the way he stops when I stop, and how he waits to see whether I'll continue." With a smile, K. followed the old man all the way up the side nave and almost as far as the main altar, all this time the old man continued to point at something but K. deliberately avoided looking round, he was only pointing in order to make it harder for K. to follow him. Eventually, K. did stop follow-

ing, he did not want to worry the old man too much, and he also did
not want to frighten him away completely in case the Italian turned
up after all.

When he entered the central nave to go back to where he had left
the album, he noticed a small secondary pulpit on a column almost
next to the stalls by the altar where the choir sat. It was very simple,
made of plain white stone, and so small that from a distance it looked
like an empty niche where the statue of a saint ought to have been.
It certainly would have been impossible for the priest to take a full
step back from the balustrade, and, although there was no decoration
on it, the top of the pulpit curved in exceptionally low so that a man
of average height would not be able stand upright and would have to
remain bent forward over the balustrade. In all, it looked as if it had
been intended to make the priest suffer, it was impossible to understand why this pulpit would be needed as there were also the other
ones available which were large and so artistically decorated.

And K. would certainly not have noticed this little pulpit if there
had not been a lamp fastened above it, which usually meant there
was a sermon about to be given. So was a sermon to be given now? In
this empty church? K. looked down at the steps which, pressed close
against the column, led up to the pulpit. They were so narrow they
seemed to be there as decoration on the column rather than for anyone to use. But under the pulpit—K. grinned in astonishment—there
really was a priest standing with his hand on the handrail ready to
climb the steps and looking at K. Then he nodded very slightly, so that
K. crossed himself and genuflected as he should have done earlier.
With a little swing, the priest went up into the pulpit with short fast
steps. Was there really a sermon about to begin? Maybe the man in
the cassock had not been really so demented, and had meant to lead
K.'s way to the preacher, which in this empty church would have been
very necessary. And there was also, somewhere in front of a picture
of the Virgin Mary, an old woman who should have come to hear the
sermon. And if there was to be a sermon why had it not been introduced on the organ? But the organ remained quiet and merely looked
out weakly from the darkness of its great height.

K. now considered whether he should leave as quickly as possible,
if he did not do it now there would be no chance of doing so during
the sermon and he would have to stay there for as long as it lasted, he
had lost so much time when he should have been in his office, there
had long been no need for him to wait for the Italian any longer, he

looked at his watch, it was eleven. But could there really be a sermon given? Could K. constitute the entire congregation? How could he when he was just a stranger who wanted to look at the church? That, basically, was all he was. The idea of a sermon, now, at eleven o'clock, on a workday, in hideous weather, was nonsense. The priest—there was no doubt that he was a priest, a young man with a smooth, dark face—was clearly going up there just to put the lamp out after somebody had lit it by mistake.

But there had been no mistake, the priest seemed rather to check that the lamp was lit and turned it a little higher, then he slowly turned to face the front and leant down on the balustrade gripping its angular rail with both hands. He stood there like that for a while and, without turning his head, looked around. K. had moved back a long way and leant his elbows on the front pew. Somewhere in the church—he could not have said exactly where—he could make out the man in the cassock hunched under his bent back and at peace, as if his work were completed. In the cathedral it was now very quiet! But K. would have to disturb that silence, he had no intention of staying there; if it was the priest's duty to preach at a certain time regardless of the circumstances then he could, and he could do it without K.'s taking part, and K.'s presence would do nothing to augment the effect of it. So K. began slowly to move, felt his way on tiptoe along the pew, arrived at the broad aisle and went along it without being disturbed, except for the sound of his steps, however light, which rang out on the stone floor and resounded from the vaulting, quiet but continuous at a repeating, regular pace. K. felt slightly abandoned as, probably observed by the priest, he walked by himself between the empty pews, and the size of the cathedral seemed to be just at the limit of what a man could bear. When he arrived back at where he had been sitting he did not hesitate but simply reached out for the album he had left there and took it with him. He had nearly left the area covered by pews and was close to the empty space between himself and the exit when, for the first time, he heard the voice of the priest. A powerful and experienced voice. It pierced through the reaches of the cathedral ready waiting for it! But the priest was not calling out to the congregation, his cry was quite unambiguous and there was no escape from it, he called "Josef K.!"

K. stood still and looked down at the floor. In theory he was still free, he could have carried on walking, through one of three dark little wooden doors not far in front of him and away from there. It would simply mean he had not understood, or that he had understood but chose not to pay attention to it. But if he once turned round he would be trapped, then he would have acknowledged that he had understood perfectly well, that he really was the Josef K. the priest had called to and that he was willing to follow. If the priest had called out again K. would certainly have carried on out the door, but everything was silent as K. also waited, he turned his head slightly as he wanted to see what the priest was doing now. He was merely standing in the pulpit as before, but it was obvious that he had seen K. turn his head. If K. did not now turn round completely it would have been like a child playing hide and seek. He did so, and the priest beckoned him with his finger. As everything could now be done openly he ran—because of curiosity and the wish to get it over with—with long flying leaps towards the pulpit. At the front pews he stopped, but to the priest he still seemed too far away, he reached out his hand and pointed sharply down with his finger to a place immediately in front of the pulpit. And K. did as he was told, standing in that place he had to bend his head a long way back just to see the priest. "You are Josef K.," said the priest, and raised his hand from the balustrade to make a gesture whose meaning was unclear. "Yes," said K., he considered how freely he had always given his name in the past, for some time now it had been a burden to him, now there were people who knew his name whom he had never seen before, it had been so nice first to introduce yourself and only then for people to know who you were. "You have been accused," said the priest, especially gently. "Yes," said K., "so I have been informed." "Then you are the one I am looking for," said the priest. "I am the prison chaplain." "I see," said K. "I had you summoned here," said the priest, "because I wanted to speak to you." "I knew nothing of that," said K. "I came here to show the cathedral to a gentleman from Italy." "That is beside the point," said the priest. "What are you holding in your hand? Is it a prayer book?" "No," answered K., "it's an album of the city's tourist sights." "Put it down," said the priest. K. threw it away with such force that it flapped open and rolled across the floor, tearing its pages. "Do you know your case is going badly?" asked the priest. "That's how it seems to me too," said K. "I've expended a lot of effort on it, but so far with no result. Although I do still have some documents to submit." "How do you imagine it will end?" asked the priest. "At first I thought it was bound to end well," said K., "but now I have my doubts about it. I don't know how it will end. Do you know?" "I don't," said the priest, "but I fear it will end badly. You are considered guilty. Your case will probably not even go beyond a minor court. Provisionally at least, your guilt is seen as proven." "But I'm not guilty," said K., "there's been a mistake. How is it even possible for someone to be guilty. We're all human beings here, one like the other." "That is true," said the priest, "but that is how the guilty speak." "Do you presume I'm guilty too?" asked K. "I make no presumptions about you," said the priest. "I thank you for that," said K. "but everyone else involved in these proceedings has something against me and presumes I'm guilty. They even influence those who aren't involved. My position gets harder all the time." "You don't understand the facts," said the priest, "the verdict does not come suddenly, proceedings continue until a verdict is reached gradually." "I see," said K., lowering his head. "What do you intend to do about your case next?" asked the priest. "I still need to find help," said K., raising his head to see what the priest thought of this. "There are still certain possibilities I haven't yet made use of." "You look for too much help from people you don't know," said the priest disapprovingly, "and especially from women. Can you really not see that's not the help you need?" "Sometimes, in fact quite often, I could believe you're right," said K., "but not always. Women have a lot of power. If I could persuade some of the women I know to work together with me then I would be certain to succeed. Especially in a court like this that seems to consist of nothing but woman-chasers. Show the examining judge a woman in the distance and he'll run right over the desk, and the accused, just to get to her as soon as he can." The priest lowered his head down to the balustrade, only now did the roof over the pulpit seem to press him down. What sort of dreadful weather could it be outside? It was no longer just a dull day, it was deepest night. None of the stained glass in the main window shed even a flicker of light on the darkness of the walls. And this was the moment when the man in the cassock chose to put out the candles on the main altar, one by one. "Are you cross with me?" asked K. "Maybe you don't know what sort of court it is you serve." He received no answer. "Well, it's just my own experience," said K. Above him there was still silence. "I didn't mean to insult you," said K. At that, the priest screamed down at K.: "Can you not see two steps in front of you?" He shouted in anger, but it was also the scream of one who sees another fall and, shocked and without thinking, screams against his own will.

The two men, then, remained silent for a long time. In the darkness beneath him, the priest could not possibly have seen K. distinctly, although K. was able to see him clearly by the light of the little lamp. Why did the priest not come down? He had not given a sermon, he had only told K. a few things which, if he followed them closely, would probably cause him more harm than good. But the priest certainly seemed to mean well, it might even be possible, if he would come down and cooperate with him, it might even be possible for him to obtain some acceptable piece of advice that could make all the difference, it might, for instance, be able to show him not so much to influence the proceedings but how to break free of them, how to evade them, how to live away from them. K. had to admit that this was something he had had on his mind quite a lot of late. If the priest knew of such a possibility he might, if K. asked him, let him know about it, even though he was part of the court himself and even though, when K. had criticised the court, he had held down his gentle nature and actually shouted at K.

"Would you not like to come down here?" asked K. "If you're not going to give a sermon come down here with me." "Now I can come down," said the priest, perhaps he regretted having shouted at K. As he took down the lamp from its hook he said, "to start off with I had to speak to you from a distance. Otherwise I'm too easily influenced and forget my duty."

K. waited for him at the foot of the steps. While he was still on one of the higher steps as he came down them the priest reached out his hand for K. to shake. "Can you spare me a little of your time?" asked K. "As much time as you need," said the priest, and passed him the little lamp for him to carry. Even at close distance the priest did not lose a certain solemnity that seemed to be part of his character. "You are very friendly towards me," said K., as they walked up and down beside each other in the darkness of one of the side naves. "That makes you an exception among all those who belong to the court. I can trust you more than any of the others I've seen. I can speak openly with you." "Don't fool yourself," said the priest. "How would I be fooling myself?" asked K. "You fool yourself in the court," said the priest, "it talks about this self-deceit in the opening paragraphs to the law. In front of the law there is a doorkeeper. A man from the countryside comes up to the door and asks for entry. But the doorkeeper says he can't let him in to the law right now. The man thinks about this, and then he asks if he'll be able to go in later on. 'That's possible,' says the doorkeeper, 'but not now.' The gateway to the law is open as it always is, and the doorkeeper has stepped to one side, so the man bends over to try and see in. When the doorkeeper notices this he laughs and says, 'If you're tempted give it a try, try and go in even though I say you can't. Careful though: I'm powerful. And I'm only the lowliest of all the doormen. But there's a doorkeeper for each of the rooms and each of them is more powerful than the last. It's more than I can stand just to look at the third one.' The man from the country had not expected difficulties like this, the law was supposed to be accessible for anyone at any time, he thinks, but now he looks more closely at the doorkeeper in his fur coat, sees his big hooked nose, his long thin tartar-beard, and he decides it's better to wait until he has permission to enter. The doorkeeper gives him a stool and lets him sit down to one side of the gate. He sits there for days and years. He tries to be allowed in time and again and tires the doorkeeper with his requests. The doorkeeper often questions him, asking about where he's from and many other things, but these are disinterested questions such as great men ask, and he always ends up by telling him he still can't let him in. The man had come well equipped for his journey, and uses everything, however valuable, to bribe the doorkeeper. He accepts everything, but as he does so he says, 'I'll only accept this so that you don't think there's anything you've failed to do.' Over many years, the man watches the doorkeeper almost without a break. He forgets about the other doormen, and begins to think this one is the only thing stopping him from gaining access to the law. Over the first few years he curses his unhappy condition out loud, but later, as he becomes old, he just grumbles to himself. He becomes senile, and as he has come to know even the fleas in the doorkeeper's fur collar over the years that he has been studying him he even asks them to help him and change the doorkeeper's mind. Finally his eyes grow dim, and he no longer knows whether it's really getting darker or just his eyes that are deceiving him. But he seems now to see an inextinguishable light begin to shine from the darkness behind the door. He doesn't have long to live now. Just before he dies, he brings together all his experience from all this time into one question which he has still never put to the doorkeeper. He beckons to him, as he's no longer able to raise his stiff body. The doorkeeper has to bend over deeply as the difference in their sizes has changed very much to the disadvantage of the man. 'What is it you want to know now?' asks the doorkeeper, 'You're insatiable.' 'Everyone wants access to the law,' says the man, 'how come, over all these years, no one but me has asked to be let in?' The doorkeeper can see the man's come to his end, his hearing has faded, and so, so that he can be heard, he shouts to him: 'Nobody else could have got in this way, as this entrance was meant only for you. Now I'll go and close it.'"

"So the doorkeeper cheated the man," said K. immediately, who had been captivated by the story. "Don't be too quick," said the priest, "don't take somebody else's opinion without checking it. I told you the story exactly as it was written. There's nothing in there about cheating." "But it's quite clear," said K., "and your first interpretation of it was quite correct. The doorkeeper gave him the information that would release him only when it could be of no more use." "He didn't ask him before that," said the priest, "and don't forget he was only a doorkeeper, and as doorkeeper he did his duty." "What makes you think he did his duty?" asked K., "He didn't. It might have been his duty to keep everyone else away, but this man is who the door was intended for and he ought to have let him in." "You're not paying enough attention to what was written and you're changing the story," said the priest. "According to the story, there are two important things that the doorkeeper explains about access to the law, one at the beginning, one at the end. At one place he says he can't allow him in now, and at the other he says this entrance was intended for him alone. If one of the statements contradicted the other you would be right and the doorkeeper would have cheated the man from the country. But there is no contradiction. On the contrary, the first statement even hints at the second. You could almost say the doorkeeper went beyond his duty in that he offered the man some prospect of being admitted in the future. Throughout the story, his duty seems to have been merely to turn the man away, and there are many commentators who are surprised that the doorkeeper offered this hint at all, as he seems to love exactitude and keeps strict guard over his position. He stays at his post for many years and doesn't close the gate until the very end, he's very conscious of the importance of his service, as he says, 'I'm powerful,' he has respect for his superiors, as he says, 'I'm only the lowliest of the doormen,' he's not talkative, as through all these years the only questions he asks are 'disinterested,' he's not corruptible, as when he's offered a gift he says, 'I'll only accept this so that you don't think there's anything you've failed to do,' as far as fulfilling his duty goes he can be neither ruffled nor begged, as it says about the man that, 'he tires the doorkeeper with his requests,' even his external appearance suggests a pedantic character, the big hooked nose and the long, thin, black tartar-beard. How could any doorkeeper be more faithful to his duty? But in the doorkeeper's character there are also other features which might be very useful for those who seek entry to the law, and when he hinted at some possibility in the future it always seemed to make it clear that he might even go beyond his duty. There's no denying he's a little simple minded, and that makes him a little conceited. Even if all he said about his power and the power of the other doorkeepers and how not even he could bear the sight of them— I say even if all these assertions are right, the way he makes them shows that he's too simple and arrogant to understand properly. The commentators say about this that, 'correct understanding of a matter and a misunderstanding of the same matter are not mutually exclusive.' Whether they're right or not, you have to concede that his simplicity and arrogance, however little they show, do weaken his function of guarding the entrance, they are defects in the doorkeeper's character. You also have to consider that the doorkeeper seems to be friendly by nature, he isn't always just an official. He makes a joke right at the beginning, in that he invites the man to enter at the same time as maintaining the ban on his entering, and then he doesn't send him away but gives him, as it says in the text, a stool to sit on and lets him stay by the side of the door. The patience with which he puts up with the man's requests through all these years, the little questioning sessions, accepting the gifts, his politeness when he puts up with the man cursing his fate even though it was the doorkeeper who caused that fate—all these things seem to want to arouse our sympathy. Not every doorkeeper would have behaved in the same way. And finally, he lets the man beckon him and he bends deep down to him so that he can put his last question. There's no more than some slight impatience— the doorkeeper knows everything's come to its end—shown in the words, 'You're insatiable.' There are many commentators who go even further in explaining it in this way and think the words, 'you're insatiable' are an expression of friendly admiration, albeit with some condescension. However you look at it the figure of the doorkeeper comes out differently from how you might think." "You know the story better than I do and you've known it for longer," said K. They were silent for a while. And then K. said, "So you think the man was not cheated, do you?" "Don't get me wrong," said the priest, "I'm just pointing out the different opinions about it. You shouldn't pay too much attention to people's opinions. The text cannot be altered, and the various opinions are often no more than an expression of despair over it. There's even one opinion which says it's the doorkeeper who's been cheated."

"That does seem to take things too far," said K. "How can they argue the doorkeeper has been cheated?" "Their argument," answered the priest, "is based on the simplicity of the doorkeeper. They say the doorkeeper doesn't know the inside of the law, only the way into it where he just walks up and down. They see his ideas of what's inside the law as rather childish, and suppose he's afraid himself of what he wants to make the man frightened of. Yes, he's more afraid of it than the man, as the man wants nothing but to go inside the law, even after he's heard about the terrible doormen there, in contrast to the door-keeper who doesn't want to go in, or at least we don't hear anything about it. On the other hand, there are those who say he must have already been inside the law as he has been taken on into its service and that could only have been done inside. That can be countered by supposing he could have been given the job of doorkeeper by some-body calling out from inside, and that he can't have gone very far inside as he couldn't bear the sight of the third doorkeeper. Nor, through all those years, does the story say the doorkeeper told the man anything about the inside, other than his comment about the other doorkeepers. He could have been forbidden to do so, but he hasn't said anything about that either. All this seems to show he doesn't know anything about what the inside looks like or what it means, and that that's why he's being deceived. But he's also being deceived by the man from the country as he's this man's subordinate and doesn't know it. There's a lot to indicate that he treats the man as his subordinate, I expect you remember, but those who hold this view would say it's very clear that he really is his subordinate. Above all, the free man is superior to the man who has to serve another. Now, the man really is free, he can go wherever he wants, the only thing forbidden to him is entry into the law and, what's more, there's only one man forbidding him to do so—the doorkeeper. If he takes the stool and sits down beside the door and stays there all his life he does this of his own free will, there's nothing in the story to say he was forced to do it. On the other hand, the doorkeeper is kept to his post by his employment, he's not allowed to go away from it and it seems he's not allowed to go inside either, not even if he wanted to. Also, although he's in the service of the law he's only there for this one entrance, therefore he's there only in the service of this one man who the door's intended for. This is another way in which he's his subordinate. We can take it that he's been performing this somewhat empty service for many years, through the whole of a man's life, as it says that a man will come, that means someone old enough to be a man. That means the doorkeeper will have to wait a long time before his function is fulfilled, he will have to wait for as long as the man liked, who came to the door of his own free will. Even the end of the doorkeeper's service is determined by when the man's life ends, so the doorkeeper remains his subordinate right to the end. And it's pointed out repeatedly that the doorkeeper seems to know nothing of any of this, although this is not seen as anything remarkable, as those who hold this view see the doorkeeper as deluded in a way that's far worse, a way that's to do with his service. At the end, speaking about the entrance he says, 'Now I'll go and close it,' although at the beginning of the story it says the door to the law is open as it always is, but if it's always open—always—that means it's open independently of the lifespan of the man it's intended for, and not even the doorkeeper will be able to close it. There are various opinions about this, some say the doorkeeper was only answering a question or showing his devotion to duty or, just when the man was in his last moments, the doorkeeper wanted to cause him regret and sorrow. There are many who agree that he wouldn't be able to close the door. They even believe, at the end at least, the doorkeeper is aware, deep down, that he's the man's subordinate, as the man sees the light that shines out of the entry to the law whereas the doorkeeper would probably have his back to it and says nothing at all to show there's been any change." "That is well substantiated," said K., who had been repeating some parts of the priest's explanation to himself in a whisper. "It is well substantiated, and now I too think the doorkeeper must have been deceived. Although that does not mean I've abandoned what I thought earlier as the two versions are, to some extent, not incompatible. It's not clear whether the doorkeeper sees clearly or is deceived. I said the man had been cheated. If the doorkeeper understands clearly, then there could be some doubt about it, but if the doorkeeper has been deceived then the man is bound to believe the same thing. That would mean the doorkeeper is not a cheat but so simple-minded that he ought to be dismissed from his job immediately; if the doorkeeper is mistaken it will do him no harm but the man will be harmed immensely." "There you've found another opinion," said the priest, "as there are many who say the story doesn't give anyone the right to judge the doorkeeper. However he might seem to us he is still in the service of the law, so he belongs to the law, so he's beyond what man has a right to judge. In this case we can't believe the doorkeeper is the man's subordinate. Even if he has to stay at the entrance into the law his service makes him incomparably more than if he lived freely in the world. The man has come to the law for the first time and the doorkeeper is already there. He's been given his position by the law, to doubt his worth would be to doubt the law." "I can't say I'm in complete agreement with this view," said K. shaking his head, "as if you accept it you'll have to accept that everything said by the doorkeeper is true. But you've already explained very fully that that's not possible." "No," said the priest, "you don't need to accept everything as true, you only have to accept it as necessary." "Depressing view," said K. "The lie made into the rule of the world."

K. said that as if it were his final word but it was not his conclusion. He was too tired to think about all the ramifications of the story, and the sort of thoughts they led him into were not familiar to him, unrealistic things, things better suited for officials of the court to discuss than for him. The simple story had lost its shape, he wanted to shake it off, and the priest who now felt quite compassionate allowed this and accepted K.'s remarks without comment, even though his view was certainly very different from K.'s.

In silence, they carried on walking for some time, K. stayed close beside the priest without knowing where he was. The lamp in his hand had long since gone out. Once, just in front of him, he thought he could see the statue of a saint by the glitter of the silver on it, although it quickly disappeared back into the darkness. So that he would not remain entirely dependent on the priest, K. asked him, "We're now near the main entrance, are we?" "No," said the priest, "we're a long way from it. Do you already want to go?" K. had not thought of going until then, but he immediately said, "Yes, certainly, I have to go. I'm the chief clerk in a bank and there are people waiting for me, I only came here to show a foreign business contact round the cathedral." "Alright," said the priest offering him his hand, "go then." "But I can't find my way round in this darkness by myself," said K. "Go to your left as far as the wall," said the priest, "then continue alongside the wall without leaving it and you'll find a way out." The priest had only gone a few paces from him, but K. was already shouting loudly, "Please, wait!" "I'm waiting," said the priest. "Is there anything else you want from me?" asked K. "No," said the priest. "You were so friendly to me earlier on," said K., "and you explained everything, but now you abandon me as if I were nothing to you." "You have to go," said the priest. "Well, yes," said K., "you need to understand that." "First, you need to understand who I am," said the priest. "You're the prison chaplain," said K., and went closer to the priest, it was not so important for him to go straight back to the bank as he had made out, he could very well stay where he was. "So that means I belong to the court," said the priest. "So why would I want anything from you? the court doesn't want anything from you. It accepts you when you come and it lets you go when you leave."

10

End

The evening before K.'s thirty-first birthday—it was about nine o'clock in the evening, the time when the streets were quiet—two men came to where he lived. In frockcoats, pale and fat, wearing top hats that looked like they could not be taken off their heads. After some brief formalities at the door of the flat when they first arrived, the same formalities were repeated at greater length at K.'s door. He had not been notified they would be coming, but K. sat in a chair near the door, dressed in black as they were, and slowly put on new gloves which stretched tightly over his fingers and behaved as if he were expecting visitors. He immediately stood up and looked at the gentlemen inquisitively. "You've come for me then, have you?" he asked. The gentlemen nodded, one of them indicated the other with the top hat now in his hand. K. told them he had been expecting a different visitor. He went to the window and looked once more down at the dark street. Most of the windows on the other side of the street were also dark already, many of them had the curtains closed. In one of the windows on the same floor where there was a light on, two small children could be seen playing with each other inside a playpen, unable to move from where they were, reaching out for each other with their little hands. "Some ancient, unimportant actors—that's what they've sent for me," said K. to himself, and looked round once again to confirm this to himself. "They want to sort me out as cheaply as they can." K. suddenly turned round to face the two men and asked, "What theatre do you play in?" "Theatre?" asked one of the gentlemen, turning to the other for assistance and pulling in the corners of his mouth. The other made a gesture like someone who was dumb, as if he were struggling with some organism causing him trouble. "You're not properly prepared to answer questions," said K. and went to fetch his hat.

As soon as they were on the stairs the gentlemen wanted to take

K.'s arms, but K. said "Wait till we're in the street, I'm not ill." But they waited only until the front door before they took his arms in a way that K. had never experienced before. They kept their shoulders close behind his, did not turn their arms in but twisted them around the entire length of K.'s arms and took hold of his hands with a grasp that was formal, experienced and could not be resisted. K. was held stiff and upright between them, they formed now a single unit so that if any one of them had been knocked down all of them must have fallen. They formed a unit of the sort that normally can be formed only by matter that is lifeless.

Whenever they passed under a lamp K. tried to see his companions more clearly, as far as was possible when they were pressed so close together, as in the dim light of his room this had been hardly possible. "Maybe they're tenors," he thought as he saw their big double chins. The cleanliness of their faces disgusted him. He could see the hands that cleaned them, passing over the corners of their eyes, rubbing at their upper lips, scratching out the creases on those chins.

When K. noticed that, he stopped, which meant the others had to stop too; they were at the edge of an open square, devoid of people but decorated with flower-beds. "Why did they send you, of all people!" he cried out, more a shout than a question. The two gentleman clearly knew no answer to give, they waited, their free arms hanging down, like nurses when the patient needs to rest. "I will go no further," said K. as if to see what would happen. The gentlemen did not need to make any answer, it was enough that they did not loosen their grip on K. and tried to move him on, but K. resisted them. "I'll soon have no need of much strength, I'll use all of it now," he thought. He thought of the flies that tear their legs off struggling to get free of the flypaper. "These gentleman will have some hard work to do."

Just then, Miss Bürstner came up into the square in front of them from the steps leading from a small street at a lower level. It was not certain that it was her, although the similarity was, of course, great. But it did not matter to K. whether it was certainly her anyway, he just became suddenly aware that there was no point in his resistance. There would be nothing heroic about it if he resisted, if he now caused trouble for these gentlemen, if in defending himself he sought to enjoy his last glimmer of life. He started walking, which pleased the gentlemen and some of their pleasure conveyed itself to him. Now they permitted him to decide which direction they took, and he decided to take the direction that followed the young woman in front of them, not so much because he wanted to catch up with her, nor even because he wanted to keep her in sight for as long as possible, but only so that he would not forget the reproach she represented for him. "The only thing I can do now," he said to himself, and his thought was confirmed by the equal length of his own steps with the steps of the two others, "the only thing I can do now is keep my common sense and do what's needed right till the end. I always wanted to go at the world and try and do too much, and even to do it for something that was not too cheap. That was wrong of me. Should I now show them I learned nothing from facing trial for a year? Should I go out like someone stupid? Should I let anyone say, after I'm gone, that at the start of the proceedings I wanted to end them, and that now that they've ended I want to start them again? I don't want anyone to say that. I'm grateful they sent these unspeaking, uncomprehending men to go with me on this journey, and that it's been left up to me to say what's necessary."

Meanwhile, the young woman had turned off into a side street, but K. could do without her now and let his companions lead him. All three of them now, in complete agreement, went over a bridge in the light of the moon, the two gentlemen were willing to yield to each little movement made by K. as he moved slightly towards the edge and directed the group in that direction as a single unit. The moonlight glittered and quivered in the water, which divided itself around a small island covered in a densely piled mass of foliage and trees and bushes. Beneath them, now invisible, there were gravel paths with comfortable benches where K. had stretched himself out on many summer's days. "I didn't actually want to stop here," he said to his companions, shamed by their compliance with his wishes. Behind K.'s back one of them seemed to quietly criticise the other for the misunderstanding about stopping, and then they went on. The went on up through several streets where policemen were walking or standing here and there; some in the distance and then some very close. One of them with a bushy moustache, his hand on the grip of his sword, seemed to have some purpose in approaching the group, which was hardly unsuspicious. The two gentlemen stopped, the policeman seemed about to open his mouth, and then K. drove his group forcefully forward. Several times he looked back cautiously to see if the policeman was following; but when they had a corner between themselves and the policeman K. began to run, and the two gentlemen, despite being seriously short of breath, had to run with him.

In this way they quickly left the built up area and found themselves in the fields which, in this part of town, began almost without any transition zone. There was a quarry, empty and abandoned, near a building that was still like those in the city. Here the men stopped, perhaps because this had always been their destination, or perhaps because they were too exhausted to run any further. Here they released their hold on K., who just waited in silence, and took their top hats off while they looked round the quarry and wiped the sweat off their brows with their handkerchiefs. The moonlight lay everywhere with the natural peace that is granted to no other light.

After exchanging a few courtesies about who was to carry out the next tasks—the gentlemen did not seem to have been allocated specific functions—one of them went to K. and took off his coat, his waistcoat, and finally his shirt. K. made an involuntary shiver, at which the gentleman gave him a gentle, reassuring tap on the back. Then he carefully folded the things up as if they would still be needed, even if not in the near future. He did not want to expose K. to the chilly night air without moving though, so he took him under the arm and walked up and down with him a little way while the other gentleman looked round the quarry for a suitable place. When he had found it he made a sign and the other gentleman escorted him there. It was near the rockface, there was a stone lying there that had broken loose. The gentlemen sat K. down on the ground, leant him against the stone and settled his head down on the top of it. Despite all the effort they went to, and despite all the co-operation shown by K., his demeanour seemed very forced and hard to believe. So one of the gentlemen asked the other to grant him a short time while he put K. in position by himself, but even that did nothing to make it better. In the end they left K. in a position that was far from the best of the ones they had tried so far. Then one of the gentlemen opened his frockcoat and from a sheath hanging on a belt stretched across his waistcoat he withdrew a long, thin, double-edged butcher's knife, which he held up in the light to test its sharpness. The repulsive courtesies began once again, one of them passed the knife over K. to the other, who then passed it back over K. to the first. K. now knew it would be his duty to take the knife as it passed from hand to hand above him and thrust it into himself. But he did not do it, instead he twisted his neck, which was still free, and looked around. He was not able to show his full worth, was not able to take all the work from the official bodies, he lacked the rest of the strength he needed and this final shortcoming was the fault of whoever had denied it to him. As he looked round, he saw the top floor of the building next to the quarry. He saw how a light flickered on and the two halves of a window opened out, then somebody, made weak and thin by the height and the distance, leant suddenly far out from it and stretched his arms out even further. Who was that? A friend? A good person? Somebody who was taking part? Somebody who wanted to help? Was he alone? Was it everyone? Would anyone help? Were there objections that had been forgotten? There must have been some. The logic cannot be refuted, but someone who wants to live will not resist it. Where was the judge he'd never seen? Where was the high court he had never reached? He raised both hands and spread out all his fingers.

But the hands of one of the gentleman were laid on K.'s throat, while the other pushed the knife deep into his heart and twisted it there, twice. As his eyesight failed, K. saw the two gentlemen cheek by cheek, close in front of his face, watching the result. "Like a dog!" he said; it was as if the shame of it should outlive him.

AMERICAN LITERATURE

Little Women — Louisa May Alcott
The Last of the Mohicans — James Fenimore Cooper
The Red Badge of Courage and *Maggie* — Stephen Crane
Selected Poems — Emily Dickinson
Narrative of the Life and Other Writings — Frederick Douglass
The Scarlet Letter — Nathaniel Hawthorne
The Call of the Wild and *White Fang* – Jack London
Moby-Dick — Herman Melville
Major Tales and Poems — Edgar Allan Poe
The Jungle — Upton Sinclair
Uncle Tom's Cabin — Harriet Beecher Stowe
Walden and *Civil Disobedience* — Henry David Thoreau
Adventures of Huckleberry Finn — Mark Twain
The Complete Adventures of Tom Sawyer — Mark Twain
Ethan Frome and *Summer* — Edith Wharton
Leaves of Grass — Walt Whitman

WORLD LITERATURE

Tales from the 1001 Nights — Sir Richard Burton
Don Quixote — Miguel de Cervantes
The Divine Comedy — Dante Alighieri
Crime and Punishment — Fyodor Dostoevsky
The Count of Monte Cristo — Alexandre Dumas
The Three Musketeers — Alexandre Dumas
Selected Tales of the Brothers Grimm — Jacob and Wilhelm Grimm
The Iliad — Homer
The Odyssey — Homer
The Hunchback of Notre-Dame — Victor Hugo
Les Misérables — Victor Hugo
The Metamorphosis and *The Trial* — Franz Kafka
The Phantom of the Opera — Gaston Leroux
The Prince — Niccolò Machiavelli
The Art of War — Sun Tzu
The Death of Ivan Ilych and Other Stories — Leo Tolstoy
Around the World in Eighty Days — Jules Verne
Candide and *The Maid of Orléans* — Voltaire
The Bhagavad Gita — Vyasa